the other boy

Yvonne Cassidy was born in Dublin in 1974. She studied English and Economics in University College Dublin and has worked in London, Australia and New York, specialising in the field of marketing communications. Yvonne currently lives in Dublin. *The Other Boy* is her first book.

the other boy

Yvonne Cassidy

HACHETTE
BOOKS
IRELAND

First published in Ireland in 2010 by Hachette Books Ireland

A Hachette UK company

Copyright © Yvonne Cassidy 2010

The right of Yvonne Cassidy to be identified as the Author of the Work has been asserted by her in accordance with the Copyright, Designs and Patents Act 1988.

'Eleanor Rigby' Lyrics by John Lennon/Paul McCartney © Northern Songs/Sony/ATV Music Publishing. All Rights Reserved. Used by permission

A CIP catalogue record for this title is available from the British Library.

ISBN 978 1444 70478 5

Typeset in Bookman Old Style and Book Antiqua by Hachette Books Ireland

Printed and bound by Mackays, Chatham ME5 8TD

Hachette Books Ireland policy is to use papers that are natural, renewable and recyclable products and made from wood grown in sustainable forests. The logging and manufacturing pro cesses are expected to conform to the environmental regulations of the country of origin.

Hachette Books Ireland
8 Castlecourt Centre
Castleknock
Dublin 15

www.hachette.ie

A division of

Hachette UK
338 Euston Road
London
NW1 3BH

For Mum and Dad

PROLOGUE

The box of tissues in the Doc's office is mansize. The black and red colours are supposed to make it look macho, so you won't feel stupid reaching for the flimsy girly contents inside. I've spent a lot of time staring at that box, directing my words at it rather than him. Focusing on the coloured cardboard makes it easier to ignore the frenzied notes he sometimes writes in his foolscap pad and the way his eyebrows crease into a frown behind his glasses. Each session lasts an hour and I probably spend at least half of it concentrating on that box of tissues. But I've never had to use one.

The other day I showed him a photograph. I don't know why, really. I just felt like it. I brought the one with the curling corners where we're at the fairground, Dad and Mam and Dessie and me. Dad's leaning down, his chin resting on my head. It must be windy because Mam's hair is blowing across her face, catching in her smile. Dessie is the only one not looking into the camera: he's facing it, along with the rest of us, but his eyes are swivelled away, looking past the white rim of the edge.

As soon as I took it out to show the Doc I wished I hadn't. He started to ask too many questions about why I'd brought it, short, open-ended questions that were meant to catch me out. I knew how to handle him, though, so I told him other things. How the candyfloss had left my mouth sticky and sweet. About the smell of petrol and sugar in the air that was so strong it even crept inside the tent where Mam and I went to see the fortune-teller. I even told him about the stripy T-shirt I was wearing, and that it had been Dessie's before it was mine.

We've talked a lot about Dessie, the Doc and I. About Dessie always being older than me, stronger than me. How Dessie could always make people see things his way. I tried to explain what it was like never to be the first to do anything, or be able to find out something that he didn't already know. The Doc nodded when I said that and he made another note but I don't think he understood at all.

You know that moment between sleep and waking? When your mind jump-starts before your body? I read somewhere that the first thing that comes into your head is what you desire or fear the most. I don't know if that's fully right, though, or if there's another reason, because for years when I opened my eyes I used to think of Mark. That's stopped now, of course, but I still haven't told the Doc about it. It's not that I don't want to, I will tell him, it's just hard sometimes to understand what it means, let alone put it into words.

I told him about 'Lucy In The Sky With Diamonds'. About how, when I was seven or eight, it was my favourite

Beatles song and after tea Dad would put it on and I'd close my eyes, listening to the scratch of the needle on vinyl, waiting for it to find the music. I tried to describe how John Lennon's voice would start, asking me to imagine myself on a boat on the river where there were tangerine trees and skies the colour of marmalade. It was before I knew that the song was supposed to be about drugs, before I'd heard of LSD, even before I knew that John was much cooler than Paul. I told him how I'd sit cross-legged, humming along, making my own pictures that sat alongside John's. The Doc says that I'm very visual, the way I remember things. He asked me what happens if I can't see the whole picture and I said I didn't know. It was only afterwards I thought that maybe sometimes I use my imagination to colour in the bits around the edges and I wondered if that was what he was getting at all along.

I didn't tell him about the time Mrs Burke asked me what I wanted to be when I grew up and how the other boys all laughed when I answered, "My dad." I still remember how she tried to hide her own smile as she explained to the class that what I meant was I wanted to be a plumber, like my dad. But that wasn't what I meant at all. I meant I wanted to actually be him, to grow into him. I had it right the first time. If I told the Doc about that, he'd start to ask about Katie and Abbey and whether I felt I'd lived up to what I wanted to be. Which would be a completely stupid question, because we both know the answer to that one.

I didn't tell him about *Revolver* either — there was no point in getting into all that. Instead, I brought him back to

'Lucy In The Sky With Diamonds'. I told him about the girl who had eyes like kaleidoscopes, that I could never figure out what that meant but now I thought I could. I spent one whole session on my theory that the past is like the picture at the centre of a kaleidoscope. The picture stays the same, it's the kaleidoscope's mirrors that change it, and the past can change too, depending on where you see it from. I talked on and on that day, trying to explain it, but he didn't say a lot. He didn't even write much down, he just kept looking at me. I don't think he got it at all.

I've been seeing the Doc for a while now. Long enough that the dark branches tipping the window have a fuzz of green and the square of white-grey sky has patches of blue. There are days when I wonder if this endless stream of one-way words is making any difference at all, when it feels as if there's more point in an hour of silence. There are days when I don't want to be here and the anger pulls taut inside and snaps out like elastic. Those are the days when I'm the one asking the questions, like the one I asked him yesterday.

"What's the fuckin' point in all this? It's all over now. Ancient history. It's not like I could have changed anything, could I?"

He sat back in his chair and held his hands in an arc, tapping his index fingers together. Even before he opened his mouth I knew he wasn't going to answer me.

"That's an interesting question. What do you think, John-Paul?"

He always insists on calling me John-Paul, even though he knows full well my fuckin' name is JP.

ONE

London, 2005

We were on the highest part of the Heath. Stretched out below, the city looked like a whole other world, the squares and rectangles that made up its shape black against the darkening sky. Behind us, the father and son we'd passed on the climb up were trying to get their kite to fly. I turned to watch as they ran down the hill, the red and blue and yellow streamers trailing just above the grass, the last thing to disappear out of sight. For a few seconds their voices hung in the smoky October air and then there was silence. Just me and Katie.

"Look at St Paul's. It's like an egg in an eggcup," Katie said.

My eyes followed where she was pointing. "It does, I've always thought that too." I smiled as I said it and squeezed her gloved fingers.

"You know, I can't believe I'd never been up here before you took me," she said. "It's so peaceful, I love it."

"It's my favourite place in London." I thought of all the days I'd stood in this spot, days when the sky over the city was a bright dome of blue or a blur of rain or a wash of orangey-grey, like today. From the top of one of the office buildings a red light flashed on and off. On and off.

"Come on," Katie said, "I'm getting cold. It's time for the Oak's famous bangers and mash."

"Or we could skip it and go home?"

It was six weeks since she'd moved in, and living together still felt like a permanent holiday.

"No way, JP! We've been in the flat nearly all weekend. You promised me bangers and mash and I'm not going home until I get them."

"OK, OK," I said, touching the smudges of red the cold made on her cheeks. "Come on, then." I took her hand and turned to walk down the hill. In the few minutes we'd been up there the last light of the day had ebbed away.

"It gets dark so quickly at this time of year," she said. "You can barely see in front of us now."

"I love the autumn, though," I said.

"I like it too. But I'd like it more if it didn't mean the end of summer."

Turning off the main path, we took the shortcut through the trees that came out at the lake on the other side. I glanced at her and she was looking at the ground, picking her steps carefully. "What?" she said.

"Nothing. I was just thinking that this is the first autumn we're spending together," I said. "And that I'm liking autumn with you." I let my words hang in the air with the clouds of our breath. I wondered what she'd say next.

"I'm liking everything more with you, JP," she said, stopping, so I stopped too. "It's weird to think of life before you. It almost seems like we've always been together or something."

I smiled into the dark. "I can't really remember what things were like before you, Katie." I leaned down to kiss her, my hand finding that warm place on her neck.

"Hey! You're freezing!" She laughed, and pulled away. "Come on, you can do that in the Oak where it's warm."

As we walked on, our feet scuffing through piles of crinkled leaves, I realised that what I'd said wasn't true, that I remembered all too well what life had been like before her. Even here, on these paths, I could see a shadow of myself running alongside us, alone. Those Saturdays weren't so long ago, the Christmas days jogging past the lit-up windows of the red-brick houses until I got to the Heath, where I could crunch across the frosty grass, just me, my feet and my breath.

I turned to Katie then because I wanted to see her, as well as feel her, to know that she was really, really there. I didn't want to remember my life before her — that was what I'd meant to say, but I could never say that. I could never tell her how walking these same paths together was like erasing all those other times, creating something new. I gripped her hand tighter.

"I'm rethinking the bangers-and-mash decision," she said.

"Let me guess. Even though you've been planning on bangers and mash all day, now you're not sure if cottage pie is a better option?"

"How did you know?"

"I pay attention. I want to know everything there is to know about you, Katie Wright."

As we walked out of the forest and back onto the main path I thought about how true that was, that every single detail she told me was logged somewhere in my mind, that I never really forgot anything.

"And do I know everything about you, JP Whelan?"

"You do indeed, my love. You know everything that matters."

★★★

Walking along Downshire Hill, we played the game I always played. It was more fun playing it with Katie.

"I'd like to live in that one," Katie said. "That's my favourite."

The house she pointed at was sandblasted brick and had a big bay window with ferns spilling from a terracotta plant box.

"It's not the one you picked last time."

"Didn't I?"

"No, you said this one."

We stopped outside the house with creeper the colour of holly and a shiny black door with a silver knocker. Today it was half open, so we could see a child's red welly lying on the wooden floor of the hall. This house had always been my favourite of them all.

"Oh," Katie said, pushing me to move on as we heard the family's voices getting louder from inside, "I like them all and they're all so different. That's what makes it so hard to choose."

She was right and that was what I loved about the road too, that each house had something to like all of its own. We passed the bright white one with the new glass front that had taken nearly all of last year to renovate. Next to it was the cream one that looked more like a cottage, with its bright blue door and matching window frames.

"Oh ... I'd forgotten about this one. It's so cute, maybe this is my favourite," Kate said. "I can't make up my mind."

"You have to pick," I said. "That's the whole point."

"Why? It's not like we're about to buy one."

A thought flicked across my mind, something my boss Peter had mentioned about a possibility of a restructure next year, how it might mean the potential of a promotion for someone on the team. It was a long shot, way too early to say anything about it.

"Not today, Katie, but some day, maybe."

She was looking away from me, towards one of the houses, and for a second I wondered if she'd heard the seriousness in my voice and if it had scared her. When she turned back to me, she was smiling. "Well, in that case," she said, "I'd better start making up my mind."

I put my arm around her shoulders and pulled her closer. I had that feeling again, the one I still wasn't used to, like a wave of something warm filling me that, even after it was gone, seemed to cling to my insides. "OK, then, but wait," I said. "You like the one on the corner as well. Don't make up your mind until we get to it."

"It's funny," she said, "the way you remember them all. It's like there's a blueprint in your head or something."

She didn't know how right she was, how on the nights when sleep didn't come it was these houses I'd count. I hadn't told her that knowing this street was here, and always would be, made everything better somehow. I wondered what she'd think if I tried to tell her, if she'd understand.

"What was the road like in Dublin where you grew up?"

I hadn't seen the question coming. The flush of only a few seconds ago vanished and the October air felt cold as a pane of glass. We were nearly at the pub. I looked down at my runners, making slow steps on the flagstones, and started to walk a little faster. "Pretty standard Dublin suburbia," I said. "Your typical street — you know?"

"No, I don't," she said. "You'll have to take me some day. Are the houses two-storey?"

"Yup."

"Detached? Or not?"

I thought of her parents' house in its own grounds in Cheshire. "No, semi-detached."

"Was it a big road? How many houses?"

I hated when she got like this, but I knew that answering was a quicker way out than trying to avoid it. "Em ..." I scrunched my face up, trying to remember. It surprised me how easy it was to picture the houses, the way the names of the families jumped so quickly into my mind after all this time. "OK, let's think — the McDonnells, the Joyces, us, the O'Briens, the Smiths, the Fogartys, the O'Tooles—" I broke off. I didn't want to think about the O'Tooles.

We were standing in the empty beer garden, Katie counting on her gloved fingers. "The Fogartys!" She laughed. "I love the sound of them — like one of those traditional Irish bands. OK, that's seven? Who was after the O'Tooles?"

She looked so pretty and happy, smiling and holding up her hands in stripy gloves, that I felt something tighten in my chest, somewhere around where my heart was. "I don't know, I forget," I said. "Three more houses, probably. Now, come on, let's get inside before I freeze to death."

★★★

The heat in the pub was too much and we stripped off our layers quickly. Katie blew on her fingers, warming them, and then jumped up from the wooden bench. "Back in a second, I still can't make up my mind. You decide for me."

Watching her walk towards the loo, I thought about the first time I'd seen her in the office, laughing into the phone. Her free hand was making a comb of her fingers, lifting her dark hair up, then letting it fall again, back down onto her shoulders. She did it over and over and I remember being mesmerised by the movement, my eyes on her instead of the notes I should've been reading as I waited outside Peter's office. It was my third interview, the job tantalisingly close, but instead of focusing on it I was wondering how I'd missed seeing her during the first two and how I was going to get to talk to her.

Katie loved that story — that I'd noticed her even then. Whenever anyone asked how we got together, that was the story she liked to tell, that she'd managed to distract me from my interview and anyone who knew me would know what a big deal that was. After everything she'd been through, the split from her ex-husband Toby, it was as if that story was some kind of proof about me that I was everything he wasn't.

I took a deep breath and let my eyes hang on the football game on the telly by the window. There was something I wanted to ask her, something that had been in my mind for a while now, since before she'd moved in. These past couple of weeks it was even bigger, the size of Mount Everest, it seemed, and I couldn't ignore it any more. But just thinking about what I was going to say made my stomach drop in fear, my heartbeat uneven. I had no idea how she would react and I wondered if I really knew her at all.

"You ready?"

The waitress was in front of me and I realised under my hand I was jiggling my knee, my leg bouncing through the ball of my foot. I held my thigh steady, placed both feet on the floor. "Yes, I'll have two of the bangers and mash, a glass of Merlot and a pint of Guinness. Oh, and some of the cheesy potato skins to start."

I smiled at her but she took the menus without looking at me. Katie was on her way back now, curling her hair behind her ear and pushing in next to me on the bench.

"I decided you were in a bangers and mash frame of mind," I told her.

"Good — you getting the same?"

"Yes."

"Copycat!"

"And we're sharing some potato skins first."

"Oh, my God, JP, you and potatoes! I've been putting on weight ever since we moved in together. This has to stop!" She flattened her top across her middle to show me. She had put on a little weight but I quite liked it. Lying in bed the other night, sliding my hands around her belly, I wondered what it would feel like to hold her if she was pregnant.

"What are you thinking?" Katie said. Her freshly applied lipgloss was shiny pink and I kissed her lightly.

"Nothing — except that I felt like kissing you."

"I hope you always feel like kissing me."

"I do, especially in the office when I can't."

I was filling in words then, saying something to hold the space instead of what I really wanted to say. This kind of conversation was easy, the kind of conversation we could fill a weekend with, flirty teases and jokes, but today I wanted to talk about something more.

"Actually, I wanted to ask you a question," I said, before I could stop myself.

"Oh, really, what's that?"

I could tell she thought I was still joking with her but before I could say any more the waitress was back with the drinks. She put them on the table, slopping the Guinness down the side of the pint glass.

I took a sip and wiped my hand on my jeans. I slid the other along the back of the bench, behind Katie. I glanced at the TV — the team in blue had scored. Next to me, Katie tasted her wine. "Mm, this is nice — you want to try it?"

"No, thanks."

"Sorry, JP, you were saying something. What was it?"

Now I had her attention I didn't want it. I twisted the pint glass on the beer mat. The goal was being replayed on the TV. I had a sudden urge to pee. I took a gulp of Guinness and forced myself to swallow slowly, licked the creamy froth from my top lip. I turned to look at her and forced the words out over the knocking of my heart. "I was just wondering what it would be like if we had a baby."

★★★

Katie was lying diagonally in the bed, pushing me in towards the wall. Her breath was heavy, interspersed with tiny snores. As I climbed out over her, she paused for a second, then her rhythm was back. Creaking down the stairs and into the living room, I knew I didn't need to worry about waking her: the red wine would see she slept soundly. I walked into the kitchen and turned on the kettle.

When I pulled back the curtain it was still dark outside, not even the first traces of light yet, although officially it was a new day. I hoisted myself onto the kitchen counter, balancing my bare feet on the window-ledge. I smiled at my reflection in the glass and realised, for the first time, that what had happened was real.

The kettle gurgled behind me and clicked itself off but I didn't want tea. That wasn't the reason I'd got up, not really. I wanted to run what had happened through my mind again, replay it, make sure I hadn't forgotten any bits, that I'd got it right.

After I'd managed to get those words out Katie had looked terrified. Even though I was too, I kept talking on and on and on. It was the only way to make her see what I meant, to fill the space so there'd be no room for her to say what I was so afraid she'd say. By the time the waitress was back with the potato skins Katie was smiling and she hadn't said no. We let them go cold as we talked about why it was a crazy idea, why it was too soon, why there was no rush, but even as we did we seemed to be edging closer together, my leg squashing against hers on the bench, her fingers wrapping tighter around mine.

We never ate the potato skins, and when the bangers and mash arrived Katie's "maybe" was hovering on a "yes" and I asked the waitress if she had any champagne. She looked at us as if we were crazy and asked whether the food was all right, and Katie got a fit of the giggles and I did too, giggles that were worse once we'd popped the cork on the dusty bottle: we drank from little wine glasses that reminded me of some we'd had at home in Sallynoggin years before.

I jumped down from the counter, found a teabag and filled a mug with water. Katie and I were going to have a family. I opened the fridge and poured the milk. We were going to have a baby together. I plucked the teabag from the cup and dropped it into the sink. Katie had said there was no one in the world she would rather have as father to her child.

It didn't matter how many different ways I said it, I couldn't seem to believe it, to make the words stick. We'd talked it over and over and said we'd talk about it again tomorrow, but we'd both agreed it was what we wanted, maybe not today or next month, but soon, definitely soon. Leaning against the counter with the tiles cold under my feet and the mug warm in my hands, I fast-forwarded in my head to a house in Hampstead, pulling into the drive with Katie and a little baby in the back. I could picture it so easily: Katie, beautiful and smiling, the baby, a girl, pretty like her mum. It was so close I could taste it.

I wondered what Katie meant by "soon".

Two

None of the books I'd read had prepared me for this. Katie's face hardly looked like hers, so red and twisted in pain. I stroked her hair back from her forehead again even though I didn't think it was helping — I didn't think anything was helping. Earlier she'd been shouting, crying, roaring curses I hadn't even known she knew. Now she was worn out and silent, panting as I held her hand and counted her breaths, like we'd practised, even though this was nothing like we'd practised.

"Don't push," the midwife said. "You're doing great, Katie. Just hang on. I know you want to push but hold on until the doctor gets here."

"Where is he?" I said.

"He's on his way, Mr Whelan."

Katie was Katie; I was Mr Whelan. The midwife had been saying the doctor was on his way for more than half an hour. I wanted to do something to help Katie — I wanted to do it for her — but all I could do was count.

"You're doing great, babe, just great."

When the doctor did arrive I didn't like him. It was the way he barely said anything and pushed his way in, past me and the midwife, and started snapping out instructions. I was about to ask what was going on but suddenly Katie was being wheeled from the room. The midwife told the other nurse to get me a gown, that we were going to theatre, and I was running, following the trolley as it banged through endless sets of double doors, too shocked to be terrified.

Outside the theatre, a nurse tied up the gown as I shoved my feet into some plastic white shoes, none of us talking. By the time I caught up, they were already getting started, a green curtain stretched across Katie's stomach like some gruesome magic trick. Behind it, the doctors seemed only half human, passing tools between them that glinted in the overly bright light. Katie reached for my hand, panic soldering us together in a tight sweaty group. The doctors were talking in low words we didn't understand and there was something about the fear in Katie's eyes that made me stronger, as if all her strength had flowed into me. I stroked her hair and told her everything was going to be fine, that together we were invincible and there was no way anything bad was going to happen. Not to us. Never to us.

I was looking at Katie when I heard the ragged scream. That's why it took me a second to grasp that it was coming from the tiny thing in the doctor's gloved hands, that the milky rope of flesh was the umbilical cord I'd read so much about and that this was it, this was her, this was Abbey, our brand new baby daughter. Katie was a beat ahead of me, pushing herself up on her elbows, as far as she could go, to take Abbey from the midwife before they could even wipe her clean. As she reached out she dropped my hand, leaving it dangling by my side so it felt cold and exposed. I shouldn't have noticed that — it was a ridiculous thing to dwell on as our daughter was taking her first breaths — but somewhere the thought of how easily Katie could let me go bounced around my head and out again like a pinball.

Looking down at Abbey for the first time, where she lay on Katie's chest, this little crying thing with scrunched-up eyes and wrinkly hands, I waited to feel something change. I'd wanted her, wanted this, for so long, and now it was here it was almost too big to feel. It wasn't until I felt the wetness on my face that I realised I was crying. Katie was crying too, quiet tears that leaked from the corners of her eyes and rolled into the brown tangle of her hair.

The doctor had finished sewing her up and as he pulled off his glove to shake my hand I thought I might just love him too. "Thank you, Doctor, thank you. Thank you so much," I said, shaking hard, hanging on.

When I turned back to Katie I saw that she was whispering something to Abbey that had made her stop crying. As I looked at the two of them lying there, it hit me that this was real. They were so perfect, like something out of someone else's life, only this time it was mine.

Out of nowhere I thought of the obituaries in the back of the *Evening Press* that Dad used to buy. I was fascinated by them, how the tight, cramped newsprint summed up a person in only a few column inches. It seemed that you needed a web of people around you to make up a life — husbands, wives, fathers, sons, daughters: these were the definitions that counted in the end. Before today mine would have been blank. But not any more.

I shook the image from my mind. Today was about beginnings, not endings.

"She's beautiful," I said. "You're both so beautiful."

In my head the words had sounded right, but out loud they were clichéd and I wanted new ones that would capture what was inside, words that this room hadn't heard so many times before.

"JP, look at her. Oh, my God, look at her little fingernails."

"She's just tiny," I said.

I kissed Katie's hair and tasted salt. When I stood up, she was getting ready to pass Abbey to me to hold. I wasn't ready yet but I had to be. I leaned down to take her at an awkward angle so pain bit my knee. Our movements were jumbled up, me half bent down, Katie pushing herself up towards me. She gave a sniffly giggle and I felt laughter bubble inside me too, but before it could break out Abbey was in my arms, heavy and light and delicate and solid all at the same time.

I was gazing at a bundle of fresh chances. She'd made no mistakes yet and she never would. I wanted to trace my finger on her face to feel her skin but I didn't know how to hold her and do that at the same time and I was so afraid I might hurt her. She was so small, so new. Her eyes started to open a little and I waited for her to cry again but she didn't. The watery pupils rolled back and forth, like marbles, stopping just for a second to focus on me. They were the bluest of blues, just like mine.

"Hello, Abbey," I said. "Daddy's here."

★★★

Sitting in the Tube carriage, shuddering at speed through the black tunnels of the Northern Line, I replayed the moment when I'd held Abbey, looking at the picture of her and Katie on my phone's screen. Across from me, a woman glanced up, then returned to the safety of her newspaper. For a crazy second I almost moved over to sit next to her, to show her the picture and tell her all about my baby girl, but I knew she wouldn't care.

I stretched my legs across the carriage and closed my eyes to relive the memory, me holding Abbey, Katie looking on. It was hard to separate how I felt from how I'd expected to feel. I think I felt conscious of my feet firm on the ground, connected to the earth below and to the universe, as if nothing could ever shake me, but maybe that was something I'd edited into the memory. Something I'd always expected I would feel. Opening my eyes, I saw black and orange patterned seats, a window of darkness, and I was back in the Tube carriage. Not for the first time I wondered if shaping the memory of something could make it even better second time around.

Abbey. I smiled as I said her name in my head. I mouthed it on my lips, enjoying the feel of it. Abbey. It was the only name we'd both liked. I'd suggested Irish names like Aoife or Aisling but Katie said she didn't want her daughter living her whole life with her name being pronounced the wrong way. We hadn't decided that we would live in England for ever, but as Katie said it I realised it was true and the twinge of sadness I felt took me by surprise.

We'd hit on Abbey by accident. There it was, always my favourite of the albums, up on the wall of record sleeves in the living room, between *Yellow Submarine* and *Let It Be*.

Abbey Road sounded like somewhere special, where magic could happen. It was simple and melodic and pretty. It was perfect. As she was.

The train stopped mid-tunnel; the thin strip of light blinked, its buzzing suddenly audible. Across from me the woman looked out of the window into her own reflection from the black wall beyond. I checked my watch. Eleven thirty. Katie was probably asleep by now, exhausted after the day, but then again maybe she was awake, breastfeeding Abbey, the way the nurse had shown her. I pictured them in the private room Philip had arranged for them, more like a hotel than a hospital. Katie was delighted and I was happy too, but I wanted to be the one sorting things out for my family now, not Philip.

The driver's voice through the intercom was a long crackle of words I couldn't make out. Something about a delay and Liverpool Street. Surely not a security alert at this hour? Checking my watch again I made my sigh loud and long. In Switzerland, the men stayed with their wives in hospital, the new families together. They even brought in a champagne meal afterwards to celebrate. I'd read that in one of the books and when I told Katie she laughed and said that sounded crazy and the last thing she'd want after hours of labour was champagne. It wasn't that part I'd liked, though: it was the idea of staying with them, not having to leave. I don't think Katie got that at all because when I suggested booking in to the hotel near the hospital she said it was silly when the flat was only forty minutes away. She was probably right. In any case, they'd be home in a couple of days — but then again, she wasn't the one sitting trapped in some sooty tunnel, miles under the ground on her own.

★★★

Walking down the hill towards the flat, I passed a couple I recognised from the complex but we didn't say hello. In the porter's office the younger guy was there, reading the back page of the *Evening Standard*. He buzzed me in without looking up.

"Thanks," I said.

I caught my reflection in the glass as I pushed through the gate, hair standing up in a spike, collar open, my tie lost somewhere in the midst of the day. It was hard to believe that it was still the same day — that I'd been in work this morning before I got Katie's panicked phone call. This guy probably thought I was just another City boy on his way home from a quick half that had turned into one too many. Crunching across the gravel I heard the sounds of chinking glass and laughter wafting from the balcony of an upstairs flat. The music in the background had a heavy trumpet beat but I couldn't fully make it out. It didn't matter that it was only Wednesday: parties were a regular feature on any night of the week. Come to think of it, I'd never heard a baby crying.

The flat was cold, the blinds up letting in the night from outside. On the kitchen table a pile of copper and silver spilled from the change jar — Katie must have raided it this morning when she called her taxi. As I scooped the coins back into the glass I saw the green light flicker on the answering-machine.

"JP, it's Rebecca. Philip and I are getting the early train

down tomorrow. It leaves here at eight and it gets into Euston at— Philip, what time does the train get in? We arrive at Euston just after ten so we should be at the hospital by half past. We're staying at the Marriott. Can you let Katie know? I didn't want to call her in the room in case she was sleeping. See you tomorrow. Oh, and congratulations again. Looking forward to seeing you all. 'Bye."

The Marriott: only the best for the Wrights. Still, at least they weren't the kind of parents who'd expect to camp here. They wouldn't stay long. Philip would need to get back for work soon enough and Rebecca wouldn't stick around without him. The conversation earlier had been to the point: Philip had dealt in facts — the weight, the length of the labour. Rebecca was more relieved than emotional, moving on quickly to the arrangements for tomorrow. Abbey was their fifth grandchild and Katie their second oldest daughter, so maybe this was how things went. Still, it had been nice to have them to call and Katie's three sisters as well. Their voices were echoes of each other, full of love and excitement and questions, and already I could feel the safety net of family spin around me, just as I'd always hoped it would.

I threw myself onto the couch and pulled off my shoes. I was exhausted but suddenly starving too — I hadn't eaten since breakfast. There was no way I was cooking tonight so it would have to be pizza.

The TV images washed over me, like warm water, as I waited for the food to arrive. I checked my emails for anything from Peter about the new assistant director job. Even though there wasn't, I found myself drawn in, responding to

other people about other things before I put my BlackBerry
on the floor and out of sight. It didn't feel right after everything that had happened to be back in the flat alone —
checking email, eating pizza, it could have been any old day,
not the first day of my daughter's life and, in a way, the first
day of my new life too. I took out my phone, but it was too
late to call Katie. I started to write a text but halfway through
I deleted it. She was exhausted when I left and I couldn't risk
waking her up.

I flicked through the channels but there was nothing on.
On the shelves by the TV were the books I'd bought to
prepare us, books I'd read at night while Katie slept. The
section in Borders had been mind-boggling. I'd bought too
many and had had to pack away some of my Lennon biogra-
phies in a box to make room. It was funny how they were all
for mothers, that us dads got only a small section at the back.
On Amazon I found books meant for men with bloke-ish
titles like *My Boys Can Swim* and *Be Prepared*. I'd skimmed
those too but they weren't what I wanted: they seemed to be
aimed at reluctant guys who had been browbeaten into
fatherhood. Sex was the main topic – how late in pregnancy
it was safe to have it, what to do when it stopped and when
it would start again. I'd given up reading after that, because
it seemed like I must be the only guy in the world to persuade his partner to have a baby, to want one so badly I
would've got down on my knees and begged her.

I got up and walked around the small living room, taking
it in as if for the first time. Despite Katie's little touches —
the stuff that I called clutter and she called character — the

flat still had the feel of a bachelor pad. The cot in the spare room that would soon be Abbey's left only a strip of floor that was barely big enough for the buggy. We hadn't enough space for the stuff we'd been buying in the last couple of weeks, a pile of it still in bags under the window. We needed somewhere bigger and Katie had talked about finding somewhere else to rent, with a garden maybe, but I didn't want to rent any more. I was sick of renting, living in other people's lives. I wanted somewhere permanent.

When I told Katie about the potential promotion I'd played it down, not wanting to get her hopes up. I didn't tell her how Peter had pulled me aside on Monday and said things were nearly there with HR, that the official announcement about the job should be made within the week and to keep checking in with him, even while I was off. I wondered if that was why he'd told me or if he'd said it to the others as well. It was hard not to get carried away and only this morning I'd found myself online, checking the price of houses in Hampstead and Belsize Park, doing sums on yellow Post-its. Even if I got the promotion it would be a stretch, but it would be worth it. I could picture it clearly in my mind, the bay window, the creeper that was Christmassy green all year round. A house with a heavy knocker on a glossy black front door that, when it opened, would reveal the happy family that lived behind it.

The buzzer rang. About time — I was starving. I ran to the intercom and held down the unlock button for the outer door. I fumbled for cash, remembering, too late, that I'd forgotten to take money out on the way home. I clambered up the wooden stairs to the bedroom and rummaged through jacket pockets. A fiver and some change, pound coins. Below me he was at the door now, knocking harder.

"Hang on, I'm just coming!"

Nine pounds, almost enough – I could raid the change jar for the rest. He knocked again.

"I'm coming, I'm coming! There's no need to wake up the whole block!"

Jumping down the last two steps, I grabbed a fistful of change from the table, ran to the door and flung it open. The last thought I had before I saw him was of Abbey, and how when she cried she might wake up the whole block.

At first I didn't recognise him. I just registered that there was no pizza, that he wasn't the delivery guy, that it was someone else. Later, when I thought about that, I was ashamed it wasn't instant, that there wasn't some sort of physical connection. But it had been a long time. His hair was shorter. Thinner. He'd never had stubble before — but this was too thick to be called stubble even, it was more of a beard. And he looked so much smaller, which was stupid: he couldn't be. It was just that I had grown.

I don't know how long I stood there, a few seconds I suppose, long enough to feel my heart thumping like a basket-ball on concrete, echoing through my whole body. He couldn't be here. He couldn't. But he was. It was his voice that unlocked me.

"John-Paul," he said, reaching out his hand.

"Dessie?" I'd been holding my breath. I stepped out into the hallway in my socks. "Jesus Christ. Dessie! I can't believe it." There were so many questions in my head, too many — they got stuck there so I couldn't ask any.

"Jaysus. Look at you in the suit. All grown-up, so you are. Christ, you look great — you're the spit of the oul fella."

His accent was more Dublin than I remembered. He dropped the "t" off "great" and "grown" was two syllables.

"Dessie. Wow! Jesus. What are you doing here? What's going on?"

"Would you listen to the accent on yer man?" He laughed, shaking his head. "Very posh altogether. It's a long story — I'll fill you in over a beer. Am I coming in or what?"

He read my hesitation, the jump in the rhythm of conversation. I saw it in the way his eyes flicked away from me and back again, the way his shoulders straightened.

"Yeah, sure," I said, nodding too hard, standing back to let him in. Thank God Katie wasn't here. Thank God. He picked up a bag I hadn't seen and slung it over his shoulder, pushing past me into the flat.

I closed the door and straight away there was another knock. Who was that? Had he brought someone with him? I opened the door slowly, but it was only the pizza guy, of course it was. Tiredness was making me jumpy. I handed him all the money in my hand, too exhausted to count it.

When I followed Dessie into the sitting room his bag was already dumped in the middle of the floor. He was standing at the shelf, a picture of me and Katie in his hand. It was the one from our holiday in Portugal, a timer picture — we were laughing as I'd almost fallen, stumbling to get into it in time.

"Jesus. Great fuckin' set-up you have here," he said. "Is this your bird?"

"Yeah," I said.

"She's a stunner. What's her name?"

"Katie."

"Katie? Very nice. Shit, I hope I didn't wake her up?"

"No, she's not here. She's … staying with friends tonight."

"Not to worry. We've a lot to catch up on anyway, haven't we? I'm sure she's heard all about me." Winking, he traded the photo frame for the steaming pizza box that I was holding out in front of me and dropped it onto the table. He ripped off a slice, cupping his hand underneath to catch the strings of cheese. Watching him, my hunger vanished and all I wanted to do was lie down on the floor and sleep. He turned to me and I realised that I was frozen to the spot, staring at him, the photograph still dangling in my hand.

"C'mon, John-Paul," he said, through a mouthful of pizza. "You eating or what?"

THREE

I'm back in Sallynoggin. Me and Mark, in my house, running from room to room. First the kitchen, then the sitting room. All the rooms are empty, bare floorboards and dust. Up the stairs two at a time into Dad's room, then Mam's. Nobody there. When I turn around Mark's gone too.

And then I wake up.

I blinked hard, focusing on the duvet cover, the blinds, the stripes of light they made on the wooden floor. My throat was dry but I'd forgotten to bring up any water. Slow breaths, in and out. I always woke up at the same point, my heart and head pounding. The trick was to let my mind relax, replace the half-formed images with the familiar surroundings of the flat, the safety of home. It was ages since I'd had the dream, I couldn't remember the last time.

From the sitting room below I could hear the cheery jaunt of morning TV. Shit, Dessie. For a second I'd hoped that was a dream too. I picked up the alarm clock: eight fifty-five. I jumped out of bed, grabbed a T-shirt from the drawer, a pair of jeans that was draped over the chair. I was late already — I could shower later.

Downstairs, Dessie was sitting in the same spot I'd left him, blankets in a pool by his feet and a plate covered with crumbs.

"Do you not have to work today?" he said. He plucked at a lock of his chest hair, twirling it between his fingers.

"Yeah. No, I'm off."

"How come?"

There was something in his voice — it was as if he knew, but he couldn't know. The conversation last night had been sparse, Dessie claiming he was dead on his feet just like I was so we'd said we'd catch up this morning.

"I've got some stuff to do." I heard the evasiveness in my voice and I avoided his look, hiding behind the open fridge door. The orange-juice carton felt too light — it was empty. That fucker must have finished it.

"What stuff, John-Paul?"

I almost corrected him but I stopped myself in time. No one called me John-Paul any more. I hated its clumsy indecisive sound. That I was an echo of a pope and a religion I'd never even believed in.

"I said, what stuff do you've to do?" he called, louder. "You wouldn't be going to the fuckin' hospital by any chance, would you?"

My eyes darted to the answering-machine. The light was flashing. I mustn't have heard it ring. Dessie was staring at me, all his laughter gone. Between his thumb and forefinger he twisted the loop of his chest hair, tighter and tighter, so it pulled at his translucent white skin.

"Actually, yeah, I am. I meant to tell you but there was so much going on last night. Katie had — I mean we had — a baby yesterday. A girl."

The TV filled the gap of silence between us.

"Yesterday?"

I nodded.

"Why the fuck didn't you say anything?" He didn't move his head but stared straight ahead at the television. Even though his body was slouched I could see the hardness in it, the line of his shoulders, the tendons in his neck.

"Look, I should have but, like I said—"

He snapped his head around. "Yeah, you should. I was wondering what the fuck was going on with the cot in the other room and then I heard your one's message." He stood up, stirred by his anger, kicking the blanket away. "You would've let me go this morning without sayin' a fuckin' thing."

"No! No, I wouldn't, Dessie, I would've told you. I just ..." Halfway through the excuse I ran out of words.

With his back to me he grabbed a pair of jeans from his bag, hopped on one leg, then the other as he yanked them up. This was my chance, this was what I wanted — he was about to go so why was I trying to stop him?

I took a deep breath. On the TV a woman was on a roof, looking out across the city, the morning sun reflected from the buildings behind her. In the background I could see the tip of the London Eye cutting into the square of blue sky. She was animated as she spoke, optimistic for another day of sunshine. I grabbed the remote and snapped her into silence.

"Hang on a second, this is mad. Let's be honest. No, I wasn't going to say anything, Dessie. Why should I? I haven't seen you in — what? Twelve years? You think you'd be top of my list to call with my news?"

"How about Rita? Remember your aunt? Was she on the fuckin' list?"

The mention of Rita got me, as he'd known it would. He laughed. "Thought so."

He was distracting me as usual. This wasn't about Rita, it was about him and me.

"Look, Dessie, you show up here, unannounced, and expect me to be overjoyed? Kill the fatted fuckin' calf? I'm sorry, mate, but I've a life here. I've a job and a girlfriend and a daughter and you're not a part of that."

In the silence that followed my words I enjoyed the pounding of my heart, the freedom in the honesty. He found a shirt, pulled it on, letting my words hang between us. The short sleeve didn't quite cover the inky blue Arsenal tattoo on his right arm. "Jesus. Would you ever listen to yourself? 'Mate'? What the fuck is that about? I'm not your mate, John-Paul. We haven't been mates for a long time." He shook his head. "And I don't think half a lousy pizza that I didn't ask for qualifies as killing the fatted fuckin' calf." Laughing at his own joke he finished buttoning his shirt, pushing it into the top of his jeans.

"Listen, I should've known what to expect from you. What not to expect. The only person you ever gave a shite about was yourself. Mam said that. She didn't know how right she fuckin' was, did she?"

"What's that supposed to mean?"

"You know right fuckin' well what I mean." He stood in front of me, hands on his skinny hips, daring me to say more. An image of Mam's funeral skimmed the surface of my memory like a stone. "And by the way, those twelve years? Hardly my fault that I couldn't come and visit, now, was it? You knew where I was."

"I wrote to you," I said, suddenly remembering a sunny afternoon in Bristol writing a letter on a park bench. "I sent you a card for your twenty-first. You never wrote back."

"One poxy birthday card? In twelve years? What do you want, a fuckin' medal?"

Just like always: attack was the best defence. Don't give an inch, never show a chink in the armour. He hadn't changed a bit.

"It was more than I got from you."

"I'm not the letter-writing type." He shoved clothes into his bag and zipped it up, sat down and pulled his socks from last night back onto his feet.

"I don't know what you want me to say," I said.

"You've said enough, John-Paul. You've made yourself very clear. Crystal. You've a great life and a wife and a kid and you want me to fuck off and not mess it up."

"She's not my wife," I said. Before he could respond my mobile vibrated in my pocket. I took it out and saw that it was Katie. "Hey," I said, turning away from Dessie and walking towards the window. Pulling the curtain back, I looked into the manicured garden outside, full of sunlight and shade.

"Hey yourself, Dad!"

Katie's voice was so welcome, so normal. This was my world, her and Abbey, not Dessie. "How are you both doing?"

"We're fine, aren't we, Abbey? She was up for a couple of feeds during the night. It hurts like hell, I swear. I keep getting it wrong, JP, but the nurse says it's normal and not to worry if I don't want to stick with it. But they say it's so much better for them. I'm just worried she won't get enough food. At least I'm here for another night. Hopefully I'll have got the hang of it by then. So, where are you? You nearly here."

"I'm just leaving now, on my way out the door."

"Only now? I thought you'd be here ages ago."

"I know, I'm sorry. I overslept."

"Mummy rang from the train. They'll be here by about half past. You'll be here before then, won't you?"

"I'll be there really soon. I'm just leaving now."

Behind me Dessie laughed and I turned to see him smirk and shake his head.

"What was that? Is someone with you?"

"It's just the TV. Look, I'd better go. The sooner I'm off the phone, the sooner I'm over there."

"OK. See you later, then. Love you."

"Me too. 'Bye."

When I turned back to Dessie his bag was hitched over his shoulder, ready to go.

"So, what did you call her?"

It took me a moment to work out what he was talking about.

"Abbey."

"Abbey," he repeated, the name sounding different in his accent. "That was always your favourite, wasn't it?" He gestured to the wall with Beatles album covers making their own wallpaper. They butted against each other, a mosaic of music and memories. Winter Sunday afternoons and board games that I loved to win.

"Yeah, it still is."

He nodded, his eyes scanning them. Side on I could see his forehead eating into where his hair had been. Just like Dad's used to. Just like mine was starting to.

"I was checking out your music collection earlier. I couldn't figure out the order at first and then I realised it was by year of release. Just like the oul fella used to have his."

I shrugged, unsure if it was a question or a criticism.

"But I was surprised to see you had that new Beatles one, though, the *Love* one. Wouldn't have thought you'd be into messing around with the originals. You being such a purist and all."

"I haven't listened to it much. It was a Christmas present."

That was a lie. I hadn't listened to it at all, hated the idea of the mish-mash of songs out of the order they were intended. I didn't tell him it was from Katie but I couldn't shake the feeling that he had guessed. I looked away. Even after all this time there were parts of me he still knew better than she did. I hated that too.

"So, where are you going?" I said.

"Not sure yet. A lad I met inside lives in north London somewhere, a bit farther out. I might look him up."

I wondered had he seen Rita, if she'd let him stay with her, but I didn't want to get into that conversation again. "Right, yeah. You should go and see the new Arsenal stadium. It's not officially open yet but a guy I work with says you can see it from the road. It's meant to be fantastic. Do you remember when we did the tour of Highbury that time with Mam and Rita?" I pictured him in his Arsenal jersey, like a skirt to his knees, the excitement in his face reflected in the glass-fronted pictures of the retired players on the walls. The tour seemed to go on forever. Even the gift shop was an ordeal — Dessie had taken ages fussing over which programme would be the best to buy as a souvenir for Dad.

"Ah, I wouldn't be bothered with Arsenal any more. The game's all about the money now."

"I suppose."

"Jesus, remember that holiday, though? Tough enough spot where Rita lived. Remember those lads in the park?"

I remembered a forgotten memory: the panic of being jumped, two boys older than me who came from behind. The heavy weight of a knee in my back as I squirmed on the ground. A sharp knock of pain in my forehead as my head hit the concrete. Voices laughing in my ear, calling me a thick Paddy. "Those little bastards."

"I was just coming along behind when I saw them. I knew they were going to jump you. The way you took them both on, I didn't think you had it in you."

I squinted, remembering, but the more I tried to focus the fuzzier the image became. One minute I was on the ground, my nose and teeth squashed into mucky grass, the next I was standing, my hands pushing back, full of tracksuit and skin. He was taller than I was and his hands were hurting me, punches and slaps to my head and shoulder but I kept pushing forward into the pain. I can't remember what I did but it must have hurt him too because he ran off and next thing Dessie was there, grabbing the other. He locked his body tight around him, holding him still so I could hit him. I didn't know how to hurt him most and Dessie said to headbutt him in the stomach so I made my head into a missile and charged.

"They had you pegged for a wimp and you should have seen the look on your man's face when you pushed him up. It was class. He saw the red face of temper on you and he knew he was fucked."

I laughed along with him and felt the knot in my chest ease a little. Katie'd said she'd be in hospital for one more night. Maybe one night wouldn't be any harm to let him stay — we could catch up a little, put things to rest.

"Look, Katie's going to be in hospital till Wednesday so you can stay tonight, if you're stuck."

"Ah, I don't know …" He put his bag down.

"Look, it's only for tonight. You'll have to find somewhere else then. With Katie and Abbey we'll have a full house."

"To be honest, John-Paul, you'd be helping me out, a lot."

"Sure it's fine. No big deal. It's only for one night."

I wanted to make sure we were clear on the scale of the favour.

"That's great, gives me time to sort myself out. And sure we've loads to catch up on. And I can meet Katie and the little one."

I searched for words that wouldn't start the row again. "Look, Dessie, don't take this the wrong way but I'd rather you met them another time, if that's OK."

I saw his expression change so I rushed on, explaining, "It's just that Katie had a very hard time yesterday, in labour. It went on for hours until they decided to do a Caesarean in the end. That's why they're keeping her in, to monitor them both."

"Look, maybe I should just fuck off out of your way."

"No, no. It's just I think she should get some rest. When they're home and you're settled you can come over. What do you say?"

The words slipped easily from my lips. I knew that would never happen and I wondered if Dessie knew it too.

He nodded. "OK, then."

The video clock said it was a quarter to ten. There was no way I was going to make it in time. The last thing I needed was to give Philip another reason not to like me. "Look, Dessie, I'd better leg it. I said I'd be over first thing. Just make yourself at home."

He threw his bag onto the couch. I followed its arc and noticed his jacket was on the arm of the chair, a pair of trainers poking out from just underneath it. His cigarettes and lighter were on the shelf next to the TV. He wasn't ready to go at all. He'd been playing me, just like he always had.

"John-Paul, do you have a spare key I could use? I wouldn't mind having a shower before I head out."

"Yeah. Of course. Sure." I rooted in the drawer under the phone, hoping he hadn't seen my hesitation. Maybe I was wrong and he'd just forgotten to pack the shoes. I found the key and handed it over.

He slipped it into his pocket with a smile. "That's great. Thanks, John-Paul. And before I forget, congratulations." His handshake was hard against mine, rings cutting into my fingers. He pulled me into a rough embrace and for a second we held it, him slapping me hard on the back. "I was just thinking about those lads in the park. You'd been scared shitless of them the whole time, hadn't you?"

"They kept staring over at us," I said, remembering. "I knew it was going to happen, that the first time they got me on my own they'd jump me."

"That's the thing about bullies, though, the thing they rely on," Dessie said, heading into the kitchen and picking up the kettle. He turned around to wink at me. "They can smell your fear."

He held my gaze for a little too long before turning to the tap, losing the echo of the words in the rush of the water. Suddenly I didn't want to leave him in our home, with our things, but it was too late now. I swallowed the feeling, turned and waved goodbye before I could change my mind.

After the suffocation of the flat the air felt good and I took a deep breath. The July sunshine was reflected back at me from all around, the narrow iron-framed windows, the water in the pond and the slow, glittering carp below its surface. All at once, the need to be with Katie and Abbey was physical. I started to run.

I ran like a man possessed. Crunching, urgent steps across the gravel of the courtyard. Out past the security gate and up the road. Pounding the concrete in front of me, feeling it shudder through my bones. I ran up the hill and past the yellow flashing light of the minicab office. I ran under the shadow of the bridge where the filthy pigeons roosted and crapped on people below. I ran and I didn't stop running until I got to the station and onto the train that would take me back to my family.

FOUR

It's fair to say that Mam and I were never close. It was different being with her than with Dad. With him it was easy, like letting your body relax into a well-worn comfy chair. With Mam the conversation was fractured, the timing always slightly off. She didn't laugh at my jokes the way she did at Dessie's. I'd have to explain them until there was no point because the fun had been flattened out of them by then anyway. Sometimes I caught her looking at me when she thought I wasn't watching, her expression curious as if she was wondering how I'd got to be her son at all.

The time I was caught stealing from McCarthy's shop is the first time I remember us fighting. Dessie had told me that no one ever got caught. He told me he'd wait for me, no matter what happened. When McCarthy marched me out, his hand on my shoulder, like a claw, I looked for Dessie but he wasn't there. There was no one on the stretch of empty tarmac, the only sound the wrappers flapping around the overflowing bin.

I remember Mam answering the door, still in her navy dressing-gown, which she wound more tightly around her when she saw McCarthy. I remember the way her skin pulled taut over the angles of her face as she apologised, explaining how she had had a busy morning of housework, but when we went into the kitchen the table was still covered with crumbs and dirty plates from breakfast.

Mam gave McCarthy the money for the sweating chocolate I had to line up on the table but it ended up in the bin anyway. I can still see her, dragging it across the floor, lifting its broken lid with one hand and sweeping the bars off the table with the other so half of them landed on the lino. I was six years old and I'd seen her angry before but not like this — at least, not with me. "Jesus, John-Paul, what the hell were you at? You of all people. I'm so disappointed. Do I have to start worrying about you now, on top of everything else?"

Her voice was a shout but it wasn't like Dad shouting because when Mam shouted she cried too. I didn't know the right answer or what the "everything else" was and I was afraid to ask. As quickly as it came, the anger dropped out of her like wind from a kite and there was silence and that was worse than the shouting. I could hear the humming of the fridge and the sudden squeal of brakes on a bike outside as well as her crying. By then I was bawling too, tears and snot mucking my face. I wanted to tell her that it was Dessie, and not me, but I knew that no one liked a tattle-tale and that would make it worse. I tried to say something but she wouldn't look at me and then she covered her face with her fingers, like at Mass. I tried to squeeze between her and the table, kneeling beside her so my head was in the lap of her dressing-gown. I ached to feel her hand on my neck, for her to stroke my hair and tell me everything was going to be all right.

"I'm sorry, Mammy," I said. "Dessie made me." I waited
for her to say something but she didn't answer. Instead, she
pushed her chair back to free herself from my snivelling. She
slammed the kitchen door behind her and left me with my
tears and a Kit Kat in the bottom of my pocket that had
escaped McCarthy's beady eyes. Shoving it too quickly into
my mouth I almost gagged on the burning chocolate. I
thought that day she'd never forgive me. Sometimes I think
she never did.

I don't remember when I first found out about her
drinking. It feels like there should be one clear revelation but
it wasn't like that. I thought everyone's mam drank in front of
Coronation Street or *Give Us a Clue*, just like everyone's dad
had a drink in the Noggin Inn. I thought everyone's mam and
dad fought the way our mam and dad fought, because that's
what Dad told me and I didn't know enough not to believe
him.

Sometimes Mam would be under the weather and we'd
have to make our own school lunches and I always ended up
tearing the bread with the butter because I couldn't make it
skim straight from the fridge the way she did. The odd time,
she was still under the weather when we got home from
school and we had to wait for dinner till Dad came in from
work, but she was always better the next day.

It was just the way it was and it didn't worry me at the
time. It wasn't until Catherine Begley started laughing at me
one day in the yard that I knew I needed to be worried. "My
mam says your mam was up the pole when she got married
to your da."

"No, she wasn't!"

"Was!"

"Wasn't!"

"She was so! My mam says everyone knows! And that means your brother's a bastard."

I knew the words, I'd probably even said them, but I didn't know what they meant, not really. I knew that it was bad, though, and my cheeks flushed hot when I said there was no way it could be true. And even as the words came out, a part of me was scared that maybe it was.

That night I decided to ask Dessie. I waited until he was in bed too and the light was out so I could launch the question into the dark.

"Was Mam up the pole when she got married to Dad?"

He waited a minute before he answered and I thought maybe he was asleep already.

"Where did you hear that?"

"Catherine Begley said it."

"Catherine Begley's a little bitch."

There was silence after he'd said that and I lay there, waiting for him to say something else, but he didn't. I wanted to ask him more, to ask about the bastard thing, but I couldn't say the words. Instead I asked something else: "Is that why they're always fighting?"

"John-Paul, just shut the fuck up and go to sleep."

After that I started counting the rows. I didn't know whether they were fighting more or if it was just that I was noticing it more, but they seemed to fight all the time. I wasn't sure which rows were my fault and which were

Dessie's. Some of them were about money and I wondered if those were our fault too. The row could start over dinner or at breakfast or on our way somewhere in the van. The ones I hated most were the ones that happened after me and Dessie had gone to bed, the ones behind the sitting-room door.

And then, it all stopped, the shouting and the door-slamming. One day, the house was just quiet. I nearly thought things were OK, until I figured out that this was just a different way of fighting. That this fight was slow, stretched out over days and weeks, even, a dangerous fight that pretended things were normal before snapping out to make itself heard and going into hiding again. I tried to forget it was happening and I think Dessie did too, but it was always there and even when I couldn't see it I was always waiting for it.

The fight before we went to London was the worst — worse than the waiting, even. I knew it was coming when I got home from school and Mam wasn't there. She wasn't there when Dessie came in from football or when Dad's van pulled up outside. I met him at the gate, trying to fill the silent hall with words so he wouldn't notice there was no sound or smell of dinner. When he lifted the phone there was silence there too. Dessie said that maybe Mam had gone to call Rita from a payphone because ours had been cut off again. He said it like he was trying to be helpful, but the way he said "again" let me know he was really on Mam's side. Dad must've known that too because he slammed the receiver off the wall so hard it burst right through the wallpaper and made a dent in the plaster underneath. The O'Briens next door must have heard him roaring the F-word.

It was Mr McDonnell who brought her home that night, even though Dad had looked everywhere. I never did find out where she'd been but I remember how she sloped against him, her body a floppy slant as he helped her up the drive. Dessie had gone out and I was sent upstairs to do my homework but I couldn't concentrate, trying instead to fill the gaps from Dad's shouting below. My stomach gurgled and I thought of the sandwich I'd thrown in the bin at lunchtime, eating only the crisps. By the time the shouting stopped, the darkness had crept across the window. Dad tried to look cheerful when he came up to see if I wanted chips for tea, but the hunger was passed by then, leaving behind only an empty swish of unease.

The next morning at breakfast it was like nothing had happened, Dad hidden behind the paper, Mam's hands wrapped around her mug of tea to keep them warm. I buttered my toast, pretending to watch the knife as it scraped across the crunchy surface, but really I was watching them. Dessie shovelled down his cereal quickly, like he was refuelling rather than eating. He was getting up to go when Mam made her announcement. It was the first thing she had said and she made herself smile. "I've got a surprise. We're going to London to visit your Auntie Rita and Uncle Ted."

I'd never been outside Ireland. Dessie had been to Holyhead with the Scouts and gloated over it for weeks. I was too caught up in the thrill to notice the false eagerness in Mam's tone. To see that Dad hadn't put down his paper.

"Are we going on a plane?"

"No, we're getting the ferry," Mam was saying. "We're

going to leave next weekend when you boys are finished school."

"How long for?" Dessie asked.

"A month."

"A month? Four whole weeks?" I repeated. "Does work not mind you being off work for four weeks, Dad?"

That was when I realised Dad wasn't coming. I knew before he folded the paper and I could see his face properly. I knew that I was stupid not to have figured out that this was part of the fight too. Dad's mouth smiled but his eyes didn't, and he explained how he couldn't get time off, that we would have a great holiday and he was sorry to be missing it. I wasn't listening, though, my mind instead imagining four weeks with just Mam and Dessie, four weeks without hearing Dad's voice, his laugh. Four weeks without him.

It was a Saturday morning when we got the ferry and Dad dropped us down in the van, trying to be cheerful. Me and Dessie were in the back with the cases and Dad was joking with Mam, fast-forwarding *A Hard Day's Night* until it got to the song he said was their song.

"There you are now, Marie, 'Things We Said Today'. Do you remember dancing around to that in my mother's living room?" He looked across at her but she was staring out the window, her chin on her hand. "Remember I used to sing this to you?" He glanced from the road over to her and back to the road again, singing the first bit of the chorus. I started to sing along too. "That's right. You know all the words, don't you, John-Paul?"

"Yep!" I kept singing, wishing that Dessie would join in,

his silence loud beside me. Mam still wasn't singing either. She just sat there like a statue and I wanted to shake her. "Did you forget the words, Mam?" I said. "Will I tell you the next line to help you remember?"

She didn't turn but when she answered her eyes caught mine in the rear-view mirror. "People don't always want to remember things, John-Paul. When you're older you'll understand."

Dad went silent after that but I kept on singing the next song and the one after and the one after that, filling the silence until we pulled over on the double yellow lines beside the ferry terminal. There were people everywhere, families going on holidays all together, no one staying behind. Dessie had dragged the cases from the back, starting towards the boat before I was even out of the van properly. Mam held my shoulder ready to go too, when Dad slipped a tight-folded square of English money into my hand.

"Thanks, Dad." I didn't look at it but pushed it down into my shorts pocket so I could feel the hard corners of it against my leg. Suddenly I didn't want to go. I wanted to stay with him, but Mam was already pushing me into the crowd, following where Dessie had gone, leaving Dad behind.

"You're to share that with your brother," Dad called after me, "and don't spend it all in the one shop."

On the ferry, Dessie had found seats already, by the window, but I didn't want to sit down. Instead I ran through the maze of passageways and up narrow stairs looking for a way onto the deck. I banged my shin off one of the iron steps but I didn't stop running, pushing my way through the crowd, overtaking the slowcoaches. At last I was out, the air like the sea in my face, and I scoured the shoreline for Dad. The engine rumbled through the floor and into my feet. My eyes moved too quickly and I skimmed over him at first but then I saw him, standing in the shade of a tree behind the turquoise railings. I waved my arms together and then he saw me and gave me a sailor's salute. I saluted back and then I waved again. I waved until the houses on the shore became smaller and smaller. I waved until the ferry turned the corner of the harbour, away from home and into the big breadth of the sea.

Later, after Dad died, I thought that maybe those four weeks were like practice, a dry run to get me ready for a time when I'd have to do without him, but they hadn't been like that at all. I'd loved London, staying with Rita and Ted and their cat Snowy in their flat on the fourth floor. I fell in love with the city, the bigness, the noise, the people. I'd never seen so many people, men and women of different ages and colours, rushing along streets, into shops, down escalators, crossing roads. Every day on the Tube Mam gripped my hand in a sweaty grasp, afraid of losing me in the crowd. I pulled away from her because even though I was a scared to be around so many people, part of me was excited too.

Dessie had no other friends around so he was nice to me and we played football in the park together. He showed me how to hang upside-down on the climbing frame that left blisters of rust on your hands. Mam and Rita talked and talked. I'd never seen Mam talk so much — I hadn't known she'd had so many words locked up inside her. When they sat together with their heads close and voices low, stopping when I came over, I knew they were talking about Dad.

One day when I went into the kitchen to get some orange, Rita had her back to me and kept talking. "You don't have to go back, you know, Marie, there are other options," she said, before Mam made a face to tell her I was there. Pouring my orange into the glass, I could feel their eyes on me, the words still real in the room, and I concentrated on not letting the cold bottle slip.

That night was one of the hottest. Dessie slept — he could sleep through anything — but lying on the couch with the cat hair I was wide awake. They were planning for us to stay in London and never go back to Sallynoggin. I tried to imagine living here, going to school here, with all those other people, only seeing Dad on holidays or at Christmas. It was hard to imagine the two places at the same time, as if Sallynoggin was only real when I was there, that Dad was too. On the phone when he rang he sounded different, his voice, the things he said. Despite myself, part of me was excited at the idea of living with Rita and Ted in London. Another part was scared by how quickly I'd forgotten I'd wanted to stay at home. How easy it might be to get on without him.

FIVE

The Royal Free was supposed to be one of the best hospitals in London but it smelled like any hospital I'd ever been in, that mix of disinfectant and fear that hit me as soon as I came up the steps and through the sliding doors. Abbey shouldn't have been born here: our postcode decided that she was an East End child. Right now Katie and Abbey should be in some overcrowded ward, but Philip had known someone who could sort it out. He always did.

I paused outside the room to catch my breath, flattening my fringe against my forehead. It was only my second time meeting them and Katie wouldn't be happy that I was late. When I opened the door it was Philip I saw first, his dark grey suit like a shadow in the bright sunlight, and I was conscious suddenly of my T-shirt, clammy from my run up the stairs. A pink and silver helium balloon blew into his shoulder, and as I pushed the door wide I saw that the room had been transformed overnight: it was crammed with flowers and cards. Rebecca was sitting on the bed, holding Abbey in her lap. Next to her Katie was leaning over, making a silly face, her tongue sticking out. Both of them looked up when they heard me and I noticed for the first time the likeness between Katie and her mum, that they were older and younger versions of each other.

"JP!" Katie said, smiling. With makeup on and her hair washed, she looked like my Katie again. I crossed the room and leaned in to kiss her, conscious of our audience.

"Hey! Look at this place. Where did it all come from?"

"I know! Isn't it fab? Mummy and Daddy brought the teddy over there. And Rachel sent those flowers with them — aren't they gorgeous? The basket is from the girls at work. Alison knows I've got a thing about helium balloons."

I followed as she pointed out who had sent what and immediately forgot. Rebecca was smiling at her granddaughter. Abbey's eyes were open and I wanted to kiss her but I made do with stroking her little arm where it poked out over the blanket.

"What took you so long, JP? I thought you'd never get here."

Letting Katie down in front of her parents was Toby's old role. I felt the three sets of eyes on me, waiting for an explanation. The lie came so easily. "I know. I'm sorry. It was the bloody Northern Line. Some guy decides that today is the perfect day to throw himself under the train and it would have to be my train."

"JP, that's an awful thing to say." Katie touched my arm and glanced at Rebecca. "The poor man."

Not only was I late, I was embarrassing as well. Before I could respond, Philip was there, his hand outstretched. His handshake was solid and I gripped it hard, trying to impart something that my words seemed to be failing to do.

"Good to see you again, JP. Congratulations. You must be over the moon."

"Oh, yes. Completely. It's amazing."

"Yes, congratulations, JP," Rebecca said. "She really is an adorable little thing."

I bent down to kiss Rebecca on the cheek, her own kiss for me landing somewhere midair. Her perfume was sweet and strong and caught somewhere in my throat. For an awful second I thought I might cough all over her but I swallowed it back, stood up and took a breath.

"So, Philip. Are you catching up on some business while you're down here?" I said, nodding at his suit. Before the question was fully out I knew it was the wrong thing to say. Katie looked at Rebecca who looked at Philip, waiting for his reply. Folding my arms I bounced on the balls of my feet, my trainers squeaking in the uneasy silence.

"Not too much, just one meeting," he said. "You know how it is. There's a retailer down here I've been meaning to see for ages. May as well kill two birds with one stone."

Rebecca sighed. "You can see your father's still a workaholic," she said to Katie. "Some things never change."

"Rebecca, one meeting hardly makes me a workaholic," Philip said, laughing. "Does it, JP?"

I laughed along but I didn't answer. Instead I gazed down at Abbey who seemed to be looking around but I knew she couldn't see anything properly yet. More than anything I wanted Philip and Rebecca to go so we didn't have to share her.

"How many times have I heard that over the years? I only hope JP's not as bad, Katie, or he won't see too much of this little one growing up."

Rebecca spoke as if I wasn't there. I opened my mouth to defend myself but held on to the words. This was Katie's moment to step in, not mine. When I'd met them before it had been slightly strained, small-talk over roast pork, and Cabernet from chiselled crystal glasses. Philip and Rebecca had smiled but I knew they were sizing me up, comparing me to Toby, deciding why they wouldn't like me. Now Katie broke the silence: "Here, Mum, let JP hold Abbey for a minute."

"Of course — sorry, I should've offered. She just seemed so peaceful. Here you are, JP," Rebecca said, taking Abbey into her arms and standing up slowly. I didn't care that her smile didn't reach her eyes, that she didn't want to hand me her granddaughter. This was the moment I'd been waiting for since I'd put Abbey down last night, maybe even before then. My moves were more confident than before as I lifted her gently from Rebecca.

"Hello, Abbey, Daddy's here."

Her eyes fluttered open and closed. Her hand outside the blanket was curved into a fist the size of a marble, the clench of strength surprising me. Without any warning her mouth opened so wide that the gaping pink gum seemed to take up half her face. Her cry was shrill and sudden, sounding as if it hurt her little throat as much as my ears.

"What did I do?"

"Are you supporting her head properly?" Rebecca said.

"I think so."

I shifted my elbow to make sure. There was a second of silence before she was squirming and whimpering again, and I knew I was doing something wrong. The whimper became a howl and then another screech. I heard Philip's voice — he was on the phone and I hadn't even heard it ring. He mouthed something at Rebecca and ducked out into the corridor.

"He's not even meant to have that on in here," she said, over the noise.

Abbey's crying was getting louder, just when I didn't think it could get any louder. I rocked her gently but everything I did seemed to make it worse. Her face was red, her eyes tiny slits. "I don't know what's wrong with her," I said, hearing the panic in my voice.

"Come here, I'll take her," Katie said, stretching out her arms. "She's probably hungry. Poor baby Abbey, are you hungry, darling? Sssh. Come here."

Katie started to unbutton her nightie and I watched in fasci-nation as she soothed Abbey into silence with her words and her touch, moulding her into the softness of her body for food. There was something about it that was so natural, so instinctive, that everything else seemed to mean nothing at all.

"Did you notice she's even more like you when she's upset, JP? Look at the way her little forehead creases up." I leaned over and saw what Katie had seen. Abbey's face already had ripples of my own, of Dad's, of Dessie's.

Abbey was brand new yet she was already part of something ancient, of a family who would pass things on, right from the start, without even knowing it. Faces, values, nurture, love. As I stood watching Katie feed our brand new daughter I couldn't help thinking about the things that shouldn't be passed on, things that should be held back. Things that she might need protection from. I'd always be there to protect her. She could count on that.

★★★

It was just the three of us again. Rebecca might have stayed longer only Philip ushered her away to a table booked for lunch in a Belsize Park bistro, saying we should have time on our own. Katie's sisters would be here in a while but for now I had them to myself.

"Look at her. I can't believe she's ours."

I murmured the words into Katie's hair, careful not to wake Abbey who had fallen asleep against her breast. Sitting behind Katie with my arms around her, I felt I was in the right place, the largest in the family of Russian dolls.

"Me neither," Katie said, turning so her mouth brushed my cheek, ending the words in a kiss. "I mean, it's weird. You know that at the end of all these months you're going to have a baby, but now she's here it's like this massive surprise. That sounds stupid …"

"No, it doesn't." I tightened my arms around her. "You're right, that's exactly it."

"I was afraid I wouldn't connect with her. You read these stories, where mothers just don't feel anything, that they're given their child and there's just nothing. I was afraid that might happen to me."

Rubbing my chin along the smooth skin of her shoulder, I smiled at the outpouring. It was just one of the fears she had voiced along the way. "I knew you'd never have to worry

about that. You're such a softie, Katie — you can't watch
Coronation Street without crying sometimes."

"Shut up!"

"It's true and you know it — sure you even stock up with
tissues when we go to the cinema," I teased. "What was that
film we watched on TV a few weeks ago, the one with River
Phoenix?"

"Oh, don't start me off!"

"*Running On Empty*, wasn't that it?"

"JP, honestly, don't!"

"What's that line? Where the parents decide they can't
expect River to be on the run with them forever, so they
leave him behind?"

"I don't know."

She stuck out her bottom lip, shaking her head in
defiance, but I could see the laughter creeping up into her
face and feel it spreading in a tremor through her shoulders.
I smiled as I remembered her cuddled up against me on the
couch, after the film, tears still in her voice as she tried to
make me see why the film was so sad, unable to understand
my lack of response.

"You do know. Go on — it's when they're all about to go
on the run again. And the dad turns and says something to
River about taking his bike out of the back of the pickup
truck so he can go off and live on his own."

She was giggling but I could hear the threat of tears in her
voice. "God, I'm so crap, I've seen that movie eight thousand
times and it still makes me cry."

I kissed her ear. "Exactly, so how could you ever have

worried about not loving this little one here?" I wanted to tell her how much I loved her mix of softness and strength. Her ability to purge herself of emotion so she could regroup and make herself stronger. Before I could find the words, Abbey let a small cry escape from her lips. We waited for more but she stretched and relaxed again. In silence, we watched her tiny chest rise and fall with short, shallow breaths. I timed my breathing to hers and then slowed, inhaling from my stomach, letting my shoulders fall as well. Calm dissolved through my body, I tightened my grip around Katie.

I'd never been so happy.

★★★

"Does it hurt?" I asked.

Katie adjusted Abbey at her breast. She couldn't seem to get her in the right position and Abbey's mouth gaped, missing the dark pink flesh of Katie's nipple. Any minute now she was going to cry.

"Yes," Katie said, not looking up. "I can't get her to latch on properly. Can you call the nurse in for a second?"

"Do you want a drink of water?" I said, holding out the glass. "The book said that if you drink cold water it can help."

"I've already drunk gallons and now I'm dying to pee as well. It's not that, JP, I'm doing something wrong — it's not supposed to hurt like this."

"Maybe if you moved her up a bit."

"JP, she's about to start screaming. Just get the nurse, will you?"

Her mood had turned all of a sudden and I couldn't keep up with it. Stamping to the door, I sighed loudly to show her she wasn't the only one who was stressed out by the whole thing. Escaping into the corridor, I found it was nice to be away, even for a minute, from the confines of the room and have a task to do. On my way to the nurses' station I checked my BlackBerry. It had been vibrating all morning but Katie had already caught me listening to a voicemail from Peter so I was afraid to check it in front of her. The nurse was one of the older ones whom I hadn't met before. I stood there while she read something from a chart in front of her.

"Hi, I'm sorry to bother you. I was wondering if you could give my partner a hand. She's having a bit of trouble breastfeeding. She's just down the corridor here." I smiled but she didn't smile back.

"You're not supposed to have those things on in here," she said, her eyes on the BlackBerry in my hand.

Before I could apologise she was already walking away and I hurried after her down the hall. As we got nearer I could hear Abbey's cries, louder than before, and another baby farther along the corridor joining in. The nurse disappeared into the room without waiting for me, and by the time I came in there was silence. The woman was leaning over Katie, who was frowning in concentration.

"You see, if you hold her in that position it's easier for you and her, especially when you've had a Caesarean. You don't want to be resting her where it's tender."

When the nurse pulled back I saw that Abbey was half under Katie's arm, only the top of her head visible with

Katie's fingers holding it in place at her breast.

"The clutch position," I said. "I read about that."

If they heard me they didn't acknowledge it, both staring at Abbey as she fed.

"Thanks so much," Katie said. "It's just if I know she's not getting fed, I start to panic, and that makes it much worse."

"Ah, now, don't be silly, duck," the nurse said, patting Katie on the arm. "We all get that panic thing the first time around. And she'll pick up on it. If you need me, just ring that bell. I'm only at the end of the hall." She winked and turned to leave.

"She's lovely, isn't she?" Katie said, when the door closed.

We sat in silence for a minute, both of us watching Abbey, whose eyes were closed now so I couldn't tell if she was sleeping or feeding. I didn't notice my leg bouncing up and down until I saw Katie look at me. I held it still.

"What's wrong?"

"Nothing," I said, shrugging.

"You look on edge."

"I'm not."

"Look, I'm sorry I snapped earlier," she said. "I hate it when I can't do this right. It feels like something I should just be able to do."

"I know. And you are." I reached over and squeezed her hand.

When she looked at me she was crying again. "What if this happens when we get home? If I can't feed her? There won't be a nurse around to show me then. If it wasn't for Daddy we'd be home already — can you imagine?"

Her voice spiralled higher with each sentence.

"Don't worry about that now," I said. "We'll take it one step at a time. It'll be fine — you heard what the nurse said, everyone goes through this. And if for some reason it doesn't work out then we'll bottle-feed her. She's not going to go hungry, that's for sure."

Katie was dead set against bottle-feeding, wanting to do everything the way her sisters had with theirs. The books recommended breastfeeding, but some small part of me felt like giving up on the whole thing. At least if we were feeding Abbey with bottles I'd be able to do something instead of just being a spectator. Abbey would be our baby again, instead of just Katie's.

"I know you're right. I'm just being silly." I handed Katie a tissue and she blew her nose. "I won't be worrying like this for the next eighteen years, I promise."

"Well, if you still haven't got the hang of it by then, we're definitely moving over to bottles."

It was a feeble joke but it was rewarded with a little smile that changed her face, softening the lines of tension. I reached my arm across her shoulders and rubbed my finger along the smoothness of her neck, playing with a loose strand of her hair. "Don't you worry about a thing, Katie. We're going to be the best parents in the world," I said. "Just you wait and see."

★★★

Hampstead Heath was empty, London empty. A man with a Labrador that sniffed in circles around him. A panting woman pushing a baby in a buggy, a toddler in tow. Those daytime people I never saw, and today I was one of them.

I lay down, stretching out, enjoying the springy heat of the grass against my back. In the corner of my vision I could see the grey hulk of the hospital pushing tall into the blue sky. Katie's two sisters had arrived from Cheshire and I was surplus to requirements. Girl talk — nappies and nipples. Any minute Rebecca would be back too. There were things I could do to help and I would do them. But not now.

So much had happened in less than twenty-four hours and I needed time to think it through and put a shape on it. The night before ran on a loop through my head. The same pictures again and again, yet still I couldn't fully get it; I didn't fully understand. After all this time. What did Dessie want? Why now?

A thought had formed in my mind this morning that I couldn't seem to shake. What if this wasn't a coincidence? What if he had known about Abbey and had been waiting? Biding his time. For what, though? It was crazy, this whole thing. I pushed myself up from the grass and onto my feet. I had to walk. To move. To get away from these paranoid fantasies. It was just everything happening together, Abbey being born, seeing Dessie. It was enough to mess with anyone's head.

Walking made the thoughts more ordered. One by one I could examine them and put them back; one by one I could deal with them. The last time I'd seen him was at Mam's funeral. A day we both wanted to forget. A day when the sun was too strong for the heavy black suits we both wore and his prison officer was never far away, like a shadow on the hot concrete. I don't know where he was when the fight broke out: it had been Uncle Ted who'd had to prise us apart, who pulled Dessie off me and held him until the officer reappeared with handcuffs. After years on the building sites, Uncle Ted was strong enough to pin back Dessie's arms and fists, but even he could do nothing about the shouted accusations that rang out and filled the hall and sometimes still fill my head.

I realised I'd stopped walking so I started again, pulling myself out of the memory. I'd been over that last time enough in my mind. He said I never visited him in prison but he was wrong. The first time I went with Mam to see him I was almost excited. The big gates. Metal detectors and buzzers. It was just like a film. Only it was real. I thought there might be reinforced glass with telephones but there wasn't. Only tables, blue plastic like in school. It should have been loud in the room with all the people talking at the same time but it wasn't, just full of heavy whispers and choppy silences.

The walk had taken me down to the lake on the other side of the Heath. My whole body was suddenly exhausted and I leaned against a tree, grateful for its shade. On the opposite bank the bathing huts reflected back at themselves. There was only one person in the water today, a red-capped head that bobbed up and broke the surface before disappearing again. Some day soon I'd be teaching Abbey to swim, passing it on.

Dad taught me in the old baths in Dún Laoghaire, a pool with crumbling grey stone instead of tiles. He made it look so easy, gliding across the water, and I wanted to get it right for him, to make him proud, to be a big boy and not cry when the water stung my eyes and got stuck in my nose. I remember standing by the edge, and the cold emptiness on my arms where the water wings had been. The older boys jumped in, their knees tight against their bony chests, yelling curse words that disappeared with them into the noise of the splash. I made myself jump in too, pushing myself blindly towards the middle, choking on the water and the fear that welled up inside. I was rising up towards the top, the panic ebbing away just before I felt the hand on my head, forcing me back down. In the underwater silence I pushed up but he was too strong. I couldn't breathe, my lungs were going to burst, I was going to drown — and suddenly I wasn't. It was my ears that told me when I burst from the surface of the water, not my tight-shut eyes. As I flapped and gasped and swallowed, I heard the laughter all around and Dessie's was the loudest.

I couldn't tell Katie about Dessie. Not when she thought I was an only child, that I had no brothers. I had made her a promise when we knew the feeling between us was on the cusp of becoming more, something bigger than us both. I remembered how she looked, crossing Tower Bridge, pulling her cream coat tight around her. I remembered her voice, her words blowing away on the breeze as she said them, disappearing into the river below.

"I need you to promise you'll always be honest, JP. Never lie to me, will you?"

I had known about Toby, about the wedding and the split. Office gossip was good for filling in the blanks. But I didn't know until then how much he had hurt her, until I saw it in the hunch of her shoulders as she pushed herself onwards into the wind.

"I promise," I said.

And I didn't lie to her, not really. She wanted to know all about me, what it was like growing up as an only child, compared to her houseful of sisters. She wanted to know more and more and I had to tell her, adding details so that life without Dessie started to become real. I used the times he'd been sent away to imagine what it would have been like if he'd never been there. It was easier making up that story than talking about what it was really like. The real story was in the past and it wasn't for Katie or Abbey. What happened before was nothing to do with them.

I turned from the lake. Back up the hill towards the hospital, my legs ached, but my head was clearer. Katie wouldn't understand how I could have lied. I wouldn't be able to explain how easy it had been to forget Dessie. Easier than remembering. It wasn't like on telly, like the soaps she watched, where they wake up one day and decide to disown a brother. I don't think I ever decided that, not really. He just slipped away, bit by bit, out of my life, out of my head, until he was gone. But he wasn't gone.

That was my big mistake. I should have let him leave this morning when I had the chance. The hurt expression, the regret in his voice. It was an act, just like all those times before when Dad had caught him stealing, joy-riding, worse. I had to make myself remember how he could trick me. How he could manipulate me. It was dangerous to forget all that.

The Other Boy

When Mam died I was only a boy. Things were different now. I had a family to protect. A baby. Despite the sun I shivered. I had to be tough like he was. I didn't want him anywhere near either of them. I wasn't going to let him hurt them.

He was my past. Abbey and Katie were my future. He had to go.

Six

It was the kind of pub I would never come to with Katie. This was a real East End boozer, a world apart from the bleached organic microbreweries that were sprouting up around the park. Even though I'd never been here before, there was something about the flashing poker machines and sticky carpet, the haze of blue smoke over the sheen of the bar that made it feel like home.

"There we are," Dessie said, spilling some lager as he lowered the glasses onto the dark wooden table.

"Thanks. You should have let me get the first round."

"They're not big on beer mats over here, are they?" he said, shaking spilled beer from his wet hand.

"No, I suppose not," I said, remembering how I used to notice that too.

"Anyway, cheers! To my little brother, the new father!" Dessie raised his dripping pint and we chinked glasses.

"Cheers." I swallowed a gulp of the cool lager and it felt good. I licked my lips. I knew what I had to do. Just not yet. "So, what did you get up to today?" I asked.

"Ah, you know, this and that. Wandered onto the Tube into Leicester Square. Jesus, that place is a hole."

"Yeah, I know. Only the tourists go there. When I first

moved down I used to hang out there a bit, at some of the Irish pubs. Huge places with glass cases of old fashioned groceries and farming tools. But I'd never go there now."

"When was that?" The crack of a match punctuated his question as he lit his cigarette. He blew a line of smoke, thin and straight, catching in the sun.

"God, it's nearly eight years ago. I can't believe it's that long. The time's flown by."

There was a pause before his next question. I could see him forming it in his mind.

"You been back at all? Home, I mean."

Home. A narrow street with houses butting together. A lane with a shop at the end. Cycling in figure eights on the green. "No." I shook my head.

He nodded. Maybe he already knew that. I fumbled for something more to say but he got there first. "Mam always wanted to live in London — do you remember?" He smiled. "She said there was a real buzz about the place, that if she hadn't met the oul fella when she did she'd have followed Rita over."

I hadn't remembered but I nodded anyway. I didn't want to talk about Mam. "I came down for a year when I was at uni in Bristol," I said, "with my mate Paul. It was part of the course to get a work placement. We'd fuck-all cash but we had such a laugh."

Across from me Dessie's face was unreadable, his pint already half gone.

"We thought we'd died and gone to heaven. Out every night after work — there was always something going on.

We'd sit there nursing our pints until the others felt sorry for us and included us in the rounds, so by the end of the night we staggered out more hammered than anyone." I laughed, remembering. The world of drunken snogs and waking in co-workers' flats seemed like someone else's life now, not part of mine. "So, how about you? What have you been up to since you got out?"

"I only got out last month."

"Last month?" I took another drink of beer, doing the maths in my head. He'd only got seven years so that didn't add up.

Before I could ask more, he bounced the conversation back towards me again, with a little flick of a question. "So, how long have you been with Katie?"

"About a year and a half." I waited for him to ask about Abbey, whether she was planned or if we'd been caught out. I got the words ready to make sure he knew she wasn't an accident but he asked something else instead.

"Where did you meet?"

"In the office. We work in the same company. BHB, an investment bank."

"You do the same job?" he asked.

"No, not really. She's one of the administrators. I'm a financial analyst, a numbers guy." I'd almost said "senior financial analyst" but caught myself just in time.

He swirled the remains of the lager in his glass, yellow with flecks of white. "So, what does a numbers guy do, then?"

"Analysing companies to decide if they're a good bet or not, and then I present the investment opportunities I think are good ones to my clients."

"How do you do that? Is it difficult?"

I checked for sarcasm but he seemed interested, actually listening. "It's a challenge, but you get to know your sector and read the signs. Mostly I look after commercial property – that's one of the biggest areas. Sometimes stuff goes wrong and you can make a loss but you balance it later. That's the idea, anyway."

My words hung in the air with his cigarette smoke. I'd said way too much. This wasn't Philip I was talking to. I wasn't trying to impress Dessie.

"Big bucks?"

"Ah, no, not really. It's decent and the long-term prospects are good but it's nothing like some of the traders make. My friend Paul, the one from uni, he's been on six figures since he was twenty-four."

He raised one eyebrow, a trick I could never copy no matter how hard I tried. I needed to change this conversation. The last thing I wanted was Dessie thinking I was loaded. "And rents in London are so damn expensive — it's crazy. Eats up about half of my salary, even for our tiny flat. And now we've got a baby we'll have to tighten our belts."

I was explaining too much but he didn't seem to be listening now, already on his feet, waving his empty glass at me. "Same again?"

Before I could respond he was on his way to the bar. From behind the tall brass taps the barmaid watched his approach, flicking her blonde curls out of her eyes. Dessie rested his elbows on the counter, leaning in close to say something to her. Whatever it was had the desired effect and a laugh broke across her heavily made-up face. What was it about him? How could a scrawny Irish guy with half a beard make her smile at him like that?

I could feel the beer starting to work its magic, the giddy swish in my stomach. I should have eaten first. Questions rolled in my head. Why had he only got out last month? What had happened in prison? I remembered his face, thin and white, at Mam's funeral. The marks on his arms. My mind expanded with possibilities. Assault? Drugs? Worse? I had to know.

"Here we go, thought I'd get a little something to wet the baby's head," Dessie said, smiling.

This time there were two small glasses as well as the pint, a golden liquid clinging to the side. He pushed one towards me, the smell of whiskey so strong it was nearly a taste.

"Jesus, Dessie, I'll be on the floor. I'm not used to drinking like this any more. And it was my round."

"Ah, come on, Johnny, it's not every day I'm celebrating being an uncle. Down the hatch!"

Johnny — I'd forgotten he used to call me that when he was in a good mood. Johnny, John-Paul, JP. Sometimes Katie liked to call me Jay. How could I be just the one person with so many names? Across from me Dessie closed his eyes and snapped the contents of the glass back in one motion. Before I could think about it too much, I followed his lead, the hot liquid catching in the back of my throat and making me gag.

"Nothing like a chaser," Dessie said, lifting his pint.

I wiped some sticky dribble from my chin with the back of

my hand. My insides tingled. Dessie was an uncle. How had I managed not to think about that until the second he'd said it?

"So, tell me, Johnny, what's a gorgeous bird like Katie doing with a loser like you?"

He grinned and so did I, knowing that in his way he was paying me a compliment.

"Christ only knows — I ask myself the same question every day." The words were honest, surprising me. "She's great. We get on really well, hardly ever fight. Don't reckon her mam and dad are too keen, though."

The beer was cool after the burning whiskey. I forced myself not to gulp too fast. Behind me there was a breeze as the door opened and a few of the market traders from outside drifted in.

"How come? You being a hot-shot numbers guy and all."

"Fuck off. I don't know, probably because her divorce isn't even through. And I get the impression they're not too keen on the Irish thing either."

Dessie's forehead rippled with the unspoken question. I'd given too much away again but I couldn't take it back now.

"Katie was married before, to some public-school prick from Cheshire with an ego as inflated as his bank account. He treated her like shit." I heard the venom in my voice. It felt good to talk about Toby instead of tiptoeing around him. I didn't need to explain to Dessie why I hated guys like him because he'd understand. Despite all the years apart, something that united us was still there. Something that time hadn't eaten away.

"They mustn't have been overjoyed at the pitter-patter of

tiny feet, then," Dessie said, his face pulled into a smirk. He pulled another cigarette from the box, shaking one out for me too. He lit the match for me as I leaned in, inhaling.

"You can say that again. They were convinced for ages that it was an accident. But it wasn't. We both really wanted a baby. Well, she did mainly, and I didn't mind."

I felt the redness of the lie creep into my cheeks. Then the smoke caught in my throat and turned the words into a cough. I sat back from the table, hitting my chest in an effort to stop. A deep breath of air and the coughing fizzled out. Across the table Dessie was having a good laugh at my performance. His image blurred through my watery eyes and I remembered my earlier resolve. I was talking too much: it was time to turn the tables.

"But enough about me. How about you? How come you only got out of prison last month? Seven years, wasn't it, five for good behaviour?"

"Ah, now, John-Paul," he shook his head and winked, "you know as well as I do that good behaviour never was my strong point." His laugh was loud and strong, amused by himself as always. It was a laugh that carried most other people along in it but it had always made me feel afraid.

"So what happened?"

I timed the question all wrong so the words cut across his laughter. I wondered if he'd heard the fear in it.

"Jesus. What is this? The Spanish fuckin' Inquisition? You weren't even going to tell me about your kid but suddenly you deserve to know every fuckin' detail about me?"

The alcohol made me brave, bringing me back to the row

this morning. We were heading towards another and this time I wouldn't stop him leaving because it would save me saying what I needed to say.

"It's hardly every detail. You're staying in my house and I think you should be honest with me. Last time I saw you, you were on drugs. It's only fair that I know what's going on."

"There's nothing fuckin' going on. Is that what you're so het up about? I kicked that shite years ago. I'm clean now for five years."

As he spoke he unbuttoned his cuffs and pushed up his shirt sleeves. There was a dangerous edge to his voice. "Have a look if you don't fuckin' believe me."

I glanced quickly at the white skin of his upturned forearms, brandished across the table at me. He'd forgotten I'd seen them this morning and I knew before I looked that they'd be as smooth as my own. "I never said I didn't believe you."

"You didn't have to. For fuck's sake, it was written all over your face."

I sat in silence as I watched him button his sleeves again and rescue his cigarette from where it furled smoke in the ashtray. Was this more of his lies or the truth for once? Something in his face made me believe him. I needed to find something to say.

"Fair play on giving up," I managed eventually. "I'd say that was incredibly tough."

The words were wrong, better suited to winning a game of squash, not kicking heroin. If he thought so he didn't comment.

"Fuckin' hardest thing I've ever done in my life," he said. "But the best thing too."

I wondered how he could define the best thing in his life as giving up something that had been his fault in the first place. This conversation could lead to dangerous places but now he'd started he didn't seem to want to stop. "I'd never have managed it on my own," he said, fiddling with the cigarette, rolling it back and forward between his thumb and forefinger. "I'd tried a couple of times, but the thing is, inside, it's everywhere. Easier to score in there than out here."

I nodded, draining my beer. I was going quicker than him now — he still had some left.

"If it wasn't for Shay I'd never have managed it. He made me see the error of my ways, as they say." He put on a fake voice, hiding behind the humour.

"Who's Shay? A counsellor?"

My question brought a snorting laugh, a real one this time, and he had to put a palm up to his mouth to keep the beer inside.

"Shay? A counsellor? He'd get a laugh out of that. No, he was my cellmate. An old lad. He'd been in there forever. He was caught up in an armed robbery when he was twenty. Petrol station, one of the other lads shot a guard by mistake. Killed him. Shay was the one who got sent down."

"Jesus."

"He was fuckin' sound, though. Never held a grudge against the other fella. Said it was just one of those things, that shite like that happens to people all the time. You're in the wrong place at the wrong time and then bam — you're fucked. It's nobody's fault."

Across the table I held Dessie's gaze. His eyes were glassy, challenging me with what he said next. "Shay taught me a lot. He was the one who made me realise about all that shite with Mark. It just fuckin' happened. It wasn't my fault."

I couldn't look at him then so I focused instead on the table, the glistening rings made by the glasses on its dull surface. Anger throbbed in my head. I didn't trust myself to speak. The silence stretched out between us and when I finally raised my eyes he was looking out of the window at the last of the market traders folding their stalls away under plastic canopies for the night.

"What do you want, Dessie?"

"What do I want?"

"What made you come and find me? Is it a loan you need to get back on your feet?"

His expression changed as he studied me. Without his jokes it was harder, all lines of skin on bone. His ring clinked against the empty glass. "Is that what you think, John-Paul? That I'm here for your fuckin' money? Who's been paying for the fuckin' drink all night? I haven't asked you for a penny, have I? Have I?"

His voice was louder, a rough edge to it that made my heart hop despite the pints, despite the crowd around us. I pictured Katie and Abbey, safe in the hospital. So much had happened, Dessie couldn't pull me back into the past just like that.

"No, but if it's not money, then what?"

He rolled the empty glass between his fingers, from one hand to the other. I waited for him to answer and when he did he seemed calmer again. "If the truth be told, I don't fuckin' know why I'm here." He held my gaze. "I just found myself on Rita's doorstep. Like going back in time, the same chiming ring on the doorbell. All the same fuckin' ornaments on the shelf. Little windmills and china fuckin' cats. She's still the same."

I pictured her living room easily, the detail more vivid than the flat where I lived now.

"She started talking about you. She said she hadn't seen you for years. She wasn't even sure if you were in London still. That she'd had your birthday cards sent back from your old address. It was the landlord there that gave me your new one."

I pictured Rita selecting a birthday card from the corner shop, writing it carefully, her dismay as it came back weeks or months later through her own door. Guilt swam in my stomach. What must she think of me? It wasn't her fault — but it wasn't mine either. She was just caught up in all this, like I was.

I cleared my throat. I knew I needed to respond. "It's been a while. I must arrange to see her. I've been really busy at work. You know how the time flies by."

"So you keep saying," he said, pushing his stool backwards before turning away and striding towards the toilets.

★★★

The pub was fuller now. There were men waiting to be

served, pulling their money from the pockets of worn-out work jeans and holding it in front of them across the bar. Somewhere behind me there was the clack of snooker balls. The six empty pint glasses in front of us made patterns on the table in the late-evening sun.

"What do you think?" I asked. "Same again?"

Dessie crossed his arms, frowning, as if there was a decision to be made. "Ah, go on then. Twist my rubber arm."

The forgotten expression brought a smile to my face as well as his. I was halfway to the bar when I heard him call me. I turned and squinted, trying to make out his face, his shape just a black shadow against the light of the window. "What?"

"Get us some peanuts as well, John-Paul, will you? And some Pringles, if they have any."

"Anything else?"

"No, that's it," he called. "Actually, do they sell Marlboro here? Get me a pack of the red ones."

"Jesus, sorry I asked."

"John-Paul?"

I turned back again.

"It's beginning to sound like you were right. Maybe I am after your money."

I laughed and it felt good, hearing him laughing with me. I shouldered my way through the crowd and the blonde girl serving behind the bar winked at me. That meant I'd be next. Someone turned the music up and the piano chords were ones I knew well. 'Let It Be'. One of Dad's favourites. Maybe it was a sign, maybe I should. Just for a while.

★★★

It was dark outside. Across the table Dessie's impression of our old headmistress made me laugh, so the beer fizzed up my nose.

"It's Mzzzzz Mulcahy. Not Mrs. Not Miss." He imitated her nasal voice perfectly.

"There was no way she was ever going to be a Mrs with a face like that. If she was the last woman on earth, I'd rather chop me own bollix off than go near her."

"Remember someone smashed the wing mirrors on her car and everyone said they broke because she looked in them?"

"Who d'you think did that? Got the rear-view one inside too, had to jimmy the door and nearly got caught, but it was worth it." Dessie drained his glass, leaking beer into his stubble.

"I should have known." I shook my head. "I'm surprised she never found out."

"Oh, she knew it was me all right, course she did. She just couldn't prove it. That was her problem."

"Just as well — Dad would have gone ballistic!"

Too late I realised my mistake. It was almost the end of the night and we'd made it this far without mentioning Dad. The anger in Dessie's face was instant and I knew that was what I'd seen a flash of earlier, that it was always there, hiding just behind the humour. Somewhere deep inside, I felt a worm of fear.

"There was a lot he never knew about. Fuckin' prick."

"Dessie, come on ..."

"Come on what? He was a fuckin' prick and a bully."

A bubble of his spit landed between us on the table. His gaze was fierce, daring me to disagree.

"Dessie, seriously, don't say that."

"Why not? That's what he was. And he never gave a shit about me."

His voice was getting louder but I thought no one would notice over the music and the talking that had risen to almost a roar. I'd chosen this pub for a reason. "Look, I know you didn't always see eye to eye. Maybe he wasn't always the easiest to get on with. But he tried his best, Dessie, you know that."

"He tried with you, John-Paul, he never did with me. He blamed me for everything. Believe me, I've had a lot of time to think about this and I know he never gave a shit."

He reached forward and lit another cigarette, half turning in his seat so I couldn't see his eyes. As I watched him I thought of a Christmas Day I'd never forgotten; Dessie had been given a brand new bike, with thin wheels that clicked when they moved. I got Dessie's old one, wrapped up, hidden under a coat of blue paint with a sparkling new bell.

"Dessie, this is bullshit! I thought you'd be over this bullshit. Of course he gave a shit. Do you not remember that Christmas when you got the racer and I got your old cast-off just with a new fucking bell?"

"For fuck's sake!"

"Well, why would he have done that if he didn't give a shit about you? Spent money that he couldn't afford?"

"One Christmas? Is that all you can come up with? A bike doesn't make up for everything else, John-Paul."

"Meaning what?"

"Nothing, meaning nothing." He shook his head as he reached for his pint again.

"You're not going on about that stupid football match again?"

"It was the under-12s' final. The first time the school had ever made it, and I was the fuckin' captain." The look on his face was identical to that of the boy who'd thrown his hard-earned medal into the corner of our shared room two decades before.

"He had to work. For fuck's sake! I can't believe you're still going on about it, that you're still holding it against him."

"Jesus! It's not about the fuckin' match. You were the one who brought up the match." Dessie ground his cigarette into the ashtray too hard so embers and ash sparked up around his fingers. "Look, forget it. I don't want to talk about him. That's all ancient history. What I'm saying is, I hope you make a better father than he did. I hope we both do."

The glaze in his eyes was alcohol or sincerity. I almost laughed, but the idea of Dessie having kids was too scary to be funny. I opened my mouth, ready to defend Dad, to refresh Dessie's memory of what had really gone on and have the same argument over again. The words were there but they wouldn't come out. They were old words, well worn. They'd never reached him before and they wouldn't tonight either. Let him think what he wanted. He was the one who was screwed up, Psycho Whelan, everyone knew that. And tomorrow he'd be gone and it wouldn't matter anyway.

As I stood up from my stool I stumbled slightly, gripping the edge of the table to steady myself. "Let's forget about it. They just flashed the lights for last orders. Same again?"

★★★

The chips were good — salty and hot. Towards the bottom of the bag they were wet with vinegar and my fingers broke apart their soggy mess. I had to tell him. Every step we took was just delaying the inevitable. I had to tell him tonight.

"They don't give you any drinking-up time in this country," Dessie said.

"Dessie, I've got to tell you something."

"Oooh, never a good start to a conversation, John-Paul. Let me guess … you're gay?"

"Fuck off!"

He put on a shocked expression, then doubled over in a crease of mirth. The laughter bubbled inside me too, jostling alongside nerves and beer.

"Have you any more chips there? I'm still starving. Do you've any food back in the flat?"

"Nope, nothing."

"You'd think now your bird would have stocked up before going in to have the kid — she must be a right selfish cow."

"Shut the fuck up."

"Ah, Jesus, John-Paul, I'm only joking." He was suddenly remorseful. "You know that. Don't start getting all serious on me. She sounds class. You're dead lucky. I can't wait to meet her. Do you remember Trisha Kelly? From Pearse Villas? I was seeing her for a while when I was out a few years back. She was a class bird too."

I remembered the Kellys. A gaggle of sisters in minis and corkscrew perms. I didn't know which was Trisha.

"When I ended up back inside she went off and got married. Wrote me a letter to tell me. Some fella from Stepaside! Stepaside was fuckin' right. Stupid bitch."

I bundled the greasy chip bag into a ball and threw it at the bin. It bounced off the top and rolled away, coming to a stop against the kerb. The pace of my heart was out of time with my actions. I had to say something.

"Dessie, listen. I don't think you're going to meet her."

The words weren't definite enough and he hadn't understood. In the orangey streetlight he was looking at me but thinking of Trisha Kelly. I spoke again. "Katie, I mean. You mightn't get to meet her. I mean, you won't."

Confusion crossed his face and was replaced by a slow smile. "Ah, I get it. You're afraid she'll fancy me." He nodded, straightening his walk into a strut. "It's understandable, she is only human after all. And I can't say I wouldn't be tempted. But don't worry, John-Paul, she'd be off limits. I swear."

I wondered if there was a grain of truth in his joke. It didn't matter anyway. I was halfway there: I had to say the rest or I never would. "No seriously, Dessie, I mean it. You'll have to go tomorrow before Katie comes home. I'm sorry."

Every word was sobering me up.

"I know, so you said. That's grand. I don't mind waiting a few days till you're all settled."

It wasn't really a question but it felt like I needed to answer it all the same. Something gurgled in my stomach and for a second I thought I was going to be sick. A loud beery burp pushed its way out. "Excuse me," I said automatically.

Dessie stopped walking and I did too.

A car appeared over the bump in the hill, its headlights blinding me for a second, engine roaring. We both turned to watch it speed up the road, listening as the sound faded into the night.

"Look, I'm sorry, Dessie …"

"Why'd you keep saying you're sorry? What's the fuckin' story, John-Paul?"

We were nearly at the gate and I could see the porter's office, the shape of Ahmed's head on night duty. The warmth and fun of the bar were miles away from this and I cursed myself for getting carried along by it. It was way harder to tell him here, on this silent, empty street, than it would have been earlier. The only way to say it, was to say it quickly and say it all.

"Look, Dessie, there's no easy way to say this. Katie doesn't know I have a brother. She thinks I'm an only child." I laughed as if it was a joke. The alcohol buoyed me along, making the laughter real, maybe it was a joke. For a second Dessie joined in and then he stopped. Something in my face had told him I wasn't lying.

"You told her you're an only child?"

"I didn't tell her I was an only child …"

"She made it up her fuckin' self, did she?"

"I never told her. She just assumed." I hated the whine

that crept into my voice. Dessie heard it too. I couldn't read the expression on his face: it looked like anger but it might have been pity.

"For fuck's sake, John-Paul! Listen to yourself, 'she assumed'. What the fuck?"

"Dessie, I should've told her but I didn't. And now it's too late ... so I can't ..." I stared at the path, at the white tips of his trainers visible underneath the dark denim of his jeans. When I looked up he was facing the other way, up the road towards the Tube station. Maybe he was going to leave right now, without his stuff, even, but I wanted him to understand before he did. "You'd been inside for so long and we hadn't even spoken. I may as well have been an only child. What was I meant to tell anyone about you? Her family ... they're real fuckin' snobs ... and her friends ... It just happened ..."

"It just happened," Dessie mimicked, turning back to me and nodding.

"It was one of those things — what was the point in telling her when I thought I'd probably never see you again?"

"What was the point?"

"I didn't mean it like that. You know what it's like — don't say it's never happened to you. You start off with one thing, an exaggeration, not even a lie, and next thing you know you're stuck ..."

There was a glimmer of something in his eyes and I thought I was making progress. "She'd ask me what it was like, you know, growing up, so I'd tell her. And it wasn't a lie, really, because you were hardly ever there. But she has this thing about honesty — I told you about her ex. He was having an affair for ages before she knew. If she found out I'd lied to her ... I don't know what she'd do." The words were coming easier now, filling the space between us. What I was saying made sense. He had to understand. "Jesus, Dessie, I don't know, she might even leave me."

"And take your kid with her."

His words went where my thoughts had been afraid to and I felt the vomit rise again, hitting the back of my throat. I swallowed it down. She couldn't, she wouldn't. I took a breath and it was better: she wouldn't take Abbey because she wouldn't have to know. I wasn't going to tell her.

Dessie's hands were in his pockets. He bounced up and down on the balls of his feet. "So, what now?"

The question was normal, as if he was asking what pub we were going to next. Maybe he understood. Maybe it was going to be OK.

"You can stay tonight. That's fine. Totally fine."

"But I've to be gone in the morning, sneak out early, maybe?"

He was sort of smiling, as if it was a game and he'd just learned the rules. I didn't like the way he jerked his head when he said the word "sneak".

"No, not that early," I said. "I mean, we can have breakfast and stuff."

"And after that?" He raised his eyebrow, and the recently remembered gesture made me feel sad and guilty at the same time.

"I don't know. If you need help to get back on your feet I can lend you some cash. I don't mind," I offered. "Maybe we could catch up every now and again. Next time you're over we could go for a nice meal, a few beers. My shout. Somewhere decent in town, not like that kip of a boozer we were in tonight."

The funny thing was I actually meant it. Some part of me really thought it would be nice to meet up the odd time, find out how he was doing. About Rita and Ted.

"A few beers?"

He was repeating everything I said, twisting the words to make them sound weak and insulting. I shrugged. I should have realised then but my guard was down, lowered by laughter and alcohol. I was waiting for him to say something else, to shout and curse at me, maybe even storm off.

"You're a smug little prick, John-Paul."

I didn't see his hand making a fist, only the swing of movement before the impact at my temple that pitched me sideways. At first it was shock and not pain I felt as my legs gave way and my knees smacked the concrete.

"You fuckin' cunt! What else didn't you tell her? Did you tell her all about Mam or did you pretend she didn't exist either?" Breath caught in his words. Another blow came, a kick this time. That was when I felt the pain, a burst of it in my side that knocked me flat onto the ground. Instinctively I covered my face, rolling onto my front, away from him.

"That's why you don't want me around, isn't it? 'Cause I remind you of a few fuckin' home truths."

Below me the cold path smelled of piss. On my back I felt Dessie's foot pushing in hard to the base of my spine.

He bounced it up and down, snatches of pain. Any second it would snap.

"Dessie, please …"

"Listen to you, snivelling, you're nothing but a fuckin' coward."

I pushed myself onto all fours, my knees and fingers clawing at the concrete, remembering too late it was the wrong thing to do. I'd given him space to find another kick and he pounded his foot into my side, flipping me over so I landed on my back. This pain was different, cold and warm at the same time, and I cried out as I remembered the curve of green glass I'd noticed only seconds before. When I opened my eyes Dessie's shape loomed large over me, a shadow magnified by the streetlight overhead.

"I should've fuckin' done this years ago."

Above me, in slow motion, he raised his foot. I could see the rippled pattern of his trainer sole. Turning my head away, I snapped my eyes shut, as if they alone could stop the force of the impending blow. In the second before the impact everything paused. I heard the gate open. A voice calling, a slice of hope, running footsteps on stone.

And then the stamp came, an explosion of blood and snot and agony. I remember the sound of my voice screaming in the dark, sounding as if it came from someone else. I think I remember someone laughing.

And then I remember nothing.

SEVEN

Dessie was always a legend at St Lawrence's. He'd been held back in fourth class and that had made him the oldest in his year. He was always first to do everything: to get suspended, to get his hole. To spend time inside, even if it was only two nights. He was captain of the under-18s when he was sixteen, and when he was eighteen he was playing for the under-21s. He was hard as nails, he'd take on anyone. He'd no fear; everyone said so.

It was different for me. I'd to follow in his footsteps instead of making my own. Teachers already blamed me for things I would never do. The lads in my class couldn't make me out. For some of them I wasn't like Dessie enough but for others I was too like him. I wasn't tough enough for the tough lads or square enough for the squares. I was a loner. A nobody.

That was how I ended up being paired up with the Tool that day, for the trip to the museum. When Miss Donnelly saw me trying to hide she picked him out straight away, standing alone by the wall. No one called him Mark; to everyone he was the Tool. He lived on our road and I saw him walking to school. He was always on his own, too, but we never spoke. At break times he sat on the steps reading

James Bond books behind thick black glasses. He was always the one without a partner.

We didn't say anything on the way to the station, hanging behind the rest until Mr O'Leary came up behind us and told us to get a move on and not be Paddy Last. As we walked faster his breathing was heavy so you could hear the air coming through his nose. It got on my nerves, the way he breathed so loud like that, and I remember thinking that it must be because he was so fat.

I might have enjoyed the museum if he hadn't been there. I liked the cold, heavy air and the smooth, curved marble stairs worn by thousands of footsteps like ours.

Miss Donnelly stood on the step counting us out loud. "OK," she said. "Today we're going to look at the Bronze Age. I want you all to pay attention because there's going to be a project that you'll be doing afterwards. You'll work in pairs so make sure your partner's paying attention too."

With the word "project" we let out a groan. This was the ransom for the trip. Somewhere near the back someone started to hum. Another hummer joined in and another, and the hums rumbled louder. Beside me Mark O'Toole sniffed. Short, leaky sniffs. He delved into his pockets for a tissue but finding none rubbed the ooze along the soft cuff of his jacket. An afternoon together I could just about handle, but a project? No way.

We followed Miss Donnelly around the display of glinting copper behind fingerprint-smeared glass. Each time Mark squeezed to the front, his chubby face a reflection of awe, her speeches got more excited, as if they were directed personally to him. Behind me, there was a tremor of conversation, muttered voices getting louder. I thought I heard my name. A snort of laughter. I never looked around.

The next day, standing on the front step watching his fat navy shape fumbling for keys behind the bubbled glass of their porch door, I could taste my hate for him. For everything about him. The "No Smoking Zone" sticker peeling from the glass. The staggering predictable piano scales that leaked through from the open window of the sitting room, stopping and starting, back to the beginning again. They all tumbled together into a tight ball of hatred in my stomach that flowed through my body and into my mouth, like saliva. We'd get the project done in one afternoon, I'd already decided. And that would be that.

He didn't smile as he closed the door behind me. I followed him down a dark hall, copying his tiptoe past the piano sounds. He opened another door, and the kitchen was big and bright behind it.

"My mam's a piano teacher," he said. "I have to be quiet when she's giving lessons."

"I kind of figured that one out."

"Do you want some orange juice?"

"OK."

He disappeared into the yellow light of the fridge and I looked around the room. It felt bigger than our kitchen, even though all the houses on the road were the same. The press doors were white and glass instead of wood. Around the table a bench was built into the wall and lined with checked cushions. There were photos everywhere, in frames on the windowsill, on the cork noticeboard, even on the front of the fridge. A younger version of Mark's mam smiling with a baby in her arms, Mark's dad's arm around her shoulders. Another one on a beach, close up, three round faces squinting into the sun that bounced back off their glasses. The coolest was one of Mark and his dad in a dinghy wearing orange lifejackets. It must have been raining because their hair was wet and slicked back but it didn't stop them smiling into the camera.

"There you go."

I didn't say thanks, just gulped, swallowing the icy liquid as if it was its fault I was stuck there.

"We can do it here or in my room," Mark said. "Which do you want?"

"I don't care."

I switched the word "mind" for "care" just before I said it. I sounded like Dessie did and it felt good.

"In my room we can listen to music, but we can't down here. 'Cause of the piano."

"What music do you have?"

"Mostly old stuff. Bob Dylan. The Rolling Stones."

His cheeks were red as he listed the names. He had stopped ignoring me. Here in his kitchen, surrounded by his photos, he wanted me to like him.

"You probably don't have any Beatles?"

"Yeah, I do. Loads. The *White Album's* my favourite."

"*Abbey Road's* better. Do you have that?"

The words were out of my mouth before I could stop myself and that was how it happened: somewhere between

Bob Dylan and the *White Album* I forgot to hate him. He had a record player in his room, his very own, and lots of albums. On the shelf above his bed there was a tape recorder as well, covered with dust.

"Do you never use that?" I asked.

"Nah, I prefer the records. The sound is better and, anyway, Dad gave me all his old stuff. It'd cost loads to buy it all on tape."

I wandered around the room, taking in the shelves of books neatly lined up by height rather than title. The Liverpool poster on the wall that matched the duvet on the bed.

"You can borrow it if you want," he said to my back, as I paced around. "The tape recorder. I hardly ever use it."

I imagined Dessie getting his hands on it. There was nowhere to hide anything in the room we shared.

"No, thanks. I share a room with my brother. He's got one already."

Mark looked away when I said that. Neither of us mentioned Dessie by name. He pulled a record from its sleeve, shiny plastic vinyl. "I'll put on *Abbey Road*. What's your favourite song?"

We started walking home together. It was easier that way, and we had to work on the project. Sometimes Mark bought me chocolate with his pocket money. He was an only child and Mam said he was spoiled rotten. Sometimes his money had already been nicked at school so there was no chocolate for either of us.

He preferred The Rolling Stones to The Beatles. Mick Jagger to John Lennon. We argued for hours about it. We played songs that would prove our point, pretend groaning and smacking our heads when the other couldn't see what was obvious. I could make him laugh — that was simple. His laugh was contagious, funny and high-pitched, and I loved coming up with a sarcastic comment or an imitation of someone in school that meant I'd hear it. Dessie was the funny one, not me, but that didn't stop Mark, and soon I was laughing too, at his crazy laugh as much as my joke.

I remember pretending I already knew when he told me that 'Lucy In The Sky With Diamonds' was about drugs — LSD. His dad had told him so it had to be true. He talked about his dad a lot. More than I did about mine, even. His dad sold insurance and had a silver grey Sierra that was the newest car on our road. On Friday nights his mam and dad went out together for a meal or to the pub; mine never did that. On Saturdays when his mam taught piano, Mark and his dad went driving in the Sierra, to the Sugar Loaf or as far as Wexford. If it was sunny they stopped for ice-cream but mostly they just drove and listened to music.

He annoyed me when he went on like that. Boasting. Rubbing it in that they had more money than us and that his dad didn't have to work on Saturdays. That they had a new car instead of a van.

"I sometimes have a pint with my dad," I told him once, making my voice casual.

"No way!"

"Way!"

"He lets you have a pint? Really?" Behind his glasses his eyes were saucers. He believed me.

"Yeah, sometimes." I nodded.

"Wow!"

That was the thing about Mark. He believed everything I said. Sometimes when I said things to him I started to believe them myself. I even started to imagine that I drove around with Dad on the weekends, went to work with him in the van. One day when everyone was out, I took his Beatles records and laid them out all over the sitting-room floor, pretending he'd given them to me, listening to a track off one, then another. But by the time he came home I'd made sure they were lined up neatly on the mahogany shelf in chronological order, where they belonged.

★★★

It was my fault for not being home on time but it was Mam's too. Usually she'd never notice I was late, or even know where to look for me. And she'd never sent Dessie out to bring me home before.

That night Mark's dad brought home the surprise, and with all the excitement I forgot the time. I really liked Mark's dad — he was always friendly, making jokes and smiling — but I never knew what to say to him. I wanted him to like me too much and around him words dried up on the roof of my mouth and funny comments I knew would have made him laugh only came into my head afterwards, when it was too late. Once, when I walked into the kitchen, he was kissing Mark's mam, hugging her and kissing her right on the mouth even though she was wearing a stripy apron with flour all down the front. Mark came in behind me and saw them too, and I was embarrassed for him and for them. He just walked past and opened the fridge door as if he hardly noticed, and they just laughed and it was like I was the one of out synch with everything.

I remember that night, his voice calling up the stairs — we just about heard him over 'Tangled Up In Blue'. Mark was more into Bob Dylan than I was but I was starting to come around. At first his voice was too grating, not as melodic as Paul's or John's, but I noticed after I listened that fragments of his words were left in my brain, making pictures long after the music had stopped.

Mark opened the door onto the landing and his dad's voice was clearer now: "Come on down, Mark, and bring John-Paul. I've got a surprise for you."

I was almost as excited as Mark was, coming into the kitchen to see his dad with a plastic bag in his hand that looked as if it had a box inside. With his other he pulled something from his pocket and handed it to Mark.

"Here you go."

Mark turned it over in his hand, confusion and disappointment in his face. "Batteries?"

His dad smiled, and I knew then. I knew before Mark did what was in the bag.

"Yep, thought you might need some new batteries for your calculator or something."

I thought Mark was going to say the calculator took different-sized batteries but he saw his dad's wink and his eyes moved towards the bag.

"Yeah, right! What is it, Dad? What's in the bag?"

Mark's smile was huge as he pulled it open, but his dad's was even bigger as he watched him rip the lid from the box to reveal a bright red Sony Walkman. Some of the older boys had them and I'd seen them on the ads but I'd never been so close to one before, seen the polystyrene that protected it under the sleeve of clear plastic.

"Wow! Thanks, Dad, it's so cool! I love it!"

Mark held it in both hands, gently removing it from its packaging before passing it to me so I could admire it too. I opened the red door, turned the black spool with my finger. I could smell its newness.

"I know it's not your birthday or anything, and your mother will probably kill me when she finds out, but there was a really good sale on," Mark's dad was saying. "And I knew you'd like it, but you have to look after it."

"I will, Dad, I promise I will. Thanks a million, it's the best present ever."

Mark's dad leaned down, making himself ready for the hug that he knew was coming. I picked the batteries up from the table and opened the plastic hatch on the back where they should go, careful to put them in around the tiny ribbon. I didn't look at their hug, I didn't want to see it, but I could feel it next to me — the family that, no matter how hard I tried, I could never be part of.

Mark got a Rolling Stones tape from upstairs, loaded it into the Walkman and, after a minute, he passed it to me so it was my turn to listen. Under the spongy headphones the intensity of the music was magic. I could still see Mark and his dad and the warm steam that trickled on the windows but the music flooded from the headphones and filled me up so it was all my own. That was why I didn't hear the doorbell, why I saw Dessie coming in with Mark's mam before I heard him, why I felt the cold from his jacket in the warmth of the kitchen before I heard him speak.

"Hi, Dessie," Mark's dad was saying, when I snapped the music into silence. "Sorry John-Paul's a bit late. We were just getting a bit excited trying out Mark's new Walkman. What do you think of the sound, John-Paul?"

Dessie was waiting for my answer. The sight of him standing there, in Mark's kitchen, made me realise I needed to piss. "It's great," I managed.

"Here, let Dessie have a go," he said, taking the Walkman from me and handing it to Dessie. "See what he thinks."

"No, it's grand, we've to go," Dessie said, ignoring his outstretched hand. I caught his eye and saw something in it that made the need to piss more urgent.

"Why don't you boys stay for dinner?" Mark's mam said. "We usually get fish and chips on Fridays so it's no problem."

"Yeah, I'll go down now. I can pick up a couple more singles. You could run over and tell your mam you're staying," Mark's dad said.

I wanted to say OK, to stay, and try out the Walkman with Mark and make chip sandwiches, but I knew we couldn't.

"Thanks, but our mam has made dinner for us," Dessie said, in a formal voice that didn't sound like him. "So, we'd better go."

It was then I realised that since Dessie had arrived Mark

hadn't said anything, that he seemed to have almost disappeared, pushing himself into the gap between the fridge and the table.

"Not to worry, maybe next time," Mark's dad said. "We're terrible gluttons on Fridays in this house. Are you going to come with me to get the chips, Sparky?"

The nickname hung exposed in the warm air of the kitchen. The smile was still on Mark's dad's face as his hand kneaded Mark's shoulder, unaware of the feeling in the room that only three of us understood. I'd heard him call Mark Sparky before but I hadn't said anything and I willed Dessie not to now. I saw that Mark was staring at the lino while Dessie gazed around the room, seeming only now to see the photos everywhere, a strange look on his face.

When we got home, Dad wasn't there yet and Mam was fussing with his dinner, putting a plate over it that didn't fit properly so the sauce from the beans seeped out around the edge. We always had to wait for him, that was the rule, but it was late and Dessie kept saying how starving he was after training and that the mashed potato would be horrible if we didn't eat it soon, so eventually she let us go ahead. The mashed potato was horrible already, stuck together in lumps, and I thought about the chips I could've had. I ate it quickly to avoid what I knew Dessie was going to say.

"I can't believe you're hanging around with the Tool."

"I'm not hanging around with him. I'm doing a project with him." I looked at Mam for support, to change the subject. She was moving the food around her plate instead of eating it.

"Project my arse," Dessie said. "Why not invite your new best friend over for dinner one night. You wouldn't mind, would you, Mam?"

"Have who over for dinner?" Mam hadn't been listening, glancing instead from the clock to the door.

"Why, Sparky, of course!" The sarcasm made Dessie smile as he slowly let the name unfold from his lips.

"What's he ever done to you anyway?" I said, my cheeks burning. "He's not that bad." I kept my eyes on my plate. There was a fish finger left but I didn't want it. Dessie opened his mouth wide, as if he was in shock. He looked to a mock audience for confirmation of what he'd heard. He loved this, playing to the crowd. The best thing to do was to ignore him. I'd learned that a long time ago.

"Not that bad? He's like your man out of *Grange Hill* — what's his name? Roly Poly! Big red face on him like his fat fool of a father."

"Shut up!"

"No wonder his oul lad goes around buying him stuff like that — it's the only possible chance he has of maybe bribing some eejit like you to be his friend."

Mam still didn't say anything. Dad would have made him shut up by now.

"He's not my friend."

"Trust you to have a new best friend who's the biggest fuckin' gobshite in Lawrence's. That's why he's such a target. Just don't expect me to bail you out when you become one too."

Even Mam couldn't stand by and let him curse at the

dinner table. "Dessie, watch your language," she said. "Leave John-Paul alone, let him make his own friends."

I remembered Mark's face the previous week – he'd looked as if he might cry when he showed me his recorder. Someone had stamped on it. The mouthpiece was cracked down the middle and a piece was missing. I still had it in my bag to see if Dad could fix it. I hated what Dessie was saying. I hated the part of me that knew he was right.

"How many times do I have to say it? He's not my friend!"

I shouted the words at her, at them both, pushed my chair back and stormed towards the door. Out of the corner of my eye I saw Dessie lean over to my plate and shove the fish finger into his mouth in one go.

★★★

Dessie went on and on. How I shouldn't hang around with Mark, how it was asking for trouble. What a spoiled little cunt he was. It wasn't like me to ignore him — I think it was probably the first time I ever did. And it wasn't as if the threat of being picked on by bullies didn't scare the shit out of me. It did. It was just that somehow, with everyone else — Dessie, Mam, even Dad, I felt as if I was somehow faking it. That the times when I was with Mark were the only times I was really myself.

That was why I was waiting around for him that day when it was his turn to clean out the locker room after PE. I was listening to the new tape he'd got, The Smiths. Mark wouldn't stop talking about it but I wasn't sure I liked it yet.

101

I needed to listen to it again but the Walkman batteries were starting to go and Morrissey's voice was even more droney than it had been before. I clicked it off, then back on again. For a second, it was normal and then too slow. I switched it off. The yard was starting to get dark. In Mulcahy's office a yellow light was left on. Mark should be finished by now.

I heard it before I saw it. When I snapped the tape off the silence wasn't just silence: I could hear something. The same sound repeated. A thud. I lifted the sponge from my ears and there were other noises too. Muffled words, someone crying. Another thud.

It was coming from the passageway, the short-cut between the yard and the teachers' car park on the other side. I'd only been in there once, running to catch a ball that had skipped down the steps. It smelled of cold concrete and piss. It would have been easy to put the headphones back on, to leave the yard and say I'd waited. But even I couldn't do that. Not then, anyway. Maybe it would have been better if I had.

Inside the passageway it was dark. I hesitated on the step, peering in. The noise was louder now and I could see there were only two of them. I didn't need to wait until my eyes turned the black into grey to know who was there.

Dessie's kicks were quick and well placed. Well practised. Mark's hands moved to cover the exposed parts of him, the soft bits of flesh that would suffer more damage than the rest. He wasn't quick enough. It was hard to see where Dessie's shape stopped and his began. Mark was crying, loud sobs that filled the tunnel bouncing off the dark walls. His cries mingled with the kicks and the noise echoed back on itself as if it wasn't enough to hear it just once. Dessie's sounds were different, short, panting breaths in time with his kicks, which were rhythmic. Methodical. Timed as if someone was calling out, "Again ... again ... again ..."

I was made of concrete, part of the step. I didn't want to be there. My bare skin touched the wall where my shirt was untucked and I shivered. Mulcahy was still in her office — I'd seen the light on. If I ran up and told her Dessie would stop. She could make him stop. I took a step up the stairs. Without turning around, Dessie knew I was trying to leave. He had known I was there all along. "Don't fuckin' move, John-Paul."

"Dessie, stop! Leave him alone!"

"I said, stay where you are." It was an order. He turned and looked at me. Even in the dark I could see his forehead was shiny and wet. "I'm not finished yet."

"Dessie, please, come on. What's he ever done to you? Leave him alone. Please, Dessie."

On the ground Mark wasn't moving. Near his head there was a small pool of blood, almost black like the oil in the bike shed. I looked up the steps and wondered how much time it would take to get to Mulcahy's office.

"I'm doing this for you," Dessie said. "Come here."

He gestured next to him, pointing at a spot on the ground. I looked but didn't move. He pulled me over so I was beside where Mark was doubled over on the cold concrete. His arms covered his face. His knuckles were buried in the wool of his cuffs but the bits of his fingers that I could see were scratched and bloody. I could see him breathing, in and out. He wasn't dead. Dessie wiped his greasy forehead with his sleeve.

"It's your turn now."

"What?"

"One kick."

"No! Here, Dessie, take the Walkman — just leave him alone!"

I took the headphones from around my neck. It wasn't mine to give but it was the only ransom I had. As I reached over to him, he smashed his fist into my arm, dislodging the Walkman so it flew up into the air, before tumbling forward out of my grasp and onto the ground. There was a horrible cracking noise as it hit the concrete, the door snapping away from the rest of it. Dessie stamped his foot down on what was left intact, shattering its magic into shards of black and red plastic. A spring rolled from the wreckage into a puddle on the concrete.

"Fuck that! Just give the bastard a kick!"

"I'm not doing it. I can't."

"Just one. Then it's finished. It's over."

"Fuck off, you can't make me!"

"OK, then, I'll keep going instead."

A smile fluttered. He was enjoying his game. This was my fault. I had to make him stop.

"I can't, Dessie, I can't," I whined, ashamed of my voice.

He swung his leg back, both arms out for balance.

"No! Stop! OK, I'll do it."

I did it because I had to. Because I wanted it to end. I couldn't look at the mound of flesh in front of me, with his leg shaking uncontrollably, vibrating to a spasmic rhythm of his fear. I closed my eyes and pretended it was football. I thought about making it gentle but I knew Dessie would make me go again. I swung back and connected with something hard. Bone. Mark yelled in pain. When I opened my eyes he was clasping his shin, skin pulled tight over his knuckles.

In my head I said I was sorry. Over and over. But the words wouldn't come out. They were stuck there in my brain.

"Good man. I knew you had it in you."

Dessie was smiling now, a real smile. His teeth looked white in the dark. He stepped back for another kick but thought better of it and skimmed the ground instead.

"Let's go! Can we just go now?" My voice came bursting out of me. I needed to be away from here and what was happening to Mark. From what was happening to me.

I let Dessie put his hand on my shoulder as we climbed the stairs back into the yard. There was no one left now, our steps the only sound. A crisp bag flapped frantically against the railings, snapping in the wind. Above us the evening sky was grey and darker grey, like half-polished metal.

He tilted his head back, looking up. I can still remember the slow calm of his voice.

"Let's get home," he said, "before the rain starts."

★★★

Mark was off school for two weeks. Some of the teachers gave me homework for him. Mr Pearse handed me back one of his essays but I left it at the bottom of my locker, until the paper got stained and torn. I waited for the knock on the door, to see his dad's shape through the lines of glass, to open it and confront his red-faced anger. I waited and waited but it never came. Eventually I realised that Mark hadn't told him. Coming home from school I didn't need to pass his house but I ran from the corner anyway, in case I saw his mam, or his dad coming in from work in the Sierra. In case I saw him.

When he did come back his arm was in a sling but it wasn't broken. His glasses were new but the same as before; the black rims hid some of the purply yellow bruises. There was nothing to hide the black stitches that gaped out from under the line of his hair.

He would have spoken to me that first day. I know he would. He wanted me to explain how it wasn't my fault and to say sorry. He was waiting for me to say something. But it was my fault, and there was nothing to say. At break it was easy to avoid him. At lunch I sheltered in the bike shed from the rain until the bell went, forcing myself to wait until everyone else had gone in and I was late for double English.

By three thirty my books were already in my bag. I had my jacket on. In the scramble of chairs and voices over the last bell I hitched my thumbs under the canvas straps of my bag and ran, pushing my way through the crowd. Out of the gate and past the playing fields where voices were calling out through the cold November air. Past the row of cottages, along the lane that took me to the corner and McCarthy's shop. On my back my books were a drum beat, the tin geometry set rattling in harmony. I don't know why I ran, I didn't need to. He would never have caught me.

I waited in Mam's room to see him come home, hiding behind the net curtain, twisting up a triangle of corner for a better look. He took so long I started to wonder where he was, but then I saw him. He might have been limping, walking even slower as he came down the road, dragging the sole of his shoe against the kerb. Across from our house he stopped to look up. For what seemed like forever he stared through the net curtain and I knew he'd seen me. Behind the flimsy fabric I held my breath. He was going to cross the road and call in. He was going to say something. He was going to have it out with me. Right when I thought he would, he must have changed his mind: he pushed on slowly up the road, towards his own gate.

That should have been the end of it. I should have just left it alone, left him alone. For a while I tried but I couldn't stop thinking about the orange juice in the fridge, the dark vinyl of the records spinning around. The way I could make him laugh without having to try.

I knew that he blamed Dessie, not me. And I knew that I could make him forgive me.

EIGHT

This wasn't how it was supposed to be. The flowers tickled my nose, almost making me sneeze, but I didn't want to move my arm because it was the position that hurt least. Abbey's bag, new and bulging, weighed down my other hand. How could a baby need so much stuff already? Beside me, Katie clutched her in the protective cage of her arms. She wasn't meant to be lifting anything yet, not even Abbey, but it wasn't the time to say it. She was walking slower than usual since the Caesarean and I was just glad not to have to struggle to keep up. Our footsteps clipped along the tiled floor, their sound taking the place of words.

The taxi driver glanced at my bandaged face, the sling on my arm, and pulled the glass between us, trapping us in our own silence. Abbey was awake now and Katie whispered something into the soft down of her head.

"Is she OK?" I asked, leaning across the bag between us to get a better look.

"She's fine," Katie said.

Outside, wet London streets slid by, Hampstead's boutiques and restaurants giving way to neon shop fronts and 'To Let' signs. The white plastic of the nose cast in the corner of my vision was getting easier to ignore now — easier to ignore than the pain. A broken nose. Two cracked ribs. A fractured collar-bone. This was what the doctor in A and E called lucky.

Rain clogged the streets with traffic and the taxi inched through Hackney, people with brollies weaving between us and the next car, making their way from one wet footpath to another. We stopped outside a red-brick school where boys in grey uniforms played football and chased each other, not caring about the rain. Opening the taxi window, I could hear their shouts and their laughter too, single voices calling out each other's names. It was the sound of excitement and I remembered what that felt like, how, after a morning in a classroom, the yard seemed to hold the possibilities of the whole world.

I'd a missed call from Peter and I needed to call him back, but Katie still looked tense and I didn't want to make things any worse. We liked London in the rain: it reminded us of that night, our first together, when we'd gone for a drink after work, when neither of us was sure if we were friends or something more. I loved remembering how it was her who kissed me first, under the dripping awning of the pub. We said we were lucky to live in London, where there was so much rain. So many chances to relive that first night together. I knew from the rigid line of her shoulders, the way she looked out of the opposite window, that our first kiss was the farthest thing from her mind right now.

Dessie was out there. Somewhere in these wet streets, he was waiting. I knew he was still here, that he hadn't gone back to Dublin. I could feel it. I pictured him in a bedsit in

Earl's Court or Shepherd's Bush. A single room with a bare lightbulb over an unmade bed. Or maybe he was with Rita — but somehow I couldn't picture him crowding the small rooms of her Lewisham flat, his fully grown body awkward among the china cats and chiming clocks.

The taxi pulled up suddenly and pain snatched through my shoulder. I breathed in sharply, biting my lip so as not to cry out. Katie looked at me, her eyes softer now, seeing me properly for the first time. The pain receded, not sharpness any more but a dull ache.

"Are you OK?"

"I'm tough as old boots, me."

She smiled. We both knew that wasn't true.

"You hear that, Abs? He's tough, your daddy, you know that?"

She leaned down to Abbey, tracing her face with a finger. I moved the bag so I could slide in next to them both, my thigh pushing up against hers. She rested her hand on my knee, squeezing it before taking it back again. It was a good sign.

★★★

I'd cleared the flat of all traces of Dessie, his bag and clothes safe in the dumpster that would be collected tomorrow. When I'd left the flat had even looked clean. But now, seeing it through Katie's eyes, I noticed the empty juice carton poking the bin lid open. The greasy pizza box on the counter, the coins and crumbs on the kitchen table.

"It stinks in here," she said, her nose wrinkled. "Has someone been smoking?"

The numb whiff of bandage was in my nose. But she must be right. Fuck Dessie.

"Yeah, I did. I had one the other night, to celebrate."

"Since when do you smoke?"

She was walking towards the window as she said it. I couldn't see her face. It was the kind of thing two people with a baby should know about each other.

"Here, sit down," I said. "Let me do that. I don't, hardly ever. Just the very odd time. With a drink, or on a special occasion."

I expected her to say something else but she didn't, turning instead to sit in the armchair, resting Abbey against her, gently kissing her head. Seeing the two of them sitting there was suddenly terrifying. This was it, what I'd been waiting for, and I had no idea what I was supposed to do next. I pushed the long window open into the rain, pausing for a second to savour the salve of the cool air on my battered face. In the grey daylight I could see Katie's tiredness. I sat down next to her on the couch, as close as I could get. Her brown hair was pulled back, but a strand had escaped, snaking its way down the side of her face.

"Is she asleep?" I asked. It hurt to talk. I resisted the urge to put my hand up to my swollen jaw.

"For now."

"How are you doing?" It was a risky question but I needed to know. It was the first time we'd been alone since it had happened.

"How do you think I'm doing, JP? Taking our baby home from the hospital should be one of the happiest days of our lives, but look at you!" Tears started to come but she talked on through them, keeping her voice barely above a whisper so as not to wake Abbey. "Your poor face! The state of you. You said on the phone you'd been in a bit of a scrape. A scrape! When I saw you come in ..." She took a deep breath. A tear rolled off her chin and landed on Abbey's blanket. When she spoke again, she was more controlled. "Poor Mum got such a shock when she saw you — we all did."

I pictured Rebecca's face, her eyes small as they scanned the swell of my cheeks and nose, the sling on my arm. It was Katie who looked shocked, not Rebecca. I thought Rebecca was going to smile but it became a frown at the last minute. She turned to Philip and shook her head slightly, their worst fears confirmed.

"She wasn't exactly brimming over with compassion," I said.

"That's not fair." Katie shook her head. "She was upset. We all were. And the way you were being so cagey about what had happened ..."

"I don't have to answer to your mother, Katie."

"Oh, fine," she said, her cheeks reddening. "But what about me? Am I owed any kind of explanation?"

In her arms Abbey squirmed and a cry escaped. We waited but nothing more came. It was the time I needed. I lowered my voice again. "Of course you are. But I told you what happened. I was out for a drink with Paul. I don't remember anything. I didn't see the guy. You know what I know."

"But why won't you report it to the police?" Frustration rose in her voice. It wasn't the first time she'd asked.

"Katie, ssh. You'll wake her. Look, this is East London, things like this happen. I know your parents would rather we were living in Hampstead—"

"Don't try that. It's nothing to do with that, JP, and you know it!"

"My point is that people get mugged all the time," I said. "You've seen all the posters on the way from the Tube station, appealing for witnesses. No one saw it happen, they'll never catch him."

"The porter, Ahmed, he saw it," she whispered back. "You told me he chased whoever it was away before he called the ambulance. Maybe he could identify someone."

"I already asked him," I said. "He didn't see properly, just that it was a white guy — it could have been anyone. It's not enough for the police to go on."

Katie didn't answer me, leaning down instead to push the blanket back from Abbey's face. She was wearing a pink cardigan that we'd bought together in Baby Gap, the sleeves rolled up. A bubble of spit formed on her lips as she slept, unaware of the disharmony around her.

"Don't you think I'd want to catch them?" I asked. "Don't you think I'd want whoever did this put behind bars? Why wouldn't I?"

Katie was listening now, digesting my words.

"I hate the thought of some guy roaming around out there free after this," I said, Dessie's image flitting into my mind again. "I hate that as much as you do, but I know

113

there's no point in wasting time at the police station when they'll never catch him. I'd rather put my time into being with you and Abbey."

"If you'd been with me and Abbey instead of out with Paul then none of this would have happened."

Words of retort jumped into my mouth but they stayed there. There was no sense taking the bait when we had almost finished, talked it through. I reached my hand out and rested it on her arm. She didn't pull away.

"It's just … the whole thing makes no sense, JP," she said. "If it was a mugger, why they didn't take your money? And how come you don't remember anything? Anything at all?" Her brown eyes scoured my face for something that would help her make sense of it all.

I shrugged. "Me and Paul probably had a few too many. But we were celebrating. I don't remember anything. I wish I did. I wish I'd never gone out that night, I really do."

The honesty rang true in my voice and Katie heard it too. She turned and held her hand lightly to my cheek, her fingers gently tracing my swollen shape. I pulled it to me and kissed her palm, lacing my fingers through hers.

"I'm so sorry, JP. I've been awful to you." Her tears came again, following the shiny tracks of the ones earlier but they were different this time.

"No, you haven't …"

"I have. It's just it all seemed so weird. I got such a shock, when I saw you … And you were so secretive about it … Maybe it's just me. My hormones and all that. The nurse said I might be a bit up and down for a while."

"I know."

"And it's selfish but I couldn't help worrying with you in such bad shape and me in bits after the Caesarean. How are we going to manage?"

Tiredness was making her fears jumble up into one. Standing up I moved to her other side, sitting on the armrest so I could put my good arm around her shoulders. "Sssh. Come here. You're just tired, that's all. We've been through a lot these past couple of days but we'll be fine," I soothed.

I pulled her back into my embrace, ignoring the ache in my shoulder joint. Shifting Abbey to her other side, Katie moved closer to me, so she could rest her head on my chest. Her voice was muffled against me but the words were clear. "I'm sorry I was horrible before, JP, I didn't mean it. I love you — you know?"

"I do. I love you too."

★★★

"JP, the phone's ringing!"

"I know, Katie, I can hear it."

"Well, can you get it, then? I've got my hands full here."

"Hang on — I'm trying to get this bloody bottle to the right temperature." I heard the snap in my voice. I lifted it from the pot of water with my good arm. Against my cheek it was still cold. "It'll only be your mum again anyway."

Rebecca had offered to come and stay and I almost wished she had. It might have been better than the seven or eight phone calls every day, which she had an uncanny knack of coinciding with times when Abbey was asleep, which wasn't often. The week and a half since Katie and Abbey had come home from hospital felt like decades. Even by my standards the flat was a tip. It was hard to find room on the counter for the bottle among the half-empty mugs of tea and dirty plates. Out of the corner of my eye I registered the washing-machine that I had started to empty yesterday, its contents still spilling out onto the floor.

Katie had made it to the phone before me, and rearranged Abbey in her arms to try to stop the whimper turning into a cry. "Hi, Mum. Yes, she's doing great. You should see her, she's changing every day. I know you're not supposed to say this about your own baby but she's absolutely gorgeous." She lifted Abbey higher in her arms, stroking the soft skin of her neck as she spoke. There was silence as Rebecca imparted what presumably were more pearls of wisdom.

"I'm really disappointed, too, but she doesn't seem to mind the bottle."

The breastfeeding plan had been abandoned and even though Katie felt guilty about it I wasn't sorry. I'd managed to convince her that her frustration and pain were worse for Abbey than the formula milk which most of our generation were raised on and she'd eventually agreed. I hadn't added that when she was breastfeeding there was nothing for me to do except get in the way. At least now I could play my part.

"Two hours. I think. Around three, anyway. Then at five ... I know, yeah."

I blasted the heat under the bottle. I wanted to take the night-time feeds: next week I'd be back at work so if I did them now Katie could get some rest. She didn't say she didn't want me to, but she still got up every time Abbey cried. It was as if she didn't trust me not to mess up even the simplest things.

"He's OK. Some of the swelling's starting to go down ... Hmm, yeah. He got the new dressing on his nose so it doesn't look as bad now."

I knew what was coming next. I could sense Rebecca's question through the hunch of Katie's shoulders.

"No, not yet." Katie sighed. "Look, to be honest, Mum, I'm sick of going over this. It's like talking to the wall. He says they'll never find them. Maybe he's right. I'd say it's too late now anyway."

The water in the pot bubbled more. Spits of water sizzled on the hob.

"I know. That's what I said."

Katie looked at me, nodding towards the phone as if to say, "There you go, Mum agrees with me." As if we didn't know that already. With every call Rebecca had asked when I was pressing charges, going to the police. She wouldn't let it go. I rolled my eyes at Katie, something I'd caught myself doing a lot in the past few days.

"Yes. I suppose ... I know," she said, turning away again. In sympathy, Abbey started to squirm. Her cry was a gurgle at first but then the rough edges came through, rising into a scream.

"The bottle's ready," I called.

"Look, Mum, I'd better go. She needs her milk. Talk to you later."

I strode across the room, holding the bottle with the

cleanest tea-towel I could find. "Do you have to talk to your mum as if I'm not here?" I demanded, above Abbey's noise. "You could take my side for once."

Katie yanked the bottle from my hand. "Since when is this about sides, JP? You were attacked, badly hurt, and you won't go to the police. Mum can't understand it — and you know what? Neither can I."

"Do you want me to hold her?" I offered, as she struggled with bottle and baby.

"No, I'm fine. This feels very hot. Are you sure it wasn't in too long?"

"I'm sure. It was cold only a second ago."

"Did you test it on the back of your hand?" she asked.

"Yes! Of course I did!"

Katie lowered the bottle to Abbey and she clamped her lips around the rubber teat. The silence was almost tangible, as if someone had switched off a light. It lasted a second, maybe two, before she pulled her head back, letting the bottle dangle in Katie's hand. The screams started again as the milk dripped onto the carpet, forming a frothy white puddle.

"What's the matter, pumpkin? Is the bockie too hot? Is it? Sssssssh, come here, it's OK, Mummy's here," Katie soothed, lifting Abbey onto her shoulder.

"It seemed fine — it was freezing a second ago."

"It was too hot, JP. I told you! You have to be careful."

"I am being careful! How am I meant to know it can go from freezing to boiling in a matter of seconds?"

"You test it on your hand, that's how. It could burn her little insides — she's not even two weeks old …"

"I know how old she is."

"Well, you should take more care, then. Look, just pour out half of it and put some cold in. There's no point in wasting it."

As I grabbed the bottle from her, the lilting ring of my mobile joined in, competing with Abbey's screams for attention. The screen flashed with Peter's mobile number. Shit. I needed to call him back with those figures he'd been emailing about earlier. I hesitated over the answer button, glancing around to see Katie watching me.

"JP, for God's sake, hurry up," she snapped. "We'll have the neighbours knocking again. Just call whoever it is back later."

Abbey's cries escalated, filling the room, bouncing back off the walls. The screen flashed urgently — even if I answered I wouldn't be able to hear a thing. I pressed the red reject button and went in search of more formula.

★★★

Abbey was asleep. Finally. It felt as if she'd been awake for days. Across from me, Katie slumped against the arm of the couch. It was dark outside and she was still in her pyjamas. I'd hardly seen her in proper clothes since the hospital. I wanted to go over and lie next to her but my body pulsed with aches that moulded me to the chair.

"Katie?" I whispered, afraid of waking Abbey. "Katie?"

Soft, heavy breaths were my response. Exhaustion had taken her over. I was glad — she needed rest and I needed to finish my report for Peter, open on my laptop since this morning. And I would, just as soon as I found the energy to stand up. Tomorrow I would be back in the office and in a way, maybe, it would make things a little easier. The two weeks had gone so fast, a smear of sharp words with brittle edges, fourteen days of frustration and tears. The cycle of feeding, changing, washing was endless. Snatched moments of sleep ripped open by crying and it started again.

We never usually fought. That was one of our things. If we disagreed we'd talk it through or compromise. Neither of us was used to the sting that words could make, the sudden way that talking became shouting. It scared me how quickly the words could avalanche, one pulling another until they were teeming down on top of us. It reminded me of Mam and Dad, and I didn't want Abbey to remember things like that. But Katie and I weren't my mam and dad. We'd had good times in the past couple of weeks too. Times when Abbey was awake and not crying. When all we did was stare at her, making faces and silly noises, waiting to see the flash of pink gum we'd decided was a smile. Or the day the three of us slept in a jumbled up pile on the bed, Abbey in Katie's arms, Katie in mine. We weren't supposed to do that, all the books said so, but for once we ignored them and fell asleep wrapped up together in a swiss roll of sleepy warmth.

My injuries hadn't helped but they were getting better. The new dressing on my nose was mostly inside now, so it didn't look as bad. The sling on my arm was replaced by a bandage across my shoulder that I could hide under my shirt. Katie had changed it for me yesterday, her touch gentle, kissing it lightly when she was done. The pain was less every day but it was still there, alongside the bubble of fear.

In empty minutes like this, Dessie filled my mind. The etch of hate in his face, the sound of his voice as he raised his foot in the air, holding it longer than he needed to and stretching out my memory of it. I was angry with him, of course I was, but I was angrier with myself. I'd been stupid, letting my guard down like that. I'd given too much away. I'd let him get under my skin and breathe life into dead memories. I should have come out with it straight away and told him I wanted him gone; there was no need to say why. A couple of hundred quid and he'd have left. It had been all he wanted, no matter what he said.

Because of my stupidity Dessie was out there somewhere, angry and raw with a key to our flat. I was afraid to leave Katie alone, even to go to the supermarket. Last night she'd caught me staring into the darkness of the window; I'd seen her reflection as she rested her chin on my shoulder, sliding her arms gently around me, taking care to avoid the bulge of bandage near my ribs.

"What's so interesting out there, JP?" she had asked. "What are you looking for?"

On the couch Katie rolled over in her sleep, her back to me now, her pyjama top riding up to reveal the creamy skin at the base of her back. I wished more than anything that she knew. The words were there, and it would be so easy to wake her and tell her. To have her put her arms around my aching mind and soothe everything away. But it wouldn't be that easy. There were things that couldn't be soothed by words. And this wasn't her problem. It was mine.

Tomorrow morning, the locksmith would come. I hadn't

found a good time to tell her and I knew having a workman in the middle of this chaos was the last thing she needed. I'd come up with a good story, that the landlord had lost his keys and insisted we change the locks. Another lie. Just like my drinks with Paul. And my taking up smoking. There were too many lies now — they were hard to keep track of, slipping out of my mouth, one after another. It was getting to the point that even I was beginning to forget what was true and what wasn't.

I decided that this would be the last. No question. After this, we could get back to normal.

NINE

Early-morning sunlight reflected around Reception, chan-nelled in from the oval atrium above. Behind the swirling glass and chrome of the desk I could see Leena was already there. Her head was bent forward as she focused on a doc-ument in front of her, one hand holding back her dark hair. The headphones rested gently on the delicate curve of her neck. She hadn't seen me yet.

"Morning, Leena!"

"Hi, JP!" She looked up quickly, her smile warm and real. When she saw my appearance it froze and faded. "Oh, my God, look at you. Are you OK?"

"Oh, I'm fine." I grinned. "Looks worse than it is. You should have seen me last week. I got on the wrong side of an East End mugger."

"That's so awful, I can't believe it. What happened?"

"It was my fault, being stupid. He wanted my wallet and I should have let him have it instead of trying to fight him off." I waved my arms to show how fine I was. I'd practised the story on the Tube. I'd be repeating it all day so it was best to have it as short as possible.

"You shouldn't have tried to be brave, JP," Leena said, smoothing a strand of hair behind her ear. "It's not worth getting hurt over money. And what bad timing with the new little baby. What did you call her?"

"Abbey."

"Abbey? That's gorgeous. I love that name. How's Katie doing?"

Her words were slow and rounded, as if every one was perfectly chosen just for me. There would be people who would ask about Katie and wouldn't listen for the answer, but not Leena. She was the kind of person who made everyone interesting. Talking to Leena was like basking in the sun; it was hard to leave her behind.

"She's fine," I said. "More than fine, she's great. Well, to be honest, we're both a bit at sea with it all. Takes a while to get used to."

"I can imagine," Leena said. "Tell her to bring Abbey in one day. I'd love to see her."

"I will." I nodded. "That's a great idea, I'll do that."

In my office everything was just as I'd left it. The to-do list from that last day was still there, a Post-it with a scrawled number that was never called back. Some opened letters rested across my keyboard.

I hung my jacket on the back of the door and sank into the chair, twirling around, inspecting the place. It gave me a thrill, having an office. Even though it was the smallest on the floor, it was still an office and it was mine. Katie had said I would enjoy being back at work and partly she was right. She knew how much I loved the order, the routine. The chance for recognition. Knotting my tie this morning, I was struck by the image of Katie and Abbey reversed in the mirror behind me, snuggled together on the white duvet. At that moment something inside me twisted and I almost didn't want to leave them, not to go to work, not to go anywhere. But Rebecca was coming for a few days, and the evenings with the four of us under one roof would be enough. And, anyway, they didn't need me — I was only in the way. Not like here.

On my way back from the kitchen I counted three other people in already, heads bent over files. Closing my office door behind me, I took a gulp of coffee and settled down behind my desk. There was just over an hour until the meeting and I had enough time to read through the final report, to make sure the details were indelible on my brain. Peter had taken a chance, leaving the analysis and recommendation up to me. It was my biggest project yet and I wasn't going to mess it up, not with a potential promotion around the corner. I watched as it printed, feeling a ripple of satisfaction at the tidy bulk of pages, the ordered lines of type. I'd started it weeks ago, putting the final changes to it late last night as Katie and Abbey slept. I knew Peter would be impressed that even with a baby I hadn't missed a deadline. The work was good and I knew it. I couldn't wait to get in there and present it.

★★★

"Knock-knock?"

The Scottish voice jerked me from my own words. When I looked up Alison was already halfway around the door, her nose scrunching up when she saw me.

"Good Christ! And I thought Katie was exaggerating," she said. "You look terrible! Oh, congratulations, by the way."

Laughing I stood up to receive the air kiss that wouldn't smudge her lipstick. On my cheek I felt the light frizz of her hair. Her blunt honesty had once robbed me of words but I was used to it now.

"I'm fine," I said, pulling back and leaning against the window-ledge. "It looks worse than it is."

"That's good, because it looks pretty awful. According to Katie, it's a lot better than it was," she said, a frown making the thin lines of her eyebrows into a V. "A least you had a couple of weeks off to recover. Katie was dead worried about you."

The grating twist of Alison's accent made her words an accusation. I decided to ignore it. "Yeah, I know. But she's fine now. Great. They both are. I can't believe you haven't seen them since the hospital. When are you coming round?"

"I thought tonight, actually," she said. "If I get out of here at a decent time. It's been manic. Peter's worse than Santa Claus at Christmas, pulled this direction and that. He's on to me every five seconds, asking me to drop everything and focus on something mega-urgent. Next minute he wants me to do the complete opposite. It's enough to drive you round the bend. But hopefully I'll get to see your girls tonight. I haven't seen Rebecca for an age either. It'll be lovely to catch up."

I went to the printer, picked up the copies of the report and counted them out onto my desk. She was only blowing off steam: she and Peter were thick as thieves. She was much more than a PA to him.

"Any news on that new assistant director job?" I asked, keeping my voice casual, straightening each report into a tidy bundle before stapling it together.

She glanced over her shoulder at the open doorway and we both watched Richard heading by towards Peter's office, a file under his arm. "I shouldn't really say anything," she lowered her voice, "but I think he finally got the green light from HR. He might bring it up at the meeting."

"Really? That's great."

I smiled, nodding to myself, as I picked up the reports from my desk. I kept my movements smooth and even so as not to give away the squeeze of excitement in my stomach.

★★★

Peter's office was easily five times the size of mine. Four of the ten chairs around the thick mahogany table were already occupied when I came in. Peter was standing by the window, looking out across the Thames at the sun glittering off the glass and chrome buildings on the other side.

"JP, welcome back," he said, turning around as I took my seat. "Congratulations are in order, I believe."

"Yes, thanks." I smiled.

Confusion skimmed his features as he registered my face. "Been in the wars?" Behind his glasses his eyebrows arched. The bowed heads around the table looked up from reading to see what he was referring to.

"Something like that," I said. "I'm on the mend now, though."

"Good," he nodded, "glad to hear it."

127

The last two members of the team came in together and the door was closed firmly. Sandra sat down next to me. "Congratulations, JP," she said, squeezing my arm. Her smile was genuine, creasing up around her eyes. "A little girl, I hear? That's great news."

I remembered being in her office and the framed choreographed photos of white-blonde children just like her. "Thanks."

"Right, well, let's get down to it. Gary, do you want to start us off?"

A hush fell with Peter's words and the meeting kicked off at its usual pace. Gary was my old boss and one of my allies at the table. His voice was decisive and clear as he took us through the events of the previous week, giving the right amount of information but not too much. Highlights. Lowlights. Potential issues. I concentrated hard, jotting down notes. I'd learned there was a fine line between asking a relevant and timely question and putting the meeting off course. After Gary it was Richard's turn.

"Thanks, Peter. As I'm sure you all know it's been a good week for retail. Contrary to the forecast, we've actually got some sunshine this summer, which has bolstered trade in the non-food sector."

His joke got the mild laughter it sought and he moved on. Every word brimmed with confidence and he fielded Peter's questions with ease. His shiny baldness made it hard to guess his age but he'd been there as long as Katie had. She'd told me that everyone had been surprised when Peter was brought in as a director over him. If he still felt resentment he hid it well.

"All sounds good, Richard." Peter nodded. "Nothing we need to be concerned with, then?"

"Not at all. Tesco, Sainsbury and M&S have all recorded higher footfall than this time last year. In fact, the future's looking very bright just now." Richard took out a small cloth and polished his glasses.

"Good news, Richard, well done."

The meeting moved on. Ben was talking about volatility in the high-tech sector. Two more people and then it would be my turn. I felt the paper in my hands become hot and clammy. I knew he'd have some tough questions for me. Against my chest I felt a buzzing vibration. My mobile. Gently, I pulled it from my shirt pocket and held it on my knee under the table.

Home flashed up at five-second intervals. *Home. Home. Home.* I watched the screen and then it was gone. The phone silenced. It wasn't like Katie to call me in work, especially not during the Monday meeting. The clock on the wall said it was ten forty-five. Something must have happened. An image jumped into my mind. Dessie outside the flat. Dessie at the door. Dessie with Katie, with Abbey.

"Excuse me for one second," I managed, pushing myself out of my chair. Ben stopped mid-sentence and seven pairs of eyes were on me. Peter didn't say anything, his expression unreadable. No one excused themselves from the management meeting.

"Sorry, I'll just be a minute." I made my voice sound firm, backing out of the room, closing the door softly behind me. I was sure I'd seen Richard smile but I didn't care. My heart hammered as I dialled quickly and jammed the green button. The rings stretched out lazy and slow. Come on, come on, pick up.

Six rings, seven rings, eight. Where was she? Oh, Jesus Christ, what was happening?

"Hello?" It was Rebecca's voice, smooth and polished, as if she'd been practising her vowels before picking up the receiver.

"Rebecca? It's JP. Is everything all right?"

"Oh, JP, hello. How are you?"

Rebecca was always more pleasant to me on the phone.

"Is everything OK? Katie called. Is she OK? Is Abbey all right?"

Already I knew by her voice that the worst hadn't happened but the questions tumbled out anyway. I needed her to say it. I needed to be sure.

"Katie and Abbey are just fine. In fact, we've got Abbey in the pushchair now and we were just about to set off for a little walk."

"Is Katie there? Can I talk to her?"

"Well, we're just about to leave, but you can have a quick word if you like." She sniffed.

"Can you put her on for a second, Rebecca? I want to find out why she rang."

"Oh, that was me. We were just wondering if you could babysit tonight. Alison was on and she's coming around later. We thought it might be nice to go for a glass of wine and some pasta in that new place by the park."

"Rebecca, I'm at work. I was in a meeting." I tried to keep

the irritation from my voice but I knew I wasn't succeeding.

"Well, you could have called me back later, you didn't need to call now," Rebecca retorted, in her reasonable voice. "If it's too much trouble …"

"JP?" It was Katie's voice on the phone now. "What's up? Why aren't you in your meeting?"

"I am … I was. But your mother rang about bloody babysitting."

Katie laughed, a stilted sound, and I knew Rebecca was listening. "Well, is that OK?" she said.

"Yeah, of course. Could it not have waited until later, though?"

"She left a message. I didn't think you'd pick up — you never do. You didn't need to call back now."

"Well, I didn't know if something had happened."

"Like what?" Katie's voice was more confused now than angry and I realised the conversation had nowhere to go.

"I don't know." I looked at my watch, ten to. I had to get back. "Look, Katie, I've got to go. I'll call you later. OK?"

"OK, then."

I hung up, irritation replacing the relief that only seconds earlier had flooded through me. A few heads turned as I re-entered the room as quietly as possible. Sandra seemed to be taking her time, explaining her ongoing projects in more depth than usual.

"So, to sum up, we've done as much as we can at this stage and there should be nothing to stop the merger going ahead next week. Fingers crossed, anyway." She smiled, shuffling her papers together.

"Thank you, Sandra, a little more detail than we might have needed, but good to hear," Peter said. "You'll send on those statistics you were talking about to the whole team?"

"Sure, no problem."

"Good. Right, JP, thanks for joining us again. You're up next."

My cheeks flushed at the mention of my absence. In front of me my notes were out of order now and I fumbled for the summary sheet.

"It's more than a general update this week, though, isn't it? You should have that completed report on the best property opportunities if I'm not mistaken."

"You're not mistaken and I have it here. Sorry I had to duck out."

He held my gaze, waiting for me to elaborate, but when I didn't he nodded at me to go ahead. I took a copy of the report and handed the bundle to Sandra to pass around. I started to read too quickly and I hoped the wobble in my chest wasn't audible in my voice. I concentrated on the words, gaining momentum as my thoughts came back to me, strong and clear. I looked up, around the table, catching the eyes of my colleagues one by one as I explained the problems we were facing. I didn't need my notes any more: I could picture the words in my head, the way the logical argument built towards the conclusion of what we had to do.

Around the table some people scribbled in their margins. Gary gave me a smile. Peter's eyes locked on mine; his forehead creased into a slight frown the way it always did when he was concentrating. Richard's hand flew across his page and I knew he was coming up with ways to challenge me. I spoke for ten minutes. When I finished there was silence.

"So basically what I'm hearing, JP, is that we should increase investment in retail property, especially in the regions," Peter clarified, when I had finished.

"That's right. The north looks particularly promising, with a couple of new developments I think we should go for. But you can see it in the full report — I've broken it down region by region."

There was a flurry of pages as people turned to that section.

"I have a question for you, JP." Richard cut in across the rustle. He pushed the report away from him across the table and tapped it with his pencil. "This all sounds a bit familiar, doesn't it? I, for one, remember the eighties when people couldn't give their property away. Paying huge mortgages on places that weren't worth half of it. You'd be too young to remember but it was a terrible time for this country, a terrible time."

A few heads around the table nodded. Richard smiled. He'd managed to get into the same sentence my age and that I wasn't British.

"I know what a terrible time it was." I added a smile so I wouldn't sound defensive. "But it was a different economy. The interest rates are much more stable now."

"The ECB has just announced yet another interest rise and there's set to be more." Richard turned to Peter with an incredulous face. "We're going to have to increase ours too. That doesn't seem too stable to me."

"Yes, but a rise of a quarter of a per cent," I argued, "at a time when interest rates are at some of the lowest rates they've ever been. And the commercial property market is a very different animal from residential, Richard."

"That's very true," Peter interjected. "I'm inclined to agree with JP on this one, Richard. It's apples and oranges. And we can't afford to play it a hundred per cent safe because of a quarter of a per cent."

"But it's a good point, Richard," I said, keeping my expression neutral. "I considered it myself. If you turn to section five of the report, I've done a like-for-like comparison between then and now. I've taken into account the interest rate, inflation, unemployment, some other global trends. You can see the list there — do you think I've left anything out?"

There was silence as everyone scanned the list.

"I'd have to have a proper look afterwards," Richard said. "I'll come back to you."

"Great. Thanks." I let myself smile.

"OK, right. Thanks for an excellent summary, JP. It's great to have some young blood on the team, some fresh ideas. I'm sure we all look forward to reading the report in full and making a final decision at next week's meeting," Peter said, looking at his watch. "Right, Melanie, over to you."

Now my part was out of the way it was hard to pay attention to the rest. Peter's endorsement swelled pride inside me but I couldn't let it show. He'd said in my review last month that I was one of the strongest on the team but recognition in front of everyone was better.

We were through the agenda with fifteen minutes to spare. Peter coughed lightly, clearing his throat. "Before we go into any other business I have an announcement to make." He stood up from his chair, pacing to the window. He knew he had our full attention. "As most of you know, the increased internal focus on forecasting has created a heavy workload for us and I've been trying for quite some time to get the way paved for a new role to provide additional support and strategic input. We've won a lot of new business over the past twelve months and that's a reflection on everyone here but, quite frankly, if we don't get more hands on deck we're in danger of dropping the ball on something."

Several heads around the table nodded. Here it came, this was it. Alison had been right as usual.

"So, you'll all be glad to hear that we've been able to create a new role in the team for an assistant director of Financial Planning and Analysis. There's a few of HR's *is* to dot and *ts* to cross but Gordon's approved it so that means it's definitely going ahead. I'm hoping to get the job spec online by Friday, or next week at the latest."

"That's great news," Gary said. I nodded, murmuring my agreement, scanning the rest of the table quickly for their reactions. Across from me Richard was polishing his glasses.

"Yes, it is good news, for the department and for me," Peter laughed lightly. "And obviously it's a great opportunity for someone here. HR have these policies, of course, that anyone from the company can apply, but we all know that the best-placed people for the job are around this table."

He waved his hand in an arc, following it with his eyes. Was it my imagination or did they rest on me for a second longer than necessary? It'd be a total long shot for me to get the role but maybe that was what he needed, the department needed. He'd said it himself earlier. Young blood. Fresh ideas.

I let myself slip into the fantasy. If I was assistant director before I was thirty, I should make director by thirty-five, like Peter had done. I pictured the red-brick house in Hampstead, this time with a shining black Audi outside, a new Mini for Katie that we'd buy with my money and not Philip's. Plenty of money for the future, for Abbey — she'd never have to do without anything.

I shouldn't get carried away. There'd be stiff competition for the job, and Richard was the obvious favourite. It was tenuous at best, a fragile picture, but it felt within my grasp. I could almost touch it. And I wasn't going to let it go.

Ten

The narrow lanes between the wharf buildings were cool despite the warmth of the evening. Hurrying along the cobblestones, I turned the corner to step out into the sunlight again, the glare from the river so bright I had to squint. It was definitely longer going this way than by the main road but I loved the walk by the water, the way its gentle swish softened the remains of the work day from my mind.

It was hard to believe it was the end of my second week back. Each day was so full, exhaustingly so, but that seemed to make them pass even quicker, one sliding into the next. We were settling into a routine, Katie and Abbey and I. Abbey was sleeping more, four, sometimes even five hours at a time. She cried less, or maybe it was that when she cried we knew what to do. She was already more than four weeks old, and even though she was still so new to us, some part of me felt as if we'd always had her.

I strode past the bar on the corner and smiled at my reflection in the plate-glass front. My bandage was gone and even though my nose was still tender I was starting to look myself again. A gang from the office had gone down earlier, but I'd no urge to brave the crowd to find them. Too many nights had been wasted there already, nights with sleeves rolled up and jackets shed as alcohol blurred the lines between co-workers and friends. Nights that were indiscernible from one another and gave me nothing more than an empty wallet and a headache. I didn't need that any more. I had a family now, a place I needed to be.

Katie had called just as I left to ask me to pick up a bottle of wine on the way home. She was so much more relaxed now that Rebecca had gone and the breastfeeding had been totally abandoned. She was such a good mum, already able to second-guess Abbey's needs. She held her like she'd always held her and I loved watching them together, moving around the apartment like one person. I loved listening to the silliness of the running commentary Katie made while she splashed water over Abbey's tummy in the bath, or lifted her little legs with one hand, changing her nappy with the other.

I was getting better too. On Wednesday night I'd found a new trick to calm her, holding her to my chest against the drum of my heart, making circles on her back until her cries became choppy breathing and eventually silence. It was starting to feel like it should feel, being a dad. It was easy, once you stopped being afraid.

At the bottom of the steps to the Tube station the flower stall was a swirl of colour. The crowd sidestepped the stainless-steel buckets with their bursts of purple and orange, pink and white that formed a stark contrast to the grey brick all around. That first week that Abbey was home we'd run out of vases in the flat but the flowers were all gone now. I stopped and hesitated, my eyes bouncing from one type to the next. Behind a wet wooden table a blonde girl looked up, wiping her hands on a green apron. "Hi there. Can I help you?" she asked smiling.

"Hi. Yes. I'd like these ones, but I'm not sure what they're called."

"They're gorgeous, aren't they?" she said. "They're pink peace lilies. They go really well with the white roses. Do you want me to make you up a bouquet?"

The peace lilies sounded expensive, but what the hell? "Ah, yeah, go on. That sounds nice." I smiled back, checking my wallet. "Just keep it under sixty quid — that's all I have on me."

"No problem."

Like ingredients for a recipe, the girl chose flowers with care, her forehead creased in concentration. She held colours together, pausing over the green fern, reaching back for some more. She took them to the table in the back and lined them up, snipping the end off one of the lilies. Something in the way the task absorbed her drew me in and I watched in fascination as the crowd spilled past behind me. Her movements and her certainty reminded me of Dad, finding exactly what he needed in the jars of nails and washers and screws that lined the walls of the shed. He had made me a kite one day. I remembered watching from my perch on the workbench, its splintery wood catching my legs where my shorts ended. She was a perfectionist just like he had been, fussing and changing the angles of the flowers until she was satisfied. She cut a length of cellophane from a roll next to the table, gathering it around the delicate bundle, finishing it with brown paper and a curl of green ribbon.

"Here you go," she said, just a pair of hands and a voice behind the huge bouquet.

"Wow, they look great!" I said, imagining Katie's face when she saw the flowers.

"I've put some water in the bottom so they don't dry out on your way home. That'll be fifty-five, please."

"Thanks." I reached into my wallet for the money.

"Is it a special occasion?" the girl asked.

"Not really, it's—"

"His girlfriend's just had a baby."

His voice came from behind me, robbing me of the rest of my words and my breath. I didn't look around.

"Oh, really? Congratulations. A boy or a girl?"

The flower girl was talking to me but I couldn't seem to find my voice and he answered for me. "A girl," he said. "Abbey."

"Oh, that's such a pretty name."

Their conversation went on around me, each word sounding farther away than the one before. I'd been so stupid, allowing myself to think with each passing week that he might have gone back to Dublin after all, that he might really have left me alone. I wanted to turn around, to check and make sure it was him, but I didn't seem to be able to move. I could feel his closeness, the heat from his body on my back through my shirt, and I pushed forward, leaning against the table of flowers. That was when I realised the girl was looking at me, waiting for some kind of response.

"I can put it on a card if you like," she said.

"Sorry. No. It's fine. Here." I fumbled with notes. "Keep the change."

"Are you sure? Thanks a lot."

She handed me the fragile bundle. It felt surprisingly heavy.

"You're welcome."

I had to turn around — there was nowhere else to go. I held the bouquet in front of me, creating space between us. Through the crinkle of cellophane I saw his face, his smile in the middle of the darkness of his beard.

"Nice flowers, John-Paul," he said. "You shouldn't have."

I had to get away from him. Pushing the flowers out in front I stepped around him, into the flow of people swarming towards the Tube. Fear made my movements jerky, my foot catching on the heel of a woman's shoe in front of me. Under my shirt I could feel a bead of sweat slide down my side. The cellophane was slippery in my hands.

"John-Paul, what's the hurry? Hang on there."

His voice sounded close and when I glanced back I saw he was only two people behind me, wearing a football shirt. For all his talk, it was an Arsenal one, the bright red standing out like a bloodstain among the dark clothes of the crowd. In front of me the entrance to the station was a bottleneck. Two at a time I mounted the steps, ignoring the looks thrown at me as I pushed past. A station worker in a high-visibility vest was pulling the metal grille across the entrance, shouting something about a security alert. If I could only get through before he closed it, if I could get to the other side, I'd lose him.

"John-Paul," he said, closer this time, his voice almost in my ear. His fingers grabbed my arm, a tight, firm band of strength. "I said, hold on."

He pulled me around to face him and I saw his smile was gone now. His eyes were as hard as the tight clench of his fingers. Over his shoulder there was a sea of faces coming towards us. Hidden behind large circular sunglasses I saw one I recognised, the one I really didn't want to see. Alison was on her mobile, engrossed in conversation with someone, maybe even Katie. She hadn't seen me yet.

"Come on," Dessie was saying. "We're not getting anywhere here. Let's head down this way."

He turned, pushing against the wall of people behind. A man with a white beard cursed at his change of direction but Dessie didn't hear him as he shouldered past, heading straight towards Alison. In a second they would collide with each other. If he saw I wasn't behind him he'd come after me, call out. Behind me the crowd was locked between the growing swell of people and the half-closed gate. I followed Dessie's retreat, pushing through the crush.

"JP, what's going on?" Alison called over, snapping her mobile closed.

"They're not letting anyone in," I said. "I'm going to grab a cab instead."

Her voice disappeared as she was carried past me. "This is typical of a Friday night, it'll be fine in a few minutes. I'll take my chances."

Dessie had stopped to wait and followed my gaze. "JP? What kind of fuckin' name is that?"

"What do you want, Dessie?"

"Don't worry, I won't lay a finger on you. I just want to talk. That's all. Come on."

"I'm late. I've got to get home."

"It won't take long," he said.

I paused, weighing up the options. Behind me I heard an announcement. Waterloo Station and Liverpool Station were on high security alert. Delays on all lines. The crowd started to surge the opposite way. I could drop the flowers and run — I knew the place better than he did. I could lose him in the mass of people who looked just like me. But in a second Alison would be back. I couldn't afford a scene. And even if I lost him he'd only find me again.

Waiting for me, he raised an eyebrow, reading my thoughts. "Don't even fuckin' think about it," he said.

★★★

Sitting on the bench we might have looked like two ordinary brothers. Having a chat. Catching up. I balanced the flowers on the ground between my feet and loosened my tie. Dessie flicked ash on the flagstones and it blew away, dancing by the railing.

From the pub behind us the crowd spilled out onto the path. It was full now with people abandoning their journey home in favour of a swift one that would turn into more. We were close enough to hear their laughter, snatches of their conversation carried over by the wind. He couldn't hurt me: there were too many people around. I wasn't going to let him hurt me.

"So, how's fatherhood?" he asked, inhaling sharply. "You any better than the oul fella was?"

The words smacked but I wasn't going to rise to him. This was a game he enjoyed. He was good at it. I needed to stay focused, to figure out what he wanted and how I could get rid of him for good.

"What do you want?"

"Not in the mood for a chat? You never did have the gift of the gab, John-Paul." He shook his head, laughing. "Mam always put that down as the reason you had no friends."

On the water a boat passed by, I could hear the voice through the Tannoy, filling the tourists with tales of the Tower of London. I strained to listen and replace Dessie's voice with the tour guide's patter. I'd never been on one of those boats.

"What did you tell your bird about what happened to your face?" He paused, putting his cigarette out under his trainer. "I bet you made up some cock-and-bull story — you always had an imagination, John-Paul. There's no way you'd have told her the truth, you're too much of a fuckin' coward." The wind from the river made ripples in the shiny material of his football shirt. "I'm not fuckin' sorry by the way, in case that's what you think I'm here to say. You deserved it. The way you treated Mam. And me. You had it coming."

I sucked my teeth, tilted my head back. A plane was flying low, its fumes making a trail of white on blue, like a giant zip in the sky.

"Thinking about it, I don't know why I was even fuckin' surprised," he said. "You were always full of shit, living in your own world. Disowning your family is just the kind of thing you would do."

"Let's not pretend we were a happy family now, Dessie. Let's not rewrite history."

"No, you're the one who does that, John-Paul." He smiled, winning the point easily.

"Dessie, what do you want?" I tried to make my voice sound bored. Like I didn't care. Like that was all behind me now.

He stood up and walked to the railing, hoisting himself up onto the bars, blocking the view of the boat. His feet hooked under the lower bar, keeping him balanced, the way a child would balance. It would have been so easy to push him backwards into the Thames.

"Should I call you J-fuckin'-P now? Poncy fuckin' name." He laughed. "Then again I suppose John-Paul doesn't sound flashy enough for a young high flyer like yourself. An investment wanker and all."

"I have to go," I said, standing up.

He swivelled on his seat, looking away across the river to the banks on the other side. When he looked back the play-acting was gone, the sarcastic voice replaced by his real one.

"When you're inside, the thing that scares the shite of out you the most isn't the other lads. Or the screws — no one's scared of them. No, it's that you've already been written off. Forgotten. That life will trundle on better without you and that no one will even fuckin' notice."

I wanted to interrupt him. I didn't want to hear what was coming next but my mouth was dry and empty of words.

"That's what has all these fellas so fucked up, the ones with the wives and the kids, because they know that, no matter what they say, sooner or later they'll be replaced. You know what I mean?"

I nodded and he nodded too. I remembered the girl he'd talked about, Trisha. Maybe if I apologised, explained the situation, it would help. Maybe he'd leave me alone. "Dessie, look, I'm sorry, I—"

"Shut your fuckin' mouth, John-Paul." He jumped down from the railing, landing in front of me, too close. "I'm sick of hearing you say sorry. 'I'm sorry, Dessie. I'm sorry, Mam.' For fuck's sake, it's all you ever say!" Standing so close I could smell his smoky breath and behind the smoke I could smell the beer too.

"Sit down."

I sat. In only a second his face had changed, and I recognised the signs I'd been too slow to register the other night. Now I could see it, the rage that was almost physical, always there underneath his laughter or his words, waiting to resurface the second he unleashed it. It was in his voice, in the jerk of his body as he shoved his hands into his pockets. I forced myself to swallow, pushing away the image of Dessie standing over me the second before the pain. I kept my face blank.

"I know you too well, John-Paul. You're a coward. You don't want any trouble, me messing stuff up for you. You'd do anything to get rid of me."

I avoided his gaze, looking out instead across the river.

"I knew you wouldn't have come clean to your bird. Don't even pretend that you did. I bet the first thing you did was throw my stuff out. Imagine what she'd say when she found out about all your lies. Or those poshy parents of hers."

I didn't want to imagine it. "Dessie, just tell me, what do you want?"

He started to pace again, up and down, his hand gently touching the top of the railing. "She'd probably start imagining that you'd lied to her about all sorts of stuff. Jesus, she'd probably think you were having an affair. You're not having an affair, are you, John-Paul?"

The joking Dessie was back now and he winked. He was enjoying himself, playing with me. I couldn't take much more of this. "Dessie, just get to the fuckin' point. What do you want?"

He stopped in front of me, leaning forward, his hands on his knees. "How much is it worth, John-Paul?"

His face was so close to mine our noses almost touched. His blue eyes were my eyes, Abbey's eyes, and I hated that I would look at her and see echoes of him.

"What do you mean?"

"How badly do you want to get rid of me? How much is it worth?"

With a quick flick he twitched his head forward, a rush of blood, and I panicked, snapping my eyes closed, pushing backwards into the bench. The flowers crumpled beneath my leg and leaked icy water into my shoe. I waited for the impact and the pain but none came. When I opened my eyes he was laughing, thin cables of saliva joining his top and bottom lip.

He stood up and I took a breath. I didn't want him to see that I was shaking, that he could still make me do that after all this time. "How much do you want? I can give you a few hundred to get you back on your feet again."

"A few hundred? Are you having a fuckin' laugh?"

I felt the flecks of spit land on my face. "OK, a grand.

Two grand. I could manage two." The words spilled out of me in a rush before I could think through what they meant.

"Two grand? That's an insult, John-Paul. With that job you're raking it in, seventy or eighty grand a year I'd say, at least." He scratched his stubble as he thought. "And that's before we mention bonuses. Or that promotion — word on the street is you're in with a good chance."

"What? How the fuck ..." I bit the words back in time. This was a bluff. I couldn't fall for it. He couldn't know. "Dessie, I don't earn that much, I swear. With the baby and all, it's tight ..."

"Yeah, sixty quid on flowers — that's tight, is it?"

"Two grand is the best I can do. It's a lot of money, Dessie. In euros that's almost three grand. That'd go a long way in Dublin."

"Easy to tell you haven't been home in a while. You could spend that in a night in Dublin now. And why would I be going back there? I've spent too long in that kip. The birds are all fuckin' tight bitches. Not like over here. Nah, reckon I might head away for a bit — I quite fancy Thailand. I'll need more than two grand, John-Paul."

I waited.

"I'll need fifty." His face was serious as he said it.

"Fifty grand? Are you insane?" The figure made me laugh. I was almost relieved. If he'd said ten I'd have had a decision to make, even twenty, but fifty? No way. "I couldn't get my hands on fifty grand, Dessie, even if I wanted to."

He sat down next to me on the bench looking out across the water, a smile on his face. "I think you can, John-Paul.

JP. Smart fella like yourself. A numbers guy. Maybe Peter can help you out."

"What?"

My heart started to drum faster. I hadn't mentioned Peter the other night. I couldn't have. I didn't think I had.

"Isn't that his name? The fella with the glasses? Your boss. Nice car. You should see about getting yourself a car like that."

I snapped my head around and met his gaze. Cold fear flooded my stomach. He wasn't bluffing, but how could he know?

"It's a small price to pay to keep your little secret, I reckon," he said. "To keep me away from Katie and your precious fuckin' Abbey."

It was hearing him say her name that boiled up the rage that pushed me to my feet, closing the space between us. "You stay away from Abbey! Don't even say her name! You'd never touch her."

"Wouldn't I? Then tell me why you changed the locks, John-Paul, if you're so sure."

He was on his feet now, his grinning face too close to mine. I backed off, realising as I did that I was standing on what was left of the crumpled bouquet, the plastic wrapping leaking the remains of the water onto the concrete.

"Don't play me for a fuckin' eejit, John-Paul. I know all about you, more than you think. You'd give anything not to lose that baby, and right now, right at this moment, you are shitting yourself, absolutely shitting yourself, that you already have."

I opened my mouth and closed it again. He bounced lightly on the balls of his feet, his eyes glued to mine, penetrating me. I was a coward. And he knew it.

"Fifty grand, John-Paul."

"Dessie, there's no way ..."

"Fifty grand," he said again. Nodding. Confirming it, as if we'd just struck a deal. When he turned away from me, his face was in darkness.

"Fifty grand? Dessie, you're crazy. How am I supposed to get that? I don't have that kind of money ..."

But he was already walking away. His voice wafted back over his shoulder to me. "You're the clever one in the family, I'll leave you to figure that out."

I watched him as he walked towards the bridge, a leisurely walk as if he had nowhere special to be. His hand reached out and caressed the railing, his fingers lightly bouncing off the rusting bubbles of paint. From behind me the voices in the bar were louder, buoyed by pints of Stella and Bacardi Breezers.

My eyes followed him under the shadow of the bridge and around the corner out of sight. I leaned over the railing, clutching its solid frame, letting my head fall so my chin pushed into my chest and my forehead rested on the cool metal.

In the warmth of the summer's evening I was shivering.

ELEVEN

It wasn't the ringing of the phone that woke me, or even the thud Dad's bare feet must have made on the stairs. It was his voice, loud in the quiet hall, barking into the night. "What? Yes. Yes, I'm his father."

Turning to check, I saw the sheets on Dessie's bed were flat and unmade since this morning.

"When? No, no, I didn't."

Crawling from the end of the bed I opened the door so I could hear better. Behind me there was a noise and Mam was up too, her makeup a streak on one side of her face. "What's going on?" she said.

I didn't answer, trying instead to listen to Dad's voice below.

"Jesus," he said. "Yes, of course I can. I'll be there in ten minutes."

The receiver gave a little ring as Dad replaced it. He walked up the stairs slower than he'd come down, his white vest stretched across the expanse of his middle.

"What's happened, Des?" Mam's voice was quiet, as if she was holding her breath.

Dad was at the top of the stairs now, his hands on his hips, shaking his head in time with his words. "I'll kill him. I'll fuckin' kill him. The little shit."

That was when I started breathing again, when I realised that Dessie mustn't be dead already if Dad still wanted to kill him. Mam and I stood in his bedroom doorway as he pulled on his jeans and sweatshirt, telling us what happened. Dessie and some of the other boys — bowsies, Dad called them — had stolen a car. The guards had seen them and followed them on their joyride through Dún Laoghaire. They'd crashed the car but no one was badly hurt. They were at the station now. This was serious, not kids' stuff any more. This was it. This was the last straw.

"I'm coming with you," Mam said.

Dad was sitting on the edge of the bed, pulling the laces tight on his workboots. "No, Marie," he said, without looking up. "This is man's stuff. You stay here with John-Paul."

"I'm his mother and I'm coming."

There was something in her voice that meant he didn't argue and he smoked a Benson in the hall as he waited for her to get ready, the front door open letting the night in. I sat on the second step from the bottom and tried to think of something to say but I couldn't find any words at all. We both listened to Mam's dithering footsteps upstairs, the opening and closing of drawers. Her voice low as she talked to herself.

I didn't like the empty way the house felt after they'd left and I didn't want to go back to bed. The clock in the kitchen said it was almost three, and as I cut the last of the cheese in the fridge for a sandwich I tried to imagine the police station, if it would be like it was on TV, and if Dessie would be scared. Maybe he was getting used to it — he'd been caught lifting stuff in town a few months back. Mam believed him when he said it was his first time but I'd known all along what he was doing, not to go near the bag he kept hidden under the bed. Dad knew, too, and ever since then the fights had been even worse. They couldn't be in the same room without fighting now. Carrying my plate up the creaky stairs, I thought about what would happen if Dessie was sent to prison this time. I decided that it would nearly be a relief.

The second time I woke up the light was already on, snatching my sleep away in an instant. Before I knew what had woken me the noise came again. It was loud, a crash. A hard noise. Sitting up in bed, I was rigid, my whole body listening, and I heard the voices then. Shouts between the bangs and the thuds.

"Did you hear what I said? Are you listening to me?"

Bang. Something fell.

That was Dad's voice, and Mam's came next, but I couldn't make out the words because she was crying. Quietly, I opened the bedroom door, stepping out onto the landing. The sitting-room door was half open and I could hear everything then, the noise channelled up the stairs so it was all around me.

"Des, stop! Stop it! Leave him, Des!"

The next bang was louder, a kick on wood.

"Des! Dessie! Both of you, stop it! Just stop!"

Mam was screaming now, hysterical, calling at Dad and Dessie to stop over and over. In science we'd learned about fight or flight and I recognised the energy pulsing through my body making a drum of my heart. Adrenalin: the trick was to harness it and not panic. I put one foot on the top stair. Before I had decided, the door flew open, smashing against the sitting-room wall.

"Look what you've done! Get out, just leave us alone!" Mam was sobbing, her voice lower now. I couldn't hear Dessie.

"Look what I've done? Jesus Christ, Marie!"

"Just go, Des, will you? Please!"

"Don't worry, I'm going, Marie. I can't take this any more. I just can't. I've had it with him. I've had enough."

Dad's voice was lower when he said that, tired. The shouting was gone and that made it scarier. I pulled back into the shadow of the landing. His boots clattered on the tiles, down the hall and past the end of the stairs. He yanked the front door open and closed it so the glass panes rattled.

I ran to the landing window to watch him, not caring if Mam and Dessie knew I was there. I can still picture him, head down, shoulders bent forward, striding across the grass. The van didn't start the first time and for a second I hoped it wouldn't start at all. But then the diesel roared, lilting into a constant sputter, and it jerked away from the kerb, past the hedge and up the road. I remembering standing on my toes to watch it go, my eyes glued to the roof as it rounded the corner, past McCarthy's shop and around by the playing fields. I'm not sure how long I stood there, maybe half an hour or maybe more, but it was long after the exhaust fumes had evaporated into the early dawn brightness and the van still hadn't reappeared in the empty street.

★★★

Dessie slept downstairs that night on the couch and in the morning the sitting-room door was still shut.

"Don't turn the radio on," Mam said. "I don't want to wake your brother."

Her eyes were still red from crying but I pretended I didn't notice.

"How come I have to go to school and Dessie doesn't?"

Mam sighed and shook her head. "Just hurry up and eat your breakfast."

"Where's Dad?"

"I already told you, I don't know."

"When's he coming back?"

"For Jesus's sake, John-Paul, if I don't know where he is how can I know when he'll be back?" Mam pulled her dressing-gown tighter around her.

I waited a minute before I asked again. "What happened last night?"

"John-Paul, you already know what happened. Your brother did a very stupid thing, a ridiculous thing, taking that car. He's lucky not to have been killed. And if anyone asks you in school don't say anything — just say you don't know anything about it."

I ate my toast slowly, it tasted of nothing.

"I know that," I said. "I meant, what happened afterwards?"

Mam looked at me for a second before standing up from the table and dumping the dirty dishes in the sink with a crash. "John-Paul, just get ready for school, will you, and stop asking so many questions."

The Other Boy

The story had got around school already. Dessie, Alan Farrell and Damo Mulvaney. They were the three who'd done it. None of them were in school and they'd probably be expelled. Suspended at least. The guards were going to come down hard, make an example of them. Rumours multiplied, each a different version of the last. They were all in hospital. None of them was in hospital. Dessie had been driving and he was in hospital. The facts and rumours spilled into each other submerging the truth. All day people who never spoke to me spoke to me, rummaging for more details, something they could bring back to the crowd and claim as their own. I didn't enjoy the reflected glory, giving only the briefest of answers to their questions. My mind was full already, thinking about Dad, playing back his words from the hall last night.

At break time I saw Mark looking at me and I thought he was going to come over but he turned in the opposite direction and went off somewhere with Trevor Henderson, the biggest square in the class, his new best friend. It was more than a year since what had happened in the tunnel and the scars on his face were well gone now but we hadn't spoken since. It was stupid to think he would want to talk to me after everything or that he'd ever understand. I knew he wouldn't get it at all. His mam and dad were perfect with their Friday-night dinners and their kisses in the kitchen. He said they never even fought. Alan Farrell's brother was in my class and I wondered what had happened in their house, what his dad had done, but I knew I'd never ask.

That day was the slowest day but eventually it was four o'clock. Two hours at least before Dad came home, but what if he didn't? My head was bent as I walked up the road, not looking where I was going. That was why I heard him before I saw him. His voice cut through the shouts and shoves around me. "John-Paul!"

When I looked up he was there in the evening sunshine, hands shoved in his pockets, leaning against the van. He'd never picked me up before and I knew then that things were even worse than I'd thought. "Dad, what are you doing here?"

"Buckle up! We're going for a drive," he said, holding the door open.

"Where?"

"Not far. You'll see. Magical mystery tour!"

I scanned the van for clues but found none. The pack of Benson tucked into the battered sun visor didn't give anything away. His toolbox was there, a length of pipe rolling into it with a clang every time we went round a corner. As we hugged the side of the narrow windy roads, ivy brushing the window, I tried to remember the questions I'd vowed to ask if I ever saw him again. Now that I had him all to myself, they wouldn't come, and we drove in silence.

The mystery tour ended in Bray. He stopped the car in front of the old bandstand. Two children ran around in a circle, the wind catching a streamer behind them. I followed him over the grass through a gap in the rusting turquoise railings down towards the sea. Together we sat down, pummelling into the clacking stones facing the spike of small peaked waves dancing under the dark clouds, like icing on a Christmas cake.

This was the way I had pictured Mark and his dad, parking up the Sierra and talking to each other over the hiss of the waves. I'd imagined it lots of times, me and Dad hanging out on the beach, but in my imagination it had never been like this.

It was ages before he spoke.

"I wanted to talk to you, John Paul," he said. "I wanted to talk to you about what happened last night." He cleared his throat and reached to light a cigarette, cupping his hand against the flame to beat the wind. I picked up a small stone and held it tight between my fingers. Dazzling white, it felt like silk, and when I turned it over there was a stripe of black down the back. I pushed it hard into my finger and thumb so the skin turned paler where it had been. I could hear his voice in my head before he said the words: I knew they were coming and there was nothing I could do to stop them.

"No doubt you heard all the gory details at school about the joy-riding." He glanced over at me.

"I heard they nicked a Fiat," I said. "That they crashed it into a telegraph pole down the seafront. And Dessie was the one driving."

He nodded. "That's about the sum total of it all right. Could've least picked a decent car. Fuckin' eejits!" He laughed and I joined in. The wind blew his hair back flat. There was more forehead than he had before. "And I'm sure you heard us. Last night, when we came in. You probably heard us fighting."

"Yeah."

He squashed his cigarette butt against a stone; embers flew into the breeze. He breathed in deeply, the salty air catching his teeth and making a whistle. "I'm sorry, John-Paul. I'm sorry you had to hear that. I just saw red. I don't know what the fuck goes on in that boy's head. I really don't. Time after time he seems to waste every fuckin' opportunity." His voice was getting louder and he stopped himself, letting the wind carry the words away before he started again, quieter this time. "The thing that gets me is that he's no respect. Not for me, anyway."

He grabbed a fistful of stones and let them trickle free, one by one. "I lost my temper. You know what it's like when you lose your temper, John-Paul?"

I remembered a time in primary school, after Christmas, coming in on Dessie's old bike when I'd told everyone I'd have a new one. Noel O'Malley was first to notice, pointing at it, saying the only thing my dad could afford this Christmas was a coat of paint for Dessie's cast-off. I didn't say anything at first, the other boys' laughter echoing in my ears, but when he bent down to lock his racer I kicked him. The kick was wrong, too hard and in the wrong part of his back at the base of his spine. I could feel it through my shoe and he fell forwards, crashing into his spokes, crying out like a girl. No one laughed at him, though. Instead Ray Healy went to help him up and turned to me saying it was only a slag, that I should've just slagged him back.

"Yeah, I've lost my temper, Dad."

"Well, I lost mine last night. I went overboard, I know

that, and I'm not proud of it." He didn't look at me, his eyes on the stones in his hands. "It's just that sometimes I think it's the only language Dessie understands. My Da, your grandda, he had his belt and he wasn't afraid to use it if you set a foot out of line. I'm telling you, John-Paul, after that you wouldn't set foot out of line again."

I thought about Granddad Whelan looking out from behind the glass in the photo frame, his face a dark smudge next to Nana and three little boys. I couldn't remember who told me the story of how he had died, how Dad had had to leave school to be the man of the house because Uncle Mike and Uncle Steven were too young and his mam was looking after their little sister who died after. I didn't know why he was bringing it up now, what it had to do with me or Dessie or Mam. All I could think of was that he was leading up to the part where he was going to tell me he was never coming back, and what I would say when he did.

"Your mother, she doesn't get that," he said. "She doesn't understand, but sure then she's in her own world half the time, isn't she?" He turned and gave me a half-sad smile and I couldn't hold the question back any longer.

"Are you leaving, Dad?"

The words burst out all over the beach.

He looked at me, confused. "What?"

"Are you and Mam getting separated?"

It was "separated" that did it, my voice making it halfway through the word before it cracked and the tears I'd been holding back all day finally came. I was thirteen then, too old to be snivelling like a baby, but Dad didn't say that. Instead he moved closer and put his arm around me, I loved its heaviness, its strength.

"Ah, John-Paul, don't get upset, will you? What makes you say that?"

"You said it. Last night. That you were going, that you'd had enough."

He squeezed my shoulder. "Look, people say things when they're annoyed. Amn't I always telling you that? They don't always mean them. Do you mean everything you ever say?"

My lip trembled and my nostrils flared wide, filling me with sea air. I shook my head. "So, you're not leaving us?"

"We've been through a lot lately, John-Paul, we all have. This stuff with Dessie, and your mam not being herself." He paused, as if he didn't know where the sentence was going to end. "It's a bad patch. But don't worry, we'll be grand. This'll all blow over."

I waited for him to say of course he wasn't going anywhere, that he would never leave us. Things blowing over wasn't the same thing. The waves breathed in and out, churning over the stones. He squeezed my shoulder again before letting it go. It felt cold where his arm had been.

Sometimes it still does.

★★★

At home Dessie didn't talk about what had happened — in fact, he didn't talk much at all, except to Mam. At school, he wouldn't shut up about it, describing the crash in detail, holding court in the yard to a semi-circle of boys hanging on his every word. He demonstrated how he was half turning when they hit the pole, how the steering-wheel gouged into his side. It was probably the shock that meant he didn't feel the pain until the next morning when he went to St Michael's and they took the x-ray that showed up his three cracked ribs.

The brief said he'd more than likely get a custodial sentence and he was right. Dessie got two months in St Pat's, Damo got one and Alan got a suspended sentence for a first offence. For a while the house was quiet. Dad dropped Mam and me up to see him every Sunday but he didn't go in. Instead he sat outside, reading his paper.

The drives there and back were the worst, me trapped between them in the front seat of the van. I remember the radio was broken so we didn't even have that to claw at the silence. I racked my brains for stories of school, of TV, of anything that would fill the journey without starting another fight. Dad would answer usually but Mam said hardly anything, her head turned away towards the fogged-up condensation on the window.

They didn't get expelled. Alan Farrell's dad was on the committee and got Ms Mulcahy to give them another chance. Mam thought it was brilliant, kept going on about what a fantastic place St Pat's was, how they'd kept Dessie up to date on his schoolwork so he'd still be able to sit his Leaving Cert next year. At the time she thought that school was the best place for Dessie. It was a real stroke of luck that he got to stay, she said over and over. I don't think

I thought too much about it then but I've thought a lot about it since. Hardly a day goes by when I wonder what would have happened if Alan Farrell's dad hadn't been on the stupid committee, if Dessie hadn't been allowed back in.

It's easy to get stuck thinking about how, if Dessie hadn't come back, it would have changed everything.

TWELVE

Abbey was hidden under the buggy's hood, its grey felt protecting her from the glare of the sun. In the gap where it ended I could just about see her tiny striped socks and the white waffle blanket that was bunched up under her feet.

"She's pushed it off again," Katie said, leaning down to straighten it. "Isn't it funny how even at five weeks old she can tell us what she wants?"

"Personally, I think screaming her lungs off has been an effective method from day one," I said. "She can have anything she wants when she starts that."

Katie laughed, nudging her hip into mine. "Uh-oh, already I can see how spoiled she's going to be, a real little daddy's girl."

I put my arm around her shoulders, locking her tightly into me, holding the buggy handle with the other. It was one of the good days, should have been one of the good days, but all weekend I'd been out of synch, my movements a beat behind, my words lines from some script instead of being my own. The hang-up calls from the withheld number had started last weekend and I knew it was Dessie. Twice, three times a day, every day, until Thursday when they'd stopped as suddenly as they'd started. Somehow the silence was scarier.

A jogger was bearing down on us, bouncing onto the grass at the last minute to avoid a collision.

"You know, I'm going to have to try to get some exercise," Katie said. "I'm like a blimp still."

"No, you're not." My words came automatically.

"Yes, I am, JP. Just look at me, or maybe you shouldn't. I'm still wearing my maternity jeans, and your old *South Park* T-shirt. How attractive!"

She shook her head, pushing her hair behind her ear. Her comfy happiness in the oversized T-shirt was sexy. The guy jogging past had been checking her out and she hadn't even noticed.

"I like you in *South Park*, babe," I said.

"No, you don't, you're only saying that to make me feel better. The doctor said I'm OK to start exercising again so I might look at going back to the gym. They have a special class for new mums to get into shape."

She was going somewhere, waiting for me to say something, but behind her sunglasses I couldn't read her expression.

"That sounds good," I said.

"It'd mean putting her into a crèche a couple of mornings a week, though, and I know we hadn't budgeted for that while I'm off. Can we afford it?"

So that was it. Money again.

"Of course we can," I said.

"But you don't even know how much it is yet, silly!"

"I know that it's worth spending whatever it takes for you to feel good," I said, and meant it.

She snuggled closer to me, leaning up to kiss my cheek. "You're so sweet, JP, I'm really lucky," she said.

I smiled, hoping it would cover up any strain in my face. I didn't want her to worry too, to see that I was doing the maths in my head of how much three mornings in a crèche might cost for the rest of her maternity leave. If only HR would pull their fingers out and speed up the promotion process we really wouldn't need to worry about money. It had taken much longer than Peter thought for approval and the job specs had only just gone online. It would be a week or two yet before the interviews, let alone a decision.

"Oh, look, JP, there's the ice-cream man. What about a 99?"

"What about the health stuff?" I laughed. "I thought it was all about gyms and losing weight."

"Exactly," she said, smiling, pushing her glasses up so they held back her hair. "And what better way to celebrate my return to fitness than with an ice-cream?"

"Go on then, I'll have one too."

I watched her half skip, half run towards the waiting queue. If having Abbey in a crèche a few mornings a week would bring my happy Katie back, it was worth all the money in the world. She missed her friends from work, I knew that — she was used to being in the centre of things. It'd be good for her to meet other mums at this class. Under the hood Abbey started to whimper, as if she could feel her mum's absence already, even in her sleep. I pushed the buggy gently back and forward on the path.

"Sssh, Abbey, there, there. Daddy's here. Daddy's here."

I reached down and held her little foot, feeling her kick against me. I'd caught myself doing that a lot lately, touching and holding Abbey when I wanted to ground myself and chase Dessie out of my head. Since the day by the river, he was in my head nearly all the time, his words rolling around like marbles. Last night he'd been in my dreams as well, a younger Dessie who held me down and wound Dad's fishing line tighter and tighter around my finger until the top of it went red and purple and then nearly black. I stroked Abbey's leg, the skin so white and soft it was like satin. There was no way I would ever let him touch her.

In front of the ice-cream van the queue stretched across the path and onto the scorched grass. I squinted into the sun to make out Katie but I couldn't see her. Careful not to jolt the buggy I pushed Abbey slowly up towards the van, scanning the crowd. At the window a lady in a grey cardigan counted out change with one hand, while a little boy hung from the other, whining for his ice-cream. Behind them a group of girls in clingy tracksuits and trainers displayed their impatience with shakes of their head and flicks of their hair. A man knelt down to wipe fizzy orange from where his daughter had spilled it on her dress. There was no sign of Katie.

Turning around to where we'd been, I thought I might have missed her — maybe she had looped back. But, no: behind me the path was empty.

"Where's Mummy gone?" I whispered to Abbey. "Where is she?"

I ignored the erratic beat my heart was making under my T-shirt. It was Victoria Park at five in the afternoon on a

Sunday. She was just here. She couldn't have gone far.

My hand shaded my eyes and I looked around me, turning a full circle. Beyond the fountain a group of lads were playing football. There was a shout from one and the ball went high into the air in the direction of the swings. Nearly every bench was full. Couples. Teenagers. A woman reading a magazine. I flicked my eyes around each, registering the images quickly. None of them was Katie.

I swallowed the bubble of panic and reached for my mobile. Halfway through dialling I remembered she'd left hers on the shelf at home. I let it ring anyway, picturing it ringing out in the empty flat, only hanging up once I heard her voicemail. Checking that Abbey was still asleep, I turned the buggy around again and strode purposefully back towards the ice-cream van, pushing through a gap in the growing queue and onwards towards the peeling wrought-iron gates.

Through the pillars I could see a rectangle of high street, traffic and people and noise. She wouldn't have left the peace of the park for the clamouring Mile End Road but with no other plan in mind I kept walking anyway. As I got closer I saw it, the nose of a white car, just visible, illegally parked on double red lines. As the pillar moved back I saw a hand on the steering-wheel, white knuckles against black leather. There was an arm with a tattoo that disappeared into a red sleeve. The sheen on the window hid his face but I could see he was twisted around, leaning over the headrest and into the back seat. Through the glass there was the shine of red slinky polyester. He was wearing an Arsenal shirt.

The bubble of panic burst. My feet acted first, pounding

across the concrete in time with my heart. I tried to make out who was in the back, who he was reaching out to, but all I could see was the street's reflection. In front of me the buggy bounced over the path, the hood falling back on itself. Glancing down at Abbey I saw she'd woken up, her eyes wide open. Maybe she was too shocked to cry.

I was through the gate now, down the cobbles onto the path but the winking light of the indicator was on. He must have seen me.

"Hey! Hey! Stop!" I yelled, breathless, conscious that people were turning to stare. "Stop him, someone!"

Abbey's delayed cry came. A howl like I'd never heard before. A quick look down and I saw her face was dark red, nearly purple. I wanted to take her out, to pick her up and run, but there wasn't time to undo the straps. Snatches of pain pulsed from my damaged ribs. The car was pulling away, into the flow of traffic. My breath caught. He had her. He was going to get away with her.

"Stop!" I shouted again, my voice ripping against my throat. "Somebody stop him!"

My eyes were on the car, drinking in every detail of the traffic. I didn't see the edge of the pavement come up until we were right on top of it. Skidding down on one knee, I felt my jeans strain against my thigh and I pulled as tight as I could, veering the buggy sideways towards safety. It took every ounce of energy I had left and for a second I thought it might tip over. I watched it as if it was disconnected from me, not sure if it would stop until it did, one of its rubber wheels teetering on the kerb.

Letting go, I ran past it, into the traffic but it was too late: the car merged with the rest and I hadn't even caught the registration plate. A red car beeped at me and swerved and I stepped back onto the pavement. Gasping for breath, I ran my hands over my hair looking in vain for someone, anyone who could help.

I didn't hear her calling until she was right beside us.

"JP!"

I spun around, my eyes needing to check what my ears told me was true.

"JP! What's happened? What are you doing? My God, what's happened?"

The break of relief was almost physical, she was there. Katie was beside me, on her hunkers, on her knees, untangling Abbey from the buggy straps.

"Jesus, Katie, thank God." I looked from her to the car. I could make out the white roof, stopped at the junction lights. "Thank God," I said again.

My breath was shaky and I realised I was trembling. Abbey's cries punctured the fug of my thoughts. Angry distraught cries. I turned again to look at the car, but it was gone. For now at least.

"Abbey, come here, my poor darling, my poor baby. Sssh, sssh, it's OK. Mummy's here now."

Katie had Abbey in her arms, her hands gently feeling her little body for signs of damage. With her palm she held the back of her head, kissing her forehead over and over. Abbey was crying still but the earlier screech was gone. These cries were the kind I'd heard before, big breathy sobs mixed with gulps of air. One of her socks was missing and her foot dangled in the sun, white and exposed.

I put my hand on Katie's shoulder but she pulled away. "Fucking hell, JP! You almost pushed her right out onto the road! You almost pushed our child into the traffic! What the hell's going on?"

I'd seen Katie angry before but not like this. This anger was hard behind her eyes, the kind I couldn't control, that there was sometimes no way back from. In the jumble of traffic the white car was gone.

"Katie, I'm so sorry. I thought—"

"Thought what? Look how upset she is, JP. Oh, my God. What were you thinking? You could have really hurt her."

"I thought you were in trouble." I changed my words at the last minute realising how close I'd come to saying I'd thought he had her. "You went off to get ice-cream and then you vanished. I couldn't find you — you weren't anywhere," I rushed the words out to explain. "I thought you were gone."

"Gone? Gone where? For heaven's sake, JP."

"Well, where the hell were you? What was I supposed to think? You can't just go running off like that."

Her chin rested on Abbey's head. The anger was starting to melt into tears that made black smudges under her eyes. Just a few minutes ago she'd been so happy. Dessie couldn't even let us have an afternoon together. She was watching me, taking her time before she answered. There was something else in her face now. It was fear. I knew that feeling:

"I went to the bank machine, JP." She made her words

slow and clear, as if she was talking to a child. "I didn't have any cash on me so I went to get some out. For the ice-cream."

Against her chest Abbey whimpered and Katie rubbed her back in tiny circles. She bit her bottom lip, waiting for me to answer. The pain in my ribs throbbed with every breath. I plucked my T-shirt from my shoulder realising for the first time it was drenched with sweat. "You should have told me."

"I was only going to be a minute. Less, even."

"You were gone longer than that. It takes more than a minute to queue up at a bank machine." I knew it was petty, a minor detail, but I had to say it. I had to make her understand. "I had time to walk up to the van and back again, down as far as the fountain … and all the way up here …"

The detail brought the emotion back and my voice edged higher. Dessie had been in that car, I knew it. Watching us, just like he'd watched us changing our locks. We'd been lucky this time but we mightn't be so lucky again. Katie opened her mouth to respond but something made her stop. She pulled her eyes away from me and rearranged Abbey in the crook of her arms. "Come on, let's just go home," she said.

★★★

It was forgotten but it wasn't forgotten. I made us dinner, seafood pasta, but the ingredients I'd so carefully selected at the market the day before didn't taste like I'd imagined they would. We both made an effort to talk, about Abbey and things to do to the flat, maybe a holiday later in the summer, but all the time it was there, this thing between us, under the words, waiting to surface. When I cleared away Katie's plate she'd eaten the prawns but left the scallops, hiding them under a sticky swirl of spaghetti.

"You never ate your scallops," I said.

"I don't really like them, always find them a bit rubbery."

All night Abbey was cranky and unsettled. Katie said it might be the heat but we both knew it wasn't. Moonlight edged around the corners of the blinds so the bedroom was shades of grey. Beside me I could tell from Katie's breathing that she was still awake. I knew what was coming, that I should be the one to bring it up first and not her. But still I hadn't thought of words that would explain it away.

"JP?"

"Hmm."

"Are you awake?"

There was no point in pretending. I couldn't avoid her question any longer. I rolled over onto my back. "Yeah."

There was a silence then, as we stared at the ceiling. We were close but not touching. We hadn't had sex since Abbey was born and despite everything I felt myself stirring, hoping maybe that was what she wanted.

"What happened today? In the park. What was that all about?"

Katie always whispered in the dark. Even before Abbey was born. I used to tease her about it, asking her who she was so afraid of waking up. Not tonight.

"I'm sorry. I didn't mean to scare you. Or Abbey. I over-reacted, that's all." My words floated into the darkness and I could almost hear her mulling them over. Distilling them. Making her own words in her head before she responded.

"I know. And I don't want to keep going on about it but you scared me, JP. There was something about the way you acted ... with Abbey ..."

"I said I was sorry about a million times. What more do you want me to say?"

"Calm down, for God's sake. That's not what I mean, I know you're sorry. But the panic, when you thought I was gone, I've never seen you like that before. What are you so afraid of, JP?"

Before I could answer she spoke again. "I mean, it's not just that. You've been acting so weird all the time lately. Like today you didn't even want us to go to the park at first, you wanted to spend this gorgeous day cooped up in the flat ..."

"I was tired."

"And then earlier when I talked about bringing Abbey into the office to see the girls you weren't keen, trying to put me off."

"Why would I try and put you off?"

"I don't know. I can't figure it out. But it's all weird. The new locks. Checking the doors and windows fifty times before you come to bed ..."

"I do not!"

"You do! Even tonight, you got up a minute ago to check."

"I was going to the toilet."

She sighed. "I heard you, JP."

I hadn't thought she'd noticed so much. She was right.

Earlier, lying in the dark, I'd imagined I'd left the kitchen window open, the long one by the cooker. Anyone could climb in. I sat up and fumbled for the lamp, snapping the room into blinking light. Next to me Katie rubbed her eyes. Her skin was pale against the white cotton sheet.

"I didn't know I was under such scrutiny. In case it's escaped your attention I was mugged. Remember that? I'm sorry if I'm a little jumpy." I sat up, resting my elbows on my knees, and ran one hand over my hair. "These things don't just go away, you know. They have after-effects. It's not so easy just to forget what happened."

She heard the truth in my words and slowly sat up, easing herself closer to me. "I know. I can't imagine what that's like. But maybe you should talk to someone about it."

"Who? Some fuckin' shrink? No way! I'm fine now anyway. It's over."

The words were harsher than I'd meant and she pulled away, crumpling her knees up into her chest.

"I'm sorry, Katie, I didn't mean to say that. I just meant I need some time to work through it on my own." I moved in closer, gently resting my hand on her shoulder, enjoying its round smoothness. "I'll be fine — you just need to give me some time."

Slowly she turned towards me, tracing a finger down the side of my face, catching in the day-old stubble. "If you won't talk to someone else maybe you could talk to me about it. That might help."

If she only knew how I longed to talk to her about every-thing. How easy it would be to rest my head on her soft pyjamaed breasts and let everything come flowing out. For a moment I let myself imagine it, her hand rubbing my head, her gentle whispers telling me everything would be OK. If I told her, we could face it together. She would understand, surely she would.

"Oh, Katie ..." I started but then the words stopped. She looked at me, waiting for what would come next, her head leaning to one side, her hand absently pulling her hair flat against her neck. She was everything I'd ever wanted. What if she didn't understand? What if I told her and she never looked at me like that again?

"It's this job thing," I found myself saying. "The promotion. What if I don't get it? What if Richard gets it, or one of the others?"

Leaning into me, she kissed my arm and then my shoulder. "If you don't get it, you don't get it, JP. We'll manage. It's not the end of the world. Just do your best, that's all."

Do your best ... just like Dad used to say.

"But what if my best isn't good enough?"

Across my back I felt her hand smoothing the material of my T-shirt, moving in big and then small circles. The movement stopped and I realised she was crying, small silent sobs.

"Hey, what's wrong?" I turned to face her, pulling her into my chest.

"It's not the job, is it? I can tell you're not being straight with me. It's me, isn't it? It's us. You haven't been the same since Abbey was born ..."

"Sssh, Katie, stop. Of course it's not you. That's crazy. Sssh." I cradled her against me, rocking her slowly from side to side like she'd done with Abbey only a few hours before. "That couldn't be farther from the truth. I swear. I'm so sorry I scared you today. I really am. I was just a bit freaked out about the mugging thing, that's all."

Against me she started to shake. Words and tears spilled out together and I held her tighter, trying to make her stop.

"I thought … I keep thinking that your moods … all this stuff … maybe it's because of Abbey … that you're not happy being a dad …"

The words stabbed me and I held her even tighter. "No. No, no. Sure I was the one who wanted a baby in the first place. I love Abbey and I love you. I love us."

She pulled herself back against the pillow, so she could see me, make sure I was telling the truth. Her eyes were swollen red. I had done that, made her feel like that. I was never going to hurt her again.

"Honestly? It's not all too much for you?"

"Honestly. I swear. Come here, you silly thing."

"And if you ever felt differently you'd tell me, wouldn't you?"

"I won't ever feel differently."

I pulled her towards me again. Her words were muffled in the warmth between us but I still heard them. The words I'd heard her say before.

"Just promise me you'll always tell me the truth, JP."

Without hesitation the words came.

"I promise."

THIRTEEN

"Hi, JP, I've got two beautiful girls waiting in Reception for you! Shall I send them up or are you coming down?"

I could hear the smile in Leena's voice, and in the background, Katie's voice too. Hearing her brought a giddy excitement and I realised, suddenly, just how much I missed not having her around at work. Getting the Tube in together in the morning, the little goodies she sometimes left on my desk when I hadn't made it out to lunch. Even on the days when we hardly had time to speak to each other it was somehow enough just to know she was there.

"Thanks, Leena. Give me two secs, I'll be right down."

As the lift descended I studied myself in the mirror, practising a smile. Katie was more upbeat since she'd joined the gym, enjoying getting out, friends already with every other mother in our postcode. She hadn't brought up the incident in the park again and neither had I, but I knew it had been on both our minds. There'd been no hang-up calls for nearly a week but I still couldn't enjoy the uneasy sense of peace, knowing too well that it was part of Dessie's game. Katie had been pleased when I'd suggested bringing Abbey up to Cheshire to see Rebecca and Philip for the weekend. It wasn't my ideal destination, but at least it was safe.

The rugged tyres of the buggy looked out of place on the sleek marble floor. Next to it Katie had Abbey in her arms, holding her over the Reception desk towards Leena. Two other girls were there too. I didn't know them but they were laughing at something Katie was saying and she was laughing too, her hair a shine of brown and lighter brown caught in the sun from the atrium above. I'd booked the appointment at an exclusive King's Road salon as a surprise and the transformation was worth every penny. She hadn't noticed me yet and I let myself enjoy her as a stranger for just a second longer. It still amazed me when I saw her like that, to think someone like her would choose someone like me.

"Hi! Abbey, look, there's Daddy!"

Seeing me, she smiled. She'd dressed up for the girls in the office, the oversized *South Park* T-shirt replaced with a bright dress that swirled as she turned, showing off the smooth curve of her legs in high-heeled sandals. Holding Abbey's hand she made her wave at me and I waved back. One of the girls was on her mobile, smiling over as she headed towards the door. The other kissed Abbey goodbye before following her. In the space they left I saw someone else there too, someone whose profile had been hidden up till then.

"Hi, Abbey!" I called.

As I came closer the figure came into focus. A guy dressed in leathers with a crackling radio clipped on the strap across his chest. A large brown envelope in his hand. Dark hair like mine. Thick stubble, bordering on a beard. He was the same height as Katie in her sandals. The helmet and gloves on the counter must belong to him. As my feet clicked towards them the smile on my face tightened.

It couldn't be him but somehow it was. It was Dessie.

"She's so gorgeous," Leena was saying. "How old is she now?"

"She's six weeks — I can barely believe it!" Katie said. "It's going so fast."

"I love her outfit. That dress! And the matching little shoes are so cute."

"Aren't they gorgeous? She doesn't need them, of course, and usually I don't bother putting shoes on her but I couldn't resist today. JP was laughing at me this morning with all her clothes laid out, weren't you?"

There was a smudge of lipstick on Katie's front tooth as she smiled. The overfull vase of lilies next to her had powdery stamens that threatened to fall, a dusting of pollen already evident on the glass sheen of the counter. Dessie turned away to talk into his radio. I managed to breathe. They were looking at me, waiting for me to answer. They were talking about clothes, Abbey's clothes.

"Yeah, I was," I said. "You're turning her into a right fashion victim."

"Just like her mum. I love that dress, Katie, where did you get it?"

"Hobbs," Katie said, one hand smoothing the material against the curve of her thigh. "I was only supposed to be looking, I wanted to wait until I'd slimmed down but I was sick of wearing JP's old T-shirts. So, this is my motivation dress! I figure if I look better then I'll feel better and it'll be easier to shift the weight. And JP was really sweet — he booked me into Strands to get my hair done."

"Strands on the King's Road?" Leena raised her eyebrows. "Very nice. I was reading about them last week. They did a gorgeous job." Tipping her head to one side, she smoothed her own hair between her hands. "Mine is way too long at the moment. Maternity leave sounds great, shopping and hair appointments. When are you coming back to work?"

"That's not exactly a typical day," Katie said. "Just trying to look half human coming in here. I'm not back till January, may as well enjoy it while I can."

"Please come back before then," Leena said, laughing. "Half the calls that come through here seem to be for you. They're all lost without you upstairs."

Behind them Dessie had stopped talking. If Katie turned around her face would be inches from his. A trickle of sweat launched from my armpit and snaked its way down my side. It was a coincidence that he was here. It had to be. He'd drop off his envelope and then he'd go.

"Sorry to interrupt, Leena, that was the gaffer, checkin' up on me. Said there's something else for collection, from the fourth floor, I think."

"Fourth floor, that's marketing," Leena said. "I'll check for you now. Oh, sorry, this is Dessie. Dessie, this is JP and Katie, and their new baby."

"Howya," Dessie said, dropping the envelope on the counter. "Nice to meet you."

The grating Dublin vowels sounded exaggerated. Why was Leena introducing him to us?

"Hi," Katie said. "Nice to meet you, Dessie."

I watched in fascination as he shook the hand she held out to him. His knuckles had the remnants of picked purple scabs. Were they from when he'd hit me or someone else? Katie had had her nails done. When he turned to me my reaction was automatic. A firm shake. Eye contact. A slight raise of his eyebrow that only I would notice. His hand was sweaty in mine. The leather courier uniform looked strangely right on him.

"JP, is it?"

"Yeah. Hi," I said.

I waited for their reaction. For someone to notice. Leena spoke first. "Dessie's been a regular fixture in here this past week or so. I'm surprised you haven't met yet. We've been relying on him for almost everything we send out."

"What happened to the other guy?" I asked. "What was his name again?"

"Charlie? I don't know, he left or something. Is that right, Dessie?"

"Didn't show up one morning apparently," Dessie said. "Same day that I knocked around looking for a job. Suppose I was just lucky, in the right place at the right time."

"Well, it's been lucky for us too," Leena said. "You know what Gordon's like about security, that we always need the same people. Dessie's been a godsend — he's the only person who seems to be able to get things to where they're supposed to be when they're supposed to be there."

"Ah, Leena, stop, you're embarrassing me now." He smiled. "Getting a few parcels out in time hardly means I was sent by God! So, who's this little one here?"

Leaning in towards Abbey he touched her head gently, his knuckles grating lightly against the soft firmness of her scalp.

"This is Abbey." Katie smiled. "Say hello, Abbey."

"She's gorgeous, so she is, just like her mam."

Katie flushed at the compliment, laughing it away.

"Dessie!" Leena giggled. "Not everyone's used to the Irish charm."

"Oh, you're Irish?" Katie said. "I wasn't sure about the accent. JP's from Ireland too."

"Gosh, are you Irish, JP? I never knew that," Leena said, frowning. "Dessie's from Dublin. Where are you from?"

How did Leena know so much about him?

"Me too." I nodded. "I'm from Dublin."

"What part? Dublin's quite small, isn't it? Imagine if you were from the same place."

Before I could answer Dessie's response was there. "Ah, Dublin's a big place these days. Something about JP's accent tells me we're from different ends of the city altogether. I'm from a place called Sallynoggin — it's a bit like Streatham. That's why we get on so well, Leena, you and me. We've a lot in common."

The wink he gave Leena took any bitterness from his words and she laughed along with him, her brown cheek fusing with a hint of pink. I'd never thought to ask where she was from. As I watched how she smiled at him the realisation was blunt and obvious. I was so stupid thinking Dessie's comments from the other night were lucky guesses. His double bluff had worked. He'd known about me all along: he was in and out of here, the place where I worked, all the time.

183

Pumping Leena, lovely, gentle Leena, for information he could use against me. Anger swelled inside and I was conscious of the hot stinging redness in my cheeks. The glass all around us was letting in too much sun, glinting and bouncing off the chrome and the marble into my eyes.

Dessie was the focus now and Katie was half turned towards him. Abbey had her back to me. Her creamy white neck had a crease of pink. Under my fingers it felt bumpy and raw. "Katie, look, Abbey's coming out with a heat rash on her neck — it's too hot for her in here."

"What? Oh, that." Katie swivelled around to look. "She's had that for a couple of days. They all get things like that. I put some cream on it this morning."

"Well, the sun here can't be helping. We should get her upstairs," I said.

"Don't worry so much, JP, she's fine. He's such a worry wart sometimes," she said to Leena, raising her eyebrows towards me.

"You know what would sort that right out?" Dessie said, examining the mark. "Eucerin. It's just a moisturiser and I don't know what's in it but it's good stuff. Use a little bit of that and she'll be right as rain."

His fingers were on her skin, touching her. There was black dirt trapped under his square nails. Abbey squirmed away, her face crumpling ready to cry.

"There, there, sweetheart, you're fine," Katie said, nodding, her new hair bouncing with the movement. "Eucerin? I haven't tried that but I will. Thanks. Do you have any children yourself, Dessie?"

"Not yet," he said, still looking at Abbey. "But I do have a niece, a lovely little one."

"Katie, are you coming upstairs or what?"

My voice cut across their chat. The words were timed all wrong, words that were too loud and made everyone stop and look at me. In the silence the phone rang. Leena waited a second before slipping her headphones on to answer it. Katie looked from me to Dessie and back to me. Her forehead rippled, creasing her makeup. "I was going for lunch with Alison first," she said, "and bringing Abbey up on the way back."

"Bring her upstairs now, everyone's dying to see her. And you. People have been asking me all morning what time you're coming in." I clapped my hands, wringing them together, sliding in their own sweat. The action felt wooden. I reached for the handle of the buggy, a prop to hold on to and smooth my jerky movement. Smiling, I turned it away from Dessie and towards the lift.

"But she's on her way down," Katie said. "Leena called her right after she called you. That's probably her now."

Before her string of words could become a meaning, I registered the soft bing of the arriving lift. That was Alison, I knew it was. Alison, who never failed to pick up on anything, who would see the resemblance in a heartbeat. Alison, who had seen us together on the steps of Tower Hill Tube station. I turned in time to see the doors slide open. Three people pushed out. Two guys from Accounts. Lauren from HR. Lauren waved and I willed her not to come over but she did anyway.

"Katie Wright, I hope you weren't going to bring this

little darling in here and not come and see us?" she said, kissing Katie first and then Abbey.

"As if!" Katie said. "I've just got here."

"Great. Listen, I'm running really late for lunch but I'll be back by two. Can you pop down after?"

"That's perfect. I'll see you then. I can't wait to hear all the news."

"Me too," Lauren called out, as she rushed towards the door.

The second lift was on its way down. The black screen showed a neon number six that became a five. That was Alison's floor. The screen still said five. Someone must be getting in.

"I think Alison's caught up in something upstairs," I improvised, the galloping of my heart threatening to drown out my words. "I saw her on the phone. There was someone waiting to talk to her at her desk. Something urgent, some emergency with Peter, I think. Come on upstairs and wait. I'm dying to show you both off."

Showing them off did it. I should have said that first. Katie shrugged at Leena. "Looks like I'm wanted upstairs."

Stretching across the counter Leena kissed Katie goodbye, her finger stroking the soft curve of Abbey's cheek. "So long now, baby Abbey, come back soon, won't you?"

"Nice to meet you, see you again," Dessie said, raising his hand.

The buggy wheels squeaked on the shiny floor. I held my finger on the glass V of the up arrow, scanning the numbers above them both.

"Hang on, JP. Why the mad hurry?" Katie asked, catching up.

"There's no mad hurry."

I smiled. Jingled the change in my pockets. I let go of the button, leaning over to kiss Katie first and then Abbey. Where was the damn lift?

"Is this a bad time? You seem really stressed. Maybe I should just wait here for Alison, let you get back to work."

Behind her, Dessie was still there. He looked comfortable leaning against the Reception desk, his envelope and helmet abandoned. Leena was laughing again, straight white teeth and pink gum. He was the only one with her now. After we left, the two of them would be alone.

"No, don't be silly. Come on, here's the lift now."

If Alison was in it we could get in anyway. We could say we had to go upstairs. She wouldn't have to see him. The line between the doors pulled back into a rectangle of space. I closed my eyes for a second and opened them to see fake walnut walls and a mirror reflecting the three of us back on ourselves. The lift was empty. Above the white of my shirt my cheeks were in flames. I flattened the peak of my hair.

The buggy got caught — it was almost too wide to go in. My hands slipped on the handles as I shoved it over the metal runners. Katie was chatting about how it was strange to be back in the office again. As we waited for the door to close I saw Dessie's hand stretch across the counter towards Leena. She looked down and back up, leaning in towards him.

"I rang Mum to tell her we're coming up on Friday," Katie said. "She was delighted, busy already lining up millions of people to see us. Or to see Her Highness here, really."

"Great," I said. "Sounds good."

"Look, Abbey, there's another baby. Who's that baby?"

Abbey started to cry and Katie turned away from the glass and followed my gaze to Dessie and Leena. "Looks like he's more than just the courier," she said. "He's sort of attractive, in that rough-around-the-edges kind of way."

I snorted. "She'd want to get a grip of herself. Imagine a client coming in and that's the first thing they see. Peter would freak out if he knew."

Katie didn't answer and I watched as she gently rocked Abbey from side to side, her hand stroking the place on her neck where only minutes before Dessie's rough fingers had been. What had just happened couldn't really have happened and yet it had. He was getting closer, too close, and I'd done nothing whatsoever to stop him. The lift doors shut and I discovered I'd been holding my breath. He was gone, temporarily, but for how long? I reached out for Katie, my hand finding the small of her back. She turned to me and smiled. I smiled a smile I didn't feel. I couldn't keep ignoring this, ignoring him. The time had come to do something.

Fourteen

Behind the stainless-steel counter a chef whirled dough around from one hand to the other, watched by the queue of people waiting for tables. Katie had been right about needing to book: it obviously wasn't just her favourite restaurant but all of Cheshire's as well.

Across the table she was telling me a story about a school-friend of hers who used to work here. She started to laugh before she got to the punchline, just like she always did, laughing even more when she noticed she had screwed it up.

"Oh, God, JP, I'm so crap at telling stories! And jokes, I've never been able to tell jokes."

"I like how you always mess up the ending. I think it's cute."

"I don't know about that." Katie shook her head, cutting into her pizza. "Anyway, I didn't mean to get so sidetracked telling you all that. Now that I have you to myself for once I wanted to ask how you feel about next week. About the interview."

"The interview?" I hadn't been expecting her to bring that up. I shrugged. "OK, I suppose. I mean, it'll be weird being interviewed by someone I already work for, but it should be OK."

She was waiting for me to say more, but there didn't seem to be any more to say. Even though I'd been focused on it for so long, lately the whole idea of the promotion seemed unreal somehow.

"Just do your best, JP, and you'll be fine," she said, smiling. "I was thinking, with the interview on Friday, we need to make sure you get an early night on Thursday, give Abbey an extra shot of Calpol."

She laughed, her whole face lit up by it and I did too. She looked so beautiful when she laughed.

"I think we should get married."

That wasn't the way I'd planned to say it. Practising the words in my head, they sounded different. Better. I'd planned to take my time, to build up to it, but there was something about how she looked right then that made the words just come out. Across the table Katie froze, a triangle of pizza dangling from her fork where it hung in midair.

"I mean, why not? We've talked about it before. It would make things more official for Abbey and you know we're good together. I love you." I was babbling now. I should have said that first. At the start. The tables were a snug fit and I didn't have to look at the couple next to us to know they were listening. The waitress arrived to refill our water glasses with a dripping jug.

"How is everything?" she asked.

"Delicious, thank you," I said.

"Fine," Katie said.

She filled our glasses and turned to the table next to us. My pizza wasn't delicious at all. It looked great but didn't really taste of anything. I wanted to love it, for it to be my favourite too, but the truth was I preferred our local

Domino's to this. Katie was staring at me, her expression hard to read. I needed to say something.

"Sorry — Jesus, I didn't mean to blurt that out. I've scared the shit out of you now."

"No, no, you haven't."

Even though she said that I knew I had. She grabbed her glass, took a long drink of water. At the door a hen party had arrived, ten or twelve of them in pink T-shirts and tinsel. The noise of voices and laughter seemed to expand to fill the room, floating above our heads, pressing against the exposed beams of the ceiling. I cursed myself for being so stupid. Cuccino's on a Saturday night was not the place for a marriage proposal.

"OK, you did," Katie said. Her laugh was nervous now as she spoke. She pushed her chair back and dabbed her mouth with the napkin. "Are you being serious?"

It wasn't the words she said but the way she said them that told me this wasn't going to go well. That I shouldn't have brought it up again and that nothing had changed since the last time. My appetite was gone now and I pushed the remaining half-pizza to the side of my plate. "What — you think I'm joking?" The words sounded defensive.

"No. Well, I don't know. Did Mum say something? Or Dad? I bet Dad said something to you while I was upstairs getting ready. He did, didn't he?" She nodded to herself thinking she'd found the trigger, got to the bottom of where this was coming from. While she was getting ready I had walked Abbey around the garden, showing her the different flowers, wishing I knew all their names. Through the sheen of conservatory glass Philip had been reading a paper. Once when I looked round he was watching us, but he never came out.

"No, he didn't. Neither of them did. Do you think that's the only reason I'd bring it up?"

"No, of course not, it's just …"

"Just what?" I shrugged to make the question lighter.

She aligned her knife and fork on her plate and took a sip of wine. Her eyes were on mine but I couldn't read her expression. I was about to speak when she leaned across the table and looped her fingers around mine. "You know I can't get married, JP. The divorce isn't through yet."

"Yes." I nodded. "But we could still get engaged. And you said it might be through by the end of the year."

"Might be. It mightn't be till next year."

"Yeah, but the point is we could get engaged now and then arrange the wedding once it comes through." I rubbed her finger in the place where her engagement ring would be. She squeezed my fingers and let go.

"Why do you suddenly want to get married, JP?"

There was a little V in her forehead as she asked me. This wasn't sudden and she knew it. She glanced at the table next to us and I did too. The man had gone to the toilet leaving the woman on her own. She might as well have been sitting in between us.

"Look, it's not a good place to talk about this."

"Clearly, but you brought it up."

I swallowed. It was important to find the right words. I shouldn't have started this until I'd figured out what I wanted to say. "Because of Abbey …"

"Having Abbey's not a good reason to get married."

"Would you let me finish? I was going to say because of Abbey and you. Us. I want us to be a family."

"We already are a family."

"A proper family."

"What's not proper about us as a family?"

Over her shoulder I saw the waitress weaving through the narrow gaps in the tables. She placed a basket of steaming garlic bread between us, next to the wine. "I'm so sorry you've had to wait for that — it's just a madhouse here tonight," she said, refilling our wine glasses. "Is everything OK? Can I get you anything else?"

"No thanks." Katie smiled.

When she left there was silence between us. It was my turn to speak.

"It's not that we're not a proper family, Katie. It's just that I love you and Abbey so much. I want people to know we're together because we want to be. That Abbey was planned instead of being some accident, like people could assume she was." Even as I spoke, Catherine Begley's voice echoed somewhere in the back of my head. Maybe kids didn't call each other bastards in the playground any more but I wasn't going to take that chance, not with my daughter. "When Abbey grows up I want her to know that she was wanted, as well as knowing she was loved. I want us to be … to be permanent. You know?"

That was better, Katie was nodding. But in the bouncing shadow of candlelight on her face I couldn't read what she was thinking.

"I know, JP. I do. But … how can I say this without you getting upset? Marriage is not what makes things permanent. I of all people should know."

Leaning across I picked up a piece of garlic bread. As I broke it in half, crumbs of crust fell onto the table and I followed them with my eyes. "Look, this wouldn't be the same as with him," I said, avoiding his name. "It'd be different this time."

"But we talked about this before, JP. We agreed. You agreed. That weddings are all a sham, the cake and the big white dress … that it isn't for us."

"I know, but it's different now we have Abbey. And we don't have to have some big cheesy wedding, we can have something small somewhere. Just the two of us. I don't care about the actual wedding. I really don't. I just want to marry you."

The words were slipping out too fast, the warmth of the wine sliding one into another. What exactly was so wrong with wedding cakes and white dresses? With wanting permanence and making promises? I was saying too much. Begging. I reached across the table and held her hand again. "Do you not think there are just certain things about getting married that you can't have if you never do it?"

"Like what? You're not religious so it's not that. Legally once we buy a place that'll be a joint mortgage, which is the same thing."

"Not that stuff, other things."

"Like what?"

"I don't know — the speeches, I suppose. And the song." I took a sip of wine.

"The song?"

"Yeah, you know the first song. Getting to choose it together."

"For Christ's sake, that's so corny! Who cares about a song?"

"I do. I just think it's nice. Something you'd always remember. You know, every time it came on it'd be something special."

Katie was laughing. She thought I was joking.

"I bet you remember the song you and Toby had."

"What's that got to do with anything?"

"What was it?"

"For God's sake. I can't remember." She lowered her eyes to the table.

"Come on, of course you can remember. What was it?"

"It doesn't matter."

"It matters to me. What was it?" I sat back in my chair, watching while she kept her eyes on her hands and fiddled with her napkin. I took another sip of wine while I waited.

"'Endless Love'."

"'Endless Love'?"

Hearing the scorn in my voice she looked up and I could see anger in her eyes. I didn't know if it was meant for me or him.

"Yes, you know the one. Christ, I don't even know who sang it. Lionel Richie or someone. How ironic — that's what I mean about it all being a complete sham. Here we are dancing around to 'Endless Love' and after only a year he's shagging some girl from his office. Obviously the definition of 'endless', these days, is less than twelve months." She laughed but her hands were twisting the napkin, shredding bits of red paper onto the brown table. She was upset, but I was still glad I'd asked. Glad it was a shit slop of a song that I'd always hated.

"I always thought we could have The Beatles song 'Something'," I said.

Katie looked up, her eyes not registering. She reached for the bottle and filled her glass with what was left.

"It's from the *White Album*, one of George Harrison's." I started to sing it, but before I could get halfway through the first line Katie cut across me.

"I know the song."

"I just thought, if we ever did get married, that maybe it could be our song," I said, feeling stupid now that the conversation had somehow come down to this.

As she drank her wine her eyes held mine over the rim of the glass. "Why is that our song?" she asked, when she put the glass down.

"I don't know — I like it. It reminds me of you."

"Why?"

I shrugged. I knew where she was going with this and I had walked right into it. I should never have brought it up. Why were we arguing about the song instead of the real issue here?

"I bet you liked it before you knew me."

"Well, yeah, I've always loved it. But now it reminds me of you, of us."

"That proves my point. It's exactly what I'm saying. That

196

song isn't about us, it's just some song you always loved that you've suddenly decided is about us. If you met someone else you'd still love it and it'd be about her. That's what I found out is at the core of every bloody wedding tradition, JP — building the couple up into some fantasy with all these romantic notions that don't mean anything in reality. What we have is stronger than that. Better. We don't need a song or a dance or a speech or a wedding."

Katie's voice was getting too loud and even though the couple next to us had their bill they made no move to leave. I caught the woman's eye and glared. She had the decency to look away. Katie was still talking.

"I know you're a romantic, JP, and I love that mushy side of you, I do. But marriage isn't about songs. It's about honesty and trust and putting the other person first. Isn't that what we already have? It's more than most marriages have."

This happened every time we talked about it. She was so convincing she'd persuade me that it was OK, that we were OK, that we didn't need someone else's validation on our relationship. She could make me believe her, like I was believing her now, but it didn't last. When I was on my own, I couldn't make the arguments stack up the way she did. The reasons for not getting married were slippery and vague and I couldn't hold on to them. No matter how I looked at it there was only ever one answer that floated to the front of my mind.

"You don't love me enough to marry me, do you?"

The words rolled onto the table. They were there, between us, a little grenade of sounds, between the wine and the garlic bread. She reached across the table but I pulled my hand away before she could get there. She took hers back, curling her hair behind her ear instead. I knew we should end it now, stop before it was too late to stop, but we'd already gone too far. No matter what it meant I needed to know.

"I love you, JP," she said. "You know that. How could you not know that?"

I picked up my glass and took a mouthful of wine, drinking it too fast so it burned my throat. Her eyes were trying to hold mine but I looked away.

"How I feel about marriage has nothing, absolutely nothing, to do with that — to do with you. I thought you understood that, JP."

When I looked back, she was leaning towards me, her chin resting in the cup of her hand. In the wobble of her lip I suddenly saw Abbey.

"I want to explain this to you properly, JP, and it's hard. If this was the other way round I probably wouldn't get it either but I need you to try."

I waited.

Watching me, she took a deep breath. "I don't know how to explain this. It's like from the time you're a little girl you learn about weddings. Story books, Disney movies. That's where they all end up — the princesses, the poor servants — at the altar. You plan it out, talk about it with your friends. Who you're going to marry, who'll be your bridesmaids, what dress you'll have, all that bullshit." The curse wasn't like Katie and she swallowed it back with some wine.

"It must be different for boys — you probably never gave it a second's thought — but for girls it's like your wedding day is your be-all and end-all."

I pictured Mam and Dad's wedding picture on the windowsill in the kitchen. The two of them with eyes closed behind confetti rain. Grease thickening on the glass dulling the colours behind. How I'd always wondered who would be in the picture with me. "I don't know, I suppose I assumed I'd always get married some day." I shrugged. "I never really thought about it."

"I had my day. I had the big cars, the church. The cake and the speeches. And you know what? I found out it's all crap. All that stuff they tell you when you're a kid. It's all lies. It's like Santa Claus or the Easter Bunny but worse, and you don't find out until it's too late."

I opened my mouth to interrupt but she was on a roll, her fingers scraping furrows in the sheen of her hair.

"When Toby and I split up, that was the hardest thing of all, remembering that day. It was awful — I just wanted to forget it. But everything is about making sure you remember it — the photos and the cards and the bloody video! God, I remember the night he left I pulled all the bloody tape out. I was sitting there with all this tape everywhere — there was so much of it. And once I'd pulled it out, I wanted to fix it and I tried to push it back in but it was twisted and torn and I couldn't do it. Not that it mattered. I didn't need the tape to remember it. I can still hear the words from those bloody speeches, his fucking lies ..."

The image was too vivid. I could picture her sitting there, surrounded by ribbons of shiny black tape, tears rolling down her face. I wanted to kill the bastard. I hated how the memory of him hung over everything we ever did.

"Katie ..." I reached for her hand, squeezing tight so we were locked together, our fingers and eyes a chain in the flow of her words. Tears were in her voice but they hadn't come yet. Behind her the waitress was on her way over but, seeing me, she took a last-minute change of direction.

"I can't do it again, JP. I'm not doing it again. Not even for you."

"Sssh, Katie, it's OK." I rubbed the back of her hand but she pulled it away, reaching for a tissue. In my jeans I found one and passed it to her under the table. I waited while she blew noisily.

"God, I hope I don't see anyone I know," she said, glancing around her. "How mortifying, having an emotional breakdown in the middle of Cuccino's."

"It'll probably be on the front of the *Cheshire Chronicle* tomorrow," I said. "'New finding: Garlic Excesses Reduce Girl to Tears'."

It was a poor attempt at humour but she giggled and I did too. The air around us lifted. I reached for her hand again. "I can't imagine what it was like to go through what you did with him. I really can't. But it would be different with us, I know it would ..."

"JP ..."

"It's not about the wedding or the day. It's about us being a part of each other's lives, Katie. Being a family. About me being a part of Abbey's life, being her dad, no matter what happens."

As the thought became words I knew I shouldn't have said them but already it was too late.

"What do you mean 'no matter what happens'?"

"I don't know, nothing, just that I want it to be official."

"Official?"

"Official's the wrong word ..."

I was making a balls of this. Only I could make a marriage sound like a custody battle. Leaning my head back I stared at the wooden beams and sought for the words that would put everything right.

She beat me to it. "JP, I think I know what you mean. The permanence thing you said before, the family. I get that."

I nodded.

"You haven't had a family and now you have us, Abbey and me."

She understood, she really did. Even though I could barely explain it to myself she understood what I meant, what I felt. She smiled and I smiled back. Maybe this was what it was about, understanding each other. Maybe she was right, that we didn't need some piece of paper, or a ring, or a song, that this was what was important.

"When I got married to Toby ..."

"Jesus Christ, can you leave him out of it for just one second?" My hand slammed on the table, making the glasses rattle, surprising us both.

Katie bit her lip and the tears made her eyes shiny in the candlelight. I knew I should stop, that I should apologise, but somehow I just couldn't. Half turning from the table she blew her nose again. When she looked at me her eyes were harder, as if in a split second she'd made a decision.

"Why do you want to get married now, JP? You're not even happy at the moment."

"What's that supposed to mean? I'm the happiest I've ever been. And with Abbey, it just feels like the right time."

"We can't get married for Abbey. What about us? God, sometimes I feel like I'm just a vehicle for you to become a dad or something."

"That's ridiculous! For God's sake, I've spent the whole night telling you how much I love you."

"Well, lately you've had a funny way of showing it. You're so moody all the time. Losing your temper every five seconds. Stressing about work and that bloody promotion. Since Abbey's been born there's been days when we barely speak. You're not happy, you won't tell me why but I know you're not. And that's one thing Mum always said to me about marriage: 'It won't make you happy, you have to be happy already.' It's true, JP."

"That's rich, coming from someone who's permanently pissed off, especially with her husband."

I waited for her to jump to her mum's defence but she didn't say anything, responding with a sigh instead. She looked away towards the door, and side on she seemed tired — and I was too. Of Rebecca's advice. Of fighting. Of always saying and doing the wrong thing. Slumping in my chair I realised how jaded I felt, I let the heaviness fill my limbs. Across the crowded room I caught the waitress's eye and motioned for the bill. Nodding, she pulled a docket from her black apron and headed towards us.

"OK," I said.

"OK?"

"Let's just forget it. Forget about getting married."

"That's it? You want to just forget it?"

I shrugged. "What else are we supposed to do?"

Before the waitress could drop the bill on the table I handed her my card. "That's fine," I said.

"Thanks. Can you follow me to enter your PIN?" she asked.

I stood up and jerked my jacket from the back of the chair. I was doing what Katie hated now. Clamming up. Shutting her out. I didn't care. She stayed sitting down while I pushed my chair in, watching me as if I was a stranger.

"Do you want to go for a walk down by the river?" she said. "It's gorgeous out still. Mum and Dad aren't expecting us back so early. We can talk through this."

She was the one with a desperation-tinged voice now, not me. I knew what was coming next: she'd want to talk about this for hours, to go over every angle from the outside in and back again. What did she want me to tell her? That I was afraid of losing her? Them both? She knew that already, so what good would it do? And no doubt Rebecca'd have some saying about being afraid too. Some bullshit rhyming couplet that sounded great and meant nothing.

At the counter the waitress was pointing at the credit-card machine.

"I'm really tired, it's been a long week. Let's just go home."

FIFTEEN

The Monday-morning air along the river was fresh and felt good after the claustrophobia of the weekend. Katie and I hadn't talked about what had happened on Saturday night. Playing happy families under the watchful eyes of her parents and the endless stream of visitors all the next day had been torture. Aunts and uncles, Rebecca's bridge friends, women from Philip's work, they all showed up to see Abbey and I couldn't wait to get out of there, to breathe. It wasn't until we were trapped in the car, just the three of us, inching in silence along the M1, that I'd realised things could get worse.

Taking the office steps two at a time I was glad to be coming in, glad it was the start of another week. Something about the schedule, the familiar predictability, was comforting, as if being in work was the only time I was who I needed to be.

Leena was in already and she called me over. "JP, I've an envelope for you here. Or should I say, John-Paul?"

Her smile was warm but suddenly I felt freezing.

"I never knew what JP stood for before. You should use your full name, it's nice."

"God, no, I can't stand it," I said.

I reached out and took it from her. It was heavy brown

paper with my name printed in square letters in black marker: "John-Paul Whelan". Leena was about to say something else when the phone rang and I mouthed goodbye. Walking across the atrium I folded the envelope in two so it fitted deep into the pocket of my suit jacket. Waiting for the lift I took it out again, flattening it back into one piece and turning it over in my hands.

The floor was empty — not even Peter was in yet — but I closed my office door anyway. I looked at Dessie's writing and took a deep breath before I tore the flap open with my finger. I groped inside, finding nothing at first. It was empty. But no, there was something, something smoother to my touch, that fluttered free onto the desk. A white-rimmed square photograph with curling corners. At the top a hole was punctured, circled by the indent of a thumbtack.

I remembered the photo. The four of us too close to the camera, the blur of the fairground behind only visible through the gaps between us. My eyes scoured the faded image, breathing life into the memory. The quiet hum of my office filled with the whirr of the waltzers, the smell of petrol and sugar. Dad's smile was the widest, his eyes crinkled up at the edges. I had only taken one photo of him with me when I left. It was of him on his own, smiling into the camera, but younger than I remembered him, with long hair and sideburns that almost reached his moustache. The man in this photo was my proper dad.

On the back Mam's slanting writing said "Courtown 1986" in faded blue biro. The summer before Dessie was in St Lawrence's. When he would still help me with my Airfix planes, even if it was when no one else was around. In the bottom corner there was another sentence in black marker, square writing like the print from the envelope. The words were neat and straight to the point: "You have until Friday." Friday, the same day as my interview. It was almost as if he knew but even he couldn't have known that. I checked inside the envelope again for something more, a letter, more instructions, but that was it. There was no reference to the money but what he wanted was clear. There was no mobile number, no way of getting in touch, so he obviously planned on paying me a visit.

Friday. At first it was nearly a relief to know that I would have four whole days before I would see him next, easier to have some kind of marker instead of all this waiting. I sat down in my chair, spinning around and around again. Four days, though. Four days. How was I supposed to find any kind of solution in four days?

I buried my head in my hands, breathing deeply through my nose. Dessie, the interview, what was happening with Katie, it was too much, I couldn't deal with this, I couldn't fix everything in four fucking days.

"Fuck you, fuck you, fuck you!"

I stood up, needing to move, and paced in circles around the tiny office. I made a crumple of the envelope and threw it towards the bin but it sank to the ground before it made it, rolling beneath the shelves. I stopped pacing and kneaded my temples. I had to think. A clear head and I could sort this out. There was a way to sort it out. There had to be, there was always a way.

Through the narrow window I could see the rain. It had just started, flicks of water thrown from the smoky clouds over the river. The flicks joined up and became lines. The lines became rivers, funnelling their way down the glass, like bars. I willed my brain to think, to figure out a solution, but it was stuck. A blur of images running into one just like the rain. My reflection blinked back at me, my tie hanging loose, just like it always had in school. I hadn't changed, I looked the same. I hadn't been able to save Mark from Dessie: what if I couldn't save Katie and Abbey either?

"Fuck it!"

I kicked out hard. My foot connected with the desk, dislodging the phone and making it clatter to the ground and skid across the carpet.

"JP? What's going on? Is everything all right?"

There was no mistaking the harsh Scottish voice that demanded an answer. I turned to see Alison in the doorway, leaning against the frame. Her glasses were pushed up, holding back her hair.

"What's happened?" she said again.

I turned to pick up the phone, keeping my movements slow. How long had she been standing there? Why was she in so early? I heard her close the door behind her.

"Sorry, Alison, I didn't know you were there. I'm fine." I turned back to her, making myself smile. I flattened my hair down on my forehead and leaned against the desk.

"JP, you're not fine. Sorry to just barge in but what on earth's happened? Whatever's the matter?"

Her voice was tinged with concern but underneath that

there was firmness too, as if I had no choice but to tell her the truth. The idea of spilling everything to her, to organised, capable Alison, was suddenly appealing. There was nothing she couldn't sort out, no problem too complicated, no deadline too tight. Alison was one of those people who could make the impossible possible and make it look easy.

"Nothing's the matter, it's fine ..." I let my voice trail off, as if there were more words to come that I just hadn't said yet. Some part of me wanted her to ask me, to push me to open up to her. She reached out and put her hand on my arm. I could feel its warmth through my shirt.

"JP, it's not nothing. Anyone can see you're upset. What's the matter? Is it something to do with Katie or Abbey?"

That was it, of course, the reason for her concern. It was for Katie, not for me. She was Katie's friend. I must be losing it, thinking about confiding in her. I pulled my arm away, pushing my hands deep into my pockets. "Yeah, she's fine. Everything's fine," I said. My voice sounded more like my voice now. More in control. Her eyes were holding mine and I wondered how much Katie had told her about what went on between us. Probably everything. I wondered if she already knew about my botched proposal.

"It's just this interview," I said, walking to the other side of the desk, putting some distance between us. "It's on my mind. Being interviewed by your own boss is the worst. What if I screw it up?"

Her face relaxed into a smile and something that looked like relief. "Ah, c'mon now, JP, you of all people won't screw it up. You have till Friday and you're always so well prepared for everything, so organised. I'm sure you've got it all worked out already — you've probably rehearsed all your answers and everything. Don't tell me you haven't!"

She was teasing me now, bringing lightness into the conversation, but I couldn't laugh it off yet. She'd seen me lose it completely — I couldn't let it go so soon.

I shrugged. "You can't really prepare for an interview like this and it depends on how everyone else does. I know Richard's going for it. He's the obvious choice and he can't stand me. He'd love to put me in my place. What if he gets it?"

The words spilled out and I could tell she was believing me. I was believing myself because mostly it was true.

"I shouldn't say this," she said, dropping her voice lower despite the closed door, "but I honestly don't think he will. I'd be really surprised if he did. There's way too much history there, JP. Peter puts up a good front, but underneath I don't think he's got too much time for Richard either."

"Really?"

"Don't get me wrong. It's not like he's said anything. He never would. But you should see the emails between them sometimes, and Richard's always trying to get snide remarks in about Peter in front of the other directors. Peter would never say this to me but I don't think he'd trust someone like Richard. He'd prefer someone more loyal, someone who'll be straight with him and who he can trust. Someone like you."

Alison had never let me into her confidence like this before. She knew Peter better than anyone, and what she was saying made sense. I hoped she was right. I wanted her to be right. I needed this job. Katie and I needed this job.

"I don't know," I said. "It could be a case of keep your friends close but your enemies closer. I really want it for Katie's sake. It would be so nice to have that bit extra every month so she could treat herself more, get nice things for Abbey, and we can find a bigger place."

She waited a second before she answered, reaching up to drop her glasses from her hair down onto the bridge of her nose. She was wearing green ones today to match her blouse. She tilted her head to one side as if I made an interesting study. "But you know Katie, she couldn't care less about that, JP. I suppose she'd enjoy some extra cash — wouldn't we all? — but at the end of the day she wants you to get this job for yourself. If you're happy, then she's happy."

The words hung in the air between us and I nodded. They echoed Katie's from the other night and I knew she wasn't just talking about the job any more. I couldn't hold her gaze and I looked away. My eyes came to rest on the photo in front of me on the desk, lying face up in full view. Four faces smiling out, two faces that looked like me. When I glanced up Alison had seen it too – she was leaning over to get a better look. Too quickly I grabbed it, crumpling it into my palm, knocking against the penholder. It wobbled and fell forward spilling highlighters and pens across the desk.

"What was that?"

"Nothing." I shook my head.

"Was that you in that photo?"

I forced a laugh. "OK, you got me. It's just this really

awful picture of me. I hate it and I don't know how it got there. Next stop the shredder!"

"Come on, let me have a look …"

She reached out towards my hand but I snatched it away. "Just leave it, Alison!"

The words were too strong, almost a shout. I tried to laugh, to think of something to say that would explain it away, but there was only silence.

"Sorry," Alison said. I waited for her to say something else but she didn't. Standing back from the desk she folded her arms.

I walked back around the desk, picking up the spilled pens, turning them so they each faced the same way. "So you think Richard hasn't much of a chance, then?"

"It's hard to say." She watched me even out the pens, stuffed back into the holder.

"Yeah, course it is," I said.

"I shouldn't have said anything, really, it's not my place."

The shower had stopped and sunlight dappled the desk, shining into Alison's eyes so she squinted behind her glasses. In my hand the photo was greasy with sweat and I folded it into my shirt pocket. She was watching me, waiting for an explanation that I didn't have. Before I could think of one the phone rang. It was her cue. "I'd better let you get that. I've a tonne of stuff to get through this morning too."

"No rest for the wicked," I said, reaching for the receiver.

"Oh, and don't forget you're babysitting on Wednesday. I'm taking Katie out on the town — remember?"

The Other Boy

I'd already picked up the phone and nodded my agreement, giving her a thumbs-up for good measure. Katie had mentioned it but in the middle of everything else that was going on I'd completely forgotten. A voice down the line was talking about a deal I couldn't afford to miss: a half-built commercial-property opportunity in Docklands needed a capital injection to complete. With the phone in my hand I stood up, pacing the small space in front of my desk. Through the glass I watched Alison make her way across the floor, weaving around the desks in the direction of the toilets. When she was almost there she looked back and I tore my eyes away just in time, giving the door a gentle kick shut.

Sixteen

That day, I knew something was wrong right from the start, as soon as I opened the door and saw it was just Dad and Dessie in the kitchen. It was months since Dessie was back home — the whole winter had gone by and I'd never seen them in the same room, even on Christmas Day. If one of them came in, the other left. That was the rule.

"What's going on?" I said, dumping my schoolbag on the chair.

Dessie was sitting at the table, pulling his long fringe down past his chin and letting it bounce back up again. Dad had his arms folded across his chest.

"Nothing," he said, "there's nothing going on."

I read the signs, the house quiet, no dinner on, and I thought it was about Mam, that she'd gone missing again. As I poured myself a glass of milk, that was what I was waiting for, bracing myself for.

"I was just telling Dessie that I saw the doctor today, that I've to have a bit of an op."

I stopped pouring and turned to watch him properly as he talked. He tried to smile as he spoke and I heard what he was saying — clichés about early-warning signs, how they could be a good thing, the tests he'd had done. I heard every single word, but I couldn't make one of them stick.

"There's nothing to worry about," he said. "The technology they have, these days, they can do these operations in their sleep."

He seemed to have finished before I'd even started to understand. I looked from him to Dessie and back to him. "When do you've to go in?" I asked.

"Thursday."

"Thursday? This Thursday?"

He nodded.

"Why so soon?"

"Ah, you know, the sooner they get these things sorted, the better."

"And the operation, what's it called? A bypass?"

"That's right, a bypass," he said. "Hope it's better than the Blackrock one — that's always clogged with traffic."

He laughed but it didn't sound anything like his laugh. I remember wondering if he'd rehearsed the joke. I thought about the picture of the heart in my Inter-Cert science book and wished I'd paid more attention. I wanted to open it right then, to learn all the details and to understand what a bypass meant.

"Where's Mam? What does she think?"

"She's upstairs having a lie-down. She thinks the same as me, it'll be grand."

I nodded, smiled, nodded again. There was nothing else to do. At the table Dessie was just sitting there. He hadn't said anything, not one word. He didn't even look as if he had taken it in. So what if he and Dad were fighting? Did he not understand what was happening? That this made everything different? I wanted to punch him, to shake him, to make him react, but I didn't do anything and he just sat there, pulling his manky fringe down as far as it would go and letting it spring back up again.

I don't remember much about the next few days or the journey to the hospital. I only remember being there, Dad looking out of place in his new pyjamas with the crisp crease down the sleeve and the leg. He insisted on sitting on the side of the bed, instead of lying down inside it like he was supposed to. On his locker the paper sat untouched, his glasses folded neatly on top. He wasn't allowed his packet of Benson.

I couldn't stop thinking about Granddad Whelan. When he'd died he'd been forty-two and Dad had been only a bit older than I was. Now Dad was nearly forty, but sitting on the bed in his pyjamas he looked more, as if he was picking up oldness from the other men in the ward already.

Mam was restless, moving too fast for the stillness in the air. She circled around the bed, picking up his pillows, pumping life into them and putting them back. Walking over to the window she fiddled with the blinds, coming back to the bed where she reached for the pillows again.

"Jesus, Marie, would you relax?" Dad said. "They're grand the way they are."

"I just want to fluff them up — they're very flat. We should've brought some from home."

"They're grand."

Mam stood still but her hands gave her away, creeping from the end of her sleeves to rest on the movable table, pushing it up and down gently with a squeak.

"You couldn't do me a favour, love, could you?" Dad said. "You couldn't pop down to the shop and get us some 7Up? I've a desperate thirst and I'm sick of that water."

Mam grabbed her bag and disappeared down the white and green corridor. Dad shifted his weight on the bed so the springs made a creaking noise. It didn't look very comfortable.

"She's on edge," he said. "Better to have her doing something."

"Yeah." I nodded. I glanced after her. I wished I had something to do too. When I looked back at Dad it was as if he'd read my mind.

"John-Paul, I need you to do me a favour while I'm in here."

"What's that, Dad?"

"There's a new set of DIY magazines coming out — I saw them on telly. The first one comes with a folder to collect the rest in. Will you pick it up for me?"

"Do you want me to bring it in to you?"

"No. Hang on till I get home, and I'll get the next ones, maybe collect the set and pick out a few DIY projects from them for the summer. Maybe we'll build a patio out the back, clear away some of those flowerbeds under the kitchen window."

"OK."

The summer felt like forever away. I hoped Dad was right, that we'd spend it building a patio together.

"And, John-Paul?" His voice was more serious, lower so the thin old man in the next bed wouldn't hear — but he didn't look like he heard anything anyway. "I just wanted to say that, you know, if anything happens — not that it will — but if it did, you'd look after your Mam, wouldn't you?"

The fear I'd been holding back flooded into my stomach. Instantly I was bursting for the toilet. Where was Dessie? Why wasn't he here? Why was I the one listening to this on my own?

"Don't worry, I'm sure everything will go grand," he reassured me, reading my expression. "I wanted to say it just in case. You know your mam can be up and down and I know I can rely on you ..."

I nodded again. I didn't trust myself to say anything. He paused so long I thought he'd forgotten what he wanted to say.

"Dessie, well, sure you know yourself, you'd never know where he is." He looked around and laughed, as if he expected Dessie to materialise from behind one of the curtains. "He's gone off the rails — and that temper of his. I can't get through to him. And I can't count on him. Not the way I can count on you, John-Paul."

"You can count on me, Dad," I said. My voice sounded stronger than I felt.

"Good man," he said, patting my shoulder. "Sure don't I know I can, that's why I'd say this to you. You're a good lad, John-Paul. But sure, anyway, this is all just pie in the sky. Won't I be home before you know it? We'll be back to normal in no time."

Before he could say anything else Mam was back, but she'd no 7Up. I was about to ask where it was but then the nurse was there, pulling back the bedclothes, making Dad get in and lie down. She was from the country, talking too much and too fast about what was going to happen the next day. Mam was nodding but I couldn't keep up and Dad looked relaxed, as if he wasn't listening properly either. I wondered if this was the same conversation he'd had with Granddad Whelan, if he'd made a promise and if he'd found better words than I had. Maybe he took his little brothers to play outside to give his dad and mam time to talk. Maybe he had hugged him or said something to make him laugh. Maybe he'd told him that he loved him.

I shook my head, flicking the images away. I wasn't Dad. I didn't have any little brothers to play with or the right words to say. I wasn't him. I was only me. And I was frightened.

★★★

Everyone said it had gone OK. Better than OK, it had gone well. That he was on the mend. In bed Dad looked tired but his smile was real and so was Mam's. They believed it and I let myself believe it too. That was why I wasn't expecting it. Even when I saw Uncle Mike outside the school when he should have been at work in the hairdresser, I thought it was something else, some other reason that he was there, taking longer than I should have to join up the dots.

The traffic was heavy on the way to the hospital and Uncle Mike cursed and banged the steering-wheel with his palm. I took one of his Murray Mints from the open pack on the dashboard, unwrapping it slowly.

"You're sure your brother wasn't in school at all?" Uncle

Mike said again. "Of all days what's he doing mitching today? We need to track him down."

The mint clacked against my teeth and I didn't say anything. I didn't tell him that Dessie hadn't been in school for weeks. The Fiat Panda in front of us stopped suddenly and Uncle Mike cursed again. "You've no idea where he could be, John-Paul?"

He might have been in Dún Laoghaire, lifting things from Golden Discs or drinking cans in the laneway behind McDonald's. He might have been in Dec's house where they went to get off their heads when his mother was at work or he might have been up the green. He might have been anywhere. I didn't care where he was.

I shrugged. "I don't know."

It took thirty-five minutes to get to the hospital. Uncle Mike ignored the no-parking sign and dumped the car across the yellow boxes outside the door so we could run straight inside to where Mam and Gran were waiting. Mam hugged me too tight and too long and kept holding my hand when I sat down next to her in a hard plastic chair. When she asked Uncle Mike where Dessie was, he shrugged, like I had, and said he'd go and phone the O'Briens next door again, in case they'd seen him.

For hours we waited, the four of us, in the corridor, sometimes speaking, usually not. The nurses came but they told us nothing. He's still in theatre. No news yet. Wait for another half an hour. Wait there a moment. Just wait a little longer. The afternoon seeped into evening and we waited. We waited as the rain cleared and sun filled the corridor.

Uncle Mike went and came back again and still we waited, drinking cans of Coke and cups of tea and squinting into the evening light.

I don't know how I managed to sleep with my body stretched out along the hard plastic ridges of the seats but somehow I did. I remember when I woke up my neck was breaking. I heard Uncle Mike's voice first.

"Jesus Christ. Half eight. How long can one operation take?"

"God, I hate all this waiting."

Another man's voice but not Dessie's. I opened my eyes a slit to see it was Uncle Steven. He lived in a big house on the other side of the city. Usually we only saw them at Christmas.

"How's Marie doing?"

"Ah, sure, she's in bits. Poor cow."

"Is she still on the wagon?"

"You wouldn't know. She's on and off, I think. Probably more off than on. Doesn't help that no one can track down Dessie."

"Where is he?"

"Who knows? He was mitching today, and by the sound of things it's been a while since he went near that school. Little gobshite!"

"C'mon, Mike, he's a teenager. Have you forgotten what we were like?"

"Dessie's different, Steve."

"But sure we were the same, always bunking off. He'll settle down, they always do."

"Do you remember the time Ma was away and Des came home and found you and Tony Cullen bunking off watching telly in our house?"

"Christ, I'll never forget it. He beat the living shite out of me! Tony legged it out of the house and straight into his da outside. He got the shit kicked out of him then as well."

Their laughter sounded like echoes of each other, followed by silence, until Uncle Steven broke it: "And I'm sure you did your fair share of mitching yourself."

"Course I did, but with us it was just messing. It's different with Dessie."

"What do you mean?"

I waited for Uncle Mike to answer but it was a while before he spoke again. Somewhere in the background a child was howling, its voice screechy in the corridor before it faded away outside.

"Ah, there's been other stuff. Did Des tell you about the stealing? The joy-riding?"

"Joy-riding?"

"He stole a car and went joy-riding. Him and some other young fellas totalled it and almost killed themselves."

"Jesus."

"He was in St Pat's there last year for it. And they got fined two grand. Two grand! On top of everything else Des has to deal with. And when I saw Dessie afterwards there wasn't a bother on him. Looked proud of himself, if anything. Des doesn't have that kind of cash. Who does?"

"Des never said anything. He should have told me. I could have helped him out with a loan."

In the gap of silence that followed I wondered if Dad had known that Uncle Steven would say something like that, if that was why he hadn't told him.

"You know what he's like. He'd never ask. I shouldn't even be saying anything now. It wouldn't surprise me, though, if the pressure of all that is why he's in here."

"Ah, c'mon, Mike. That's not fair. You can't blame Dessie for this."

"I'm not. I'm just saying Des has been under some pressure lately. He wouldn't tell me half of what goes on but I can see it in him. I know I shouldn't say it but he's a lot on his plate, what with Marie and everything as well. It's that lad there I feel sorry for."

I could feel their eyes on me and hoped they wouldn't notice the redness that was creeping into my cheeks.

"How's he getting on?" Uncle Steven asked.

"He's getting on great. He's a good lad. School's not a bother to him, comes top of his class in everything. Like his da."

"Was Des always top of his class?"

"Oh, yeah, always writing stories and poems and stuff. He should've gone on to do the Leaving. I should have been the one to get a job and help Mam. You don't need the Inter Cert to cut hair.

"He could've gone back — after, like?"

"Sure, he met Marie and once they got married it was too late then."

There was something final in Uncle Mike's words. Dad was twenty when he married Mam, and Dessie was born the same year. The way Uncle Mike described it, it sounded like that was when Dad's life was over, not just beginning.

"That's why he has all his hopes pinned on that fella there." I felt their eyes on me and lay extra still, careful to keep my breathing steady. "Des always says that he'll go far. And you know what? I think he's right."

★★★

By nine o'clock everyone was there except Dessie. Uncle Mike had collected Auntie Paula. My baby cousin Emma squirmed on her lap and a waterfall of drool fell from her rubbery lips. Chris was five and played Snap, his fingers sticky on the plastic backs of the cards as they slid from the chair and onto the floor. Uncle Steven was across the corridor on the phone, one arm leaning against the wall. Mam and Gran had gone to talk to the doctor and Uncle Mike had followed them.

In the gift shop the magazines were on a rack by the door, above the newspapers. Near the top I saw what I was looking for. On the glossy cover there was a picture of a man standing proudly on a newly built patio. I lifted it out from the holder but something made me hesitate. Buying it seemed almost like tempting Fate but it was the only thing Dad had asked for, and I wasn't going to let him down.

I don't know if I paid for it. I can't remember if I'd handed over the money before I heard the bang of the metal handle as the door on the other side of the corridor swung open bouncing into the wall and back again. The bang made me turn and then I saw them, the three of them together, Mam in the middle. I started to run and then I stopped.

Mam's mouth was open but I couldn't hear any sound. Her body sloped like she might fall only for Gran and Uncle Mike holding her steady on either side, like stabilisers.

I must have run from the shop. I don't remember. I probably called out but if I did the sounds are gone now. The memory is in snatches — Uncle Mike coming towards me, reaching me before I got to them. His hands on my shoulders, turning me away from where Mam was starting to cry. The smell of his sweat. The slidy feel of the magazine cover slipping from my fingers and onto the floor.

"I'm sorry. John-Paul, I'm so sorry, son."

I'd never seen him cry before. I'd never seen any man cry. His nostrils flared wide and red like he was trying to fight it. I knew then, before he said it. Before his arms locked around my shoulders, tight like an iron band. Uncle Mike shook, hard physical shakes, as if electric volts were pumping around his body. Through his tears he was saying something about Dad but I wasn't listening. I was remembering being small enough so he could swing me around, wondering when I'd become too tall. I hadn't noticed but now I could see over the navy wool of his shoulder where Chris was reaching for a card he'd dropped under the chair. I could see a woman on the phone behind him, laughing and twisting the cord in her hand.

Dad was dead. That was what he was saying over and over. On the phone the woman laughed and I could see her fillings. Dad was dead but everything was the same. I started to laugh too but I bit it back. Uncle Mike clenched me tighter, rocking me with him back and forth. Dad was dead.

Everything was the same but nothing was the same. Nothing would ever be the same again.

★★★

Before Dad died I'd had to write an essay about a funeral and I'd imagined that grief might be like drowning. In the essay I wrote that it was like everything was slightly blurred and out of focus until you had to come up for air and then reality would hit. I was all wrong. That night in the hospital, the lens twisted tighter so everything was extra sharp. Tiny splinters of detail lodged in my head. The bright pink of Gran's lipstick seeping into the wrinkles around her mouth. The clanging tinkle in the cup when Uncle Mike stirred his tea. Every moment was magnified, the details squeezed and embossed forever on my memory.

After the funeral everyone came back to our house. Every time I thought the sitting-room wouldn't take any more people, the doorbell rang and new voices were in the hall. Empty and half-full bottles of stout lined the mantelpiece and the windowsill. A cloud of smoke hung across the room, caught suspended in the evening sun. Twice, I'd had to run down to McCarthy's for another sliced pan and some more ham as everyone devoured Gran's never-ending supply of sandwiches.

Mam was drinking vodka and tonic, squashed on the couch between Auntie Rita and Mrs O'Leary. She was laughing at something Auntie Rita was saying, something about when they were girls, but the laugh was too loud, like it was almost a scream. Her cheeks were flushed and the earlier redness in her eyes had been replaced with a different kind.

I was doing the sandwiches and Dessie was looking after the drinks. He was the man of the house now; that was what everyone kept saying. As I watched him step easily through the crowd, his shirtsleeves rolled up and a cigarette behind his ear, he filled the part well, as if it was a role he'd been waiting for, all along.

He wouldn't tell me where he'd been that night, when we were all at the hospital, and I was the only one who seemed to care. His absence didn't stop Mam wanting his arm around her shoulders at the church instead of mine, and he was the one who got to hold the front of Dad's coffin with Uncle Mike while me and Uncle Steven followed behind. All day, he'd been in the centre of things, and as I stepped around outstretched legs to retrieve plates for Gran, I wondered if I'd always be the one out of place.

"Put the empty plates down there, John-Paul," Gran said, when I made it back to the kitchen. "I've a fresh lot here so you can head out with them. Does anyone want tea, do you think?"

"No, Gran, I don't think so."

"But did you ask? You run in there and ask if anyone wants a cup and bring in the fresh sandwiches. I'll make a few more just in case."

Gran looked at home with Mam's apron stretched over her middle, smoothing butter easily over the soft white bread. A smile played on her thin lips and I wondered if she was enjoying herself.

"I'll bring those out in a minute, I think I heard someone at the door," I said.

Outside it was better. In the garden there was fresh air and room to breathe. I wandered down the driveway and stood next to Dad's van. Along the passenger door a key or a knife had sliced its way through the red paint exposing the metal underneath. The scratch looked new and I rubbed my finger along it. Who had done it? Who would fix it now?

"Hi."

The voice behind me was uncertain and I spun around to see Mark O'Toole standing on the opposite path. He was still in his school uniform. He didn't smile and I couldn't read his expression. For the first time since the day in the tunnel, I looked at him properly. His glasses were new ones, not as bad as before. He was still fat, roly-poly, like Dessie said, but he was a bit taller too. He might even have been a little bit taller than me.

"Hi."

"I was sorry to hear about your dad," he mumbled, looking at the concrete.

I had learned what to say when people said that. You were meant to say thank you, like it was a compliment. Be polite. I didn't feel like being polite. I shrugged.

"He seemed really nice, your dad. He always beeped his horn at me and waved to say hello. I really am sorry."

I snorted and shook my head, a trick I had learned from Dessie. "Why are you sorry? Did you kill him or something?" I laughed. As soon as the words were out I wanted to take them back. Something crossed Mark's face.

"See you around, John-Paul." He turned and started to walk up his driveway.

"Mark, look, I'm sorry. I didn't mean that." I said the words to his back but he stopped anyway. "It was a stupid thing to say. I didn't mean it. Thanks."

"OK."

I'd crossed the road so I was standing outside his gate now but I didn't care who saw. I could see the porch window, the faded "No Smoking Zone" sign. The jumbled-up coats that looked like the same ones from years before even though they couldn't be.

"What was the funeral like?" Mark asked, leaning against the wall.

I wanted to tell him, to try and explain it, but all I could think of was a mix of things that didn't match. The splintery feel of the coffin under my fingers. Mr Hegarty from Dad's work hiding his burning cigarette in the cup of his hand as we passed. The line of people dressed in black and grey, like shadows against the white blossom of the trees behind.

"It was OK," I said.

"Are there loads of people over at your house?" he asked, gesturing at the cars clogging the road.

"Yeah, there's barely room to move."

"Do you not have to stay?"

"I'm supposed to but I felt like going out."

"It must be shit having so many people around and none of them being your dad."

"Yeah." I nodded. "Yeah, that's exactly it."

And that was it. In a second, Mark had expressed what I

couldn't even see. Every other time before this, Dad would be there, making sure I was doing what I should be doing, that I was part of it. I realised then that the funeral was just the start. From then on I was going to have to figure everything out for myself. Not just tonight, but forever.

The thought was too big and I felt the tears that had been cemented deep inside since Friday start to dislodge. I gulped some air, taking a step away from Mark onto the road. Right then, I knew I could let go: I could fall into the depth of the grief that was coming. But not now. Not yet. I rubbed my nose along my shirtsleeve and turned back to where Mark was standing, cleaning his glasses. Without them his eyes looked tiny.

"You can come in, if you want. Listen to some music or something."

I wondered what music he was into now, if he still bought records or if he preferred tapes for the replacement Walkman I was sure his dad would've got for him. "I don't know, I probably should be getting back." I glanced back at my own house. I waited for him to convince me.

"OK, then."

He finished polishing his glasses and put them on gently before turning his back on me and heading up the driveway. Next door's stripy cat jumped from the bonnet of the car where it had been watching us and weaved in between his feet. Across the road I could hear voices and laughter floating from my open sitting-room window and into the garden. Somewhere inside music was starting to play.

"Hey, Mark," I called after him.

He stopped but didn't look around.

"I probably could come in. If you want. No one will miss me for a few minutes."

SEVENTEEN

The picture on the TV faded into black so it was just a sound. When I jerked my eyes open it became a picture again. I tried to focus but my eyelids were heavier than the rest of my body. It would have been easy to give in, to join Abbey and tumble into sleep together on the couch. Snapping myself awake, I focused on the video clock, blinking the numbers into clarity. Eleven forty. Much too late for Abbey not to be in bed. I pushed myself up, keeping my movements smooth, holding the curve of her body still, so as not to wake her. When I put her down in the cot my chest felt cold where her warm weight had been.

Katie should have been back by now. Before she was pregnant, a night out for her and Alison could run and run, but not these days. I checked my phone again. Nothing. It was strange that she hadn't been on to check how Abbey was. The last Tube would be soon and she'd probably be on it. She always insisted on getting it, no matter how many times I told her to take a taxi. I pictured Bow Road Station, dark and empty at this hour, and in the picture I could see Dessie there too, waiting, stepping out of the shadow, his footsteps in trainers quiet behind her high heels clip-clopping on the concrete. I started a text to her, choosing words that were casual and not too anxious, but instead of sending it I hit the cancel key. Friday was still two days away: Dessie wouldn't ruin his chance of getting the money by trying anything before then. Katie was out having fun, that was all. Everything was fine.

I made a cup of tea. Stretched out on the couch I flicked through the channels. The midweek movie was coming to an end. *A Fish Called Wanda* — it was years since I'd seen it and I nudged the volume up and then down again. The last thing I wanted was to wake up Abbey. I tried to hold on to the plot but it wasn't enough to keep my mind away from Dessie.

Four days had become two and I still had no way to find the money he wanted. And even if I could, would I? What had he done to deserve it? And he'd only come back for more. I should tell Katie, I knew I should tell Katie, but where could I even start? Like handkerchiefs from a magician's sleeve, one question pulled another, each quicker than the last until they all blended into one with no sign of any answers.

The bang of the door jolted me out of sleep. My head was leaning on the arm of the couch and pain bit my neck as I tried to sit up. It took me a second to work out where I was. In front of me, Katie was leaning against the wall, her leg bent behind her as she fiddled with the strap of her sandal. Underneath her makeup her cheeks were flushed red and I registered the smell of drink as she wobbled over on her ankle.

"Youfuckinlyingbastard!"

Her words slid into each other making one big long word. She was crying. Something had happened.

I rolled myself upright off the couch, rubbing my eyes. "Jesus, Katie, what's wrong? What's happened?"

"Bastard! You're a fucking lying bastard, JP!"

She tried to laugh but it came out like a sob. Hearing what she said snatched the last fug of sleep away. She knew. She knew about Dessie — but how could she know? Before I could formulate a question, more words were coming, spat out at me through lips stained with red wine.

"I knew it, I fucking knew it. You weren't with Paul that night. You were with someone else."

"What night? What are you talking about? What's going on?"

I reached out to touch her but she jerked her arm away. I was catching up but I was buying time as well. I'd never seen her mouth twisted and sharp like it was now, never known her eyes could hold such anger.

"Don't fucking lie! Stop lying to me, JP. Gemma told me. Who were you with? Who is she?"

Slowly, the slurred words formed a picture in my brain. Gemma, Paul's girlfriend, had blown a hole in my mugging story. It was nothing to do with Dessie — he hadn't hurt her. She thought I was seeing someone else, some other woman. It was laughable, except it wasn't.

"Katie, there's no one. No other woman, I swear," I said, moving towards her again.

The rest of my sentence was swallowed up in her words, words that broke into a screech as her hands became two white fists, beating the air between us. "Get away from me! Don't touch me! Don't touch me!"

Turning towards the wall she had her back to me and I skirted around her so I could see her face, make her understand. "I love you, Katie, you know that. You know I'd never look at anyone else. You just need to calm down. You've had too much to drink, you're upset ..." I kept my voice low, deliberate and soothing, like the way she calmed Abbey when she wouldn't stop crying. I tried to look into her eyes, let her see the honesty in mine, but hers were shut tight and she shook her head over and over, little sharp motions that flicked my words away.

"Katie, listen to me. You have to believe me, I love you ..." She was saying something but I couldn't make it out. She slowed down, her energy seeming to ebb away. Her head drooped forward and I lifted it up so I could hear her. "What, Katie?"

"The flowers."

"What?" I could barely make out the words but at least she was responding. I pushed her hair back from her face and she stared up into mine, a mess of mascara and tears and snot.

"Who were the flowers for, then?"

For a split second she waited, before wrestling herself out of my grasp, pushing past me in a blur of anger. One sandal was abandoned on the ground, the other still on her foot as she ran lopsided up the stairs, a hard clatter on every second step. As it dawned on me what she was talking about, something clenched around my heart and I couldn't breathe.

"Oh, Jesus, Katie, come back. Listen to me, hang on. The

flowers were for you!" Turning to follow her, I ran into the cup of cold tea. It poured onto my bare skin and seeped into the carpet. "Fuck!"

By the time I got upstairs she had the wheelie-bag down from the top of the wardrobe. The tags were still on from when we'd gone to Portugal. I had to make her listen, make her understand, but as I watched her pull clothes from the rail and throw them at the open bag I felt myself freeze. The scene was unfolding around me but somehow I wasn't part of it, I was only an onlooker and nothing I could do would change it. What I'd been afraid of for so long was just like I'd imagined it would be, played out like every overplayed soap-opera scene. Except this one was real.

I had to get through to her. "Katie, I'm not having an affair. I swear on my life. You're right that I haven't been honest with you but it's not what you think — I swear it's not."

I said the words to her back but they didn't slow her down. Things were moving too fast, and I could feel her sliding out of my grasp. I remembered our first Saturday spent together in Greenwich and already our relationship was becoming a memory. The hot blast of air on our cold cheeks as we pushed our way inside the gaudy Mexican restaurant on the corner. How she ate her fajitas so politely with a knife and fork. Out of nowhere, I remembered Christmas before she came, waking up as late as I could, running through the quietness of Hampstead Heath, empty except for a mother pushing a little girl on a creaking swing.

"I was with my brother the night I got mugged. I mean,

I didn't get mugged, he beat me up. That's why I didn't want to tell the police."

My chest thumped through the words, making an echo in my voice. She was down on her knees, dragging jeans from a Top Shop bag at the bottom of the wardrobe. She'd only bought them on Sunday — her reward to herself for losing some of the baby weight. I'd stood outside the changing room, jiggling Abbey in my arms, while she tried them on. How had we gone from that to this?

"Katie, are you even listening to me?"

The words came out as a shout and she turned to me, flicking her hair back from her face. When she spoke her voice was singsong, as if it was all some crazy game. "Lies, lies, lies, JP, I'm not listening to any more lies."

"Katie, you have to believe me!"

"I don't have to do anything, JP, nothing at all."

"Katie, I'm not fuckin' lying!"

My fist found the wall before I knew I was going to punch it. The plasterboard caved open, cracking into the hollowness underneath. "Fuck it!"

The pain in my knuckles was sharper than I'd expected and I shook my hand to try and let it go. When I opened my eyes Katie was pushing herself backwards across the wooden floor away from me, her skirt riding high above her knees. The noise she was making was a whimper, a sound I'd never heard make before.

"Katie, listen. Calm down, you have to listen to me."

"Oh, God. Oh, God. Why does this happen — why does this keep happening to me?"

Her words were lost in more tears and below us I could hear Abbey start to join in. There was no way to get through to her, to penetrate this mess of drink and fear. And then I knew what I had to do: how I could prove it. The photo. When she saw the photo she'd believe me. I'd almost thrown it away, had been about to put it in the shredder at work, but something had made me keep it. I yanked the drawer open, my hands rifling feverishly for the evidence I'd hidden with such care only two days before. Socks and boxer shorts spilled onto the floor until I felt the shiny paper underneath my clawing fingers.

"There! See? Katie, if you need proof, there's proof for you."

I brandished the photo, throwing it at her, but she let it slide onto the floor next to her sandalled foot. I half fell, half knelt as I picked it up again and waved it too close to her face, forcing her to look at what was in my shaking hand.

"Look! There he is. There's Dessie, my brother. A happy fuckin' family holiday snap. That's it — there's no mystery woman, no affair. That's all there is."

In the gap of silence I heard the thumping on the wall from next door and realised I'd been shouting. In the mirrored wardrobe I saw myself then, a red face and a bumpy vein near my hairline as I bellowed at the woman I loved, cowering on the floor in front of me. That was what anger looked like. I'd seen it often enough to know but somehow seeing it in myself was so much worse. Leaning back against the chest of drawers I let silence seep between us, became conscious of the TV still on downstairs, the film replaced by

237

the high-pitched hum of car racing, the sound of Abbey's cries that mingled with Katie's.

The handles from the drawers dug into my spine but I couldn't move. Holding my head in my hands I could feel it coming. I thought about the day outside Mark's house when I'd fought it back, the pain or the sadness or whatever it was, and I was sick of fighting it, fighting everything. I didn't have the energy any more. Inside me, something was breaking and it had to come out — it had nowhere else to go.

It was the sound that came first and I tried to lose it in the crook of my arm but it kept coming. My body was taking over, deep fast inhalations, breath rasping out again. Now the tears had found their way out they wouldn't stop, just kept coming and coming, drenching my cheeks, my chin, my neck. I wanted to say something but there was no room for words in the purge of breathy sound. I pulled my knees in tighter to my chest and clenched my eyes closed, but the tears and the noise still came, shuddering out of me and spilling into the room.

I don't know how long it went on for. Twice I thought it was over but when I looked up at Katie and tried to talk it started again. When I was finally finished my breathing was choppy and my bum was numb from the floor. Katie was sitting next to me now, the photo in the lap of her skirt. Her shoulder was inches from mine but we weren't touching. It didn't matter: she was there.

"I'm sorry," I said. "I'm so sorry."

She didn't look up from the photo, her eyes scouring the image, her fingers flattening the crease where it had been folded in my pocket. A loud hiccup burst out of her, breaking the silence in the room, but neither of us laughed.

"I should have told you before, I know I should. I don't know, I just couldn't. I was so afraid of what you'd say, what you'd think."

She was looking at me, crying too, but I couldn't tell what she was thinking yet.

"I was ten in that picture. He was thirteen. It was taken four years before my dad died and before Dessie got sent to prison. He … he killed my best friend."

The words were out, little boy's words, John-Paul's words not mine, but at last it was said. Katie looked from the photo to me, the dark rings of mascara like tyres around her eyes. I waited for her to see the courier from Reception, to make the connection, but the colour snapshot was slightly out of focus and it was hard to see the trace of the man he would become. I waited for her to say something, anything. I wanted to ask her if she believed me, if she still loved me. A coldness had replaced the charge of emotion in the air that didn't feel quite right.

"Katie, please don't leave me. Please, don't."

I was begging but I didn't care. I put my arm behind her shoulders pulling her towards me. I could barely hear her reply, which was muffled against my chest.

"I don't want to leave you, JP."

"Then don't!" My smile broke out but it was too soon: it wasn't over yet. When she pulled back out of my grasp I could see that.

"I can't … I can't keep doing this. I just want it to stop …"

"Katie, I won't lie to you ever again, I swear. Let me tell you about Dessie and Mark. I want to tell you what happened. I want to tell you everything."

"Stop, JP, just stop. Please. My head is spinning. I need a moment ..." She was shaking her head, talking as much to herself as to me. Tears that I thought were all gone kept rolling, rivers of makeup that dripped off the end of her chin and onto her top. Her bottom lip was pushed out, turning down at the edges. When I first started to fancy her, before I knew anything about her, it was her smile I noticed first. As bright and real as the sun, it was the kind of smile that made everyone else smile too. It was ages since I'd seen it. Now she was a crying mess and it was all because of me. Just like everything else I touched, I'd ruined her too. I could tell her the truth or lie to her, it didn't matter, because in the end she'd leave me anyway. Just like everyone else.

From her handbag beside the bed her mobile phone rang. We both looked at it for a minute before she reached across and answered it.

"Hi. Sorry. Yeah, I'm fine."

She looked away from me, combing her fingers through her hair, hiding behind it so I couldn't see her face.

"What? OK, yeah. I know."

I could hear the voice at the other end, asking questions, organising. Alison. Katie stood up and walked over to the bed. Sitting on the edge she fiddled with her sandal strap, yanking it back until it snapped. The shoe fell and hit the floor with a bang. Downstairs, Abbey started to cry again. Peeling myself up from the floor I hung onto the shaky banister as I went to comfort her. My body felt weak, as if I'd exercised beyond the limits of my energy, an elastic band stretched too far. The noise from the TV warbled into the empty room and I snapped it into silence.

Abbey's Babygro twisted around her and I tried to fix it as I picked her up, her cries getting louder before they eventually softened. My hand made a circle on her back as I comforted her, treasuring the weight of her in my arms, the sound of her breathing, her smell. When I turned Katie was in the doorway, her hair tied back in a ponytail. She'd put on my grey hoody and it was miles too big for her, making her look like a little girl.

"Is she OK?"

"Yeah, she's fine," I said. "I might get her a little bit of milk to send her off."

"Are you OK?"

"I think so. Are you?"

She nodded, folding her arms across herself. "Yeah."

I waited for her to say something else but she didn't.

"Do you want to talk about it some more? Will I make us tea?" I said.

She shook her head, shivering slightly despite the warmth of the hoody. "I'm knackered, JP. Let's just go to bed."

★★★

The feeling was there when I woke up but I didn't remember why at first. It wasn't until I reached my hand across the bed and found only the empty sheet that it came back. When I sat up I saw that the wardrobe doors were open and most of the clothes were gone. The ones from the floor had been tidied away, along with the case.

"Katie?"

My feet slid on the rug beside the bed, and I took the steps downstairs two at a time. When I saw her sitting at the kitchen table the relief hit me like a wave until I realised she was already dressed. And that she was writing something.

"Katie, what's going on?"

When she looked up she was biting her lip but she didn't answer me. Her face was pale, more tired than I'd ever seen it.

"Katie, it's six a.m. What are you doing?"

I saw the wheelie-bag then, through the door into the hall, but I didn't need to see it to know. Standing just in my boxers I felt suddenly exposed — like if this was going to happen at least I needed to be dressed.

"I've barely slept," she said. "I've been awake all night."

"You were going to leave me a note?"

She pushed the paper in front of her across the table, two lines of her loopy writing, another one crossed out. I picked it up.

"'Dear JP,'" I read, "'I'm taking Abbey to Mum and Dad's for a while. I'm really sorry. I need some time to think. Things between us have been ...' Have been what, Katie?"

"I just need some time out. I don't know what's going on," Katie said, shaking her head. "I don't know what's changed. You say it's not Abbey but something has."

"Of course it's not Abbey — I love Abbey!"

"I know that." Katie smiled a smile full of sadness. "And

that's what makes this all so hard. You've been behaving so strangely and I've been walking on eggshells ..."

"Katie ..."

"And then all these lies. This stuff about your brother. I can't make sense of it. It's starting to feel like I don't know you any more. I don't know what else to do."

"You know me better than anyone, Katie. We just need to talk about it, so you can understand ..."

She shook her head again, curling her hair behind both ears. When she spoke her words were practised, but she still couldn't look at me. "No, not yet. I need some time on my own. Being here, around you ... it's scary, like I'm not in control. And I need to be in control, for myself and for Abbey."

"So, what are you saying? How much time?"

"I don't know."

I sat down on the chair opposite her, at the table where we'd shared so many meals. So many plans. And now we were sharing this, our words so detached we might as well have been talking about grocery shopping.

"OK," I said, nodding. "I understand."

Her hand stretched halfway across the table but stopped before it reached mine. I wanted to touch her fingers but I couldn't. Instead I stood up and walked into Abbey's room where she was dressed too, her little legs in stripy tights kicking under the denim dress Rebecca had bought for her. When I picked her up her head pushed into the hollow under my chin, her body resting against my chest. It was a perfect fit. In the doorway Katie was looking at us. I searched through every part of me to find something to say, something that would change things, something that would make them stay.

"Katie, please …"

The words hung in the air between us, begging and desperate. In the overly lit hall I could see each wrinkle, each shadow on Katie's face. She seemed so sad standing there, her pain so exposed, pain that I had put there and couldn't take back.

"JP." Tears broke through when she said my name and she wiped them away quickly. I felt then that she didn't want to leave either, that something else was forcing this to happen, something that was nothing to do with either of us.

"Are you driving or getting the train?" I said.

"We're getting the early train. Alison's giving us a lift to the station before work."

I understood suddenly that the plan had been arranged last night and that made it worse somehow, except it couldn't be any worse. "Do you want me to help you get the car seat out?"

She pulled her handbag up over her shoulder. "Thanks, no, it's fine. Alison can do that." Her hands reached out for Abbey, plucked her gently from my arms.

"Wait a second." Groping on the hook behind Abbey's bedroom door, I found her jacket and passed it to Katie, helped her push her little arms through the sleeves. When we'd got it on, I leaned over so my lips grazed the softness of Abbey's head and she turned back towards me.

"We'll see you soon," Katie said, opening the door, pushing the wheelie-bag through first.

"I love you," I whispered, to no one and to everyone.

As I held the door open behind them and I was left alone in the hall, I thought, not for the first time, how lonely those words could sound.

Eighteen

We never fought, Mark and I, even the first time we'd been
friends. There was never any reason to: we agreed on stuff,
we laughed at each other's jokes. The thing about Mark was
that he knew things without me having to tell him. I didn't
have to say when it was one of the really bad days, when I
missed Dad so much I was raging at him for leaving me
behind. I never told Mark what it was like to sit alone with
Mam in the evenings, while Dessie was out God knew where,
but somehow he seemed to know. And just when I couldn't
bear another night of it, Mark would tell me what they were
having for dinner, and his mam would set a place for me at
the table when we came in. I stayed there so often, the spare
room was known as my room and I liked that. It made it
easier to pretend that I lived there, with the O'Tooles, rather
than in the house with the dark windows across the road.

The fight that day, on the way home from school, was
Ray Healy's fault. Stupid Ray Healy with his gappy front
teeth in his too-wide mouth. He was the one who started it,
nicking Mark's trousers after PE and then his Walkman as
well. Making the whole class laugh as he swiped them close
to Mark's hands but not close enough, so he clapped in the
air like a performing seal.

"You shouldn't have fuckin' paid him," I said.

We were already at the lane when I said it and my voice bounced back at me off the walls, making an echo. It was the first thing I'd said the whole way home. Mark didn't say anything at first. I knew he was looking at me, could see the slight movement of his head, but I kept my eyes on the ridges of concrete under my runners. In my head I could hear Ray Healy's stupid whoopy laugh as he took Mark's shiny pound coin with one hand, pulling his stuff just out of reach with the other.

"Or at least you could've fuckin' waited until he gave you your stuff back, and then paid him." I kicked the weed tufting out from the corner of the wall and the ground for emphasis. My runner scraped the brick, making a white scuff mark. Mark still didn't say anything. I turned around to see him lagging behind, his face red, as if he was angry or upset. His mouth was half open, his breath heavy, like an overweight spastic.

"You do realise that every time you give him money, give any of them money, it just gives them more reason to do it again," I said. "You're such a fuckin' retard, Mark." No wonder they call you the Tool. Those were the words in my mouth and I nearly said them — they were nearly out there — before something stopped me. I think it was the look on his face, as if he'd heard them anyway, as if he could see what I was thinking.

"What's your problem, John-Paul?" He pushed his glasses back up his nose as he said it, so the words were half muffled behind his hand.

We were almost at the top of the lane and I could hear voices from outside McCarthy's shop. I shook my head, turning my back on him again. He didn't get it. Didn't get that his weakness reflected on me as well as him. That he made it hard not to see that clapping seal in his jocks every time I looked at him for ages after. I couldn't tell him that but I thought he knew. He had to know.

"I mean, I don't know what it has to do with you, anyway. It's my money. What I do with it is up to me," he said. "It's none of your business, John-Paul."

The last words were like a question, going up too high to have the punch they were meant to. I could see who it was now outside the shop, one of the Kelly twins and Dessie's friend Damo Mulvaney. I wasn't going to fight with Mark here. Not in front of them.

"Look, forget it," I said. "It doesn't matter now. But maybe next time try standing up for yourself. They might not take you for such a fuckin' eejit."

That was his way out. I hadn't said sorry but it was as close as I'd get and he knew it. I didn't think he'd say what he said next.

"Maybe if you stood up for me the odd time, John-Paul, that might help."

He'd been thinking that, I knew he had, but it was different him thinking it and the words said out loud, rolling between us at the top of the lane with Damo Mulvaney there to hear. The words found their target in the surge of guilt but I quickly pulled on the anger that would wash it away. "Jesus, Mark, that's the whole fuckin' point. You don't get it, do you? I'd have no problem sorting out Ray Healy but you have to stand up for yourself. It'd mean nothing if I stepped in for you."

Ray Healy was thick but he was bigger than me. I wouldn't fancy getting on the wrong side of him, but the way I spat the sentence out, you couldn't tell. I almost believed it myself. Glancing up, I saw Damo Mulvaney was sitting on the wall now, on his own, maybe waiting for Dessie. I didn't know if he'd heard me. He threw a crinkled crisps bag at the bin but it missed.

"Hiya, Damo."

"All right, Whelan."

Mark and I walked past in silence, our conversation suspended until we were nearly at my house. I knew it was teetering on the edge of something dangerous, somewhere that I didn't want it to go, and I thought we'd managed to avoid it. I was wrong.

"You think you're such a hard man, John-Paul, but you're not," he said finally, his face redder than ever. "The only reason no one goes near you is because of Dessie. That's how you get away with lickin' up to fellas like Mulvaney ..."

"I wasn't fuckin' lickin' up to anyone."

"You wouldn't take on Ray Healy and you know it. And if Dessie wasn't your brother you'd be picked on as well, just like me."

Behind his glasses his eyes held mine and, for a split second, we both knew it was true even though I couldn't let it be. Who did he think he was, saying all that? A response formed in my mouth before I'd thought it through in my head. "Let's get something straight. I'm nothing like you. Nothing. You're a fat fuckin' sad cunt and I'm only friends with you because I feel sorry for you." My voice was sneery and not like me but I couldn't stop the waterfall of words. "And if you're too fuckin' cowardly to stand up for yourself, don't expect me to do it for you."

I let the anger take over my voice and my body too, jabbing my finger in his face the way Dad's used to when he was making a point. I felt like someone else and not me and I almost enjoyed my role, like a character in a film. If I didn't recognise myself then I don't think Mark did either, his face a blur of confusion and almost tears. Turning, he hoisted his bag higher on his shoulder and crossed the road. I stood at the gate watching his funny walk as he hurried down his driveway, not looking back. Before I heard the glass door slam I was already sorry for what I'd said, wanting to take it back but not knowing how. Once the anger was out the guilt invaded, worse than before, and I wanted to rub the words out with a giant eraser or spin the world backwards, like Superman, so we could be back down the lane when things were OK.

A few minutes passed while I stood there wondering what to do but eventually I did nothing. I thought I'd find a way to make it better, make it up to him. I knew it'd be hard but the thing was I thought I'd have time to figure it out. I had no idea what was going to happen. I didn't know then that those words were the last I'd ever say to him.

★★★

Mam was in bed that morning, her door closed. Dessie was up, his mood worse than usual, almost a match for mine. I thought his fist might come through the flimsy bathroom door as he roared at me to hurry the fuck up. When I went downstairs his cereal bowl was on the table, half-full, and he'd only left only a dribble of milk in the carton for me. Next to it was the newsletter we still got from Dad's work. It was open on a middle page and even upside-down I saw the photo of Dad straight away. Turning it around I read the caption that said this month was his anniversary, a whole year since he'd died. He had three lines of cramped black type, talking about his long contribution to the company, his loyalty, his hard work and how he was missed by his colleagues. In the photo he looked younger, serious, and I couldn't take my eyes off it. I was still looking at it when I heard Dessie leaving, slamming the front door so hard it sounded like the glass might break.

I had double art that morning so I didn't have to see Mark first thing. The bell rang for little break and I didn't know what I was going to say but I was going to find him. I was first to the door but the corridor outside was clogged with bodies and noise, shouts and laughter in the distance with snatches of silence. The sound of a fight.

Holding my books tight against my chest I shouldered through the crowd. Voices floated over me and beside me.

"Who is it?"

"Psycho Whelan."

"He's lost the plot. The fuckin' eejit's going to end up expelled!"

I stepped on someone's foot, pushing on, ignoring the curse that followed. An elbow squeezed into my ribcage. Near the top of the corridor everyone was packed tighter and the noise was louder, but mostly it was drowned out by the sound of my heart.

I could see him through the last few near the front, before the crowd stopped suddenly leaving a semi-circle of space around Dessie standing at the top of the stairs. He had his back to me and I could tell by the way his shoulders knotted together that he had someone tight in his grip. And I knew that it was going to be Mark.

"So, what do you have to say about these rumours, then, you fat cunt?"

Dessie was talking too loudly to be talking only to Mark. He wanted us all to hear he'd always loved an audience. Mark tried to speak but Dessie's fist had his collar squeezed too tight so creases of grey shirt bunched together under his double chin. Mark's cheeks bulged redder and his glasses dislodged from behind one ear. The way Dessie held him he was dangling over the top step.

"What's that? Speak up there. Everyone wants to hear what the Tool has to say."

A fizz of laughter sputtered from around me. Dessie was enjoying himself. He pulled Mark closer to him so their faces almost touched.

"Nothing to say? Then it must be true, then, mustn't it? About your old lad liking little boys?"

Dessie turned around to us, raising an eyebrow as he said it. Mark twisted in his grip, opening his mouth to speak but no words came out, only a grunt. This time there were fewer laughs with Dessie and they sounded uneasy. The crowd pushed closer, wanting more.

"I always thought it was a bit strange to see your oul fella waiting for you outside the school in that ugly car of his. Window-shopping, was he? So he could get excited before giving you one on the way home?"

I didn't see his face as he spat the words out, but Mark's was almost purple, anger fusing with shame. Dessie was lying, I knew he was lying — probably everyone knew he was lying — but that wasn't the point. He'd always hated Mark's dad, and even though I liked him, some part of me hated him too. The way he was always polishing his poncy car so everyone would know it was the best on the road. The way he gave Mark too much of everything — his time, his money, his love. What Dessie was saying now were words that sprang from some twisted duct of jealousy. I knew that because it was the same twisted duct that sometimes lived inside me and I hated us both for it. I opened my mouth to stop him, to shout out that he was making it all up, but no sound came and I realised it didn't really matter what I said. Everyone had heard and nothing I could say would change it now.

Somewhere at the back the whisper started travelling through the crowd, like a flame.

"Whelan, watch it ..."

"Here comes Mulcahy ..."

It would have ended then. It should have ended then: Dessie wouldn't have risked getting expelled, not over Mark.

Distracted, he turned away, letting go of Mark for just long enough that he didn't see him pull back, get a swing in his kick, enough momentum to carry his foot high. Mark didn't need to do it, he could hear Ms Mulcahy coming just like we could so he knew he was safe: he could have escaped down the stairs, or grabbed the banister at the side. But what Dessie had said about his dad couldn't be unsaid and he needed to take him on in front of everyone. He needed to prove he wasn't just a fat fuckin' sad cunt. To Dessie, to himself and to me.

His kick was a good one. It caught Dessie hard, connecting with the top of his bony thigh. Mark gasped, a split-second smile in his face that melted into fear when he found he couldn't pull his leg back, that Dessie had trapped his ankle with both hands so he was balanced on one foot, at the top of the stairs.

In my mind the next bit is in slow motion. Dessie with his back to me, Mark's arms outstretched, flapping for balance, both of them framed by the white railings on either side, Mulcahy's voice calling out from the back of the crowd, coming closer. The slippery numbness in my limbs as I stood there, watching and waiting and doing nothing. It might have been ten seconds that Dessie held him there, suspended in time, or it might have been less. However long it lasted, it was long enough for Mark's eyes to find mine, long enough for us both to realise what was going to happen, right before it did.

It was easy for Dessie in the end. In my memory, it's a smooth, swift movement, a simple push that jolted Mark backwards, dislodging his one grounded foot on the rubber groove of the top step. His hands waved out to grab onto Dessie, to grab onto the plastic handrail, but found only empty air. I had just enough time to see the panic flood his face before he turned the top half of his body the right way around, plunging away from me, into nothing.

There must have been noise as he fell. People must have cried out, called his name. There must have been movement but all I remember is stillness. Stillness and silence except for the lonely crunch of Mark's body bouncing and sliding down the steps and out of sight.

The final thump as he landed on the hard tiled floor unlocked us. We pushed over to the railings, a swarm of shock and curiosity and fear. I was there first, the crowd behind squashing me into the cold iron of the bars. In the square of tile below, Mark lay like the hands of a broken clock. His left leg stuck out, buckled and bent at the knee like a backwards L. His right arm was missing and for a mad moment I remember thinking it had been severed until I realised it was pinned under the weight of his body. His head was turned on its side, and I could see his eye was closed above the puff of his cheek. His glasses lay a few feet from him, the lenses shattered. The force of the fall had dislodged one of his shoes, and it sat on the second last step, empty and out of place.

I became conscious of the sounds around me, the shouts from the crowd, Mulcahy's voice louder than them all. There were hands on my shoulders, turning me away, I tried to spin back, to call out to Mark, but the hands were too strong and

The Other Boy

I was in a line leading back to the classroom along with the others. What happened next is a whirlpool of images swirling into each other, one as difficult to grasp as the last. But there are pictures that pierce through the blur, crystal shards of memory that still cut. The double beep of a Casio watch punctuating the jumble of voices saying an Our Father. The flicker of blue ambulance lights reflecting back at us from grimy classroom windows around the yard. The circle of view in the fogged-up glass where I wiped my sleeve so I could see Mark, rolled out on a stretcher, squares of green plastic on either side of his head, a white mask covering his mouth and most of his face.

These are the things that I remember. These are the things I can't forget.

★★★

That night I slept in the room we called the spare room but really it was Dad's room. I couldn't be near Dessie: to be in the same room, it was as if he sucked all the oxygen away. The spare room still smelled of Dad, and in the dark I breathed deeply and tried to make myself believe that he was still there and everything that was happening was a bad dream.

When the call came from the hospital I was ready, not sleeping. I already knew. I wondered if the time someone dies is the time that their heart stops beating or the time you find out that they're dead. I remember being calm, thinking that, listening to Mam's voice in the hall. It wasn't until I saw Dessie come down the stairs, his face creased with sleep, that the rage started to beat inside me. I'd been angry before but I'd never felt anything like this, a feeling that filled my whole body with steel and made me lunge at Dessie so I trapped him in the corner of the hall thrashing out with fists and kicks, not caring what might happen. This was a feeling with no room for words, just grunts and breaths and proper punches, and it was what I wanted, to hurt him and to be hurt too. The icy water Mam threw over us shocked the feeling, stalling it into a slippery resistance that let her pull me off him. It paused it for just long enough, and afterwards it had faded a notch, but it never really went away.

Mam told me not to go to his funeral, warning me what it would be like, but I went anyway. I'd survived Dad's, I could get through anything. Mark's mam and dad knew me: they wouldn't blame me along with Dessie, they couldn't. But they did. When I went up to them they looked straight ahead, as if they hadn't seen me.

"You've no right," Mark's dad said, his voice thick, "you've no right to be here."

My heart and my head thumped but I walked past him anyway, down the aisle, finding a place to sit near the back ignoring the stares and murmurs. My knees slipped on the leather kneeler and I buried my head in the clammy warmth of my hands. I felt a tap on my shoulder and when I looked up it was one of Mark's uncles asking me to leave and not make a scene. Standing up, my cheeks were burning and even though I wanted to run I made myself walk slowly to the side door, the whispers clinging to my clothes as I went.

At school it was worse. People who had made his life a misery talked endlessly about him and I was the one with no right to grieve. Walking into a classroom the silence would snap, like someone turning out a light, so I could feel the half-finished sentences in the air. At lunch and break I was always on my own, like Mark used to be, and I spent my time hiding in the smallest bike shed near the primary school, reading the same books over and over. But even that was still better than being at home.

To be fair to Mam, she was making an effort, getting up again to clean the house and cook dinners I didn't want and couldn't taste. Dessie was never there and his dinners were left on the counter covered with clingfilm that beaded with foody sweat. She tried to talk to me about Mark and about Dessie and the "accident" while I worked through the food, but I didn't talk back. Instead I left the table barely saying thanks, heading straight out and picking my bike up from where I'd left it by the gate. Every night I headed off on breathless cycles along the bumpy gravel of the West Pier or down the steep, snaking track at the back of Killiney hill. The cycles were too fast on routes I'd never done before. Cycles that made the wheels rattle and the air pump hard in my chest until my head hurt and I was rasping for breath.

"You think it's my fault, John-Paul, don't you?" she said to my back one night, as I rinsed my plate in the sink. Turning towards her, I saw the tears that glazed her eyes as she fumbled in her sleeve for a hanky. I didn't know how to answer her.

Gran loaned Mam money to get a good brief because

Dessie was going to need it. I was dragged with them, the first time, to his office, a crumbling Georgian terrace on Mount Street, but I wouldn't answer his questions and Mam didn't make me come again. When they went to see him the house was mine, and I'd take Dad's records from their spot on the shelf, handling them with care the way he used to, blowing dust from the grooves on the black vinyl.

The *White Album*, *Abbey Road*, *Rubber Soul*. I'd play them all, letting the music spill around me sliding from one track to the next. The songs brought Mark back with them and Dad too. They brought back arguments over John Lennon and Mick Jagger. They brought back Christmases full of relations and party pieces and tins of Cadbury's Roses. Sometimes the needle skipped where there was a scratch but I never minded: it sounded as if it was meant to be there, a hidden part of the music meant only for me.

As the trial came closer Mam kept on trying to talk to me about it but I didn't want to know. I didn't care that Dessie was old enough to be tried as an adult or how the solicitor was worried about his previous offences. The O'Tooles' house had been locked up since the funeral and Mam didn't think they'd be there, but I knew different. I knew that, despite the fan of long grass in the front garden and the pyramid of letters that piled up behind the glass porch, they'd want to see their son getting justice at last.

"For the last time, will you not come with us, John-Paul?" Mam said that morning, as I lay in bed, waiting for them to leave. "I know you're still upset but we should present a united front. The solicitor says it's important."

259

I turned over, my back to her, examining the wallpaper and the way it squashed under my nail.

"And I know it would mean a lot to Dessie."

I'd managed not to speak to him for three whole months and it was easy because he didn't want to speak to me either. I waited for her to bring in the big guns, to start on the guilt trip about Dad, that it was what he would have wanted. But she and I both knew Dad would never have wanted this.

"Well, I can't force you, you're too old for that, but I just hope you don't regret it. We don't know what'll happen today. When you'll next see your brother."

That was when I knew that she didn't have a clue, that she didn't know me at all. She assumed that, despite everything, I wanted Dessie to walk. To get off so we could all live happily ever after and forget what had happened. She had no idea how much I wanted him to be sent away, to be punished once and for all for what he had done. To Mark, to Dad, to me. When I heard the front door close I sat up in bed, flicking the curtain up to watch the two of them head down the driveway towards the waiting taxi. Mam was hanging behind, checking her bag for her keys, while Dessie strode on ahead, the suit he'd worn to Dad's funeral already pulling tight across his shoulders.

I distinctly remember hoping that I'd never see him again.

NINETEEN

The day before the interview was not going the way I'd planned. My mind was disconnected from the rest of me, my reactions a beat behind, like some badly dubbed movie. I'd forgotten a conference call, sent confidential files to the wrong client. It wasn't until the meeting with Peter and Richard that I'd managed to plug myself in for long enough to defend my recommendations over next year's strategy. The debate became heated, almost a row, and for a few short wonderful minutes it had filled me and replaced everything else. But when the meeting ended and I saw Alison on the phone outside Peter's office it suddenly came back, and the weight of remembering that Katie and Abbey were gone was worse than knowing it all along.

When I got home from work I half hoped they'd be there, even though I knew they wouldn't. I told myself that over and over, hoping to trick my mind into a surprise instead. When I opened the door the stillness told me there was no surprise, no Katie, only silent memories of her. Her half-written note was folded over on the table, caught in a rectangle of late evening sun. The unfinished words still pierced and I tried to read the line that was scribbled over. After a minute I bundled it up into a ball before flattening the page out again. I felt I should keep it, just in case. In case of what, I didn't know.

I dialled her number, then hit cancel. My fingers hovered over the keys to send a text. What the hell was I doing? Katie had left me and I was going to send her a text message? In frustration I threw the phone hard, bouncing it off the couch so it disappeared underneath. I paced the room but ran out of space. My hands clenched but I didn't have the energy to punch anything and I knew it would hurt too much. Leaning against the wall I let myself sink down onto the carpet, pulling my knees to my chest. I thought I might cry again but the tears were stubborn this time. Looking up, I saw my phone in the couch's shadow next to one of Abbey's soothers that had gone missing. I scrambled on my knees to fish it out, its rubber teat sticky with fluff. Sitting with it in one hand I reached for the phone again and dialled Katie's number with the other. Abbey was my baby too; I was her father. I had a right to know how she was.

It rang twice, three times, four, before I heard Katie's cautious "Hello." The sound of her voice, her breathing, was like coming home. The tears decided it was a good time to come but I held them back with words, talking fast, asking questions about Abbey and their journey to Cheshire. At first her answers were one word, a yes or a no, but then despite herself she started to talk. It was a lifeline and I latched on, pouring out more questions, answering hers, shaping my day in the office into a self-deprecating anecdote designed to make her laugh.

To anyone listening we were like any couple discussing any day, and it amazed me how easy it was to slip into the well-worn groove of structured conversation, to make things feel normal when they were anything but.

Eventually I broke the spell. "When are you coming home?"

A beat of silence passed. It wasn't a good sign.

"JP, I just got here."

I waited for her to say more, forced myself to stay silent and listen to her breathing.

"I need some time."

"How much time?"

"I don't know, JP, I told you this morning. I need to sort my head out …"

"But you are coming back? We need to talk this through, sort it out."

This time the silence was hers. She went to speak but it was too late: I was there first. "Katie, I'm telling you the truth. You know that there's no one else. You believe me, don't you?"

When she answered me her words were trapped in a sigh. "I don't seem to know what to believe any more, JP."

★★★

My breath came hard in my chest. Short, rhythmic gulps of air. Beneath my step a rock was loose and I stumbled, a burst of pain biting my ankle. I kept running, the soreness fading to a dull throb and eventually to nothing as I ran on, leaving it behind me.

It was ages since I'd done this and I realised how much I'd missed it. I needed to do something to empty my head and focus on the interview tomorrow and I remembered how running used to calm me. It was something about my breath and the repetition of the movement that brought my body and brain into the same moment, and as I ran I wondered how I had ever forgotten how good that felt.

Beside me, the canal flashed by, the sunlight giving it a golden sheen that hid the old shopping trolleys and empty cans that lurked so close to its surface. On the opposite bank a group of young boys jeered at each other in the dark shade of the archway made by the bridge above. Their voices, echoey and hollow, filled my ears and faded as I sped past.

Before we'd met, I'd always run around the park. never come down here. It was Katie who first showed me this route. Katie, whose summer holidays had been spent on a barge in Norfolk so she was able to explain the complex system of locks and how the canal connected with other canals, stretching as far as Essex and beyond into the North Sea.

A couple were walking slowly towards me, smiling and swinging hands between them. She chattered away, her voice light and high in the summer air, and he nodded and smiled, watching her. That was how we must have looked back then, holding hands or arm in arm, stopping now and then to kiss. Maybe other people had watched us and felt a stab of envy too. I hadn't noticed, too wrapped up in Katie, in us, to think of anyone else. What if she never came back and we never had a chance to do that again? What if we'd already walked this walk together for the last time, only I hadn't known it was the last time so I hadn't enjoyed it properly?

A feeling rippled through my body, a pain that had nothing do with exercise. Ever since the tears had overflowed last night they had threatened to come again, a burning sensation where my nose met my eyes. The couple moved in closer to let me pass. I couldn't look at their tenderness, focusing instead on the bouncing path ahead.

My calf muscles were aching already, even though I was only just over halfway through. Beneath my feet the path was getting steeper; I was out of practice but I wasn't going to give up. The trick was not to let myself think about slowing down, not to give myself the option. I'd learned that the easiest thing when I felt the pain was to speed up and run through it, to show it that it wouldn't stop me. I ignored the burning in my legs and concentrated on the canal speeding by me on one side, the backs of houses on the other. Past the Old Ship where people were having beers out in the sunshine, up the granite steps and into the lane and there I was, back on the home stretch of the Mile End Road.

I couldn't blame her for not believing me. When she'd asked why I'd not told her about Dessie before, I couldn't explain it. I took too long to make the story into a shape that she would understand but she didn't give me enough time, cutting across to ask me again about the flowers and why I'd pretended I was with Paul. The pain in my legs was hard to ignore now but I was almost home. Through the breath and the sweat her words replayed in my mind.

"How do you expect me to believe you when you've told me so many lies, JP?"

The tiredness and the hangover had made her voice hoarse so it could barely cover the tears. Logic outweighed truth and I had no answer that would make it right so I had let the dead air hang on the line between us until I realised she had hung up. It was only a little thing, hanging up on me, compared with everything else, but somehow it was bigger than everything else too.

The pavement sloped downhill now and my legs caught a new boost of energy, freewheeling to a pace all their own. With the speed, a decision came too, a single thread of clear thought that penetrated the rest. I had to see her. To talk to her and explain everything. Face to face, I could make her understand. I'd tell her all about Dessie and about Mark, the proper story she wouldn't let me tell her last night. That wasn't enough, though: I'd have to tell her about Mam too. About the drinking, about the times she didn't come home. About how I'd let Dad down. Let them all down. Everything. Even thinking about it made the guilt sting. It was years since I'd spoken about Mam to anyone, more than a decade. I couldn't imagine how I would explain it all to Katie, but I couldn't let her go like this. Whatever it took I had to try.

My thoughts came faster and faster and my strides did too, each shop front a square of colour as I sailed past. When I'd told Katie the truth, told her everything, Dessie couldn't blackmail me any more. Whatever Katie said, whether she forgave me or not, he'd have no more power over me. No more control. Thinking about it now, I could almost feel pity for Dessie, coming after me to wreck what I had because he had nothing. He'd never experienced what I had with Katie and he probably never would. He might end up back inside, might never know what it was like to hold his baby in his arms. This was a chance for me to be the bigger person, to help him. Maybe I'd give him some cash to help him get set up. A couple of hundred, or a grand, even. He didn't deserve it, but he was my brother, and once I'd done that he couldn't expect anything more.

Past the garage, under the metallic rattle of the train crossing the bridge overhead, I could see the apartment complex in the distance. Making the decision left my head free, and I imagined the extra space it would give me in my mind not having to hide everything from Katie any more. It was the right thing to do, what Dad would have done. I held onto the thought and let the relief trickle in. Maybe, despite everything, he would have been proud of me after all. The wind in my face felt like freedom.

I couldn't wait to see Katie now, and Abbey too. I wouldn't stop to call her, I'd just jump in the shower and then take the car. I'd drive right through without stopping. I'd be there by eleven and that would give me five hours before I'd have to drive back. Face to face I'd be able to make her listen, make her see that there was no one else. I'd tell her everything, even if it took all night. I'd make her understand, talk to her, really talk to her, like I'd always been afraid to before. Doing the interview on no sleep was hardly ideal but I'd do a better job knowing that things between us were OK, that they were coming home. We loved each other, we had a baby together. That was what mattered, not the past, mine or hers. She knew that, she'd see that. She had to.

Seduced by my imagination, I pushed myself uphill, through the ache of the last stretch. As I reached the gates my legs slowed awkwardly, my feet slapping the pavement. Gasping, I held my hands on my knees. Sweat trickled its way from my forehead down the side of my face and made little dots of wet on the concrete below. Gulps of air filled my hungry lungs making me giddy.

The older porter buzzed the door to let me in. He was on the phone, his grey head bent over the sign-in book, checking some detail. He looked up and I raised my hand in greeting. He waved back, putting his hand over the mouth-piece and beckoned me over.

"Mr Whelan," he said through the gap in the sliding glass window, "you've got a visitor waiting for you. He arrived not long after you left for your run. I wouldn't normally let someone wait inside, but he said he was your brother."

I followed his finger where he was pointing across the courtyard. A man in a red football shirt was sitting on the bench facing away from me towards the pond. He had one arm resting on the back of the seat, his tattoo sneaking out from the sleeve. It was a second before I realised that the porter was looking at me with concern in his face, waiting for me to tell him he'd done the right thing. "Of course, that's great. Thanks," I said.

There was relief in his smile as he resumed his call. He'd broken one of the rules but Dessie was my brother; if you couldn't trust someone's brother then who could you trust? My eyes were locked on Dessie's back as I counted my breaths, waiting for my heart to slow down. He was too far away to have heard me but he turned slowly, as if he sensed me there, sliding his hand over his forehead to shade his eyes.

I'd made my decision and now it was time to make it happen. The elation of a few minutes before had evaporated, leaving behind a stone in my chest. He was here, this was it, there was no more time for excuses. Straightening my shoulders I strode across the gravel to where he was waiting.

TWENTY

Even the day I was making my promise to Dad in the hospital some part of me knew I would break it. And every year that passed after he died I seemed to break it a little bit more, chipping away at the intention of it, so not even that was left.

After Dessie was sent away, Mam's drinking got worse. I found a bottle in the press under the stairs next to the Hoover and then another behind the couch, only barely open, as if she'd forgotten it was there. The bottles I found I poured down the sink, enjoying the brief moment of power as the contents gurgled down the plughole. I remember the sweetness of the smell invading the kitchen, hoping that she'd walk in and see me, say something to me and ask me where they'd gone but she never did.

When I got home from school she was nearly always in bed. The first time I thought she was out, seduced by the silent cold house into believing I had it all to myself. As I changed from my uniform I blasted my Nirvana tape so it filled my room. I sang as I changed, drumming my fingers on the imaginary guitar. I rewound it to the start and played it over, turning the volume up to the max.

"Jesus, John-Paul!"

A bang came along with the words and my heart leaped

in my chest. I snapped the music off and in the silence I wondered if I could have imagined it. "Mam?"

I knocked on her bedroom door but she didn't answer. When I pushed it open the air in the room was heavy, a taste within a smell, and I wondered when she'd last opened the window. In the bed Mam was a diagonal hump.

"Mam? Are you OK?"

She tried to answer me but her words were lost sounds, muffled in the pillow and the blankets. The alarm clock on the locker read five. Through the staleness I smelled the sharp tang of urine. I took a step backwards. "Mam? What do you want me to do? Should I call Dr Roche?"

At first she didn't do anything and I didn't think she'd heard me until her arm freed itself and waved in my general direction, flopping at an unnatural angle and back down onto the bed. Her words were half lost in the pillow but I could make out the last bit.

"Get out and leave me alone."

After that we fell into a routine, Mam and I, of leaving each other alone. I stayed behind in school every night to study or fill out application forms for colleges in England that were cheaper than the ones at home. You were supposed to leave the building as soon as class was over but it was easy to hang back, lingering over my locker, dawdling in the jacks until everyone was gone home or out on the playing field. I'd double back to the silent classroom and let maths or history or biology take over the space in my head until the shouting on the playing fields outside grew quiet and it was time to go.

It was months before Mulcahy caught me. I realised I'd been sussed that afternoon when I heard her high-heeled clip-clop slow down outside the door — she'd seen the line of light underneath. I remember holding my breath as she opened it, my brain stretching tight to think of excuses and a good reason why I was there.

"John-Paul, what are you doing here so late?"

She always called me Whelan, never John-Paul, and I thought I heard concern mixing with the suspicion in her voice. As she walked towards me, her arms hugging a bundle of copybooks to her chest, I delved for an excuse, something that would make her turn around and walk back out again.

"I just thought I'd get some study in, Ms Mulcahy. Get a head start before I go home."

"What's wrong with studying at home like everyone else? You know you're not meant to be here after school hours. If something was to happen to you we're not covered by insurance."

"What could happen to me, Ms Mulcahy? I'm sitting here studying. That's all."

Behind her glasses her eyes were scrunched up small. I felt the heat in my face as if she could see right into my head. I looked back down at my notes.

"How are things at home, John-Paul? Is everything all right?"

Her voice was so low I barely heard her. She shifted the books in her arms and leaned on the heel of one shoe.

"Yes, Ms Mulcahy. Everything's fine, thanks."

My heart beat hard in my chest. She knew — but how

could she? Maybe someone told her, someone from the road. Maybe she'd seen Mam or tried to phone the house. Maybe she could smell my shirt — I should have washed it the night before and I resolved to do it as soon as I got home. She shifted the weight of her books again and I could tell she wanted to go. She didn't want to have this conversation either.

"Everything's fine. Honest. It's just that it's easier to concentrate here. And all the teachers have been saying that it's good to start early on the Leaving Cert stuff, not to leave it until the last minute."

She paused, making up her mind. She was ready to say something else — I could see the question forming before she pushed it away. "OK. I shouldn't really be making exceptions for anyone but at the same time it's good to see a student taking the Leaving seriously. But just make sure you don't say a word to anyone …"

"I won't, Ms Mulcahy."

"And if I hear that there's been one ounce of trouble, or if you get yourself locked in the building …" She made her voice stern but I knew she was pretending, that she had to do that so I'd know how lucky I was but that she was going to let me stay.

"You won't. I won't be any trouble, I promise. Thanks, Ms Mulcahy."

That was the only time we ever had a conversation, just the two of us. She was nice to me and I wasn't sure why. Now I can see that she knew, of course she did, but then I thought I was doing a good job, covering it up even to myself.

The Other Boy

In the evenings if Mam was at home, she'd usually be in her room, quiet except for when I could hear her crying. Sometimes in the morning she'd surprise me and be up before I was, making breakfast or cleaning the house with a frantic, frenzied energy that must have been stored up from the days in bed. On those days she was a blur of movement, washing floors, opening windows, hoovering and dusting as if her life depended on it. Her energy might last until I got home from school and there might be a dinner ready or even a press full of food. Once there were three days in a row like that. On the fourth she wasn't there when I came home. I remember that night being in bed when I heard her hand banging the glass of the hall door downstairs because her key couldn't find the lock.

I learned to cook. It was easy. I made fish fingers and beans and waffles. Or little frozen pizzas that I ate too fast and burned the roof of my mouth. Sometimes when the press was full I sneaked tins of beans and spaghetti hoops up to my room and hid them behind the old dusty runners under Dessie's bed, just in case.

Weekends were harder, with no school to eat away the hours during the day. The library was open on Saturday mornings, and I started my days there. In the narrow wooden aisles I lost myself in the pages, in the smell of dust and polish, and the silence that felt more like home than home did. When the heavy bell rang it was time to leave and rescue my bike from where it was locked at the bottom of the steps outside. Cycling out towards Bray and beyond, into Wicklow, the books rattled on my back like company as I challenged myself each week to find a new road I hadn't taken before, one that would take me deep into the country. I loved those winding, narrow roads that curved and twisted under my wheels and the trees that reached across to link their branchy fingers over my head. I loved not knowing where I'd end up, testing myself to see if I could make it home again.

I got a job as a lounge boy in a pub in Dún Laoghaire. I collected glasses and brought drinks to red-faced customers for five pounds a night and the odd bit of loose change. I wore my school shirt and a pair of Dessie's old black jeans that were too long. I could have asked Mam to turn them up but I didn't want her to know where I was going, covering up the white shirt with my denim jacket as I cycled off each night. I spent hardly any of the money, keeping it instead in a brown envelope in the bottom of the wardrobe. For what, I wasn't sure.

Sundays were the worst. We couldn't avoid each other on Sundays. Every week, no matter what, Mam insisted we went to visit Dessie, the two of us sitting shoulder to shoulder on the shuddering number seven into town, where we had to wait for the ten to take us to Mountjoy. Mam never missed a Sunday. One Saturday night I found her conked out on the step when I came home from my shift in the pub. I couldn't wake her, could hardly drag her from the cold concrete and into the hall. I had to leave her there, lying on the floor, spittle forming a pool against the tiles, stepping over her to go up the stairs to bed. I was sure we wouldn't go the next day but there she was, like clockwork, at two o'clock, pulling on her winter coat from the cloakroom, calling to see if I was ready to go. It was too big now, its navy wool shoulders slipping off hers, swinging from her narrow frame as we walked towards the bus stop, but she wore it whatever the weather.

I don't remember much about the visits. In my memory they've slid into one big long visit. Early on Dessie shaved his head and it made him look older somehow and harder, but not as hard as some of them. He never said much. All he seemed to care about was whether Mam had remembered to bring him cigarettes and he lit one after another, flicking specks of ash into a shallow tinfoil ashtray as Mam talked on and on. He didn't seem to listen to her endless stream of words any more than I did, his eyes flitting around the room, watching everything while I watched him. As Mam filled the silence I remember wondering which version was really her, the talking one for Dessie, or the silent one for me, and how it was that one person could be two people at the same time.

The Sunday before it happened I saw Fionnula Brady on the bus. Everyone fancied Fionnula and I did too. The way her long blonde fringe fell into her eyes and her tight school jumper clung to her breasts. Even though I fancied her, part of me hated her too because she knew we all did and she loved it. I saw her through the window, before we got on, but I didn't catch eyes with her. She was with another girl I didn't recognise, and as we passed them I heard their giggles squirt out and I knew it was about us. I looked at Mam and I saw what they saw. It was April by then, too hot for the ridiculous coat. With her hair stretched halfway down her back she looked like some crazy homeless woman. She walked past them, taking a seat two rows behind. I was tempted to go upstairs, to pretend I didn't know her, and I nearly did but I knew that it would make everything a hundred times worse. Sitting next to her, seeing the back of Fionnula Brady's shoulders shake with laughter, that was when I decided. The next Sunday I told her.

"I'm not going."

I was sitting in front of the TV as I said it, my hand on the remote control. I braced myself for her reply but she was in the hall: she hadn't heard me.

"Come on, John-Paul, hurry up or we'll miss the bus."

She was back in the sitting-room now, moving around quickly. The colour was high in her cheeks as she closed the top button of the coat, her smile flashing back at herself from the mirror. Watching her, I couldn't blend this person with the one who lay in her room, who wouldn't talk and wouldn't eat. One version of her for Dessie and one for me. Which did she see when she looked at her reflection?

"I'm not getting the stupid bus. I'm not going."

For once I'd got her attention. I snapped off the TV and stood up, ready to leave. She followed me across the sitting room, getting to the doorway first, blocking my way as if she thought she'd a right to tell me what to do.

"You're coming with me to see your brother."

"No, I'm not. I'm not going." The more I said it, the more I decided I should have done this ages ago, instead of being bullied by her. "I'm sick of it. Every Sunday, like a pilgrimage, to sit with him in that kip. I've had it. That's it. I'm not fuckin' going any more."

I cursed on purpose, pushing the word out right in her face. I realised suddenly my need for a fight. The thoughts from the silent Saturdays flickered into feelings and I felt the anger throb inside me. I wanted to see her anger too — I wanted to feel it, to have her shout at me, to hit me. I wanted an excuse to let my rage build and explode all over both of us.

"Ah, come on now, stop messing, John-Paul. We always see Dessie on Sundays. He looks forward to it, he needs us …" Her voice was trembling, weak. She was nearly begging me.

"He needs us!" I mimicked. "For Christ's sake. He put himself in there! What about me? What about what I need?" My fingertips were hanging on to my temper but it was slippy and I knew I was going to let go before I did. "The only time you bother to speak to me is when he's there. The only fuckin' time you leave the house is when you go on that bus to see him. Apart from going to the off-licence, that is."

Her slap was quick and hard, a snapping pain that cut across my words and stung my cheek. My hand was a fist and before I could think about it I was swinging it wide and fast, all my anger and frustration bound up in the tight clench of fingers. Something caught my eye, the rush of movement in the mirror, and I tried to stop myself but it was too late. I remember the feel of her jaw as I hit her, how it gave way too easily and her head flicked back and to the side as if it would spin off her body. I remember her skin, dry under my knuckles, skin that felt too thin, barely protecting the fragile bone underneath. I remember her eyes were closed and how, apart from her head, her body hardly moved at all. It wasn't until my arm dropped to my side and my fingers unclenched that her eyes opened again.

"Mam, Jesus, I'm sorry. I'm so sorry, Mam. I didn't mean it."

My voice broke the silence between us. It was already starting to get red where I'd struck her and I reached out to touch it but she stepped back, away from me. She brought her hand to her chin and when she took it away I could see her mouth was almost a smile.

"Mam, I'm really sorry, I didn't mean it. I don't know what happened."

There were tears in my voice but not in hers. Her face was too still, the twitching movement gone. When her words came they were calm too.

"I don't know why I'm surprised, John-Paul. After all, you're your father's son."

★★★

The day she went was a Wednesday, full of sunlight and cherry blossom. My mind was taken up with my Leaving Cert only three short weeks away, and it was late that night I realised I hadn't heard or seen her all day. Pushing her door open, I saw her bed was a tangle of stained sheets.

I didn't wait up for her — it didn't even cross my mind — but I remember not being able to sleep for ages, lying in bed with the house's noisy silence all around me, waiting to hear her come home but I never did. In the morning, her bedroom door was still open onto the landing and she wasn't there. Pausing in the doorway, I surveyed the room, wondering what to do next. On the dressing-table the photo of her and Dad lay amid the half-empty cups and dusty jewellery and I put it back in its proper place, under the rim of the mirror.

I was sure she'd be there when I got back from school. I made myself later than usual, cycling the long way, down around the seafront and back up the hill, buying time, just to make sure. I called her when I came in but all I heard was the sound of my own voice, lonely and afraid. Taking the steps two at a time, I checked her room but nothing had changed. Leaning against the wall I let myself slide onto the floor, resting my hands on my knees.

She wasn't back on Friday either, and I messed up a load of orders that night, not concentrating properly on the names of drinks so they slipped from my head as soon as they'd been said. I had to pretend to Eamonn the barman that some of the customers had changed their minds but I knew he didn't believe me. Despite my mess-ups it was the best night for tips I ever worked, with Mr Fogarty from down the road tipping me a fiver at the end of the night, placing the note slowly on the tray with a flourish to make sure everyone saw.

It was midnight when I came home and the curtains still hung open onto dark rooms so everyone on the road could see our emptiness. I called out to her before I turned on the light but she didn't answer. Even though I knew she wouldn't be there I went up to check her bedroom and Dad's old one too. I swallowed my panic, methodically looking in the bathroom, the sitting-room, the kitchen and the garage, as if it was some crazy game of hide and seek. The shed keys weren't in the drawer where they were meant to be and it took me ages to find them. I knew before I opened the rusty, sticking padlock that it was impossible that she had locked herself in but I had to try anyway. The bulb inside had long gone and it was eerie in the spidery darkness with Dad's jars of screws and nails glinting in the half-light, like some relic of a prehistoric existence. My hands trembled as I pulled the door shut tightly, sliding the bolt across and locking it again. In the kitchen I turned on all the lights and gulped back a glass of water. She'd never stayed out all night before, and this would be the third. I had no idea what to do next.

In my imagination I'd been inside the police station loads of times. When Dessie had been caught I'd pictured it in my head, good cop and bad cop, the action and the excitement. In real life it was different from what I'd expected, more like a dentist's waiting room than anything from TV. A bobbled glass shutter was closed but I could hear voices behind it and see the navy blue of their uniforms. When I rang the bell it sounded too loud and it was a few seconds before a hand opened it up and the face appeared of a guard not much older than me.

"Yeah?" he said, leaning down to see me through the hatch.

When I tried to speak my mouth filled with saliva instead of words and I saw the flicker of impatience in his face. When I finally spoke I sounded like a scared little boy and not like me at all. "It's my mam. She's gone missing, I can't find her."

The guard's name was Kevin and he made me some tea with sugar in it, sitting me down in a grey room where he wrote out the whole story. When he asked why I hadn't rung Uncle Mike I didn't have an answer for him, couldn't explain why that had been so hard since what had happened with Dad. It must have been only ten minutes between Kevin making the phone call and Uncle Mike arriving down, his pyjama top sticking out from the bottom of his jumper. I was so glad to see him, to see him look the same, that I nearly cried but I stood up to shake his hand and the moment passed.

It's funny how your mind can work. Despite everything hanging over us, those next two days felt like a holiday. The lie-in on Saturday morning, waking up to the smell of sausages frying downstairs. Playing Nintendo with Chris. Helping Uncle Mike in the hairdresser's, sweeping up the fuzz of hair and counting the money from the till at the end of the day to make sure it balanced. Every now and then when we were on our own, he started to ask about Mam, what it was like at home now, apologising for not being in touch. I could tell he felt bad but I didn't want to talk about all that and ruin everything. Being with him wasn't quite as good as being with Dad, but it was the closest I was going to get.

When the call came it was Sunday night, during *Glenroe*. Auntie Paula turned the TV down and we heard Uncle Mike's voice, a low mumble in the hall. He seemed to be on forever and I watched the ads with the sound down, trying to guess what the next one would be. When he came back in he looked at Auntie Paula first before he turned to me, his hand kneading the back of his neck like Dad's used to do.

He told me on the way to the hospital. Someone had been found in the harbour, near the wall of the pier. Two young men out sailing had seen the body from the boat. It probably wasn't Mam, they just had to make sure. It wasn't going to be Mam, there was no way, and even if it was her, it was an accident. It must have been an accident.

They didn't want me to see her. I waited on a hard chair in a bright corridor. Dad was dead. Now Mam was too. I knew before they told me, before Uncle Mike had to give the final verdict. The knowledge floated above me. I could see it but it wasn't part of me, not yet. Poor Uncle Mike was the messenger not once but twice.

I had no one now. The thought washed into my mind and out again. No one to try and keep and no one to lose. I pictured the pier — stone and sunshine and small children on bikes. Families and couples strolling past skinny tracksuited boys with dangling fishing lines. I closed my eyes and I could see beyond them into the white, glistening water where the boats jostled side by side. Mark had told me their names, shown me the difference between the squibs and the lasers and the yachts, explained how the sound I thought was bells ringing was really the halyard hitting against the mast. We both loved that sound, the noise of all the boats' halyards clanging together in the harbour, and I could hear it now, along with the call of the gulls, disappearing into the wind.

The image didn't fit. This couldn't be the place that Mam had jumped or drowned or fallen but it was. Uncle Mike came out of the room and his face told me so before his words did, his hand cupped over his open mouth, the other supporting him against the doorjamb. He started to walk towards me but I didn't see him any more: instead I was seeing the picture in my head, this time with the bulk of the car ferry behind the other boats slowly slipping out of the harbour, taking people to Holyhead and London and beyond. And even as he looped his arms around my shoulders I was trying to figure out how many weeks it would be before I could be a passenger on that ferry again, and leave him and all this behind.

Twenty-one

The clothes horse was a jumble of drying work shirts with gaps where Abbey's Babygros had been. Katie's note lay on the table and I nudged one of the supplements from the weekend's papers over it. Dessie seemed oblivious to the chaos, heading straight to the couch. Sitting down, he crossed his legs so one foot rested on the other denim knee, moving the cushion to find Abbey's pink teddy bear underneath. He lifted her with a tinkle of the bell inside, turning her once in his fingers before dropping her onto the floor.

I didn't sit down. I wanted to stand. To show him I was in control, not panicked like before. Looking down at him, sitting there with his thinning hair and rounded shoulders, he was suddenly only an older version of me.

"Your note said I had till tomorrow," I said. "What are you doing here? You can't just show up here, Dessie."

"They're not here, so what's the problem?"

"You didn't know that?"

The statement became a question but he didn't answer it, picking instead at a loose thread in his trainer. He had known. He was still watching us. Through the glaze of sweat I shivered.

"They're coming back in a couple of days. Katie's just taken Abbey up to see her folks."

I wished I hadn't sounded so defensive. I needed him to know I was relaxed, that he couldn't bother me any more. My aching legs reminded me I hadn't stretched and I pulled my knee up into my chest, holding it there and twisted my ankle around. The familiarity of the motion, the strength in my body felt good, and I repeated the stretch with my other leg.

He pushed his hands down on his knees and stood slowly until he was almost level with me. Before I could say anything he broke our held gaze and turned his back to me, looking instead at the collection of Beatles album covers on the wall.

"Look at all this shite — it's like a fuckin' shrine."

His bait dangled but I wasn't going to take it. Not this time.

"Dessie, I told Katie," I said. "Last night, I told her everything. It just came out."

He didn't turn around but I could tell by the way he held his head that he had heard, that he was weighing up his answer. I was about to speak when he turned to face me. "So, what did you tell her?"

Taking a deep breath I exhaled the words. "Everything. She knows about you. About Mark and—"

He cut across me, rolling his eyes at the mention of Mark. "Did you tell her about Mam?"

"About Mam?"

I was buying time. I wasn't ready to answer him. Leaning against the wall, scratching his stubble, the way he said it was too casual. Too offhand.

"Yeah, Mam. Remember Mam?" He pushed himself away from the wall, walking towards me, his slow pace in time with his words. "The woman who gave birth to you. The one you never gave a shite about."

He was getting too close. My heart bounced against my ribs, its speed at odds with his slow, deliberate movement.

"Of course I cared about her, Dessie, that's a load of bollox …"

"No, that's a load of bollox!" His sudden roar made me jump. "She was dying and you were stealing from her. Is that what you'd call caring about her? Well, is it?"

His voice was too loud, filling the narrow band of space between us. I felt his spit as it landed in my face. I tried to turn away but there was nowhere to go. The need to piss was so bad I thought I might wet my shorts. For a second he stayed there and I steeled my body, pulling my strength in tight waiting for his fist to come, but the anger that had blown up so quickly seemed to fall out of him until he sank into the couch again, empty and deflated.

I eased myself into the chair opposite him. I needed to defend myself, to tell him how it really was. This was the confrontation I'd been afraid of since he'd come back — but, no, that wasn't true: I'd been afraid of it since long before then. There was so much to say, years of pent-up words, but now the time was here there seemed to be so little.

Before I could say anything he was talking again, softer this time, his fingernails whitening where he kneaded them into the wooden arm of the couch. The motion was in time with his words, only I couldn't seem to hear them properly any more. The more I looked at him, the veins on his hands, the square-cut nails of his fingers, the less I heard. It was as if I could look or I could listen, but not both.

I fought my brain to tune in, to focus. He was still on about Mam. About how I let her down. How I stole from her when I should have been helping her. He was making a list of things I should have done, things he would have done. That wasn't how it had been. He didn't know, he wasn't there. This was some patchwork version of the truth made up from Mam's Sunday visits, sewn together with his own thread of guilt. I should rip it apart, tell him what was what. But when I opened my mouth, there were no words to say.

Ahead of me, the gallery of album covers stood out from the stark white wall.

I loved them all, the story they told. The way the simple two-tone photographs of the early days gave way to rainbows and cartoons and psychedelic flowers. The fact they were in order of release date made the seesaw of colours imbalanced, black and white on one side, colour on the other with the *White Album* like a missing tooth in the middle. I laughed at Katie when she'd suggested rearranging them. Dad always said that it was only right that *Let It Be* was back to four simple pictures on a black backdrop. That, even though it wasn't really the last album, it closed the loop, and the cover was a coded message for proper fans like him. Fans they knew would get it. I used to nod, agreeing with him when he said that, but even though sometimes I thought I knew what he meant, I don't think I ever got it at all.

"John-Paul, are you even listening to me?" Dessie said.

I looked back at him and he was waiting for me to respond. *A Hard Day's Night.* 1964. A class cover, always made me smile. Soundtrack to the film with the same name. The first album to be entirely made up of self-composed and self-performed Beatles compositions. So it said inside the sleeve. Two of their biggest number ones on that album, 'A Hard Day's Night' and 'Can't Buy Me Love'. They weren't our favourite songs, though. No, me and Dad preferred 'I'm Happy Just To Dance With You'. I used Mark's tape recorder to make him a tape of it and he played it in the van all the time until the stereo broke. He said it didn't matter how bad the traffic was, 'Things We Said Today' would always put him in a good mood.

"Don't you have anything to say for yourself, John-Paul, for fuck's sake?"

Dessie's calmness was giving way to something else but it wasn't anger. His voice was higher, a tinny echo of its usual self, as if each word was a fishhook being ripped from his throat. I needed to say something. Anything.

"It wasn't my fault, Dessie," I said. "You can't blame me for what happened."

"Nothing's ever your fault, John-Paul, is it?"

I didn't like the way he was looking at me then, like he knew something I didn't. "You don't know what it was like. You weren't there."

"Course I know what she was like! For fuck's sake, wasn't I the one looking after her for years? I know she wasn't easy to deal with but, Jesus … she was our mother!"

"It was different, Dessie. She wasn't the same." I tried to gather my evidence, to line up why it wasn't the same as

289

before, but the images slid away, just out of reach. I knew it was to do with Dessie and Dad being gone, with the red graffiti that sprayed out the word "killer" on the white pebble-dashed wall outside, with the phone being cut off because she forgot to pay the bill, but somehow I couldn't make the pieces into a whole picture. Dessie was talking again, listing out more options I'd had and didn't take. The one-sided unfairness of the allegations stung, igniting anger from guilt.

"I was fourteen, Dessie, a kid! It wasn't all down to me. If you were so sure something was wrong why didn't you do anything?"

"I was in jail for fuck's sake! And you were seventeen when she died. I did what I could. I tried to help her." He was shouting at me again, the words loud and well rehearsed, too close to the surface not to be. "I called you from prison, remember? I tried to sort it out, but you were too wrapped up in yourself, just like always."

I did remember. Dessie's voice on the phone, silences and words said over each other. Twisting the phone cord in my hand so tight it almost pulled from the rectangle of plastic that held it into the wall. The detail was so vivid I could see the numbers on the dial, the dent in the wallpaper that Dad had made all those years before. How come I could picture that but not Mam's face?

"Dessie, Mam was different that time. Worse." I tried again to make him understand. "Maybe it was you being in prison, maybe it was grief over Dad."

"Grief? Are you fuckin' serious?" Dessie's laugh was loud

and long, almost sounding real. He slapped his hands on his knees. "Jesus Christ, what's scary is the fact that you actually believe that. I can see it in your face. What's wrong with you, John-Paul? Don't you remember what it was like? The fights. Them going at it hammer and tongs while we were lying rigid in bed upstairs, shitless the bastard would get us too?"

His pupils were bigger and darker than usual. Dilated, that's what that was called. I held them with my own. A catch in my chest and I realised I'd forgotten to breathe. The new air was a relief. I timed my breaths slowly, careful to round their jagged edges. In and out. In and out.

Abbey Road. 1969. The last of the originally recorded albums. My firm favourite of them all and second on Dad's list. Each song was part of my soundtrack. 'Octopus's Garden' was scrunching up small in my own warmth under the covers listening to the rain and the wind lash against the bedroom window. 'Maxwell's Silver Hammer' was Dad with his toolbox out, when he should have been hanging a picture or mending a shelf but instead he was pretending to hit me on the head with his real hammer instead.

Dessie was still talking. On and on. About some time when Dad had lost his temper and pinned his arm behind his back until he apologised. He bent his head forward so it rested in his hands, his fingers rubbing the spot where his hair was thinner. I was catching up with what he'd said earlier. It was too late to answer his question, but I did anyway. "They did fight. I know they did. They fought about you," I said. "Dad could never get why she stuck up for you, how you could wrap her around your finger."

"That prick didn't need a reason to fight," he said, his words muffled. "He was a nasty bastard, a bully ..."

"Not to me."

"That was because you spent your whole life pussy-footing around him! Doing anything to keep the peace. You were always scared shitless of setting him off."

When he looked up there was something wrong with his face and it took me a second to realise he was crying. He'd lost the plot now. I loved Dad. I adored Dad. He was jealous of our relationship. Even the apartment was like a shrine to him, Dessie had said so himself.

I wanted to stand up but my legs were too heavy to move. Through the open window I heard a girl laughing, a light, high laugh, a one-sided flow of words into a mobile phone.

"We should have done something, John-Paul. We should have saved her. What if she was waiting for us that night? What if she was waiting for us to come and find her and bring her home?"

He was in jail. If Mam was waiting for anyone, she was waiting for me. His voice had cracked again on the word "home". Mam used to cry at the first line of 'Golden Slumbers', the one about finding a way back home. 'Home', such a safe word, only four letters, and yet it seemed to twist barbed wire around all of our hearts.

I watched him cry.

I don't know how much time passed. There were more noises outside. The squeaking of birds. A motorbike. Voices loud and then fading. Inside, the sound of his crying was nearly silence except for sniffles and breath. I felt as if I couldn't move, not even to blink. That I was pinned to the chair, my legs spread across the rug in front of me. That this would be the position I would remain in for the rest of my days. My eyelids were weights and I let them slide closed. I didn't think I slept but I must have because when I opened them again, he was standing in front of me, the tears gone. Something had changed: the sadness was replaced with an edgy energy. With a flick of his lighter he lit a cigarette.

"So, how much did you take?" he said.

My mind was sluggish, like my body, a beat behind his. For a second I thought about denying it. I pushed myself straighter in my chair before I answered.

"I can't remember."

"How much, John-Paul?"

He slammed his hand against the wall. *Help* dislodged and fell face down onto the carpet.

"Not much. There was hardly anything to take. A few hundred or something."

Eight hundred and eighty-three pounds. And fifty-five pence.

"A few hundred? How long did it take you to stash that? You little bastard. She knew you were stealing from her, you prick. She told me."

I hadn't known that before now. The realisation made the weight of shame a little bit heavier, sinking lower inside me, resting below my ribs. He wouldn't understand how easy it had been. How finding a fiver in her purse had felt as if it should be mine. How five became twenty. How easy it was to forget what was mine and what was hers as the bulge of the brown envelope in the wardrobe became the fulcrum of my future, bigger than her, and than me too. There was no point in telling him because he wouldn't get it, or maybe he would. Maybe he'd get it all too easily.

"It would only have gone on drink anyway," I said.

He blew smoke at the ceiling, watching its straight grey line with detached interest. I stood up slowly, hoping he didn't see the shake in my legs.

"I can give you a grand," I said. "It's way more than I owe you but you're my brother and it's the right thing to do. It'll help you get back on your feet, give you some time to find a job. Or whatever."

I sounded like a bad actor, stilted and over-rehearsed.

"Fuck your poxy grand and your guilt money! Fifty grand is what I want, and I'm not leaving until I get it." He strode across the carpet, closing the small distance between us, his finger stabbing the air with every word. Stumbling backwards I found myself pinned against the table and my fingers wrapped around its edge to steady me.

"Dessie, there's no way, I can't—"

"Don't give me that bullshit — that Paki bitch has a big mouth. She told me, so I know how much you lads rake in."

It took me a second to register he was talking about Leena. "Dessie, for fuck's sake, don't call her that."

He put on a confused face, as if he didn't know what was wrong. "Why not? That's what she is. I've never had any Paki pussy before. I thought they're meant to be tight, those Indians, but I got that wrong. She'll let me have her however I want. I like taking them from behind. Listening to her

English accent, I can imagine I'm riding your Katie."

He let Katie's name drip slowly from his mouth, holding his hands out to hold her imaginary arse, thrusting slowly back and forth. Anger leaped inside me like a flame and before I knew it my hands were on his chest gripping his T-shirt into a bunch. "Take that back, you filthy bastard! If you ever say that about Katie again, or go near her, I swear I'll—"

"You'll what?"

Close up, I could see the tiny web of red veins threaded across the whites of his eyes, the yellow nicotine stains on the edges of his teeth. His lips folded into a smile and as he raised his eyebrow, I realised, too late, that I was being played. My grasp loosened. Laughing, he stepped back. Hands in pockets, he bounced on the balls of his feet, grinning, enjoying my discomfort. "Looks like maybe it's not just me and the old man with the temper, doesn't it, John-Paul?"

Swallowing, I took a deep breath, running my hands over my hair. I needed to be calm now, to listen to him and explain so that he understood. This had to be sorted out tonight.

"Leena's just the receptionist, Dessie. She's only been there since Christmas. She wouldn't have a clue what I earn." I sounded like I was explaining it to a child. "Would I be living in a rented flat in the East End if I'd cash like that? Don't you think I'd have some flash car parked outside? You've seen our car, a Peugeot, it's eight years old. And it's not even mine."

His smiles and laughter were gone now, and I saw a twitch of doubt dance across the certainty in his features. His eyes held on to mine and I felt as if he could see into my mind, as if he knew about the deposit I'd been saving up for mine and Katie's future, but he couldn't possibly know.

"OK, so you might not have it but you can get your hands on it," he said, nodding, convincing himself. "Access to all that cash, a whole bank of it. You steal once and it's easy to do it again, You know that as well as I do, John-Paul."

This was his trick. He wanted to pull me back into the past again but I wasn't going there any more. I needed to make him understand that there was no chance of getting that kind of money, not now, not ever.

"Dessie, I don't have it. I swear. But even if I did I wouldn't give it to you. I've told Katie everything so nothing you say can make any difference now."

Shaking his head, he turned towards the door. He stretched his arms up in the air and I heard a click from his shoulder. For a second I thought he was going, that I had won, until he walked back towards me again, his face as hard as his voice. "What if it's not just talking I want with Katie?"

The impact of his words didn't hit me straight away. My stomach seemed to understand before my brain did, dropping to become an echo chamber for the frantic rhythm of my heart. "You go near her and I'll call the police."

The words burst out of me and he shook his head slowly. "Now, that sounds like something Katie might say. The police! You and I both know that the pigs are about as much use as a rubber johnny in a convent. Will the police be able to monitor her every move? Will they be there when, say, she's a bit tipsy on her way home after a night with the girls?

It's very dark under that bridge, you know, anyone could wait there."

I wasn't going to look at him. To listen to him. Shaking my head, I pushed his words away, staring out across the courtyard to the windows on the other side.

"Or what about when you have to work late at those boozy banker dinners? Will they be there to reassure you when you come home and find the door unlocked?"

The pain in my chest was there again. Breathing. I just needed to breathe in and out. In and out. I closed my eyes. I didn't need to look at the covers to picture them.

The *White Album*. 1968. Officially called *The Beatles*. Double album released after their trip to India. For some fans it was a new beginning, for others it was the beginning of the end. Dad said it was the greatest musical achievement in his lifetime. He said the contrast made the album, but some of the critics saw the difference between 'Ob-La-Di Ob-La-Da' and 'Happiness Is A Warm Gun' as a tear between the band's old and new influences. Between Lennon and McCartney. Critics saw the inconsistencies as a flaw, that it was an album released by individual artists pretending still to be a band. They didn't realise, Dad said, that the brilliance was in the contrast, the extremes nestled side by side in grooves of vinyl.

"You're all talk, Dessie. I'm not a kid, you don't scare me."

He waited a beat too long to respond. When he did I could hear the smugness of the smile in the words that floated from behind me. "Was it talk that broke your nose then?"

My hand rose inadvertently to my face and I remembered the smash of his kicks, the frightening up-closeness of his trainer right before it plunged. Looking down, I saw he was wearing the same ones. Was my blood still lined in the rubber creases? He knew he could breathe life into the fears that floated under the surface of my mind. He knew how to make me doubt myself and question my decision, even question my memory. He didn't deserve a penny from me, one thousand pounds or fifty thousand. I just wanted him gone.

"Get out of my flat."

He turned around so I was talking to his back. Looking up and down, he seemed transfixed by the blur of colour from the album covers.

"I said, get out, Dessie. Get the fuck out!"

I walked into the hall and held the door open. The new air diluted the pressure chamber so I could breathe. I was about to say it again but he came away before I had to. He stopped opposite me, in the narrow doorway. He was close enough to smell my cold sweat. "You're missing one," he said. "You don't have the complete collection there."

Through the open sitting room door I followed his gaze to the record sleeves. We both heard the pause before I spoke. "What?"

"I knew there was something that bugged me. I always hated them but you couldn't help pick up stuff in that house by osmosis. They had twelve original albums, but you only have eleven up there. *Revolver's* missing."

"Dessie, just go."

My heart drummed faster.

"Supposed to be the turning point for them, wasn't it? Bit of an omission for the fan of the century?"

"Dessie, I said get out."

He wanted to say more but he stopped. I took a deep breath and held my voice steady, pushing each word out slowly. "I don't want you ever to come near me or my family again. Ever."

Before he could reply, I started to close the door, forcing him out along with it. Turning, he leaned in, so his face was sandwiched between the closing door and the frame. He pushed the words through the gap, and somehow the quiet way he said it made it worse than anything he'd shouted before.

"I want what we agreed, the fifty grand. It's not worth risking it all for, John-Paul."

I leaned against the door with all my weight. When it clicked closed, I let my head rest against the wood, enjoying its coolness. I listened to his footsteps fading along the hallway, slow at first, then faster. At the end of the corridor the outside door creaked open slowly before slamming shut.

I'd been holding my breath and I exhaled slowly. He was gone.

TWENTY-TWO

I winked. The guy in the mirror winked back. I smiled. His smile looked fake, like a smile in a photo that's been held for too long. Stretching in, to get a better look, I flattened down my hair to cover the expanse of forehead that was eating into the hairline above. Close up, I could see the rims of my eyelids were pinky red but that was the only tell-tale sign from the night before. My tie was too loose and I pushed the knot up against the hard collar of my new shirt. In the mirror I was a smartly dressed City guy heading to the office, straightening his tie. The smoothness of the movement and the expression on my face bore no resemblance to the jerky panic that bounced around inside.

I leaned back against the wall, the bathroom tiles cold through my shirt. Sliding down slowly, my arse found the hard floor and I rested my arms on the triangle of my legs. I was late. I couldn't be late, not today of all days. I should be going, I should be gone, but somehow I couldn't seem to make myself care. I sat there. I closed my eyes and then I opened them again. Grabbing a bath towel from the rail I folded it over and buried my head in its soggy softness. I didn't cry.

By the time Dessie had left it was too late to drive up to

Katie and I didn't call her either. I told myself it was because I didn't want her to hear the fear in my voice, the sharp edges I knew she'd pick up on. But really it was more than that: after Dessie had left, the earlier certainty I'd had went with him. Now I had no idea what to tell her. I only knew that whatever I had to say, whenever I had to say it, I wanted to be calm and in control, to use words that wouldn't frighten her. And frighten me.

I'd gone to bed thinking I'd lie awake, but the second I lay down I felt myself tumbling into a dark abyss of sleep, the pull so strong I thought I might never wake up. The dreams were vivid and everyone was in them. Dad, Dessie, Katie, Mam, even Leena. Something jerked me awake, and when I drifted off again, it was a self-conscious sleep, too uncomfortably close to waking to offer any rest. When I pulled myself out of it, the sheets were tangled around me, tightening with every move. The clock said it was three eighteen, too much of the night still to go to stay there. Making tea was comforting, the ritual and the warmth. Turning on the TV, I found a *Fawlty Towers* repeat and it seemed to suck me in so I was part of the crazy colour and sound, the thin membrane between what was real and what wasn't dissolving into nothing.

Sitting on the floor of the bathroom I took a breath, held on to the towel rail like a ladder as I pulled myself into a stand. Deep breaths. I just had to remember to breathe. I made it out of the apartment, up the road and onto the Tube, as if it was any morning. It was fuller than usual, the height of rush-hour, every millimetre of space jammed with

someone's body, someone's smell, someone's breath. The
tinny rasp of someone's soundtrack. Outside Tower Hill
Station it stopped, the lights flicking us briefly into darkness.
Unease spread through the crowd as the driver announced
the delay. Fuck it, anyway. I wanted to check my watch but
my arm was locked in a grip on the handrail overhead, as if
I'd become melded into the train itself, a hunk of metal,
unable to move. I tried to think about the interview, what
Peter might ask and what I should answer. Before I could
hold on to the thought it slipped away, replaced by a dislo-
cated TV image from the night before: John Cleese skulking
behind the Reception desk as his wife's voice cut through the
jangling canned laughter, calling out, "Basil, Basil," over and
over.

I got to the office. Some of the stragglers were still coming
in, chatting in twos and threes, carrying coffee in ridged cardboard cups. I weaved through them, mounting the steps two
at a time. Dessie's words about Leena were on a loop in my
head. He was angry. I'd made him doubt what she'd told him.
He'd tried not to let on but I could see it. What if he had
gone straight to her flat? What if his anger for me had found
her instead? I bounced into someone's elbow and they called
after me to watch where I was going. Pushing through the
revolving doors I was afraid to look at the Reception desk in
case I saw a stranger where she should be. I was halfway across
the floor, almost at the lift, before I risked a glance, but she
was there after all, the silver headphones bright against her
black hair that spilled down onto the desk as she read something in front of her.

"Good morning, JP."

The voice was Richard's. He smiled and fell into step with me, our feet clicking across the marble, like a well-rehearsed routine.

"Richard, hi. Fantastic morning, isn't it?"

They were the first words I'd spoken since ordering Dessie out and they sounded normal. A memory flickered of a time before Katie, when sometimes I wouldn't speak out loud between leaving work in the evening and arriving again the next day. Just like it had then, my voice responded with sparky ease, finding words I didn't need to look for, a mix of instinct and practice taking over.

Richard's response was even brighter, outshining mine. "Glorious. It's the kind of morning that makes you glad to be alive."

The lift doors opened and we took our places inside, our fledgling conversation swallowed into the rest of the crowd. When we reached our floor he turned towards his office, but I found myself calling him back. "Richard, listen, I know you're going for the interview today as well and I just wanted to wish you the best of luck."

His eyes behind his glasses held mine. He smiled and put out his hand. I leaned over and shook it.

"Thanks. And the same to you, JP. I've no doubt Peter will choose the best man for the job."

Turning away, I smiled to myself. He couldn't figure me out and I knew that despite himself he would waste time wondering over my motives. He'd probably think I saw the position as a foregone conclusion, that I was trying to suck up to him already. My smile stretched further. The rhythm of the office was inside me and this was better. I could feel myself responding to the energy and noise that pushed everything else away. Here, there was an order, a team, a goal, and I was part of that. There were people I needed to speak to, and people who needed to speak to me. Things that had to be done and only I could do them. As I approached my office the phone was ringing and I speeded up to answer it. Leaning on the desk, I responded to the clipped, short demands with the firm confidence of someone who had handled this situation a thousand times, because I had. Relaxing into the familiar, words and jokes and the right answers found their way into my mouth. I was an actor in a role I knew well, cajoling and soothing and making him laugh. In less than five minutes the client was over it, agreeing to increase his portfolio with us at the expense of one of our biggest rivals. As the challenge faded, my mind started to wander. I looked up to see Alison outside, mouthing something through the glass. I gestured for her to come in, miming the caller's talking with my hand. She shook her head and made a face.

"Hi," I said, when I hung up. "Sorry about that. It was David Gilroy from Bennett's. All panic as usual. What's up?"

I shook off my jacket and slung it over the back of my chair in one movement. I'd mostly managed to avoid her since Katie had left and I didn't want to be reminded of everything. Not here.

"You look sharp today — new tie?"

"And shirt. Have to make an effort this being a big day

and all." I put my finger under the collar, flicking open the button so I could pull my tie down a fraction.

"Very nice. I just wanted to let you know you've been bumped from eleven until twelve this morning. Peter had this conference call that ran over. I mean, he should have allowed time — they always run over, those calls."

"Oh, yeah, the steering group. The AOB on those always goes on for hours." I nodded in agreement.

"Tell me about it." Alison rolled her eyes. "It's Muggins here who has to take the minutes. Anyway, the upshot of all that is that Richard was pushed from eleven till twelve, and you're after him."

"When's he seeing Sapna?"

"Oh, I thought you'd have been on top of that. He saw her yesterday. Don't think it went too well, to tell you the truth. She was in and out in just over half an hour. He must have raced through it. He's all over the place, meetings with Gordon and this new budgets thing. Everyone keeps asking me about the merger, not that I'd know anything about it."

Alison would know all about it, more than me, but that wasn't the right answer so instead I nodded, folding my arms. Office conversation was always like this, clichés with a timed script and no real meaning, like answering prayers at mass. I could have a conversation and be somewhere else entirely, but still listening enough so as not to be caught out, my face and body language a mask of interest. It was easy. Until she crossed the line.

"How are you doing anyway, JP? Have you been on to Katie?"

As she spoke she made her voice softer than usual, the slow words, like bait, meant to extract some nugget of insight that she could go running back to Katie with. She gently pushed the door closed. Now that I was trapped with her tangible anticipation the office seemed to shrink. She knew exactly how things were with Katie, when we'd last spoken. If she wasn't Katie's best friend and Peter's PA, I wouldn't have had to answer her. I could tell her to fuck off out of my office, that I was busy and it was none of her goddamn business anyway. But she was, and that wasn't an option.

"I'm OK." I shrugged. "We spoke yesterday evening and she seemed fine." My words sounded fake, scratches of noise; the timing was off. I took a breath and started again. "I mean, there's still a lot we need to talk about. I haven't been around much. We're both getting used to Abbey being in our lives. There's been some miscommunication that we need to sort out, you probably know that. I think we need to work through this together, figure things out."

I threw in the miscommunication bit on purpose, so she'd know that I knew how much of what had happened was her fault. This time I made a better job of it: the words sounded real, adult expressions of what people in relationships did. It was my fingers that gave me away, fiddling with the blinds, twisting them open and closed again. When I turned around her expression was moulded into concern and I knew I hadn't satisfied her yet. The bloodthirsty bitch needed more.

"Look, JP, I feel awful if I've had any part to play in all this."

"No, no." I shook my head.

"I mean, I only said to Katie what I saw. The flowers, and the photograph, and you seemed to be acting so stressed all the time ..."

She let her words hang, pushing her glasses up into the frizz of her hair. Her eyebrows knotted in concern, in a face that told me I could open up to her. That I could tell her anything. I wondered what would happen if I did, at what point the balance would tip from empathy to gossip. I pictured how her expression would change if I told her about Dessie, if I told her what he had said about Katie and Leena. For a second I toyed with telling her, imagined the shock and disgust that would pour through her features and peel the mask away.

I realised she was saying something and I folded my arms, my head to one side. When I tuned into her hesitant words I wished I hadn't. "I know you don't want to hear this, but I don't know if she ever properly dealt with the break-up with Toby. It was just such a shock. I know you never met him but they were just one of those couples who seemed unbreakable — you know? They were so close ..."

"For fuck's sake!"

The curse burst out before I could stop it and hung in the air along with the dust motes caught in the morning sun.

"I'm sorry. I didn't mean that to sound the way it did. I just thought that if you knew ... Look, sorry, JP, it's none of my business. I shouldn't have said anything."

The pause stretched between us, Alison looked down at her shoes and my gaze followed hers. It was my turn to speak, to tell her I knew she was only trying to help, but I wasn't sure I believed that anymore, so instead I returned to the script.

"So, is Peter seeing anyone after me?"

"I was just trying to explain why ..."

Our sentences clashed, stopping us both. Mine offered a way back to where we should be and she grasped it tightly, her briskness pumping through the words as she answered. "No, you're the last. Gary was in yesterday too. You know none of the others are going for it? It's just you four. After you, Peter's got lunch with Gordon and then he's at an offsite for the rest of the day. I could be wrong but I'd say he'll make the decision tonight."

"Wow, that'd be quick but you're probably right," I agreed. "He probably already knows who he wants. But, listen, thanks a million for the heads-up. I really should crack on and get some work done for this thing, get my head together."

Turning, I walked around the desk and sat down so it was between us. I felt her eyes on me as I picked up a document in front of me, plucking off the yellow Post-it note on the front.

"OK, I'll give you a shout when he's ready for you."

When I looked up, her hand was on the door handle and I thought she was going to say something else so I nodded and looked back down. As she pushed it open the sounds of voices and phones ringing outside swirled around us and I could breathe again. The second time I looked up she was gone.

After she left I tried to read the document but the pages were heavy and moist in my hands and the words slipped just out of reach. I read the first paragraph twice before moving down to scan the rest. Rolling my eyes down the pages, the rows of Times New Roman became neat black lines as the words bled into each other. I couldn't shake the feeling that they didn't matter anyway, that these words were only the choice of some given person on some given day and that they could be erased at any time, their meaning deleted forever.

Dropping the pages back on the desk I turned to look out of the window. The sunshine showed up the smears on the glass, the film of dirt on the other side. Down below on the street there were cars and people walking, talking to other people on phones at the other side of the city, at the other side of the world. Connected and disconnected. Real and unreal. You could lose anything in a city like this with its whirlpool of lives. If Dessie took Katie I would never find her but he always found me. I let myself imagine his voice on the end of a phone. He was laughing. A distant echo of jangling music playing in the background. I closed my eyes, kneading them with my thumb and forefinger so all I could see was a speckled black mosaic. Underneath my ribcage there was a knot, a hard kernel of something I didn't understand yet, and I tried to breathe through it, slowly, in and out, counting as I pushed the air through my nose like I'd taught myself to do. Then the phone rang for real, and I knew before I answered it that it was going to be him.

"What do you want?"

"JP?"

"Katie?"

"JP, what's wrong?"

It was Katie — of course it was Katie. I realised I was standing up. My shirt was damp against my skin. My breathing had speeded up in time with the relentless drum of my heart inside my chest.

"Katie, sorry. I thought it was going to be someone else."

"Who did you think it was going to be that you answered it like that? Is everything OK, JP?"

"No one, sorry. I just had an argument with one of the brokers."

"Which one?"

"Jesus, does it really matter who it was? Are you ringing to interrogate me or what?" The words were wrong, serrated instead of soft, and instantly I wanted to pull them back in.

"I was ringing to say good luck," she said, not hiding the bruising from her voice. "I shouldn't have bothered."

Sitting down again I ran my hand over my hair. Swivelling my seat towards the window I remembered who I needed to be. Breathe, I just needed to breathe. In and out, in and out. I made myself sound as she expected. "Hey, I'm sorry. I was only joking. I've had a crazy morning and I'm a bit wound up about the interview. Peter bumped me from eleven till twelve. It's great to hear your voice, though. How's Abbey?"

There was a second of silence on the line before Katie answered. "She's fine. Well, she was acting up a bit this morning. I think it's thrown her routine, being up here. She's not sleeping as well as she was before."

"That makes two of us," I said. "I miss you."

The pause that followed was too long. We both heard it stretching over the dead air of the phone connection. It was Katie's turn to speak next.

"Look, we need to talk, JP, to sort stuff out. I thought it would help being up here but I don't think it is. Mum's driving me batty. And I was thinking about what you said and you're right. We're not going to get this sorted with me up here and you in London. If you have things you want to talk to me about, then I want to listen."

My mind had become detached from her voice but I forced myself to tune back in. What she was saying was brilliant, words I'd been longing to hear that should have made my insides hover. Words that should have brought relief and a beam that stretched across my face.

"That's brilliant, Katie," I said. "I can't wait to see you. Both of you." I meant it, I knew I meant it, but somehow the notion of her and Abbey coming home was strangely abstract. I filled my voice with the excitement I knew I should feel but it wasn't there, as if the place it should be had died.

"Well, you won't have to wait too long. Daddy's driving down now. He's got a meeting somewhere near Waterloo this afternoon and I thought we might come with him. I could take Abbey to the park and meet you after work."

The park. Stuck here I couldn't protect them from what might happen in the park. There were too many places to hide. Dessie could watch them from a bench or an idling car outside the gate, waiting and watching as he had before.

"This afternoon? That sounds great," I said. I was stalling, looking for a reason to find fault with the plan. And then I found one. "I was just thinking, though, you left the car seat in Alison's car, didn't you?"

"Oh, that's OK. Daddy bought one. You know what he's like, it's a top-of-the-range thing like a throne, much better than the one we have. So, that's all sorted. I might ring Alison and ask her if she'd be free to babysit later. We could take some time together, go for a meal or something. Talk through everything."

This time the pause was on my side as I struggled to find something to say that I meant. Something that was true but wouldn't scare her or crack our fragile alliance.

"How about if I drove up to you in the morning instead? You won't even want to see me tonight — I'll be shattered after the interview, no good to anyone," I said. "But if I left early tomorrow I'd be with you before lunch and we could have a proper chat, come back together on Sunday. It'd be nice — what do you think? You know I love going up to Cheshire."

The last line was a mistake.

"What are you on about? You can't stand it up here, couldn't wait to get on the road last weekend, acting like the place was on fire or something."

"Katie, that's not true!"

"And we won't get any privacy to talk up here, you know that. What's going on with you, JP? One minute you can't wait for me to be back, the next you're fobbing me off with some stupid excuse. You need to decide. Which is more important — your job or your family?"

The trembling question made her voice crack. Rebecca would definitely have overheard that and I pictured her smiling to herself, nodding that she had been right all along. I walked around the corner of the desk, looking out across the office. The red light of the other phone line flashed Alison's extension number. It was time.

"Look, Katie, that's Alison on the other line. I've got to go and see Peter. Can we figure this out later?"

I held the phone under my chin as I shuffled my jacket onto my outstretched arm. In my reflection in the window my hair was standing up again and I pushed it down flat on my forehead.

"No, we can't, JP, there is no later! Daddy's about to leave and I can stay here or go with him. You decide now. Which is more important?" Katie wasn't bothering to keep the tears from her voice now.

The other phone line had stopped flashing and looking up, I saw Alison outside the office, pointing at her watch through the glass. I gave her the thumbs-up. There was only one answer. "Katie, you know you and Abbey are. Come down with your dad and we'll sort this out. I've got to go. I'll call you later. I love you."

Alison was on her way back to her desk. Through the open door I saw Richard emerge from Peter's office, a black folder under one arm.

Katie was starting to say something else but I'd hung up too soon so I lost her truncated words. I tried to put her voice out of my head as I strode towards Peter's office. On the way I passed Richard. He was smiling.

***

Peter didn't see me at first. Leaning against the window he had his back to me, surveying the river below and the mismatched skyline of buildings on the other side. The mahogany table loomed long and empty, a series of water rings from a discarded cup the only evidence of Richard. I rapped lightly on the already open door and he turned around with a smile. "JP, come on in."

"Thanks."

"Grab a seat."

Closing the door behind me, I took a deep breath. This was it. I walked past where Richard had sat and took the chair second from the top, next to where Peter's papers were strewn across the table's shiny surface.

"So, how's tricks, JP?"

Hands in pockets, he smiled down as I sat back and crossed my legs.

"Great. Couldn't be better. Bennett's are expanding their portfolio by a couple of hundred K so that's good news. Oh, and I got a call from Anthony Waters this morning, sniffing for info on the Capital deal."

"Ha!" Peter threw his head back and laughed. "He's a bit too late in the day on that one. We were on to it weeks ago."

"Yeah, I know. Didn't tell him that, though. Thought I'd keep him guessing." I tapped the side of my nose with my forefinger, sending two snatches of pain through me that triggered Dessie's words from last night. "Was it talk that broke your nose, then?" Peter was talking again and I needed to listen. To remember that, no matter what Dessie said, there was no John-Paul any more, only JP.

"Good stuff, JP." He nodded. "Let them waste some time while they suss it all out. Keep them off our backs for a while."

"Absolutely."

"Right then, I guess we should kick off," he said, taking his seat next to me. I waited while he picked up a sheet of paper, a crease furrowing his brow as he read. His fingernails were immaculate, shiny pink squares cut with a neat white edge. Dad's nails were cut too short, so squidges of finger spread out from underneath. I remembered him in the steam of the bathroom, washing the smell of work away. No matter how hard he scrubbed with the plastic nailbrush there was always a black rim of grime left that he couldn't reach, deep under his cuticles like an outline in a drawing. Peter was speaking and I blinked the image away.

"So, how do you feel you've been getting on since joining the management team, JP? You're not finding yourself too overwhelmed by things, I hope?"

I pulled myself back to the table, focused on his stare behind his glasses. I made my face serious like his was.

"No, not at all." I shook my head. I took a breath and remembered to pause in the right places. "I'm really enjoying it. Taking on new clients. Getting exposure to other areas of the business. I mean, it's been a learning curve for sure but I always enjoy new challenges."

Peter nodded, his hands forming a diamond as he listened. "And the hours, you're not finding them too much with your ... new situation?"

It was a funny choice of words, as if having Abbey was something that had happened to me by accident. It was the first time he'd referred to her since the day after she was born. On his desk I could see the backward frame of a photograph of his own family but he never mentioned them either. "I'm lucky." I smiled. "Katie understands how important my career is and she's a great support. We've discussed it and, really, it's just about being flexible. Abbey's in a crèche now too so that helps."

I only realised it was a lie as I said it out loud. We'd never discussed the promotion, not really. She'd called to wish me luck, she must want me to get it, but we'd never really talked about what it would mean, with me at work more, at home less. When Dad worked late we'd all had to wait to eat until he got home, that was the rule. I remembered Mam fussing with the oven, putting plates over dinners that had dried out long ago, Dessie's voice moaning about how he would die of starvation. The tight ball under my ribcage that had been there all day felt like the hunger that seemed to peak just before the scrape of the door over the hall tiles that signalled Dad's arrival.

"Yes, that's a good idea," Peter agreed. "Don't get me wrong, it's not that I've seen a change in your attitude — quite the opposite, in fact. If anything, you seem more driven than ever. It's just that this new role would be more intensive, as you'd expect. I'm hoping to cut back on my travel so there'd be a fair bit of that and so on. I'm off again to New York on Sunday, second time this month. Going forward, I'd like to hand over some of those reporting sessions to whoever gets the job. And some of the Tokyo trips. It's just good to have these expectations clear up front."

"Absolutely."

New York. Tokyo. The travel made my heart sink and jump altogether. I hadn't thought about that. A hotel-room phone heavy in my sweaty hand. The powerlessness of listening to it ring on and on, unanswered. Nights spent stretched out trying to find sleep in aeroplane seats, cramped and awake and wondering. I held my face still, careful not to let my fear spill out. In front of me Peter opened his mouth to speak and closed it again. Taking his glasses off, he started to polish them and I waited for what was coming next.

"I may as well cut to the chase," he said. "You're well respected here. You know that. You're very bright. You work hard. You're loyal. I like loyalty." Pausing, he caught my eye and I smiled slightly, acknowledging the compliment. He nodded and started to polish again. "For me, one of the things that's difficult about this role, for the whole team, in fact, is getting the right mix of youth and experience. We need someone who's got the energy, got the drive, but who's willing to learn and ask for help when they need it. You know what I mean, JP?"

"Sure." I nodded, frowning slightly. "You don't want someone who's going to run off half cocked, but at the same time you don't want to be bothered with every little detail."

"Exactly," Peter nodded firmly, agreeing with his own hackneyed phrases quoted back to him. "That's it exactly. I'm sure you know what I'm about to say, JP?"

I made my face a mask, clasped my fingers lightly in front

of me on the table. My heart was marching faster again and I couldn't slow it down. This wasn't what I was expecting: Peter was doing all the talking. I tried to concentrate on his words but my brain was finishing his speech before he did. He was going to tell me that I wasn't what they were looking for. That someone like me would never make assistant director. Beyond the door I could hear voices, a phone ringing. He was about to tell me I had a nerve even to think of going for it.

"I know I should go through the whole interview thing but I think that HR stuff is all baloney. It's a waste of everyone's time, really. I've known from the beginning who I wanted for this job, JP, and that's you. You've proven yourself to me time and time again. You've got the kind of energy and commitment that we need on the team. You're a great example to everyone else. I want to offer you the position."

He was sitting back, waiting for my reaction, his hands clasped behind his head so I could see small leaks of sweat in his armpits. His words rolled around me. I hadn't taken them in yet. He was smiling. I smiled too. The meaning of his last sentence drip-fed into my brain. I imagined telling Dad. Telling Katie. I opened my mouth, forcing the words, any words to come.

"Peter, I don't know what to say. Thank you. Thank you so much."

"Don't thank me, JP, it's well deserved."

That was a mistake. I shouldn't be too grateful. I'd worked hard and I should expect this. My next line was better. "I appreciate your faith in me, Peter, I really do."

He waved the words away, standing up again, resuming his place by the window.

"It's a big job, JP, and a lot more responsibility — but that comes with considerably more reward, as you know. And, again, you deserve it. Everything's set up ready. I just need to give Payroll the nod. There's a new lady I've been dealing with, Eleanor — do you know her?"

"Eleanor?" I hated that name. Like the song, 'Eleanor Rigby'. I'd always hated that too. "No, I don't think I've met her."

"She's good. Seems deadly efficient. I'll call her after this and she'll have you sorted out in no time."

"*Eleanor Rigby picks up the rice in the church where a wedding has been.*" The broken lyric ran through my head and back into hiding. I nodded at Peter. "Great, that's great."

A beat of silence and it was there again. "*Lives in a dream.*" I tried to swallow but my mouth was too dry. The song ran on unchecked into the next stupid line about keeping her face in a jar by the door. "Who is it for?"

Peter was still talking, his voice full of energy, counting on his fingers the things we needed to do. Reaching forward I slowly lifted the plastic cup and took a sip of lukewarm water.

"The handover will take a while but in the meantime there are things we can get started on. We'll tell our own team this afternoon, before I go away, and I've written an email to send to the board. You'll want to advertise for your replacement so you can get up to speed on the portfolios across all the sectors. I've managed to hold Gordon off for the past few months because we've been under-resourced but now he's expecting to see a big upturn next quarter."

Peter was back at full tilt. I tried to follow what he was saying, picking up a pen to jot down notes and hide the tremor that had suddenly invaded my hand. I couldn't get the song out of my head and it kept going, unstoppable, into the next verse with Father McKenzie darning his socks. The kernel of tension under my ribs seemed to be replaced by something else, a cold hollowness that was taking over my whole stomach and threatened to move down into my legs as well. I scrawled words I managed to catch as he leaped from one topic to the next, the biro slippery between my sweaty fingers. I couldn't keep up, was about to ask him to stop, when Alison knocked on the door and broke his flow.

"Peter, I'm really sorry," she said. "I wouldn't interrupt only I've Gordon on the phone. He says it's urgent."

"Should I step out?"

I was already half standing, my legs shaky.

"No, JP, sit down. This will only take a minute. We've got a lot more to get through."

Alison avoided my eye as she closed the door. I wanted her to stay, to call out to her, but what would I say? My mouth, which had been dry, was suddenly wet with saliva that poured in from all sides, so thick and fast and sudden that I thought I might be sick. I reached forward for the glass of water. My hand was shaking worse than before and I spilled some on my shirt, tell-tale splashes of darker blue. 'Eleanor Rigby' roamed freely through my head, on and on, and I couldn't make it stop. Over the jumbled lyrics Dessie's voice cut through, so sharp the words might have been made of glass. "They had twelve original albums, but you there's only have eleven up there. *Revolver*'s missing."

Behind me, Peter was telling Gordon the news. I knew he was watching me and I flicked over my page of notes as if examining the scrawl of my writing. Breathing. I just needed to breathe. I listened to Peter's words as he described me to Gordon. "Energy." "Commitment." How I was "raising the bar for the team". This was real. This was the present that was happening right now. To me. This was nothing to do with Dessie. I hung on to Peter's voice, pulling myself back into the room, hanging on tightly to the safety rope of his words.

"Sorry about the interruption," Peter said, hanging up. "Gordon's very pleased about you taking on the new role. He wants to meet us. I'm back on the early flight Thursday so maybe then."

"That's great. Thursday sounds fine."

I had no concept of what might be happening next Thursday, couldn't seem to think beyond today, but that was OK. The main thing was that my voice sounded normal, that I could swallow again. That I could breathe.

"I'll get Alison to sort out the diaries. I've got to get off in a few minutes to a lunch meeting but before I do I want to go through the investment sign-off process."

"Investment sign-off? Sure."

I hadn't known that was part of the role and I could feel the glow of heat in my cheeks. I wondered if Peter noticed.

"To be honest, everyone's recommendations are usually

pretty sound so it can be a bit of a bore. But it's a good way for you to get to know the other sectors, and in this day and age, we need to make sure we're watertight and everything's done by the book."

"Of course." I nodded. "Absolutely."

"So, basically it means that instead of presenting to me, the rest of the team will need to present to you before doing a deal. Nothing moves in or out of this department without your say-so. I'll tell them this afternoon when we make the announcement."

"And what about my own investments? Will you still sign them off?"

Peter laughed, shaking his head. "Not at all. Your recommendations are always bang on. I trust you to sign off everyone else's so I think I can trust you to sign off your own. I know I should have waited until I talked to you but I went ahead so there'd be no problems next week while I'm away. It's already set up."

Millions of pounds went through the department every month into hundreds of accounts, meaningless flickers of numbers that moved from one screen to the next. It didn't feel like money at all, more like some complicated computer game, not linked to anything in the real world.

"So, what do you think, JP? Are you up to the challenge?"

I gave him the answer I knew he wanted. "Absolutely, Peter. I won't let you down."

Twenty-three

From behind the sitting-room door the music was loud, the metallic twang of the guitar filling the hall. 'Taxman' was the first song on *Revolver*. I shouldn't have been up, my bedtime had been hours before, but the scratch of pain in my throat had started to grate and I couldn't sleep.

The kitchen was dark but the fridge light was enough to pour the milk by, holding the bottle tightly with two hands so as not to let it slip. They hadn't even heard me over the music and I should've gone back to bed, but something made me stop outside the door. Something made me reach out and pull down the creaky handle.

Even before it was fully open I wished I hadn't. It was better when it was closed, just a white piece of wood instead of the rectangle of colour and noise that jumped out at me, like a story in a pop-up book. I rubbed my eye with one hand and it took a second for the images to make sense.

Mam was sitting down but not in a chair. She was on the floor, her knees pulled up close to her, making a triangle from her legs. I couldn't see her face through her hair. The music was louder now and she hadn't heard me yet. I pushed the door back more and Dad was there too. Standing over Mam he looked much bigger than he was. The shape of his mouth as he shouted made his skin tight and red. He had his arm pulled back over his head, his hand a fist.

I don't know what made them stop and notice me. Maybe I cried out or called Mam's name. I don't remember that bit but I remember how they both turned at the same time, trapped in my gaze like a photograph. I could see Mam's face then, her eyes that were red and puffed up from crying too much, her makeup a mess on her cheeks. She pulled her hand to her mouth but not quickly enough, I'd already seen that her lip was burst and oozing like an over-cooked sausage and the blood, dark red like paint, that covered her chin and smeared her teeth.

The music swirled around. It was too loud; sounding angry too. Dad's shout cut through it. "What the hell are you doing up? Get back to bed now, you little bastard!" His eyes didn't look like his eyes. They were red too but not like Mam's. They were bulging like Brutus's eyes in Popeye when he was really angry. I looked to Mam and she was half standing up, one hand on the radiator the other cupped under her dripping chin. She was trying to say something but her mouth wouldn't work properly so she nodded, looking over at Dad. His second yell was even louder. "I said now, John-Paul!"

A slow warmth spread over my pyjamas and too late I realised I'd wet myself. In my hand the glass slipped a little and milk slopped over the side. Dad was still shouting, coming towards me now, but I slammed the door so I wouldn't have to hear him, so I wouldn't have to see. I ran for the stairs. I ran so fast I didn't have time to check if he was behind me and by the time I reached our room the milk was nearly all spilled. I dropped the glass on the floor, burrowing under the covers, making a tunnel, elbows first then knees. In the darkness I started to count in my head to make my breaths slow. The wee was cold then and its smell mixed with the milk made it hard to breathe.

Downstairs the music was louder — I could make out the words. 'Taxman' was nearly over. I could hear Dad's voice shouting louder and I remember squashing my hands together and praying the O'Briens next door would hear and they'd come in and save us. But even then I knew they wouldn't.

In the darkness Dessie's voice sounded small and far away. "John-Paul?"

I pulled my head out from under the covers but I didn't answer him. 'Taxman' slowed into silence and the gap between the songs was like a breath of air.

"I hate him," he said.

I didn't say anything. I didn't want to answer him and I didn't want to hear him either. I pushed my fingers so hard in my ears it hurt, but it didn't work: I could still hear everything. Instead, I started to sing. It was 'Eleanor Rigby' and I knew all the words.

"*Eleanor Rigby, picks up the rice in the church where a wedding has been ...*"

My leg vibrated with the music.

"*... lives in a dream.*"

Something hit the wall downstairs and it wasn't a dream.

"*Waits at the window, wearing the face that she keeps in a jar by the door ...*"

Dessie joined in too then, his voice wobbly, like mine.

"*Who is it for?*"

Together we sang through the next verse and the chorus and the verses after that. We sang on through 'I'm Only Sleeping' and the strange foreign rhythms of 'Love You To' and the soft comfort of 'Here There And Everywhere'. We sang the bit in 'Yellow Submarine' where the needle skipped. We sang through 'Good Day Sunshine' as if our lives depended on it.

I don't remember falling asleep that night. I don't remember how old we were, but Dessie must have been small enough to be scared like me. I don't remember other nights like that one so it must have only happened once. Just the once.

What I do remember is imagining the record needle sliding over the shiny black vinyl, up and around and down and around again. I remember concentrating so hard that in my head I could see the music through the grooves. I remember thinking that if I concentrated hard enough I could become the needle, I could become the music. I could become the sound.

And if I could do that, then nothing else would matter.

TWENTY-FOUR

The taxi driver started to talk as soon as we opened the door and he didn't stop until we reached the restaurant. Normally I hated being trapped like that, in their moving soapbox, but not tonight. Down the Mile End Road, past Aldgate, over London Bridge, his rants on politics and the terrorist threat gave my head a chance to clear, his words an excuse for me not to have to find any of my own. I let my mind rest on nothing more than the London shop fronts beyond the window, leaving Katie to do the necessary nodding and agreeing.

Seeing Katie and Abbey was like a trick. The two of them, in the sitting-room when I got home, looked as if nothing had changed. Abbey in Katie's arms, her back a soft slope of red and white stripes, turning her wobbly head when she heard my voice. When Katie looked up, her smile was almost a real smile but it was just a second too late and it never fully reached her eyes.

We hugged and kissed. I held Abbey and bounced her in my arms and we both laughed when she threw up her milky sick on my new shirt. We opened champagne to celebrate my promotion. Alison arrived then and we had some more, rushing to drink the froth of bubbles before it escaped over the rim. Arm in arm we waved at Alison and Abbey, laughing in the corridor, went out past the porter's lodge and into the taxi. On the film reel in my head everything looked fine but it wasn't. There was something between us, something that made our movements ever so slightly out of synch. Something that shied out of sight every time I tried to look it in the eye. Something that was growing bigger and was almost physical. Like a tumour.

The sleek metallic restaurant was a sea of couples celebrating the start of another weekend together. Couples with faces lit up by love and candles. Couples with fingers that linked loosely across the table, so close they seemed to be part of each other. Following our waiter to our table I turned to kiss Katie but the timing was all wrong, and her kiss back was brisk and dry.

We needed to get back to the way it had been in the apartment and I ordered more champagne. The alcohol made it easier, rounding the edges of the movements and the conversation. It put colour back in Katie's face and I could feel her starting to relax.

"Remember when we came here to celebrate when we found out I was pregnant with Abbey?" she said.

"You wouldn't even have a glass of champagne that time," I said. "I think they got some of that Aqua Libra stuff for you."

"Ugh, yeah." Katie made a face. "I hated it. I think that was the first time I'd had it since I was fifteen, when I drank a whole bottle thinking it was alcoholic."

Katie giggled as she remembered, cringing at her past youthful self. I laughed along with her, loving to see her laughing again, loving to see her happy. I knew we were here to talk, that there were things I should say — but I didn't know what those things were. What had seemed so clear only last night was tied up tight in a knot again, like elastic bands wound over and over on themselves.

I topped up our champagne, and over our starters we toasted Abbey, and my new job, and Katie and even Alison. When my steak arrived it was too bloody but I didn't send it back. I was afraid of breaking the warm ooze of the spell between us so instead I ordered red wine.

We laughed a lot over dinner but I don't remember what we laughed at. After the waiter cleared the plates Katie stood up to find the Ladies. I let my eyes wander around the room, then back to the floor-length window and the view of the river below. For a moment, the heavy, settled fullness felt like happiness. Things were great with me and Katie again. I had the beautiful baby girl I'd always wanted. The job of my dreams. If it wasn't for Dessie, we'd be like we were tonight all the time and things would be perfect. Looking up I saw Katie was back already, slipping into her seat opposite me. There was something about the sense of purpose in her movement that made me sit straighter in my chair and the ease seemed to edge away.

"I'm full now," I said. "Not sure if I'll manage a dessert. Maybe some cheese though."

"You said you wanted to talk to me, JP," she said, cutting across me. "What was it you wanted to say?"

The mouthful of wine I took was too big and it scorched my throat slightly as I swallowed it. It was a good question.

What version was I going to tell her? And where would I start? Last night I'd wanted to tell her about Mark and Dessie, about Mam and Dad, and I still did. I just didn't know what that meant any more.

"Katie, I'm sorry I didn't tell you about Dessie before," I said. "I'm sorry I lied. It's just … I don't know … I almost felt like I didn't have a brother any more, not after everything that had happened."

Katie rested her chin on her hand as I tried to put words around what had happened to Mark, to put the story into a tidy coherent shape. She sipped her coffee, her eyes big over the rim of the white porcelain cup while I hacked my way around the cheese board, splinters of cracker falling from my mouth with my stumbling words. The soft sludge of Brie seemed to mould to my tongue and hold back any meaning from the stammering stories of a childhood that sounded so ordinary out loud. So unimpressive. When I stopped there was silence. I was about to try again but before I could she was interpreting for me, organising my words into things I hadn't said that made complete sense to her and to me.

"JP, what you're going through is totally natural, you know. When you become a parent you start to think about your own parents more. I know I have. Your dad meant so much to you, and you lost him so young. You want to make sure you're everything to Abbey that he was to you."

Her eyes were locked on mine. As she spoke she was nodding and I nodded along. I hadn't said anything about Dad and the mention of him made heat flare in my face, prickling the top of my nose. For a second, I thought I might cry. "He was a great dad," I said.

"I'm sure he was. It's the same way I think about Mum, that there's no way I can live up to that. I was reading this article in *Marie Claire* last week, about how the role of the father has changed so much. I kept it for you if you want to see it."

"Sure," I said, smiling. "I'd like to read it."

"It was really interesting. It said that for men it's hard to know what role to play, because when they were young their experience of their own father was so different from what's expected now. Like, it's not enough to be the breadwinner any more, you know?" She paused to drink some coffee and I thought she was finished until she started again. "This article was saying that loads of guys feel left out after the baby's born, like they're ... I don't know ... It's like they feel in the way or something."

I picked up a grape and held it between my thumb and forefinger before chewing it. Its freshness dissolved and burst on my tongue. Across from me, Katie was waiting for my response.

"Is that how you feel, JP? Do I make you feel like that?"

The grape had pips but I swallowed them anyway. Outside it was getting dark. In the warm glow of candlelight what Katie was saying made sense. It was normal, there were articles written about it.

"I don't know," I said. I took a deep breath. "Maybe. Yeah, I suppose I do a bit."

Katie reached across the table to hold my hand. I rubbed

my thumb across her fingers. She was waiting for me to say something more.

"It's just harder than I expected," I said. "I want to be a good dad to her. More than just good, I want to be great."

"I know," Katie said, nodding. "And you will be. You are."

I thought that would be enough. It seemed to be over. I thought it was. We drank more wine. The conversation seemed to have split into two tracks. Katie was pulling me back to talk about Dad and Mam, endless questions, questions, questions. I didn't want to talk about them any more: I wanted to tell her about my new job, what it meant and what it would mean. I remember the urgency in my voice as I tried to convince her to come to New York and bring Abbey with her for my first meeting. I was trying to explain it when my hand clipped my wine glass, spilling the contents in slow motion across the shine of the table so it seemed to float like mercury. I jumped up to stop it but Katie had already stemmed the flow with her napkin, its whiteness seeping first to pink and then red. It must have been after that that I remember leaning against the mirror in the Gents, the beads of sweat my forehead left on the glass, like tears.

When I came back I'd sat down before I realised Katie had called for the bill, which was sitting on my place mat in a teak box. I left too much, not waiting for my change as I hurried to keep up and follow her as she swayed between the tables and towards the door.

The fight was definitely the taxi driver's fault, the idiot taking us towards Borough instead of Bow. It was Katie who noticed that we were going south instead of crossing the river. She leaned forward to ask him if he was going the right way and when my eyes focused I realised the wet streets lined with houses and cars looked nothing like the neon shop fronts of the East End.

He was the one who shouted first, even though I knew it was a scam. I'd heard it happen before and I wasn't afraid to say so, to tell him I knew he was trying to rip us off. When he jerked the car to a stop I jammed my face off the headrest in front, the wash of alcohol not enough to stop the sudden burst of pain from my nose. I shouted back at him then, our voices clashing in the small hot car, his a high-pitched discord of foreign sounds as he jabbed his finger at the square black boxes on the inside cover of his A–Z.

I didn't see Katie getting out of the car. It wasn't until I saw her through the window, her arms pulling her jacket tight around her that I noticed she'd gone. Flicking the catch on the door I stumbled out after her, ignoring the taxi driver's frenzied shouts for payment. A violent roar erupted, filling my ears and head, and I realised he was leaning on his horn. A light came on in the darkness of the building across the street.

"For Christ's sake, JP, will you just give him some money?" Katie said, rooting in her handbag.

"Why should I? It's not like he took us home."

"For God's sake!"

More lights were coming on and I heard voices from the house behind us. Katie had found her purse and handed over a note that he pocketed without offering her any change.

The back door was still open and I leaned in to shout one final insult at this asshole who had ruined our night. I'd just about managed to slam it closed before he revved his engine and sped away.

"What a wanker," I said, turning towards Katie. Her eyes were following the red lights of the car disappearing into the dark and she looked as if she might cry. "Hey, come here, we'll get another taxi."

I reached out to put my arm around her but she snapped her body back before I could touch her.

"*He's* the wanker? *He* is? Christ almighty, JP!"

I reached out again but with her elbow she pushed my touch away. In the streetlight I could see only half of her face. Half of her anger.

"Katie!"

"Don't 'Katie' me! I'm sick of it! 'Katie, we need to talk', 'Katie, we can sort this out'."

It took me a second to get that the deep growl of her accent was an imitation of me.

"You're full of shit, JP! You don't want to sort anything out. What's wrong with you? You're so angry all the time. Since when do you have to get shit-faced to have a meal out with me? When did you turn into the kind of lout who shouts racist abuse at taxi drivers in the middle of the street?"

Swinging away from me, she walked towards the lights at the end of the road, her whole body bent forward as if she was leaning into a storm. I stood there for a minute, watching her leaving me. Her anger was scary: she couldn't control it and neither could I. It felt like a scene from a film but I had to act, to do something, so I ran after her, my breath pumping hard, latching onto the only handle I had.

"I'm not a racist," I said. "It was his fault! He started shouting at me."

"He did not."

"He did, and then he slammed on the brakes on purpose. He could have hurt us, hurt you …"

"Don't pretend this is about me," Katie said, pausing for long enough to spit the words at me before striding on again. "A fight's been brewing in you all night. He just got in the way."

"Why are you taking his side, Katie?"

I heard the whine in my own voice and it pulled her up too, slowing her down enough to turn and look at me, as if she didn't know me at all.

"For Christ's sake, JP. This isn't about sides. It's not even about him. It's about us!"

It was the "us" that did it, that cracked open the emotion that had tightly repelled and bound us together all night, letting it seep through into the night air. Without waiting for my response, she turned away again, the energy of her rage propelling her down a dark lane ahead, her high heels awkward on the cobblestones. I walked behind her and we emerged on the smooth walkway of the riverfront, lit with old-fashioned lamps from Sherlock Holmes's London, that was designed for lovers on night-time strolls to hold hands and admire the view.

In front of me Katie was walking faster now, her footsteps a brisk clip-clop on concrete. The air was colder here, somehow snapping me awake. Blinking, I looked across the water where the black lines of the city were brought into sharp focus against the night sky that was never dark overhead.

"Katie, wait."

My voice was a mumble and my body was moving too slowly to make any dent in the growing distance between us. I lifted my feet faster but they barely caught the end of her long shadow that stretched out behind her. I tried to shout again but when I opened my mouth nothing came. Instead that feeling was there again, itchy heat at the bridge of my nose. I sniffed it back but it spread further, down into my nostrils. I opened my mouth to take a deep breath of city air but it was too late. The tears were already behind my eyes and in my eyes and when I blinked they were on my face too.

"Katie," I called. "I'm sorry!"

Something in my voice made her turn around. The lights on Blackfriar's Bridge were a swimmy blur. Against it, she was a shape made of shadow. I had to make what I said next count.

"Tonight … it should have been perfect," I started. The tears were a hot burst that soaked my voice as well. I tried again. "You've come home. I was so scared you wouldn't. I love you. I love that restaurant. It should have been perfect." I rushed the words out, pushing them between us. She didn't walk on. I couldn't see her face in the darkness but she seemed to be walking back. Very slowly, but still it was back. I tried to move towards her but the alcohol in my limbs made me stumble sideways so my side caught the hard edge of the river wall. I felt myself sink against it.

"I'm so sorry, Katie. It should have been perfect and I fucked it up. Katie, why do I always fuck everything up?"

She was so close now that I could see she was crying too. She was coming back. She was nearly close enough to touch. In the quiet, I could hear the river licking the bank below, just about louder than silence. I didn't think I'd ever been in London when it was quiet enough to hear that but the sound wasn't new: it was as worn and familiar as a favourite taste. Leaning into the wall, I looked down at its slippery blackness rushing by. The sharp edge of stone bit into my arms just above my elbows where they took the full weight of my body.

"My mam drowned," I said, my words muffled in my jacket sleeve. "My mam killed herself."

Katie's hand was on my neck, the coolness of her fingers a better answer than words. I didn't turn to see her. Leaning farther forward, I inhaled the river's air, breathing it in so I could get out the rest of what I had to say.

"I should have saved her. I didn't save her, Katie. I should have. But I just wanted to get the hell out of there."

Crying washed the rest of the words away. Katie was holding me tight from behind, her arms wrapped around my chest. Her head was on my shoulder. I could feel her hair on my neck. In my ear she was ssshing me. My words leaked out between tears and breath, gappy and slow like a telegram.

"It was … only me, Katie … she needed me. I promised Dad … I was supposed to look after her … Dessie … he would have looked after her."

As she held me she started to rock me, rocking us both in time with her ssshs. My body seemed to deflate and I clutched her while I cried and neither of us spoke. When the sobs stopped the hiccups came, popping me full of air and snapping it back again. All the time we stayed there, leaning against the wall, rocking to our own rhythm.

Eventually I had to stand properly. My back and arms ached. When I turned to face her she reached for me again and pushed my hair back from my forehead. With her other hand she held my cheek, making me look at her, so I'd see what she said next as well as hear it.

"It wasn't your fault, JP."

My eyes slipped away, looking beyond her to a stretch of grass, but hers found me again, deep brown pools brimming with trust and love.

"You know that, don't you? Whatever happened, it wasn't your fault. You couldn't have done anything. You weren't your dad, you were only a kid."

I thought the crying was over but that was all it took, her mention of Dad. I bent my head onto her shoulder so she wouldn't see. I don't know if I was shaking from the cold or the crying or the drink, but whatever it was, I couldn't stop.

"I loved my dad," I said.

Her arms circled my waist, pulling me to her softness.

"I know you did, I know, sssh."

"I loved my dad," I said again, over her shoulder, the words disappearing into the London night.

Twenty-five

The laptop screen was frozen, the low hum of air the only indication that it was working at all. I double-clicked the icon again but nothing happened. I took a sip of water from the plastic cup on the desk but it wasn't enough to wash away the residue that still coated my mouth from last night. Checking my watch, I saw that it was still only seven thirty. I didn't need to be in this early — it wasn't like there'd be anyone here on a Saturday.

I'd forgotten to turn on the light so the office looked both the same and different. In the right-hand corner of the screen a red window popped up with an alarm bell that rang through the silence. My hands jerked on the keyboard before I realised it was only my anti-virus software alerting me that it was out of date. I clicked it closed and three versions of the program I needed opened — the computer was confused by my impatience.

I worked quickly. I didn't need to; I was simply activating an investment and drawing down payment. There was nothing unusual about it. Still, imagine if Peter came in, wanting to get something finished before his trip tomorrow. I could play up my dedication, my eagerness to get started, but even he might think it strange to see me here. Maybe I should've waited until later, but once I'd decided what I wanted to do, I needed to do it quickly, to get it done, so I could forget about it.

It took me a few seconds to find the account I needed and when I opened it the laptop paused again, the arrow turning into an egg-timer. It wasn't usually this slow. The achy rattle that had rolled around my head since I'd got up sharpened into a stabbing needle of pain where my forehead met my hair. Just when the pain became unbearable it retreated as quickly as it had come.

Katie had been sleeping when I'd left, one arm and one leg shrugging off the duvet that I gently lifted back up to her chin. She always slept with her mouth slightly open, her front teeth resting on her lower lip. When I kissed her forehead she smiled without opening her eyes, as if she didn't need to see me to know I was there. I wanted to get back into bed then, in all my clothes and shoes and everything, to hold her tight from behind and breathe in her smell and let it fill me inside.

In front of me the screen was alive again and I scanned the columns for the numbers I needed, half my mind on the spreadsheet but most of it embedded in the night before. It still had the edgy quality of a dream, a series of snapshots thrown out on a table rather than a proper flow of memory. I remembered walking with Katie for ages along the river, leaning into each other, warm and close. The café we found was too bright with white lights overhead but we went in anyway. Katie had hot chocolate and I had tea in chipped mismatching mugs, and the waitress didn't seem to think it strange to find this well-dressed couple among the track-suited teenage clientele.

And then I told her everything, from the start, sometimes directing my words into the beigy-coloured tea when looking at her face got too much. All about when Dad died and Dessie was sent away, about the time I hit Mam and the money I stashed away in the wardrobe. Telling her, listening to my words out loud, made the story somehow more and less real at the same time. Having it out there, between us, made more space in my head, and I didn't know what I was going to do with it yet but it felt like it was important to have it just the same. Out loud, the words didn't sound dirty and dark and wrong. Out loud, it just sounded like a really sad story.

When I finished, I looked up and Katie was gazing at me, but her expression was still the same. I searched her eyes, her mouth for a change, but I didn't see one. I saw only love. Hearing her sum it up made sense of it somehow. Losing the father I adored. My best friend a year later. A promise I didn't keep. It was a story with all the right parts. No wonder I was so afraid of losing Katie and Abbey too. I reached out to hold her hand across the table and I knew then how lucky I was that she was still there, that I'd broken the cycle of losing things and that I was never risking that again.

The laptop was behaving itself now, keeping up easily as I clicked between the spreadsheets, double-checking as I went. I had gone over it in my mind when we'd got home, lying next to Katie's warmth, slowing my breaths to the same rhythm as hers. My eyes open in the darkness saw that this was the only way. When Katie asked about Dessie I told her he had gone back to Dublin. It was only a small lie because soon he would. I'd texted him from the toilets in the café and he'd responded straight away, even though it was well past midnight. We were meeting on Monday night and he had agreed to leave London by Tuesday. That was one of my conditions. Katie came from a world where the police were there to solve problems like this and she didn't understand that mostly they just made things worse.

Choosing one client was the best option, only one person to notice, and Pembroke wouldn't notice. Steve Pembroke was younger than I was, and taking over his father's business had brought him more money than he could ever spend. He'd told me before to stop sending him quarterly statements because they only piled up on his desk unopened. It was only money after all and London was full of money. I had nearly twenty thousand saved already. I had planned to use it and borrow the balance but I found myself typing in fifty, the full amount. I needed it right now more than Steve Pembroke did and I'd pay him back in record time.

I was nearly finished. Seven forty-five. A bus rumbled past on the street below, the whine of its engine strangely noticeable on the city's silent Saturday streets. On screen a message in a shaded box confirmed the transaction was ready to complete pending authorisation, an arrow showing a drop-down list of authorising managers. My name and initials had already been added, replacing Peter's.

The second window opened up and the cursor winked, waiting for me to fill in the bank details. The account was new and I had to check the details on the printed card in my wallet; the last thing I needed was a mistake with the numbers. Before the funds would go through, the system would do an automatic check against the number and name on the account, one of the antiquated protection policies against employee fraud. Filling in the box for the name field my fingers shook as I typed 'Abbey Marguerite Whelan'.

If Peter found out I'd be fired. Straight away, no questions asked. But there was no way he would. It wasn't even stealing really: it was mostly just a question of cash flow. I was going to pay Pembroke back. Once my new salary came through I'd invest it in some high-return deals and replace it before he'd noticed. He'd have his money back with interest in six weeks, maybe less. There was no way I could get caught.

I was almost looking forward to telling Dessie how I'd done it, a shard of me seeking his approval for my daring. Just as quickly as the thought formed, a picture of Mam did too: confusion spilling in her face as she emptied her bag upside down onto the carpet searching for the tenner she'd seen that morning. I remembered her fingers clawing through bits of paper, tissues, bus tickets, an elastic band as she sought for what she was sure was there. The memory pulled something tight inside and I took a deep breath. Dessie said that when you've stolen once you realise how easy it is, but this was different. I was going to pay Pembroke back — he'd probably even give me the money if he knew what was at stake. This wasn't the same at all.

The system needed confirmation and I hovered for a second with the mouse, as if there were other options to consider. But there were no other options, I'd been through them all before. I remembered Dad saying that you knew what the right decision was because it was usually the hardest one. Well, this was hard but I couldn't shy away from it. Not now. My finger responded before my brain, clicking OK.

The screen changed to another and told me to wait, the egg-timer reappearing. My eyes scrunched closed I rubbed them too hard, making then water, erasing the image of Mam that lingered there. It was over now. Dessie had taken enough of my past. He wasn't going to take my future too. When I opened my eyes the egg-timer had been replaced by a green tick. Underneath it the bold letters flashed: 'Transaction complete.'

Twenty-six

Below Abbey's feet there was a bunch of white blanket that she'd shoved off in her sleep. I loved her feet, the softness of her heels, the little beans of her toes curving together. I freed the blanket from under them, pulling it up gently over her legs and her middle. She was already getting so much bigger; stretched out to her full length with her hands making tiny fists above her head, she was almost half as long as the cot.

"Give her five minutes and she'll be free of it again."

Katie's voice came from behind me and I turned to see her framed in the open doorway, her shape dark against the light from the living-room.

"Come here," I said, holding out my arm to her. Smiling, she walked over to me, smaller than me in her slippers. Her arm circled my waist and I pulled her closer so we slotted into position, my chin resting on her head. When I kissed her hair I smelled the clean sweetness of her shampoo. It smelled like home.

"It's amazing how much better she's been sleeping," Katie whispered. "I think it really knocked out her routine, being away. She seems to like being back."

"I'm glad to have her back — and you too." I said.

Katie squeezed her arms tighter around my waist and the

reassuring pressure made me smile. I stroked her hair with my free hand but didn't say anything; I was starting to understand that I didn't always need to. We'd talked so much over the weekend, shaping words around the things we'd been afraid to talk about before. I'd told her everything, nearly everything, but it was those times when we were just quiet together, those times there were no words for, that I cherished most of all.

We stood there, watching Abbey sleeping, her shallow breaths pushing the little curve of her chest up and down. The feeling that coated my insides was happiness and I let myself savour its taste, slow and viscous like honey. I thought I'd been happy before, but that was until I knew how happiness really felt. This was different. This was like cleaning a camera lens to see the depth of colour beyond and realising you'd been looking through a layer of dust all along. Anchored to Katie's strength, I couldn't get lost on the currents, I wouldn't be washed under on the waves. When I was with Katie, I knew who I was.

With one hand she flicked the elastic waistband of my tracksuit.

"Hey! What are you up to?"

"I just can't get over seeing you in a tracksuit. What time is your game?"

"Nine."

"Why is it so late?"

"Not sure, really — Paul said there's some other team playing first," I said, dropping my voice to a whisper as I saw Abbey's eyelids flutter open.

Turning away from the cot, I guided Katie with me and we tiptoed from the room, nudging the door half closed behind us.

"You playing football, that's something I'd love to see," she said, when we were able to talk again, then giggled.

"Why? What's so funny?"

"You're the one who told me what a nightmare you had playing at school. What was the name of that teacher again? The one who used to force you to play every game even though you were rubbish because he was so certain that one day you'd develop your brother's talent?"

For a second I was on the pitch again, struggling to keep the ball under my feet but losing it to the opposition anyway, Lynch's curse's disappearing into the September wind. I flinched in the memory until Katie's laugh brought me back and I laughed too. Telling her things like that, sharing even the flintiest splinters of memory, softened them so I could mould them into something else. Something that could live alongside the new ones without piercing through.

"Lynch was a bastard," I said. "Anyway, that was years ago. I'm probably much better at sport now."

"Really?" Her eyebrows raised with teasing indignation.

"Yes, really." I puffed my chest out. "In fact, I'm pretty unbeatable, these days. I reckon I'm going to score a goal tonight."

"Unbeatable? I must remind you of that next time I win with straight sets in tennis."

"You never beat me in straight sets! I win a few games."

"Maybe the odd one, when I'm feeling sorry for you."

Katie's smile lightened her words and I took the bait as she knew I would. I reached for her hips and my fingers found their way to just above the bone where I knew her tickles lived. "Take that back!"

"JP! Stop!" She was trying to wriggle away and what she said came out in a gasp. "Stop it!"

"Take it back, then!" Relentlessly, my fingers worked over her ribs climbing upwards under her armpits. Turning halfway around, she slithered out of my grasp and skipped around the armchair to the other side of the living-room. There wasn't far to go and she was cornered between the wall and the couch. She tried to double back but I'd caught up and we both knew I had her now. Planting my hands on the wall either side of her, I felt my hardness grow under the flimsy material of my tracksuit.

Folding her arms tight around herself, she begged for mercy, but I wasn't interested in tickling her any more. Instead I cupped my hand under her hair, holding the weight of her head where it met her neck. My thumb stroked her jaw. "Do you take back what you said about letting me win at tennis?"

The kiss had already started before my words had ended and I never heard her answer. I loved how we kissed, the rhythm of it, the solidness of her mouth on mine, the pausing in between, the flick of her tongue, even the occasional bump of her teeth. Right from the start the kissing had just worked, and every time we did it I wondered why we didn't do it more.

My other hand found the rest of her body. The heavy

softness of her breast, the slope between there and the jut of her hip. My kisses moved down too, over her neck to the place I loved, the hollow that gave way to the curved bone of her chest. I tasted her perfume on my tongue. I felt her exhale and heard the snap of her bra. Pushing her T-shirt up, I saw her nipples were already dark and hard, standing out against the white softness of her swinging breasts. I engulfed one with my mouth, working it tighter before moving to the other.

Above me Katie was breathing hard. Her hand grabbed my tracksuit, pushing the elastic easily off my waist, down over my arse, taking my boxer shorts with it. My finger left the warmth of her skin for the cold button of her jeans, metal wedged into denim, refusing to become unstuck. It was going to take two hands and my curse made Katie laugh as I pushed it harder, pulling it back until eventually it opened.

Falling onto the floor together, we couldn't get our clothes off in time. My tracksuit bunched behind my knees, Katie's T-shirt caught around her neck and she let go of me for long enough to rip it over her head. Pushing and pulling at her jeans we finally got them off and she wrapped one leg around me. My mouth was on her mouth, her neck, her nipples, her mouth again. I couldn't wait any more and when I entered her she let out a little gasp, like she always did. In grunts of silence we rocked together, pumping hard against the carpet, building our own rhythm. Behind the dark of my eyelids an image formed. My hand holding someone else's arse, my cock pumping into someone from behind. The image that Dessie had painted of Leena was as clear as a photograph and I snapped my eyes open to look at Katie below me and push it away. Her leg squeezed me tighter, pushing me in more but I didn't need the depth. I was already about to let go.

"Oh, Jesus."

Her words told me it wasn't too soon and the cusp of the moment became the moment. Time speeded up and paused. I was panting now. Her teeth were biting her lip to keep her noise inside, but with each thrust I pushed it out. A fleeting thought of how we might look ran through my mind before thought became only feeling and I closed my eyes and let go.

Afterwards I loved the emptiness, as if it wasn't just my body purging but my mind as well. I was holding myself slightly above her, the position awkward and uncomfortable now the intensity was draining away, but I didn't want to move, not yet.

"I love you, Katie," I said.

"I love you too."

It was the fourth time we'd made love since Friday and it seemed things were back on track — more than back on track. But still, looking down at her, I felt the pierce of shame for the image that Dessie had planted in my mind and I wanted to start all over again, to get it right this time. I became conscious of a dull pain in my knee from where it had ground into the carpet.

Katie smiled up at me and I leaned down to kiss her. Outside two men's voices passed the window, a snatch of conversation about cricket, and then they were gone. Abbey was asleep still and the noises of the flat grew loud. The humming of the fridge. The stereo next door.

"I hope they didn't hear us," Katie said. "I hate the way the walls in this flat are so thin."

"Not with the volume they have their music," I said, rolling to one side to rest my weight on the floor. "They drive me nuts with all the crap they play."

"Hang on — listen. I think they're actually playing The Beatles tonight."

I concentrated to hear better, trying to make out words and a tune from the bouncing rise of sound. "No, they're not, that's not The Beatles."

"It is, listen, it's 'Eleanor Rigby'," Katie said, laughing. "Hello? I thought you were the big fan."

As soon as she said it, I heard it. Of course it was 'Eleanor Rigby', the irritating jangle of bouncing beats — it couldn't have been anything else. Like a child's relentless reciting of a predictable poem, it went on and on. At the chorus, Katie started to sing.

"*All the lonely people, where do they all come from?*"

"*God, stop! I hate that song — I've always hated it.*"

She smiled and sang on.

"*All the lonely people ...*"

Slipping outside her, I was already deflating and a trickle of cold semen escaped onto my thigh. I didn't want her to see the shift in my mood so I joined in, singing along with the next line, forcing the words from my mouth, focusing on the sound to keep the pictures away. Katie was still singing and, rolling over onto my back, I pulled her into me so she snuggled against my shoulder. I needed to hold her, to feel her warmth against me, to push away the growing hollow of coldness inside me.

In my mind I could see Revolver's tracklist and I waited for it to slip into 'I'm Only Sleeping' but it never came. It took me a second to grasp that the rumble of bass that replaced it meant it was only the harmless drone of the radio. Katie's hand was tracing the line of hair on my stomach, following it all the way up to my chest, and I hoped she didn't notice the panicky percussion beat of my heart. I exhaled, controlling the breath. It was only music, just a song. Dessie had made it something worse, something bad, but once he was gone it wouldn't matter any more.

"I love you, Katie," I said, tracing her smile with my finger.

As soon as I said it I remembered I'd told her that just a few seconds ago and the repetition sounded wrong. I wanted to get back to that fleeting feeling from earlier when we were watching Abbey sleeping. I wished I had more words. Better words to tell her how it felt.

"Let's go up to bed, get an early night," she said. "Forget the football."

Already I felt myself stirring again. There was nothing I wanted more. I didn't want to lie to her, not now, not when I'd been so honest with her about everything. But it had been easier to tell her that Dessie was gone. She wouldn't understand why I needed to do what I was going to do, why I had one hundred fifty-pound notes tightly bound in a hard-backed envelope in the bottom of the navy sportsbag, along with a cashcard and a PIN.

"God, I'd love to. But I promised Paul — I can't let him down."

I was playing football afterwards, that part was true, but even the half-lie left a burn in my throat.

"But he won't care, will he? It's only a five-a-side."

"I know, but without me it'll be four versus five. Someone won't get to play."

"OK, then, I admire your dedication. I'm wrecked. I think I'll run a bath and have an early night anyway. Sure I can't convince you?"

Leaning over me, she pushed my hair flat, kissing the place where it stopped and skin began. When I shook my head she smiled and pushed herself up into a stand. One of her ankles clicked as she walked slowly towards the bathroom, not bothering to cover her nakedness, smoothing her hair back behind her shoulders. Watching her, I made a mental photograph, taking in the soft dip of her arse where it met her legs, the mole on the back of her knee. She didn't need to convince me: this was right where I wanted to be, not just for now, but for a lifetime. And one night was a small price to pay.

I was welded to the floor, my limbs heavy. The music next door was better now, the sleepy melody of Cat Stevens. Maybe I should stay here, maybe I could, maybe there was another way, but I'd been through this so many times already: there was no other way. I picked up my T-shirt from where it lay in a pool on the floor and slipped it over my head. Pushing my feet into my still laced-up runners, I went over the plan again in my mind. In a couple of hours this would be over. In a couple of hours I could have my life back. I could come home, get into the bath with Katie and never get out if that was what I wanted.

Taking the bag from the cupboard I unzipped it as quietly as I could, even though I knew she wouldn't hear it over the noise of the running water. My hand felt the bulk of the envelope under my sweatshirt where I knew it would be. A misting scent of roses drifted under the bathroom door, and when I opened it Katie was a silhouette in the steam.

"I'll see you later — it'll probably be after eleven by the time I'm back. Paul said we might have a drink after." I blew her a kiss.

"Good luck!" she called.

I pushed open the door to Abbey's room. In the triangle of light I could see the blanket was already a bulge under her feet.

"Daddy's going out for a while," I whispered. "I love you."

In the hall I hesitated, the door handle cold against my fingers. It was time to go but I didn't want to leave them. I wanted to stay here. I wanted to make tea in my "Dad" mug. I wanted to dunk a Hobnob in it until it was a soft gunk of oats on my tongue. I zipped up my jacket. I wanted normal things, not to be holding a sports bag full of stolen money. But this was the only way to get the things I wanted. I had come so far and I was almost there.

Just one last step, and then it would all be over.

Twenty-seven

Meeting at Liverpool Street had been my idea. Deciding the place had put me in control again and it was perfect there. Not so many people that anyone would remember us, but enough to make sure he couldn't hurt me.

When I told Dessie on the phone he laughed, saying he could never understand my obsession with the Underground. When we'd gone to London with Mam and Rita, Dessie had chosen Highbury for his day out and I'd chosen the London Transport Museum so I could explore the old Tube carriages with the wooden doors and lamps and the scent of 1940s passengers that still clung to the curtains. They tried to make me change my mind, to go to Hamleys or Madame Tussauds — they couldn't understand my fascination with it. I tried my best to explain how I loved the crowds and the speed and the noise. How the interconnected coloured lines were like a real-life game of snakes-and-ladders that you could get lost in and pop up somewhere totally different from where you'd thought you were going. But no matter how much I tried to make them understand they never really got it at all.

Tonight, the tubular corridors were almost empty except for the heat that rolled through and made the tiles sweat.

The Other Boy

Alone on the escalator, I stood still for once, taking in the repeating roll of posters for West End shows, laser eye surgery and dream holiday destinations. In the creaking silence a fragment of lyric was lodged in my brain. *"Eleanor Rigby picks up the rice in the church where a wedding has been."* The needle was stuck on that line, over and over, refusing to move on to the next. It was too slow, like a record at the wrong speed.

At the top, I hoisted my bag higher on my shoulder, turning right, down another corridor towards the Central Line. I didn't know where he was coming from and I hoped he'd find the right platform. Just before the steps a sponsored busker sang out to no one, pouring all his energy into the electronic keyboard underneath his fingers. The music he made was trapped in the stifling corridor and I plunged into it, letting my feet bounce down the staircase to his soundtrack so it replaced my own.

I had tried to be late, or even on time, but I was early as usual. I knew he'd make me wait: it was all part of the game. The past couple of months had been longer than any others I could remember. Waiting to see where he would appear next or when he would call had felt as if time had stopped. Sometimes I felt I'd been waiting my whole life.

"Father McKenzie, writing the words of a sermon that no one will hear." Jesus. Damn this fuckin' song, it just wouldn't leave my head. The bag was burning the skin behind my fingers and I switched it to the other hand. I didn't want to look at Father McKenzie working, darning his socks, but I could see him anyway, the picture in my mind, a black figure

behind a leaded windowpane. My pace on the platform speeded up, even though there was nowhere to go. Scanning the jukebox of my mind I desperately searched for another track to replace it but the playlist was empty. "*All the lonely people ...*" I pictured my iPod, headphones curled safely around it on the shelf in the living room, and cursed myself for leaving it behind. In that moment, without its help, there was no other song in the world that I knew except this one.

Dessie wasn't there yet. The platform was empty except for a young guy stretched out on a red plastic bench. As I got closer, I saw he was asleep, slumped against the constraints of his crumpled suit. Without warning he lurched forward and righted himself again too fast, smacking his head off the white tiles behind. Somewhere on his journey he'd lost his tie and half his shirt hung open. A pub casualty. I'd been there myself, before Katie and Abbey. Nights full of banter and beer, nights that had ended with the security guard prodding me awake as he did his last sweep of the station.

There was no more platform left, just a little grey gate and then the gaping mouth of the tunnel, black with promises of darker black beyond. The tingling hum in the air told me the train had just gone through. Glancing at the digital timer, I saw that the next one was only three minutes away. Leaning against the wall, I rested the bag between my legs and folded my arms to muffle the ascending knocks coming from my heart. I slowed my breathing, remembering how I loved the consistency of the Central Line, the dependability of the city's pulse. Slow, deep breaths of heavy hot air. In and out, in and out. There was no need to panic.

The Other Boy

I felt the dampness of sweat in my hair, under my arms and even on my legs beneath my tracksuit. The more I tried to block out the song the louder it got. I needed to be calm. I tried to focus my mind on something else. I pictured Katie, lost in bubbles that foamed up over the edge of the bath, wetting the ends of her hair and the pages of her book. In the next room Abbey would still be asleep in her cot. I imagined Paul, warming up in Spitalfields, heard the echo of his voice under the metal rafters above the indoor pitch as he called for the ball. I thought of Peter and the dinner he was having with the Group CEO, over in New York. I'd never met him, but in my imagination he had silver hair and even white teeth and I pictured them laughing around a table with glasses of red wine as big as goldfish bowls. I could almost hear the piano music tinkling in the background.

The images were slippery and I couldn't make them stick. They felt clichéd, like actors in some soap opera. But they weren't actors, they were real people, people who made up my life now. People who thought they knew me, who never would have thought I could do something like this. "We need someone loyal," Peter had said. Was that really only a few days ago? He'd thought I was that loyal person, and when he'd said it I had thought so too. Katie trusted me again, since I'd told her everything. Nearly everything. She'd never think I was capable of something like this and it felt as if she was right, except she couldn't be right because I was here, proving her wrong.

In my mind the thoughts were abstract, like a puzzle to be solved, as if there should be some answer as to why so many versions of me could co-exist. I wondered which version was the real one. I remember thinking that maybe I wasn't a real person at all, that I was just something malleable, a lifesize piece of Plasticine that took on the shape of everyone else around me. Maybe I needed to make sure I was around people who would shape me into the person I wanted to be.

The thoughts had cleared my head of music and I felt calmer. The timer showed a line of stars, the train was approaching and the background whine started to build into a mechanical hum. Snatches of electricity burned in the air and the hum became a roar as the train exploded from the tunnel in a burst of speed and noise and steel and glass. It slowed and I could see people behind windows flashing by, rushing by, moving by, stopping. The doors hissed open, rubber smacking on metal, spilling them out around me, their footsteps quick and decisive on the platform.

My eyes scanned the passengers but I didn't move. As the crowd dispersed there were a few stragglers. Two young black teenagers with startlingly white trainers. A pretty blonde woman pulling a wheelie-bag. A group of foreign students who stopped to huddle around a map. He wasn't there. As the thought registered a new fear bit me. What if this had been a ploy to get me away from Katie and Abbey? What if he was around there now while he knew I was here on a Tube platform, too far away to help them? Before my mind could fully distil the thought he was there after all, walking towards me, the opposite direction from the crowd. He'd seen me before I'd seen him, and I hoped he hadn't registered the fear in my face. He'd had a haircut and as he came closer I saw his beard was shaved too, the skin a lighter white where it had been. His denim jacket was closed, pulled tight across his shoulders, his hands buried deep in his pockets. He nodded to me in greeting.

"Dessie," I said.

"Wasn't sure you were going to show."

"Why not? I said I would, didn't I?"

We stood there, looking at each other. The shadowy rings of darkness under his eyes were the same ones that I knew were under my own. Without the beard he looked more like Dad, more like me. He looked at the bag between my legs and smiled, the shadows disappearing into the crinkles of his face. "So, you came up trumps in the end."

I nodded.

"Told you, didn't I? When you've done it once it's not so hard. We're more alike than you think, John-Paul."

Now that he knew I had the money he was almost jovial, bouncing his elbow off my arm, his hands still in his pockets. I hated that his words were an echo of what I was thinking.

"You didn't leave me with a choice," I said. "But I haven't stolen it. It's a loan and I'm going to repay it as soon as I can."

"Of course you are," Dessie said. "Sure there's no thieves inside, only borrowers who forgot to pay their loans back."

He laughed at his joke, but I didn't and he stopped. I plucked the bag from between my feet, holding it against my chest like a buffer between us. He took his hands from his pockets and held on to the other side. "Do I need to count it?"

I shook my head. "It's all there. An envelope with five thousand like I said, the cashcard, the PIN and all the account details and passwords so you can move the lot over when you get an account set up in Dublin."

His hands were still on the bag and his eyes held mine, his silence making my words sound like a speech.

"I told you I'm not happy with this cashcard business. Is there no other way? How do I know you won't close the fuckin' account down before I have time to move it over?"

"And I told you I can't take any more out in one go. Not over the counter in cash anyway." I shook my head. "There's no other way. You're just going to have to trust me. Anyway, you don't want to be going around with fifty grand in cash."

In the corner of my eye I saw the drunk falling sideways, his head connecting with the edge of the seat, jolting him to consciousness before he closed his eyes again. Dessie jumped, swinging around, one hand letting go of the bag and delving deep into his pocket.

"What the fuck was that? Oh, it's just your man. Jesus Christ. He almost gave me a heart-attack."

He laughed but there was relief in his face. What was he so afraid of? My eyes followed where his hand was rammed in his pocket. The bulge was too big to be just his hand. Christ, did he have a gun?

"OK, John-Paul, I trust you. Let's leave it at that. Hand it over." He reached out for the bag again, his fingers gripping the handle. "Oh, yeah, I meant to ask you, did you get a chance to pick up that missing album by the way? *Revolver*, wasn't it? Might be nice to have the complete collection."

His face was close to mine, his eyes looking straight into my eyes, the bag the only distance between us. I knew he was going to say it before he said it.

"Do you remember the night ..."

"No!"

It burst out of me, a single syllable, more like a sound than a word. Its force pushed the bag forward, carrying us across the platform. My hands were sweating, one on the bag strap, the other on the same handle that Dessie had, clenching tight.

"All right, all right, John-Paul. Just give me the bag."

The joking was gone now. That was an order.

"Look, forget what I said, it doesn't even matter. You can believe what you want. Give me the bag and it'll all be over."

It was already supposed to be over. When I'd left, it was over. When I'd met Katie. When Abbey was born. How many times was I supposed to end it? Over the top of the bag I could see it then, in his face. The anger that was there all the time behind his easy smile, the hate that was waiting to find somewhere to go. If I didn't give him the money he was going to pull out the gun he had in his pocket. If I gave him the money it could never be over.

"John-Paul, I'm not messing. Let go of the fuckin' bag now!"

Sweat glazed his forehead but I wasn't scared of his anger any more. I was more scared of waiting. Whether he was there or not, I would always be waiting for him. A figure behind the railings outside Abbey's school. Silence at the end of a telephone line. Like a shadow, only visible when the sun was at its brightest, but always there. Always there.

He pulled harder, backing across the platform so his heel was on the yellow line near the edge. My fingers gripped tighter. "*All the lonely people, where do they all come from ...*" The music was back, spinning faster. I saw Mam on the ground with blood dripping from her chin. I felt the warmth of my own piss spreading down my leg. I let myself see it, the ugliness of Dad's anger contorting his face, the face I loved so much, the shocking hardness of it. I let myself hear the frightening roar of his voice, feel again the tidal wave of terror that flooded my body. In front of me, Dessie's eyebrows flattened — the sharp angle of his jaw looked just like Dad's that night. And it looked just like me, one Sunday in the sitting-room mirror, towering over my mam.

Behind him, the red stars were starting to flash but I didn't need a timer. I could feel the buzz and snap of electricity burning the air. The whine that became a hum that became a roar. My thoughts were the speed of the train, hurtling through my head faster and faster and faster and faster. Dad, Dessie, me, we were all the same. All three of us the same. But I wasn't the same. He wasn't going to make me the same.

He heard the train too and he wanted to get on it, so it could be his escape. I knew he was about to pull the bag, a final tug to get it from my grip. He waited a second, like I knew he would, so he could catch me by surprise and tear the bag from my hands. Watching, I waited too, waiting,

waiting, until it was time, and when it was time, I pushed with all my strength. As I let go the canvas burned the soft pads of my fingers.

The push hit right when he pulled, the double force of effort jerking him backwards in a skid that jolted his anger away and left only shock behind. It was slow and then it was quick. He clung to the bag like a life-raft, leaning the top half of his body forward in desperation, trying to force his way upward through the unrelenting momentum of gravity. Shock slipped into panic as he realised his right foot hung in midair over the tracks. With his left he battled to steady himself, but the smooth, rippled surface of his trainer couldn't quite find a grip on the platform's greasy edge.

When I describe it like that, it sounds as if it took about thirty seconds but it couldn't have — it must have been less than five, or even two. After that, I stopped looking, I didn't want to see. I remember turning, half twisting my body trying to make it as far as the wall but falling on the filth of the platform instead. *"All the lonely people, where do they all belong?"* The stupid song was still there and I remember wrapping my arms around my head to drown it out. And that was when I heard the other noise. The noise that sounded so ordinary that it could have been anything, a barely audible thud lost in the rush and hiss of air and metal.

For a second, when the train stopped, there was total stillness — well, that's what I remember anyway — before the footsteps and the shouts and the sound of a woman crying out. Above all the other screams there was one that was worse than all the rest, like a voice ripping in two, as if the sound itself was bleeding. Scrunching my knees up to my chest, I pushed my fingers into my ears so hard it hurt, but I could still hear that scream, piercing its way through.

I recognised the voice, I'd have known it anywhere, and I remember thinking that Dessie must be OK — that if he was able to scream like that, he couldn't be dead.

It wasn't until I opened my eyes that I knew it wasn't Dessie who was screaming. It was me.

EPILOGUE

8 December 2010

Dear Abbey,

The Doc said I should write a letter to you. He gets me to write a lot of "Do Not Send" letters, DNSes he calls them but this isn't one of them. This one is real and hopefully some day you'll read it and maybe it might help you understand.

It feels like I've been here for half my life and yet you're still a baby, still so small. I wonder if you noticed, at the time, that I was gone. You were so young, but maybe you missed my smell or my touch. Maybe you noticed the atmosphere changed or something different about your mum. By the time you're allowed to read this, you'll be an adult and maybe I'll have already met you. I hope so, I really do, but I can't be sure, so I need to write to you now, just in case.

It's weird in here, not like I imagined it would be at all. In some ways it's not as bad as I thought, but in others it's so much worse. The routine sort of reminds me of school in a way. They take the decisions out of everything and there's something comforting about always knowing where you're supposed to be and what's going to happen next. I think I needed that at first — the routine was like a scaffold that held me up and made the days pass. And despite everything, the days do pass. Already it's December again and outside the trees are black against the darkness and another day is almost over.

The nights are the hardest. At first I thought I'd be sharing a cell, like in that old TV show *Porridge* (ask your mum, she'll remember) where they had iron bunks and itchy blankets. I expected to be in with some old codger who'd show me the ropes or something. But I have a cell to myself. God, "cell" sounds terrible — it's just like a room, really, with a single bed and a locker and I even have my own TV. There's no itchy blankets either, just a normal duvet, but it's still hard to sleep.

I'm sorry, I'm rambling. I didn't know how to start and the Doc said just to write whatever was in my head but you don't want to know about old TV programmes from thirty years before you were born. I suppose what I'm trying to say is that I think about you and your mum a lot at nights, and that's what makes them so hard. I used to have this picture of what I thought the future would be like and that's when it comes into my head. You and your mum are in the picture and it's winter, and you're still only small, but old enough to walk and hold on to my hand. We're by the lake at Hampstead Heath and the cold is snapping at our faces. You're wearing a tiny red coat with a hood that you keep pushing off and I'm showing you how to throw the bread far enough so it reaches the ducks.

Lying there in the dark, listening to the prison's noise around me, I realise that version of the future is never going to happen now. That we won't live in the house that I imagined, with the black shiny door and the silver knocker. That I'm not going to be able to teach you how to swim or ride a bike, or tie your shoelaces or even words to songs I know you'll like. And that's when I feel so homesick, so very homesick, Abbey, because I know I'll never be home again.

I'm sorry. I'm making myself upset and I'm probably making you upset as well and I don't mean to, that's the last thing I want to do. I guess what I really want to do is to try and explain, but it's too late for that, and by the time your mum lets you read this, you'll have heard lots of versions of the story already and you'll probably have made up your own. What I did was wrong, I know that, and I won't try and pretend it wasn't. I just want you to know that I'm more than what happened that day at the Tube station. I'm more than what brought me here. That probably won't make sense to you yet, but what I'm trying to say is that people aren't one thing or another, all good or all bad, the way I used to think they were. People can be good and do bad things sometimes. I wanted to tell you that, because it's taken me a long time to figure it out.

I was thinking the other day that maybe the bad bit of some people spreads like dropping ink into water. Did you ever try that? We used to do that all the time as kids. Black was my favourite and I loved to watch the ribbon of ink that wound its way to the bottom. I'd put the jar on the windowsill and watch the spidery colour unfold and spread stark against the whiteness of the water. But then after a while everything was just grey, and even though I was watching hard, I always missed seeing it happen.

I'm seeing a therapist in here, Abbey. I call him the Doc. A shrink. I wonder what my dad would have thought of that. Sometimes I think it's a waste of time but sometimes I think it might be helping me understand, just a little bit. Talking to him makes me remember a lot of things, things I'd thought I'd forgotten. Not big things. Small hidden memories that just seem to come into my head like a present from the past. There's this one that was in my head when I woke up the other day. Me and Dessie are both in it. And Dad too. We were down at the harbour on the West Pier near where we lived. It was really early — you know that time of the morning when the light still has a linger of the dark so the air feels like you have to push through it? We were going fishing. I'd forgotten that Dad liked to do that, until I remembered this. I have a feeling that he used to go sometimes on Saturday mornings early, when he didn't have to work, but I think this was the only time we went with him.

In the memory he's getting ready, finding the right hook, you know, the right bait. And he's standing behind us, a cigarette in his mouth, his forehead creases of concentration. Dessie is small, he's wearing shorts and so am I, and even though it's chilly you can tell already that it's going to be a scorcher later. We're playing around, chasing each other and pushing, laughing and making faces, but Dad doesn't give out. I remember a dinghy going by with children in orange life-jackets and now I wonder if one of them was Mark but it was before I knew him then. Opposite us, I can see the ferry waiting patiently for its passengers and it might be the same boat that we went on to London years later. Behind it the other arm of the pier is jutting out, the pier where Mam would be found on a sunny morning, just like this one. But this was before all that, before it was even a shadow of that, and we were just two kids messing around and fishing with our dad.

The game was Dessie's idea and it was a good one. He thought of it first, scooping up handfuls of gravel to see how far he could throw it off the edge of the pier. He shouted out as he cupped his hands together, letting the small stones fall like speckles, suspended for a second in the rising sun before they hit the sparkling darkness of the water below. I copied him, of course I did — I copied everything he did then. If he'd jumped in I probably would even have done that too. After a while, Dad joined in and the three of us scrabbled for more, each trying to outdo the others, swinging handfuls of stones into the sea. It was hard to see whose went farthest because the stones mingled together as they fell and became shadows on the water, then a splash and then nothing. If I close my eyes I can imagine the feel of the tiny pebbles against my hands, the swing of my arms, the opening of my palms as I let them go.

I know you won't understand why I'm telling you this and it probably doesn't make any sense. I should be explaining things properly, telling you why I did what I did, to try and make you see my side. But I suppose I'm just trying to tell you something else about me, Abbey, to give you another memory in the kaleidoscope of memories that me and Dessie shared. It's just a moment that happened in between all the other moments, and it probably doesn't sound important or special. But it's one moment when I can see Dessie as a boy, just like I was, and I can be sure, absolutely sure, that right then all three of us were happy.

I don't know if your mum still has my Beatles albums or if they're in a second-hand shop by now, or even a skip. They've a pretty good library in here with CDs as well and I'm listening to stuff I've never listened to before, like Yo La Tengo and Pavarotti and an

Australian band called the Go-Betweens. It's weird and nice, getting to know the music, not knowing what's going to happen next, putting it back if I don't like it. Music is more than music, Abbey. It can help you and heal you and make you understand. I wanted to tell you that, to make sure you knew it, but somehow I think you already do. I wonder what music will make up your soundtrack, but whatever it is you have to choose it for yourself and I know whatever it is it's going to be great. I can just feel it.

Your mum will have read this letter before you do. I can picture her face as she reads that part. She'll think it's crazy that that's the only advice I can give you but then again maybe she'll think I shouldn't give you any advice at all. She'll have said bad things about me, your mum, even though she'll have tried not to, in front of you. And that's OK. I don't blame her, Abbey, I really let her down. I really let both of you down. And me too. And if she is reading this I want her to know that I still love her, that I'll always love her, and sometimes at night we're on Hampstead Heath, laughing together, kicking our way through piles of the red and orange leaves that litter my mind.

I'm coming to the end of this letter, Abbey. It's not that I've run out of things to say but I'm afraid if I don't stop now I won't be able to stop at all. I hope I can meet you one day. I hope I can hold you in my arms. I hope you can look me in the face and smile at me and mean it. I'd like to take you to Dublin, to walk with you by the sea and show you the places where I grew up. I'd like to buy you an ice-cream from Teddy's and eat it on the wall looking out at the waves. I'd like to be there on a winter's night and show you the long line of lights from Howth that lie flat across the water on the other side of the bay. And I'd tell you how when I was very small I didn't realise it was land at all, that I thought it was a train that moved very slowly, stretching out on the other side of the sea.

Some day, Abbey, I hope we'll get to do these things. I know it's too late with your mum but maybe it's not too late for us. On the nights that are so very long, when the music in my ears isn't enough to get me through and the hollowness inside becomes my whole body, they're the nights I hope that you can find the forgiveness in your heart that I never could.

And I know that if you can do that, some day, the picture in my mind will become real.

Always know I love you, Abbey.

Your Dad

Acknowledgements

I'd like to thank the following people who helped me at different stages and in many different ways along the journey towards publication of this, my first novel: Dominic Bennett, Una Brennan, Ken Byrne, Steven Byrne, Norma Cairns, Hester Casey, Michael Collins, Yvonne Cullen, Eoin Dempsey, Orla Dempsey, Broo Doherty, Gerard Donovan, Ciara Doorley, Catherine Dunne, Clare Farrell, Paul Farrell, Grainne Fox, Bernie Furlong, Grainne Hehir, Matthew Johnston, Eileen Kavanagh, Robin Laffan, Danielle Mazzeo, Emma McEvoy, Clodagh Ní Ghallachoir, Gareth O'Hagan, Tim O'Halloran, Kusi Okamara, Karen O'Neill, Hazel Orme, Aisling O'Sullivan, Christine Peterson, Helen Ryan, Maresa Sheehan, Jane Smallman, Anthony Tierney, Catherine Wallwork and Evelyn Walsh.

Special thanks to Sue Gaisford whose faith in my writing has been unwavering from the beginning, to Ciara Geraghty for taking my novel to Hachette and to my editor Ciara Doorley for her invaluable guidance and help in making this the best novel it can be.

Thanks also to Sony ATV for permission to reproduce lyrics from 'Eleanor Rigby'.

And most of all, thanks to my family and to my friends, whose encouragement, support and love makes this all worthwhile.